Rory's Story

Konnie ELLIS

Lavonne Waldner Stradinger

Rory's Story

THE EARLY YEARS

KONNIE HOFFMAN ELLIS

TATE PUBLISHING
AND ENTERPRISES, LLC

Rory's Story
Copyright © 2011 by Konnie Hoffman Ellis. All rights reserved.

No part of this publication may be reproduced, stored in a retrieval system or transmitted in any way by any means, electronic, mechanical, photocopy, recording or otherwise without the prior permission of the author except as provided by USA copyright law.

The opinions expressed by the author are not necessarily those of Tate Publishing, LLC.

Published by Tate Publishing & Enterprises, LLC
127 E. Trade Center Terrace | Mustang, Oklahoma 73064 USA
1.888.361.9473 | www.tatepublishing.com

Tate Publishing is committed to excellence in the publishing industry. The company reflects the philosophy established by the founders, based on Psalm 68:11,
"The Lord gave the word and great was the company of those who published it."

Book design copyright © 2011 by Tate Publishing, LLC. All rights reserved.
Cover design by Kristen Verser
Interior design by Joel Uber

Published in the United States of America

ISBN: 978-1-61346-881-4
1. Biography & Autobiography: Composers & Musicians
2. Family & Relationships: Life Stages, General
11.10.19

Dedication

This book is lovingly dedicated to Mom and Dad.
You always knew it would happen.

My family; (left to right) Mom (Karol) Dad (Roland) me (Konnie) Reed, Kim, Rory.

acknowledgments

It's very hard for me to know where to draw the line when trying to think of everyone who could or should be publicly thanked for the part they played in this book's completion. Keep in mind then that this is by no means an exhaustive list but represents only a few of the people to whom I am indebted.

First of all, I must acknowledge the huge role that my family played in making this book what it is. My siblings gave me invaluable input all along the way, reminding me of details that wouldn't have made it into the story otherwise. Thanks, guys.

I would also like to thank my friend, Bobbie Kambestad, for proofreading and critiquing many of the chapters and giving me the invaluable encouragement I needed when I was getting started with this undertaking. She was one of the first people outside of my family to read the story and gave me the confidence to keep plugging away. Next time we head for Red Lobster, Bobbie, it will be my treat.

Thanks is also due to Kim Wong and Monica Tanner, the leaders of the West River Christian Homeschoolers who allowed me to post several chapters to the e-mail group, even though a lot of the material was off topic. I wanted to get the impressions of a large number of people, and WRCH provided me with just such an opportunity. I am also grateful to many of the people at my church, South Canyon Baptist, for reading the rough draft and lending their support and insight, as well as to other friends and extended family, too numerous to name individually. I appreciate you all very much, and you know who you are.

And last but certainly not least, I need to extend my sincere thanks to all of the wonderful folks at Tate Publishing. I cannot say enough about their professional expertise and advice. Especially to my editor, Hillary Atkinson, who worked so hard to see that this book was the best it could be. She gave me invaluable suggestions to improve the story, and I will certainly apply many of these to my future writing endeavors as well.

Table of Contents

Introduction	11
God's Plan	13
Music in His Blood	21
Singing for Jesus	33
First Day of School	45
Big News	59
Arrival of Reed	69
Standing on the Rock	83
Christmas Program	99
Changes and Choices	115
Rory, the Drummer	135
Passage of Time	149

Learning and Growing	157
Teaching Experience	171
Concerts and Recordings	185
Rory and Reed Visit	207
Life Marches On	217
New Horizons	229
Turning Points	237
Attack from Satan	249
Surprise Trip for Father's Day	261
Christmas Rabbit, Burned Eggs, and a Spaghetti Dinner	269
Musical Adventures	283
Climbing the Ladder	301
Texas, Here We Come	317
Just the Beginning	333
Contact the Author	349

Introduction

This book tells the story of my brother, multi-instrumentalist Rory Hoffman, Nashville studio musician, performer, and producer, as well as a two-time winner of the ICMA Musician of the Year award, and endeavors to explain how he learned to succeed and thrive without sight, in a world that was nevertheless full of adventure and opportunity.

Rory rarely followed the typical timeline for a child of his age and hardly ever learned to do things in the same way that everyone else did. He was the official drummer for the family band at age four and played on his first record album a year later. He held the guitar upside down and backward, laying on his lap, as this method was much easier for him than doing it the traditional way. Before his thirteenth birthday, he could play many different instruments, including saxophone, harmonica, piano, accordion, and banjo, just to name a few.

Rory's Story has been a long time in coming, as I have actually been working on chronicling the saga of my family since I was sixteen years old. God knew the perfect timing, however, as He always does, and I'm only glad that I didn't run out of patience and give up hope before seeing the dream come to fruition.

Many people have mentioned to my family over the years that they would love to see a book about our lives, and Rory's in particular. This story barely touches the surface, and I intend to make it only the first in a series, which will continue to portray all of the exciting adventures we have had and are currently experiencing.

My prayer is that this book will touch the lives of people throughout the nation and beyond with the truth of how it really is possible to be content in all circumstances with God's help, and that He always rewards the trust we place in Him.

God's Plan

I was nine years old when my brother was born. For as long as I can remember, it had been my dream and that of my twin sister, Kim, to have a baby sister or brother of our own. So needless to say, we were overjoyed when we learned that our wish was about to become a reality.

As it happened, having a baby brother turned out to be as good in real life as we anticipated it would be. We doted on him from the moment he was first placed on our laps as a three-day-old infant. My sister and I had been away all week at the school for the blind in Aberdeen, South Dakota, more than two hundred miles away from home, so waiting to see him for the first time was obviously agonizing for both of us.

Kim and I weren't too thrilled to learn that we had a baby brother instead of a sister at first. Some of our classmates had little brothers, and we'd come to the conclusion that when they reached about four years of age, they became a huge pain and made it their business to wreck all their older sisters' belongings. Once we met our own brother though, all of these fears vanished and there was never any question but that he would be the ideal baby and grow up to be the best little boy that anyone could ask for, with us to help mold him, of course.

To avoid Rory's welcome home from turning into a heated argument over who should hold him first, somebody came up with the brilliant idea of placing Rory on a pillow that was laid across both of our laps. And so we sat for several hours, until Mom finally said it was bedtime. The only thing we insisted on was having Mom switch the baby's position from time to time so that we could take turns having his head on our lap while the other one of us was relegated to being happy with just his feet.

The first thing I remember about Rory was his lusty cry, which he showed us immediately upon his arrival home from the hospital. He cried a lot that first night, after my sister and I had gone to bed. Mom told us he must have a mild case of colic, but we were convinced it was only that he missed our companionship.

The next morning, I quietly walked to the bassinette where he was sleeping and ever so carefully picked him up and carried him out to the other room to greet the rest of the family. My grandma was the first to notice me, and she rushed over, alarmed to see me walking with him unaided. It didn't take her long to realize, however, that she need not have worried. Kim and I were very careful with him and always shielded his head with our hands in case we should encounter an unexpected obstacle in our path.

I could tell right away that Mom and Dad were very proud of their new son's arrival into the family. Dad was impressed with his strong grip, which he demonstrated each time someone put their finger into his hand. We were all amused when Rory's hand moved over Dad's shirt pocket the first time he held his boy for an extended period.

"Are you looking for the checkbook, already, son?" Dad quipped. "Starting a little young, aren't you?"

"I wonder if he'll like music and be a singer someday," Kim mused.

"Of course he will," I assured her, as though there could be no doubt. "How else could he be in the family band?"

"He'll have you girls to teach him," Grandpa pointed out. "So I'm sure it won't take him long to learn the songs."

"And we can teach him other stuff too," Kim added, already thinking ahead to the time when Rory would be old enough to become our own built-in, ready-made student and playmate. She and I had already decided that we wanted to be teachers when we grew up, so we knew our brother would give us good practice.

We were very grateful that we didn't have to stay at the school for months at a time as most of the other kids did. Our parents had committed to bringing us home every weekend. It was hard enough to wait until Fridays to see Rory and catch up on how he'd grown while we were away all week. We couldn't wait until summer, when we'd have three whole months to be with him every day, uninterrupted. We loved helping care for and play with him. We were so proud when he made his first cooing sound, and the whole family gathered around the couch to listen when he laughed for the first time. We were glad

Mom never asked us to help change a diaper though. We would often hold our noses and make sure we were at the other end of the house when that was being done. But other than that, we couldn't think of anything wrong with our brother. In our opinion, he was just a perfect baby.

One day, when Rory was three months old, Mom told us that she would be taking Rory to have a checkup and some shots. Kim and I didn't like the idea of having our sweet brother poked and prodded with needles, but Mom had assured us that it was normal procedure and something that all babies needed to have done. She promised that the doctor would be as gentle as possible and that Rory would probably sleep through most of it and only fuss for a few seconds when the time for the shot came.

When Mom got back with Rory, however, she seemed very quiet and a little sad. We asked how the appointment had gone and whether everything was okay with our brother, and she told us he was doing just fine. So I couldn't figure out why she and Dad were so subdued.

That evening, Dad took Kim and me for a motorcycle ride, which was one of our favorite activities. When we returned to the house, Dad stopped the engine and the three of us just sat out there for a while, listening to the crickets and talking together as we often did just before bedtime.

"Soon, we'll be too big to fit all three of us on the motorcycle at one time," Kim observed. "Mom better get one before long so there will be enough room for everybody."

"Yeah," I agreed, "especially after Ror gets big enough to ride too."

"I bet he'll like motorcycles even better than we do," Kim commented. "'Cause he's a boy an' everything."

"He'll probably even wanna get one of his own someday," I said. "Would you let him get one if he wants to, Dad? When he's old enough, I mean."

Dad was quiet for a long moment. Then he cleared his throat and said carefully, "Well, I don't think he'll be getting one of his own. He'll just have to be happy riding with me, like you guys do."

"How come?" I wanted to know. "Other boys get cars and motorcycles and stuff like that when they're teenagers."

"Well, that's true," Dad admitted. "But Rory wouldn't be able to drive one."

"Why not?" Kim asked. "Couldn't you teach him?"

"I'm afraid not," Dad told her. "We found out today that Rory can't see."

"You mean he's blind like us?" we both asked in unison, a little shocked by this news.

"That's right," Dad replied. "We've actually known this for quite a while already, but the doctor confirmed it today."

"I thought the doctors always told you that if you had more kids, they wouldn't be blind," Kim reminded him.

"I guess they were wrong," I answered her, a little condescendingly. Then, turning back to my father, I went on soothingly, "but we can always teach him Braille like we taught Gramp. So then maybe he won't have to go away to school like we do."

"I still don't get why he's blind though," Kim persisted. "How do you know he can't see, anyway? He seems normal to me."

"Yes, he is a normal little baby," Dad agreed. "But he just doesn't follow movements with his eyes the way other babies do. And he doesn't reach out for a toy or anything unless we put it in his hand. So that's how we know he can't see."

Kim and I were quiet for several minutes, digesting all this information.

Finally, I said cautiously, "But, Dad, you've always said that God was going to heal us someday and make us see. So why would He let you have another blind kid?"

"I don't know why," Dad said. "But I do know that God has a reason. You know that verse I've told you so many times that says that 'All things work together for good to those who love God and are called according to his purpose?' This means God has a plan for everything that happens. He knows why you guys are blind and why Rory can't see either. He has a special purpose for all of it, and we just have to remember that and keep going the best we know how until He shows us what that purpose is."

"Maybe it's so He can work an even bigger miracle," I offered. "Or so more people will hear about our family and then learn about God. After all, I don't know of any other families that have three blind kids."

"I guess that means we're kind of a special family," Kim reasoned.

"Come on, you guys," Mom called through the kitchen window. "The mosquitoes are gonna eat you alive if you stay out much longer. It's getting late anyway and time you two were in bed."

I lay awake for a long time that night, turning restlessly from one side to the other. Finally, I decided to talk with Kim about everything we'd just learned. Maybe she could help me sort out my own thoughts better.

Unfortunately, just as I was about to nudge her and ask if she were still awake, I heard a soft snore beside me. I decided to let her keep sleeping and try to do the same myself. So I lay very still and closed my eyes, waiting for sleep to come.

It was at that moment that I heard the faint sound of voices coming from down the hall. Mom and Dad were in the middle of a serious discussion of some kind. I sat up and strained to hear what they were saying but couldn't make out the words.

Suddenly, I heard footsteps heading in our direction, and I knew Mom was coming to check on us one last time, as was her customary routine. Quickly, I lay back down on the pillow and turned my head toward the wall. I breathed deeply, just as Kim was doing. Mom must have been convinced that we were both sleeping because she and Dad no longer tried quite so hard to keep their voices down.

To my surprise, it sounded like Dad was telling Mom the exact same things he had mentioned to Kim and me earlier, about how God had a plan and that it wasn't up to us to question His reasons. The only difference was that Mom wasn't reacting the same way we had to what he said. In fact, her reaction was quite different from what ours had been.

"I'm tired of never having any answers," she said. "How much more do we have to go through? How much more does God think we're supposed to take?"

I realized with astonishment that Mom was actually crying. I couldn't believe it. I didn't think grown-ups ever cried, especially not Mom. Why, she hadn't even cried on the day when she'd left Kim and me at the school in Aberdeen by ourselves for the first time. At least if she had, I never knew about it.

"We just gotta have faith," Dad said, trying to comfort her. "What else can we do? If we don't keep trusting, what do we have left to hope for?" But even he didn't sound very confident anymore.

"I can't keep believing and trusting when there aren't any answers," Mom insisted. "It isn't fair. This isn't the way things were supposed to pan out. I just can't go through all this again."

"God will give us strength," Dad told her. "He has always brought us through whatever we needed to face. We can't give up now."

As I continued to listen, I tried to figure out what it all meant. For the first time, I realized that our blindness was really a big deal. I had hardly ever thought about it before, and Mom and Dad never seemed to worry about it much either. They just treated us like normal kids and expected us to be well-behaved and get good grades in school like everybody else. I had no idea this news about Rory would be so hard for them to accept.

"Dear Lord, won't you please heal our eyes so Mom and Dad won't be so sad?" I prayed. "They really, really want us to be able to see, and I know you can do it if you want to."

All at once, I began to feel very sleepy. I felt all warm and soft inside, like God was right there beside me, listening to my prayer. I didn't feel scared or worried anymore. God would take care of us, as He always had before. I knew I would sleep peacefully for the rest of the night and that God would help Mom and Dad feel better too, just like He had done with me.

Music in His Blood

"Hey, everybody, be quiet a minute and listen to this. You're not gonna believe it!" I cried excitedly one day when Rory was about six months old. It was a Sunday afternoon, and we were all at my grandparents' house, where Gram had just made us a big, delicious dinner, as usual, before we made the weekly trip to the school in Aberdeen.

Everyone stopped their conversation and listened quietly. I jiggled Rory on my lap to keep him awake. It was past his nap time, and I knew he'd be asleep any minute.

"Okay. Now do it again," I coaxed my brother. "You remember how to sing, right?"

Slowly and clearly, I began to hum the tune for "Jesus Loves Me," which I'd been singing to him a few seconds earlier. Rory laid his head back down on my shoulder contentedly, glad to be hearing his favorite lullaby again.

"No, you can't go to sleep yet," I pleaded, as I jiggled him to keep him awake. "First you have to sing 'Jesus Loves Me' like you did a minute ago."

Everyone continued to wait in anticipation, but nothing happened. "What did he do anyway?" Kim demanded to know.

"He was humming it," I said, in frustration. But I could tell by the silent response that no one really believed me.

"I was rocking him to sleep, and I thought he was napping, so I stopped singing," I explained further. "I guess he wanted me to keep humming it, because all of a sudden his little head came up and he started humming it himself."

"How could he know the tune?" Kim asked skeptically. "He's just a baby."

"Quiet! He's doin' it again," I exclaimed.

They all listened attentively, and sure enough, as though to prove my point, Rory began humming the song once more.

"Wow! He's really doing it!" Kim breathed in wonder. "It's right in tune and even the right rhythm and everything."

Rory hummed the song all the way to the end and was rewarded by loud and long cheers and applause from his entire family. Tickled to have so much attention, he promptly did it all over again and got the same result.

"Now do it for me," Kim insisted, grabbing our brother away from me.

Rory bounced gleefully in her arms and obligingly began to hum the entire song for the third time.

"Well, I'll be darned," Gramp declared unbelievingly. "He is singing it, sure enough."

"There's no denying that kid has music in his blood," Dad agreed.

Needless to say, we were all very enthralled with this most recent accomplishment from our very own baby. Kim and I hardly gave him any peace throughout the whole trip to Aberdeen. We kept experimenting with him to see if he'd still remember what he'd done after waking from a little snooze and to test whether he might have stored any other songs in his brain besides "Jesus Loves Me." We could hardly wait to get back to school in order to impress the other girls in the dorm with our incredibly talented little brother.

As the months went by, Rory's musical appreciation continued to become even more apparent to the family. Shortly after learning to walk, he started dancing to music. Whenever Mom turned on the radio or Kim and I pulled out the bench to play the piano, Rory would begin to spin around enthusiastically in time with the music. He'd even join in vocally as well. He invented a way of modulating his voice to match whatever rhythm was being played, kind of like having his own portable drum set at his disposal for whenever the need arose.

Soon, Rory began to accompany our frequent jam sessions with ice cream buckets and spoons. Pie plates made great cymbals and/or snare drums, and different-sized containers were used for the different-sounding drums. This makeshift drum kit could be quickly gathered and assembled at a moment's notice. He'd beat them so hard that the buckets never lasted very long, but this gave our dad a good excuse to eat plenty of dessert.

When Rory was about two, he began to travel with the family band so he could sing a couple of songs during our concerts. He loved being able to sing in the microphone and hearing all the applause. He didn't ever seem to be nervous or shy, and no one knew what he might divulge to the audience at any of these performances. Mom always joked that it was a good thing we didn't have any big family secrets because they wouldn't have stayed secret for long.

"And now I believe it's time for my little son, Rory, to come up here and do a number or two for you all," Dad might say by way of introduction.

That was Mom's cue to bring Rory up to the front.

"Testing, one two three four," Rory proclaimed loudly into the mic, as he'd heard Dad do several times during setup.

"What are you going to sing for us tonight?" Dad asked him.

"'It's Bubbling,'" Rory replied promptly. "And I have to do a good job or the girls said they would pull my hair."

This remark was followed by a burst of laughter from the people in the audience.

Dad cleared his throat and tried to change the subject. "And how old are you now, Rory?"

"I'm two years old," he stated without hesitation. "And my sisters are twelve, and you're thirty-nine."

There was more laughter, and Rory waited patiently for it to die down before delivering the punch line.

"And Mom is thirty-two," he declared emphatically.

"All right then. Thank you," Dad said above the laughter and smattering of applause. "Let's go ahead and sing your song now."

Rory subsequently did. Afterward, while the last notes were still being played and before the people even had a chance to clap for him, Rory whispered loudly, "Now can I have my bubblegum, Mom? I did a good job, right?"

"Yes, you can have your gum now," Mom answered, as she hurriedly removed him from the spotlight amidst more laughter and applause.

One day shortly after he turned three, I was sitting with Rory on my lap, telling him a story, while Kim played some familiar melodies on the piano. I could tell that he was distracted by something and not really paying attention to my story.

"What's the matter?" I asked him.

"That song Kim is playin' doesn't sound right," he said in a perplexed tone after listening intently to the music for several more seconds.

I shrugged. "It sounds pretty much the same as always to me."

"No, it should go like this," Rory said, humming the same tune Kim was playing, but in a higher key. "That's how it is on the radio."

"Oh, that's just because it must be played in a different key on the radio," I explained. Then I stopped short, as what Rory had just said began to sink in. "Wait a minute," I said incredulously. "How do you know what key the song is supposed to be in, anyway?"

"I just do," he answered matter-of-factly, as though there were nothing unusual about having this skill. "Don't you know how it should sound?"

"Hey, Kim. Quit playing a minute," I exclaimed excitedly. "I can't get over this. I think Ror can tell keys apart."

We later learned that the correct term for this ability was to have perfect pitch. At the time, though, we weren't even aware that any other humans had ever done such a thing. So Rory seemed like a true musical genius to us indeed. We did have reason to be amazed, however, because being able to identify the different notes audibly is a gift that only a very few people are innately given. And for Rory to be able to demonstrate this knowledge at such a young age was quite remarkable, to be sure.

Kim played several different notes on the piano at random, just to see if she could trick our brother. "Now, can you tell me what key you sing 'Jesus Loves Me' in at our concerts?" she quizzed him.

Without hesitation, Rory started singing. Kim found the key of C where we normally played the tune and began playing along with him.

"He's right!" I marveled. "And he didn't even have to think about it."

"Wow! This is sure something!" Kim said, hardly able to believe what she was hearing either. Then, unable to resist finding out just how much Rory's brain could take in, she played a C and told him what it was called. Then she went one note higher, and explained this was the key of D.

"Just like *D* comes after *C* in the alphabet," I put in.

(Rory had been able to recite his ABCs for a year already.)

Next, Kim played a series of C and D notes in several different octaves in order to test Rory's ability to identify them correctly. He didn't miss even one.

"I bet I know what the next note is called," Rory said triumphantly. "E!"

"That's right!" I confirmed proudly, covering his head with kisses and giving him a big squeeze.

It wasn't long before Rory could name all of the musical notes, including the sharps and flats. Often, he would remind us of where a song should be played or proudly correct his dad when he'd accidentally hit a wrong chord on the guitar.

"Dad, you have to go to a G when it gets to the chorus," Rory told him. "I think this song would be easier if you would put the capo on the second fret."

Whenever Rory heard a new song for the first time, his initial fascination was with the musical aspect. He would pick the melody apart piece by piece until he was able to tell you precisely which instruments were played in any given section. If it was a song he really liked, he usually knew exactly what notes each instrument played throughout the entire selection as well. Once he had the music down to a science, it was then time to focus on the lyrics.

One day, Mom found him sitting next to the radio, tears streaming down his face.

"Why, Ror, what's the matter?" she asked in concern.

Although he was sensitive by nature, it certainly wasn't like him to be crying without a good reason.

"That little boy is so mean to his dad," Rory sobbed.

"What little boy?" Mom asked, completely bewildered by what he said.

"That boy on the song," Rory answered through his tears. "He won't even open the door and let his dad come into the house."

"What do you mean?" Mom asked, still puzzled.

Rory sniffled and attempted to calm down a little.

"That man in the song keeps saying, 'Honey, honey, won't you open the door?' And then he says, 'This is your sweet daddy. Don't you love me no more?' And the poor man is cold and has to sleep on the floor and everything, but his son just stands there and won't let him in."

The tears began to flow heavily again as Rory recounted the tragic story.

Mom hugged him and patiently tried to comfort her own little boy by assuring him that it was just a song and that it was actually talking about a not-so-nice husband who was always trying to convince his wife to take pity on him. Rory was somewhat mollified, but the incident showed us all how literal Rory was and also made us aware of just how closely he was paying attention to the things going on around him and taking them to heart.

As Rory grew, his interest in music continued to develop even more. Looking back, I can now see that he definitely wasn't a typical three-year-old. At the time though, he was just my little brother, Ror, nothing more, nothing less. Without realizing it, we were all subconsciously helping him stretch his potential as far as it would go. He seemed always able to deliver whatever we required of him, so we simply continued to keep expecting more and more from him in countless little ways.

Before long, Rory was harmonizing with us on some of our songs, in addition to singing several of his own. One of his favorite pastimes was when Kim or I or both of us would sit down at the piano and let him join in on his kazoo or wood knockers, and even the harmonica, which was his most recent fascination.

Whenever we were on the road going to and from school or traveling to one of our concerts, we were not without music. If the eight-track player wasn't in use, the three of us kids would often burst into song ourselves, doing a three-part acapella trio.

If we weren't singing, Kim and I would spend long hours during road trips playing travel games with our brother, such as Twenty Questions or memory games. We rarely let him win unless it was deserved. As though determined not to be outdone by mere sisters, he proved to be good competition. Sometimes, Kim and I would make rhythmic patterns by clapping our hands to see if Rory could copy what we did. If he succeeded, we would make the patterns more complicated.

Besides games like this, we might keep occupied by indulging in some other form of educational activity: teaching Rory about rhyming words, opposites, synonyms, or syllable identification. When this became boring, Kim and I would sometimes become a little more mischievous with our forms of entertainment.

"Ror, do you know who I am?" I would ask in a high-pitched voice.

"Is that you, Henrietta?" Rory questioned, always eager to play with one of his imaginary friends, which Kim and I created for him.

"No. I'm someone else," I replied.

"Who are you then?" Rory wanted to know.

"Guess."

"I don't know. If you're not Henrietta, I give up."

"I told you! Guess!" I shot back at him.

"I did guess," Rory said patiently.

"No, I don't mean that!" I insisted. "My name is Guess."

"Mom," Rory called up to the front seat in frustration, "Kon is buggin' me!"

"Knock it off, Konnie," Mom warned tiredly, without much hope that her reprimand would be heeded.

"But I did tell you who I am," I said innocently to my brother. "I'm Guess."

Rory thought for a few seconds. "You mean your name is Guess?" he finally asked hopefully.

"Guess," was my reply.

"Your name is Guess," he said triumphantly.

"Why should I guess? I already know my own name," I said.

"No, I don't mean you should guess," he countered. "I just mean I'm telling you your name. It's Guess."

"Very good," I finally conceded. "You're a pretty sharp little boy. You know that?"

"Now, would you like to know who I am?" Kim asked in a similar high-pitched voice.

"Who?" Rory asked, always up for a new challenge.

"Nobody," my sister answered in the high voice.

"Oh, so you're Nobody," Rory exclaimed knowingly.

"I'm somebody. Why did you say I'm nobody?" Kim asked in an offended tone.

"You guys!" Mom scolded with almost as much exasperation as Rory must have been feeling. "Stop it now."

"I didn't mean you aren't anybody," Rory explained carefully. "I just mean your name is Nobody."

"You're right," Kim consented. "What a smart boy."

"Now, Ror, remember to sing loud and clear in the mic tonight," I reminded him sternly. "Last time, you mumbled a couple of your words and people couldn't understand what you were saying."

"And you also sang a few of your notes a little bit too high, at the beginning of 'It's Bubbling,'" Kim added. "You can sing better than that."

"I did that on purpose," Rory admitted. "Just to be funny and see how it would sound."

"Ror, you know better than that," I accused, giving his hair a tug. "You don't ever be silly in the microphone."

Undaunted, Rory took a sip from his pop bottle.

"Hey, I got this bottle to be in the key of C," he announced happily. "Kim, if you drink a little more of yours, you can make an E note, and Kon's is almost full, so she can be G! Then we can make a nice chord when we blow in our bottles at the same time."

"Or we could make C, D, and E, and play 'Mary had a Little Lamb' like we do with that neat push-button telephone at Debbie's house," Kim suggested.

When we got to wherever we were going, Kim and I would usually go off exploring the new church or building where we would be doing the concert. Rory, on the other hand, always had to be in the thick of whatever was going on up front. He was very curious and had lots of questions for Dad while the equipment was being set up, soaking up every bit of knowledge he could about all the aspects of what went on behind the scenes.

"Where do you plug in your guitar?" he might ask.

"Right here," Dad would reply, taking his hand and showing him which connection fit into which socket in the amplifying equipment.

Rory was intrigued. "So I wonder what would happen if I put it in this other hole, instead?"

Rory was always on hand to help tune up the instruments and get them balanced correctly too.

"That second string needs to be a little bit higher, Dad," he would say. "And the next one is flat, too. How did you ever tune your guitar before I was born?"

"It took a lot longer. That's for sure," Dad admitted.

"And do you still remember that new chord I showed ya the other day?" Rory asked, wanting to be certain there would be no goofs when it came time to perform.

Dad thought for a minute. "Not really. Which song was that again?"

"Remember, the girls wanted to try going to that newfangled minor chord during the chorus of 'Try a Little Kindness,'" Rory reminded him. "It's pretty much like a regular A chord, but your third finger just moves down one fret."

Ironically enough, Rory's favorite type of music as a child was waltzes and polkas, probably because he heard so much old-time music whenever he visited our grandparents' house. Grandpa began letting him experiment with his mouth organs, just as he had with me several years earlier. He would let Rory touch his face as he played so Rory could see how he moved the harmonica for the different notes, exhaling for some and inhaling for others.

Rory could often be found sitting next to Gramp as he would pick the guitar and sing his favorite songs from when he was a boy. Sometimes, Rory would kneel in front of Grandpa and practice strumming along with him.

"Can I try to do it myself?" Rory begged, as he carefully took the guitar from Grandpa and tried to wield the cumbersome object as easily as Gramp had done.

"It's still too big and heavy for you to handle," Grandpa admonished. "You'll have to wait until you're a little older."

But Rory had an idea. "Not if I do it like this," he said, as he laid the guitar down across his lap and rested his fingers on top. "Now I can get to the different frets a lot easier too. Otherwise, my hand was too little to reach around the neck of the guitar."

"Hmm," Gramp said thoughtfully. "I don't know if that will work or not. I've never heard of anybody doing it like that. And, anyway, you have it laying backward right now. You should turn it this way." He picked up the guitar and positioned it so that the neck of the guitar was on Rory's left side, rather than on his right.

Rory obligingly strummed a few notes but then decided to put the guitar back the way it had been a few moments earlier.

"I like it better with the frets over here," he told Grandpa in a matter-of-fact manner. "I guess I'm just used to it because that's how it is for me whenever I kneel in front of you. And I like strumming with my other hand more too."

Grandpa laughed. "Well, you have plenty of time to figure it all out," he said. "Just keep working on it, and I'm sure that someday you'll be a star."

Singing for Jesus

It was the first part of June, and our family was scheduled to do an hour-long program that weekend at a church about a hundred miles away. School had just let out for the summer a few weeks earlier, so we had more opportunities to play our music than we did during the rest of the year. We also had more time to learn new songs in the summer as well.

Mom had spent several hours that week copying lyrics from a gospel record she'd recently purchased. This was not an easy task when considering that there was no pause button on our stereo. She would listen for a few seconds and then stop the turntable, write down the words, and then move the needle back a bit before starting the recording up again.

The concert was scheduled for Sunday evening, but it was still necessary for us to leave well before noon in order to be all set up and ready to go when the time came. I hurried out to the van and jumped in before anyone else to reserve my spot in the very back seat. Kim usually resided in the middle seat, and Rory had a place up front, although he usually spent most of his time with one of us. When the concert was over though, it often fell to Rory to sit up by Dad and help keep him awake on the long drive back home while the rest of us dozed.

"Hey, Dad, do you think maybe Kim and I could play the piano tonight?" I inquired as he started the engine. "You know our songs don't sound as good with just your guitar as they did when there were more instruments." (Within a matter of months, the young man who had previously been playing base guitar for us had joined the military, our drummer had gotten another job, and our lead guitar picker had moved to California.)

"Yeah," Kim added. "Since the other guys had to quit, Kon and I thought we'd start helping out more. After all, we're older now and we've been playing the piano ever since we were four. So we should be good enough by now."

"Londa Lundstrom wasn't much older than we are when she started playing in their concerts," I pointed out just for good measure. "Probably even younger, for that matter."

"I don't know," Dad said doubtfully. "I'm not sure you guys are good enough yet to sing and play piano at the same time."

"That's right," Mom agreed emphatically. "I don't want you girls to mess up the new song we worked so hard on learning all week. You haven't even ever practiced playing and singing at the same time yet. Let's work on it awhile at home first, and then maybe next time we go somewhere you can give it a try."

"But I wanna try it now," I whined belligerently. "Just let us do it for one song at least. Then if it doesn't sound very good, we can stop."

"If they can do it okay, we might be able to get one of those keyboards that have a bass sound and use it in place of the bass guitar now that John isn't with us anymore," Dad suggested to Mom in an undertone.

But we both managed to hear what he said anyway.

"Yeah, Mom!" we chorused loudly. "Just one song each. Please, please?"

Mom sighed. "Okay then. One song," she relented. "But you'd better be sure to concentrate on the words and not get carried away with the piano," she added warningly.

Suddenly, I didn't know whether or not I was glad that she had given in so easily. What if we made a terrible mess of it and ruined everything? Then people would laugh at us or feel sorry for us, and that wouldn't be good at all. But I wasn't about to change my mind and back out now. God would just have to help me to do my best when the time came.

"What time is it?" Rory wanted to know.

I flipped open my Braille watch and told him it was a few minutes after eleven.

"Would you find my old-time music program on the radio, Dad?" Rory asked. "It comes on at eleven."

Dad groaned. "Do we really have to listen to waltzes and polkas the whole way?" But he was already turning the dial in his search for the correct station.

"I think we're going the wrong direction," Mom observed a few minutes later, looking up from the map she'd been studying. "This doesn't look like the right route at all."

"I'm just taking the scenic route," Dad told her.

"Oh no!" I moaned. "Not this again!" We were all well aware that Dad's famous "shortcuts" and "scenic routes" usually had the result of putting us at least a half hour behind schedule and always succeeded in stressing Mom considerably.

"Just admit you don't know where you are for once and pull over somewhere and get directions," she demanded now.

"I'll find the way," Dad replied, unconcerned. "I always do, don't I?"

"Your luck won't hold out forever," Mom retorted.

Fortunately, however, this proved not to be the day that the fates were against us. We did eventually manage to arrive at our intended destination, albeit about sixty minutes later than planned.

"This is why I make sure we're all ready to go and in the van at least an hour ahead of schedule," Mom couldn't resist reminding us. "So next time, I don't want to hear any complaining about why we have to leave so early."

Dad began unloading the equipment while the rest of us started looking around for a Sunday school room where we could get into our good clothes. Kim and I didn't particularly care for wearing dresses much, but we had resigned ourselves to the fact that it was part of what was expected of us if we wanted to play our music in front of people.

After everything was plugged in, we set about doing some final practice runs of some of the more difficult songs and testing our microphones.

"There should be a little more treble on my voice," Kim said after singing a few notes. "And could you take off some of the reverb too?"

Always our best critic, Mom sat in the back row and gave orders to everyone.

"The guitar is way too loud, and you girls need to sing out more so the music isn't drowning out the words," she informed us.

"But, Mom, just because some old ladies complain about their hearing aids, why can't they just sit in the back if they think it's too loud?"

"You heard me," Mom said with that tone that signified she would listen to no further protests.

"I think maybe we should start saving our money to put toward a mixing board," Dad suggested. "That way Mom would be able to sit in the back and adjust all the balances as need be throughout the program, especially if we end up getting a keyboard too. The more instruments you have, the harder it is to keep everything balanced."

"But she'd never put anything loud enough," Kim muttered under her breath, even though it was obvious she and I had already been outvoted in that regard.

Mom was glad to see that Kim and I remembered all the words to our new song, and we decided to let Rory chime in with his wood knockers during the chorus. We also ran through the songs during which Kim and I intended to do our piano accompaniments. To my delight, it went surprisingly well, and even I was impressed with how much this improved the overall effect of the sound. I could tell Mom and Dad liked it too, even though they weren't overly lavish with their praise. I suppose they realized that if they said too much, Kim and I would insist on playing for every song. So they wisely thought it best to leave well enough alone and not push their luck.

"I'm getting hungry!" Rory informed the room at large as we were concluding the mini rehearsal. "Where are we gonna eat supper? There's no restaurants in this small of a town, is there?"

"You're always hungry," I commented dryly. "I think you're going to have Dad's appetite when you grow up."

"The pastor invited us to his house for supper," Mom told us, as we all bustled back out to the van.

"Do they have any kids?" Kim wanted to know.

"I think they're an older couple," Mom replied. "At least that's how he sounded on the phone. So probably no kids."

"In that case, I'm taking in my Brailler," I said, starting to gather up the papers that were strewn all over the seat. "That way I can work on my story and not be bored."

When we arrived, the pastor welcomed us cordially into their home. His wife was in the kitchen, preparing a meal that smelled delicious. Within five minutes, she and Mom were talking together a mile a minute, as though they had known each other all their lives. Dad called it Mom's gift of gab, but I have come to see it as a true talent she has for making people feel at ease. I really admire this ability, especially in light of my own shyness when surrounded by people I don't know very well.

"What is she doing?" the woman asked my mom, as I began inserting a new sheet of paper into the Brailler in order to try to hopefully get a few more paragraphs written before it was time to eat.

"I'm writin' a story," I responded quickly before Mom had a chance to answer. It had always been a pet peeve of ours to have people talk about us rather than to us when we were sitting right there.

Seemingly startled to hear me speak, the woman now turned to me and gushed loudly, "Oh, are you really? How marvelous!"

At this point, Rory, who had been sitting quietly on Kim's lap, now asked in a whisper that we all could hear plainly, "Kim, why is that lady talkin' so loud? Does she think we're deaf or something?"

After an awkward pause, the woman quickly continued to gush on, but at a much lower volume. "Oh, what a cute little boy! And what is your name, young man?"

"My name's Rory Hoffman," he answered promptly. "What are you cooking for supper? It sure smells good!" Like Mom, Rory never met a stranger either.

The nice lady laughed pleasantly. "Well, I hope it tastes as good as it smells. It should be about ready, so why don't we all head into the kitchen and find out?"

After the scrumptious meal had ended, the grown-ups visited awhile longer, and then we all headed back to the church. The program that evening turned out to be more challenging for all of us than was normally the case. The audience was very reserved, which made it difficult for us to stay enthused about what we were doing. When Dad announced my upcoming piano song, I began to have a few butterflies in my stomach. Everyone was being so quiet that they'd be sure to hear any little mistake I made. And what if I forgot the words? I tried not to think about the fact that I hadn't known the song for very long and that I'd never sung and played at the same time before in front of anyone. But it was no use. I swallowed hard and attempted to ignore the lump in my throat. I didn't even remember to ask God to help me.

He definitely must have helped me though because almost before I knew it, the song was over. It was as though once I got started, God just seemed to take control, guiding my hands to all the right keys and giving me the words to sing as I needed them. Of course, it also helped that Kim was singing along with me, so I could rely on her to keep things going if I should flounder along the way.

When the song had ended, Dad said, "Let's make a joyful noise unto the Lord!"

Everyone burst into applause as though they had been waiting for just such an invitation. I felt my tension begin to diminish as I realized that the worst was over and that the people were apparently enjoying our music after all.

"Thank you very much," Dad went on as the clapping died down. "I used to sing in nightclubs and bars all over the state, and the people there weren't a bit afraid to show when they were having a good time. So I figure why should we Christians be any different? We have a lot more to be thankful for than those people did. These kids up here can't see your smiling faces the way I can. Until a few seconds ago, they had no idea whether there were twenty people in the crowd or two hundred. They couldn't tell whether you were appreciating their music or not. So I do thank you again for that warm display of assurance."

Before he could go any further, the congregation burst into another spontaneous display of appreciation even longer and more heartfelt than the previous one had been.

When the program ended, there was a time of refreshments and fellowship downstairs. Several people came up to us, shaking our hands or giving us hugs, and telling us how much they enjoyed the songs. I felt much better than I had earlier that evening. It was a good reminder to me that even though some people might not always be as demonstrative as others. It didn't mean they liked what we were doing any less. In any case, as long as we were serving the Lord and trying our best, that was all that really mattered.

Kim and I sat at a table with our brother while Mom and Dad waited in line to get us something to eat. A few minutes later, somebody took a seat across from us.

"Hi," said a voice that sounded like it came from a girl about our own age. "I'm Jennifer. You guys sing good. Your brother too."

"Thanks," we responded politely.

There was a slight pause, followed by a question from Jennifer.

"So what's it like being blind anyway?"

Of course, this wasn't the first time someone had asked that of us, but it wasn't any easier to answer now than it ever had been before. Finally, I shrugged. "I dunno. What's it like being sighted?" I countered.

Taken aback, Jennifer had to think a minute before answering. "Well, I mean, like, how do you get around and know where things are and everything?"

"It's not really a big deal," Kim informed her. "If it's somewhere we've been a lot, we just sorta memorize our way after a while and we don't even have to think about it."

"And if we've never been there before," I added, "we still don't run into things very often because Kim and I have light perception, so we can tell if there's something in front of us because it gets darker there."

"What do you mean light perception?" queried Jennifer in a puzzled tone.

"That means we can tell when a light is on," I said.

"But our brother can't see light, so he just has to use his ears more," Kim added.

"Kind of like a bat does," Rory put in. "It's called echo location."

"Very good," I told him. "You remembered that big word."

A couple of weeks earlier, I had explained to Rory all about how bats use their sense of hearing to get from one place to another. The reason I did this was that Kim and I had just tried on some new dresses, and everyone was saying how pretty they were. Not wanting to be left out, Rory joined in and told us he thought we looked pretty too. The rest of the family just tried to ignore it, but I figured it was as good a time as any to explain to him that his eyes didn't work in the same way that other people's did. So I had taken him aside and told him that his eyes were broken and that this meant he had to see things in other ways, such as using his hands and ears and nose. I said that Kim and I saw things the same way and that this made us special because we could do things other people couldn't, such as read in the dark or get around easily when the electricity went out. Then I'd explained to him about how bats function, and he thought it was pretty cool that he got to use the same methods as they did.

"So I guess blind people must have a lot better ears than the rest of us," Jennifer commented.

"Not really," Kim replied. "We probably use our sense of hearing more than most people do, but I don't think God has given us superhuman ears or anything.

"Hmm," Jennifer mused. "That makes sense I suppose."

On the way home that night, our parents finally gave in and told us we'd done a good job on the piano.

"We're really proud of you girls," Mom admitted fervently. "I didn't think you could do it, but it sounded really nice."

"How would you like to try doing every song next time?" Dad added.

"Yeah!" Kim and I shouted without any hesitation.

"But how will we decide which one of us gets to play on each song?" Kim wondered.

"We'll figure it out," Dad replied. "You girls will develop your own styles, and then we'll just see which flavor fits best for a particular song."

"And you two can start saving up for that bass keyboard," Mom said. "Then you'll both have something to play."

"Maybe it will have other sounds on it too," I said hopefully. "That will really make the band better."

"Do you think we have enough money saved up, Mom?" Kim wanted to know.

"It won't be long," answered Mom. She and Dad had agreed to divide equally any money we took in at our programs between all of us.

"Did you get a chance to count what we got tonight?" Dad asked under his breath.

Mom must have nodded in response. "It wasn't very much," she told him quietly. "They just had the offering plate sitting in the back of the church, you know. So that never works nearly as well as passing it around does."

"Did we break even at least?" Dad questioned her with misgiving.

"Well, the pastor had us for supper, so that helped," Mom conceded. "But I still don't think that was enough to make up the difference in the expenses. Especially if you consider the van and equipment breakdowns we've had recently."

"That seems to be the norm lately," said Dad dryly. "Sometimes I wonder if it's really worth all the time and effort."

"Oh, Rolly, don't talk that way," Mom chided him. "You know this is what we're supposed to be doing. We can't go by how things look on the outside, remember? Aren't you the one who always reminds me of that?"

Growing bored with the adults' conversation, I turned to Rory. "You know what's going to happen in a few days?"

"No. What?" he asked eagerly.

"Well, as soon as Kim and I get everything set up, we're gonna put you in school."

First Day of School

"So how do you think we oughtta do this?" Kim asked. "We should try to come up with some sort of schedule or something."

"Let's get started right after breakfast tomorrow," I suggested. "Do you think we should start with only a couple hours a day, or could he handle more than that?"

"I'm sure he could probably do a couple hours in the morning and a couple more in the afternoon for now," Kim reasoned. "After all, we're gonna make it so fun that he won't even know he's learning anything. I bet he won't even want to quit when it's time to go home."

By the next morning, my sister and I were all organized and couldn't wait to put our many carefully laid plans into practice. As soon as Rory had finished his last bite of Cheerios, we snagged him and announced that this was the big day. Mom had been hearing us talk to Rory about school for weeks, but we had been too busy to fill her in on most of the details.

"Where are you gonna have your play school?" she asked with interest.

"We have it all set up already, in the old house," Kim replied. "You should come see it sometime."

"Yeah. We'll have an open house one of these days so you and Dad can visit and see what all we're doing," I assured her.

Neither Kim nor I bothered to mention that in our minds, this was not a play school at all. We weren't little kids anymore, playing teacher to Gramp, who never seemed quite able to get past the first grade. This was serious business. But we doubted Mom could really understand until she started to see for herself what Rory was learning under our capable tutelage.

The old house was where Grandma and Grandpa Hoffman had lived before they moved into their trailer house, which now stood very near our own home. For many years, the empty house had served as a storage building. Kim and I intended to breathe new life into it and convert it into our very own schoolhouse. We figured there were plenty of other places on our ranch where things could be stored. And anyway, what could be more important than our brother's education?

"Okay now," I said to Rory, as we walked outside, "The first thing we're gonna do is teach you how to get to school all by yourself. When you get out the door, just turn left and follow the gravel path, like you do when you go to Grandma Hoffman's house."

"Except when you get there," Kim added, "you turn right, instead of left. Then just follow along the wall with your left hand, and it will lead you around the corner and directly to the door. Think you can remember that?"

But Rory was already well on his way to school by the time we'd finished giving him our directions. I had to run in order to get there ahead of him. When he arrived, though, I had already converted into my well-thought-out teacher persona.

"Hello, Rory," I greeted him in a professional-yet-pleasant voice, shaking his hand briskly. "Welcome to school. We're so glad to have you. Come right this way."

Rory hesitated, bashful for a change. This was school, after all, and he wasn't yet sure of the correct procedure. I'm certain that at some level he realized it was just me, but the three of us had perfected our imaginary play to the point that we were all able to enter into it wholeheartedly and then withdraw from it at will just as easily. So while he was at school, we were no longer Konnie and Kim but actual teachers and fellow students as the need arose. It's a good thing my sister and I were fairly adept at changing our voices to imitate young children as well as adult women. Since Rory didn't have the visual aspect to distract him, it was even easier for us to fool him into thinking that there were actually several people in the room when the truth was that we were the only ones there.

"I'm one of your teachers, Miss Calvin," I said, as I led him through the main entrance.

"Miss Cavin?" he asked uncertainly, not quite able to get his tongue around the *L* sound in his nervousness.

"Fine. Miss Cavin then," I agreed smoothly, eager to put him at ease as quickly as possible. "This big room that you're standing in right now is where you'll have your music class. Your teacher will be Miss Applewhite. I don't think she's here quite yet though. You'll meet her later.

"I already know a lot about music," Rory informed her.

"That's what I've heard," Miss Cavin enthused. "But you're going to learn even more about it here at school. Now, right over here, by the piano is my classroom. This is where you'll come first every morning when you get to school."

"So will I go other places too?" Rory asked, sounding a little confused.

"Yes. You'll have four teachers altogether. We each have our own classroom. But you'll learn your way around before you know it. Go ahead and have a seat right here at this table."

Deciding it was time to introduce Rory to his classmate, I switched to my Linda persona.

"Hi, Rory," Linda shouted at the top of her lungs.

"Linda, calm down," Miss Cavin admonished sternly. "You know that isn't the way we should act in school."

But Linda just couldn't contain herself. She stomped her feet and clapped her hands in sheer ecstasy. The character I'd invented as Linda was very vivacious and impulsive. I figured she'd be a good balance for Rory's more sober and thoughtful personality.

"I'm just so excited," she exclaimed, reaching over to give Rory a big hug. "I've been waiting and waiting for you to come to school. It was so boring having to learn all by myself, but now I finally have a classmate."

"How long have you been coming to this school?" Rory wanted to know.

I was grateful to see that Linda was having the desired effect of making him feel more comfortable with his new surroundings.

"Oh, a long time," Linda replied. "But Miss Cavin is a good teacher, and we do lots of interesting stuff here. I know you're gonna like it."

"Thank you, Linda," Miss Cavin interjected before the children could get too involved in their own conversation. "Why don't you tell Rory some of the things we'll be learning about?"

"Oh, we have science, where we learn about animals and outer space and stuff like that. Then we have social studies, where we read stories and talk about people from other countries. And we practice telling time with these neat clocks Miss Cavin has. Oh, and I almost forgot, sometimes we get to play store."

"How do we play that?" Rory asked with interest.

"Well, first you hafta learn to tell the coins apart and how much they're all worth," Linda explained. "Then one of us is the storekeeper and the other one is the customer. You get to say what you want to buy, and the storekeeper tells you how much it costs. Then you give them the money and they see if you did it right or not."

"And if you do a good job, you get a nice scratch-and-sniff sticker to put on your shirt," Miss Cavin added.

"Neat!" Rory said with anticipation. "I bet I'll get one every day."

"If you try hard and do your best, you certainly will," Miss Cavin agreed.

"I don't get stickers very often because Miss Cavin says I get too carried away and don't concentrate," Linda put in forlornly. "But maybe now that you're here, I'll do better."

"All right, children. It's time to get down to work. Today, we're going to have a geography lesson. Linda, do you remember what geography is?"

"Of course," Linda replied promptly. "It means learning about maps and where places are."

"That's correct," Miss Cavin confirmed. "Rory, do you know your directions, like north, south, east, and west?"

"I've heard about them, but I don't know which way is which," Rory admitted.

"Well then let me show you," Miss Cavin said as she got up from her chair and went over to another part of the room. "Come over this way, and put your back to this dresser right here."

Rory did as instructed, and Miss Cavin told him he was facing north.

"Now turn around," she directed, "so that your tummy is against the dresser. There you go. This direction is south."

"I get it," Rory said happily, as he spun around the other way. "Now I'm north,"—he turned back again—"and now I'm south."

"Very good!" Miss Cavin praised. "Now I want you to face north again and then turn left. That's it. Now put your shoulder against the dresser."

"I'll tell him the trick," Linda put in. Then she added quickly before Miss Cavin could respond, "This direction is west. A good way to remember is that if you're going north, west is to your left, and *west* kind of rhymes with *left*."

But Rory was already thinking ahead. Turning so that his right shoulder was against the dresser, he said triumphantly, "And I bet this is east."

"That it is!" Miss Cavin answered proudly. (I must confess I almost forgot about maintaining my professional teacher conduct in my excitement that he had caught on so quickly.)

Next, Miss Cavin tested Rory by first telling him to point himself in a particular direction at random. After he had completed this task successfully several times, his teacher then asked Linda to face in various directions. Rory placed his hand on her head each time, and announced which direction she was facing. Since I was playing the part of both teacher and fellow student, my knees were getting pretty tired after this little exercise, as I had to keep kneeling, in order to be the expected height of Rory's new classmate.

"All right. Now let's go back over to the table and I'll show Rory the tile board where we'll be building our maps. We don't have time right now, but when you come back this afternoon, I'll show you how to make your own pretend town on the map."

"Yeah," Linda added. "She'll say stuff like, 'Put a house in this certain part of the map,' and you'll have to see if you know where it should go."

Rory explored the tile board methodically before proclaiming that he thought this would be a pretty easy job. "So which class do I go to next?" he asked.

"It's time to meet Miss Green now," the teacher said. "Do you think you can find the doorway all by yourself?"

Rory did without much difficulty. "Bye, Linda," he called over his shoulder, as he went out the door.

Since I had already walked through ahead of him, I had to quickly sneak back into the classroom and over to the table so that the responding farewell from Linda would be from the expected location.

"Bye, Ror!" Linda shouted. "See you again soon."

"And this is Miss Green's room," said Miss Cavin, as she led Rory to another doorway. "Miss Green, are you here?"

"Certainly," said Miss Green, otherwise known as Kim, as she came to the door to greet her new pupil. "Welcome, Rory. Have a seat right there to your right, and we'll visit for a few minutes about what we'll be doing in class this summer."

"Aren't there any other kids in this class?" Rory wondered. "Linda says it's boring if there aren't other kids."

"Well, sometimes Joey will be here," Miss Green told him. "But he isn't feeling well today, so he stayed home. "Anyway, we're going to have a lovely time in this class. You'll be learning to read Braille. Isn't that exciting?"

"My sisters read Braille," Rory informed her. "But they're the only ones."

"Well, soon, you'll be reading it too," Miss Green assured him. "We'll also be learning how to write on the Brailler and how to do math using an abacus. Have you ever seen an abacus?"

"Yeah. That's the thing with beads on it, right? I've seen Kim and Kon work on theirs. They told me that the beads on top stand for five, like five, fifty, five hundred, and stuff like that."

"Very good," Miss Green replied. "Then you already have a good start. We'll be learning how to add and take away numbers on your own abacus and a lot of other things too."

"Okay," Rory agreed obligingly.

"And I'm sure you know what this is," said Miss Green, as she put his hand on a familiar object.

"That's a Brailler," he told her unhesitatingly.

"Indeed, it is," agreed Miss Green. "How would you like to learn to make some letters on the Brailler today?"

"You mean I'm big enough to write stories like the girls do now?" he asked in wonder.

Miss Green chuckled. "Well, not quite. But we can start learning the ABCs at least. And before you know it, you'll be writing words and then sentences."

"And then I can write anything I want, can't I?" Rory said eagerly.

"You certainly can," Miss Green replied encouragingly. "For now though, let me show you how to put your fingers on the keys. This big key here in the middle is the spacebar. You'll notice that there are three keys to the left of the spacebar and three to the right. So the first three fingers of your left hand should be placed on the three left keys—"

"And the fingers on my other hand should go on the right," Rory cut in knowingly.

"Yes," Miss Green said. "You've got it. Now, if you push the key with the finger right next to your thumb on your left hand, that makes the letter *A*."

"That's easy," said Rory. "Can I do it now?"

"You certainly may," Miss Green encouraged. "Push down nice and firm, like that. Now a little faster. That's better. Good job. You've written a whole line of *A*s. Now, would you like to see what you wrote?"

"These are some neat *A*s," Rory cried with excitement, as he ran his fingers over the dots. "I'm gonna take this home and show Mom."

"That's a fine idea," Miss Green affirmed. "First though, let me show you how to make a *B*."

Miss Green told Rory that a *B* was made with the first two fingers on the left hand. After that, he was so eager to learn more that she told him how to make the letter C by pushing both of his index fingers.

"You worked very hard in my class this morning," Miss Green said proudly. "And you did a fine job. This afternoon, if you still remember how to write all the letters we've learned, I think we just might make a word. Would you like that?"

"Sure," Rory replied.

"Great. Then let me get Miss Cavin so she can take you to your next class, and I'll see you again in a few hours."

"Will Joey be here this afternoon?" Rory asked hopefully.

"Perhaps he'll be better by then," she said, not wanting to make any promises. "We'll see."

Just then, Miss Cavin, who had been eavesdropping on Miss Green's class, approached and told Rory she was ready to show him where his gym class would be held.

"Your teacher is Mrs. Smith, and her room is in the playhouse."

"Oh, I know where that is," Rory told her, pulling his hand free and starting off on his own to prove it. "It's right by the swing set."

"Yes, it is," Miss Cavin replied. "I'll just let you go ahead then and Mrs. Smith will meet you at the playhouse when you get there." I was also playing the role of Mrs. Smith, so I would need to switch to a deeper voice for that character.

As it turned out, Mrs. Smith was a few minutes late, but Rory waited patiently for her by the playhouse door.

"Hi, Ror! It's me again," a familiar voice whooped joyously.

"Hi, Linda," Rory called, as she ran up to where he was standing. "So you're in Mrs. Smith's class too?"

"Yup. It's a fun class. First, we have to do boring exercises, like sit-ups and toe-touchers, and jumping jacks and knee bends, but then we get to play games. And sometimes we get to jump on the trampoline, and when we get older, Mrs. Smith says she'll teach us to roller skate and maybe even teach us how to swim too."

"Hello, children," Mrs. Smith greeted. "This must be our new student."

"I was just telling him about all the things we do here," Linda stated for Mrs. Smith's benefit.

"Fine. Then you already know what to expect," Mrs. Smith surmised. "Did you tell him about our new aerobics tape, Linda?"

"Oh no. I forgot. But, Ror, we have this neat tape with music on it, and a lady comes on and tells us different stuff to do and we get to move in time with the song."

"Let's do it now," Rory pleaded, always eager for anything having to do with music.

"Not this time," Mrs. Smith said. "I think we'll just play some games for today. Doesn't that sound like fun?"

"Will we do the tape this afternoon?" Rory wondered.

"Maybe so. But right now, let's move over to the patio. We play most of our games outside because there isn't much room in the playhouse."

"Can we play Red Light Green Light, or Captain, May I?" Linda suggested. "I like both of those."

"What are they like?" Rory wanted to know.

Mrs. Smith explained briefly how the games were played, but Rory didn't seem very impressed. "What are some of the other games?" he asked.

"Oh, we play Simon says, On the River on the Bank, Musical Chairs—"

"Yeah. Let's play musical chairs," Rory shouted.

"We don't have time to get chairs together and set up right now," said Mrs. Smith. "I'll do that during your lunchtime, and we can play it when you come back."

"Let's do that river one then," Rory conceded. "That sounded interesting too."

"All right," Mrs. Smith relented. "Then stand right here so that your feet are on the very edge of the concrete. This is the bank, and the gravel right in front of you will be the river. Can you jump into the river for me?"

Rory obeyed, and then Mrs. Smith told him to jump backward onto the bank again. "That's the idea," she told him. "Now I'm going to say, 'On the River,' or, 'On the bank,' and each time I say it, you jump to where you're supposed to go."

"Then she'll start saying it faster and faster," Linda warned. "So you'll have to listen close because sometimes she'll try to trick you and will say the same thing twice in a row. So if you're not paying attention, you'll do the wrong thing."

"No, I won't," Rory boasted. "This will be easy."

Much to his chagrin, however, Mrs. Smith succeeded in tricking him several times.

"Ha-ha. I'm better than you," Linda taunted. "Now I get to be it and try to trick you and Mrs. Smith."

"When can I be it?" Rory asked disappointedly.

"Maybe this afternoon if you get better at it," Linda tried to comfort him.

"Well, children, I think we're going to call it quits for now," Mrs. Smith put in. "Miss Green's class ran a little long today, so we're behind schedule. I'll take Rory to his last class, and, Linda, you may go ahead to yours."

"Bye, Ror!" Linda shouted. "But, remember, it's my turn to be it first when we come back after lunch."

"I bet I know what my last class is," said Rory. "Music."

"Yes, it is," Mrs. Smith assured him. "Do you think you can find it?"

"I think so," he answered. "You better come along though to make sure."

Rory managed to get there unaided without too much difficulty. Miss Applewhite was waiting for him by the piano when he arrived.

"Good morning, Rory," she greeted warmly.

Rory paused a moment in the doorway.

"Are you Miss Applewhite?" he questioned.

"Yes, I am," she replied.

"You sounded like Miss Green for a minute," Rory said. "Will you teach me how to play the guitar?"

Miss Applewhite hesitated for a beat before responding. "Well, probably not quite yet. But we'll be learning a lot of other interesting things." Before he could protest further, she rushed on. "Do you know what intervals are?"

"No," Rory admitted, seemingly surprised that there were some things about music he did not yet know. "What are they?"

"Well, sit down here on the bench beside me and I'll tell you all about them. Then I'll play some intervals and see if you can tell me what kind they are."

Rory was all ears now, anxious to consume any knowledge having to do with his favorite topic. Miss Applewhite told him about harmonic versus melodic intervals and then explained how they were identified by number. "If I play a C and a G, you count from C up to G: C, D, E, F, G; one, two, three, four, five. So C to G is a fifth interval."

"Oh, I see," Rory said eagerly. "So C to E would be a third interval because C, D, E; one, two, three."

"Yes. Very good," Miss Applewhite acknowledged.

"Now you play some and let me guess what they are," Rory challenged excitedly.

But Miss Applewhite couldn't trick him. Even when she started with notes other than C as the root, he still didn't miss even one. The teacher sighed. They had only been in class for a few minutes, and already he had mastered what she'd planned to cover that day. She would need to come up with something else, and in a big hurry too. She had Rory's rapt attention and didn't want to risk his losing interest already.

"Well, I've heard that you know about major and minor chords. But what about augmented and diminished ones?"

"Only when Dad tells the girls to quit wanting to play everything in the key of R diminished," Rory replied seriously.

Miss Applewhite laughed. "Well, I'm sure your dad was joking because there's no such key as R diminished. But let me show you how these chords sound."

So Miss Applewhite went on to explain how lowering or raising the top of a major chord changed it to a diminished or an augmented respectively. He was enthralled by this concept, even though he claimed that none of the songs his family sang had such fancy chords.

"Maybe someday you can teach them," Miss Applewhite smiled. "At any rate, I think we'll stop a few minutes early today, but when you come back this afternoon, we'll begin learning a new song I picked out for you. It's called 'I'm Little, But I'm Loud.'"

"That sounds like a silly song," Rory deduced.

"I think you're going to like it," Miss Applewhite predicted. "It will be a good one to start doing at your concerts once you get it all learned. So hurry back right after lunch."

Mom had macaroni and cheese waiting for us when we got back to our house.

"Did you have a good time?" she asked.

"Yeah, and Linda was there, and I Brailed some *A*s and played 'On the River,' and I'm gonna learn a new song," Rory told her breathlessly.

"Hmm. That sounds like fun," Mom said.

"We'll make report cards for you and everything," Kim told her. "That way you'll know what kind of grades he's getting since you won't be able to read his papers."

"Oh, that will be great," Mom enthused. "I'll be sure to save them in my scrapbook. Right now, you all need to hurry and eat your macaroni though because we're going to town as soon as you get done."

Normally this news would have been greeted with cheers because visiting Gramp and Gram was always a treat. But that day, we were disappointed that the afternoon classes would need to be cancelled.

"Can't we wait until three?" I asked. "We wanted to have Rory's afternoon classes."

"Oh, you guys will have all summer to play school," Mom said. "You don't need to teach him everything in one day."

"You mean I can't go back to school till tomorrow?" Rory asked worriedly. "Somebody better go tell my teachers. Do you think they'll be mad?"

"I'll go over and explain it to them," Kim offered. "I'm sure they'll understand.

All in all, Kim and I were quite pleased with how the morning had gone. It was obvious to us that Rory was eager to learn, and we couldn't wait to see what the summer would bring. Little did I know that this was just the beginning of all the exciting things that were about to happen to our family during the next eighteen months of our lives.

Big News

"Gramp, can you go bowling with me now?" Rory asked, bursting into the bedroom where Grandpa was reading *By the Shores of Silver Lake* to Kim and me.

"Ror, go away," I told him. "Gramp is almost done with this chapter."

Gramp laid his book aside, however. "No. I just started another chapter, remember?" he corrected me. "Ror has been very patient, so I think it's his turn now."

"Well, he just woke up from his nap," Kim pointed out. "So it's not like he was wandering around bored all afternoon or anything."

"I've read to you girls long enough," Gramp insisted. "Maybe after supper I'll read another chapter, but right now, my eyes are getting a little tired anyway."

"Girls, give Grandpa a break," Mom called from the other room. "Come out here a minute. There's something Gram and I want to tell you."

"Oh, goody. That means I get to go bowling," Rory said, as he headed for the basement, where Gramp had constructed a pretend bowling alley for him made of scrap lumber and pop cans for the bowling pins.

Kim and I sat side by side on the couch, waiting impatiently for Mom and Gram to tell us whatever it was they wanted to say so that we could be on our way and find something interesting to do. As the silence lengthened though, I began to get the idea that their news must be more serious than I'd at first thought.

"Well, what did you want to tell us?" Kim finally blurted out.

"Can't you guess?" Mom asked.

I could tell that she was trying to sound cheerful but wasn't exactly succeeding in the attempt.

"I don't have any idea," I replied, after thinking it over a few seconds. Mom hadn't hinted at any sort of upcoming surprise, and I could think of no reason for this sudden conference.

"Just tell us," Kim said. "We can't guess."

After another moment had gone by, Gram decided to spill the beans.

"Your mom is gonna have another baby," she announced somewhat bluntly.

Kim and I sat there, completely stunned by this revelation.

At last, I found my voice. "Really? I just can't believe it."

"When did you find out?" Kim wanted to know.

"Just a few minutes ago," Mom admitted. "That's what the doctor told me."

"Boy, I just can't believe it," was all I could think of to keep saying.

"Are you guys happy?" Mom asked almost hesitantly.

"Yeah," Kim said a little too quickly. "I'm just so shocked is all."

Gram laughed. "Well, you shouldn't be. Babies are born every day."

"Wow. Another baby," I breathed as the news began to sink in. "Just think. We might get a sister this time."

"I can't get over this," Kim added.

Trying to picture having another little brother or sister, besides Ror, was difficult to imagine. As far as we were concerned, our family was just right already, and we didn't know what adding another member would be like.

"You girls are so quiet," Mom said worriedly. "Don't you think you'll like having another baby in the family?"

"Of course," I said with more enthusiasm than I was feeling right then.

Mom was acting so strangely and seemed to be needing some encouragement and support, so Kim and I tried to force ourselves to be as upbeat as we could manage.

"It's just taking us a minute to get used to the idea," Kim said. "But Ror's growing up so fast. It will be nice to have a baby in the house again."

I couldn't help but remember, though, how different it had been when Mom and Dad had told us the news that Rory was on the way. Everybody had been so happy, and it wasn't at all like the sober discussion we were having this time around. It was hard to act very excited when Mom and Gram were being so quiet and serious themselves.

On the way home that night, Kim and I tried to explain to Rory that another baby was coming. He was a little bewildered by the news at first.

"Will it go meow like the kitties?" he asked in a confused tone.

"No. It's not a pet, silly," Kim told him. "It's a baby, a really small person, just like you, except littler."

"Or it could be a girl," I put in. "Then you'd have a little sister and you'd be the big brother."

"Where is it now?" asked Rory.

"Inside Mom's tummy," Kim informed him. "It will keep growing in there until it's big enough to come out."

"Will it go to school like me?" Rory asked.

"Not right away," answered Kim. "The baby won't be able to do much of anything at first."

"Then what are they good for?" questioned Rory curiously.

"They're fun to hold and play with and stuff like that," I replied.

But Rory didn't seem very impressed.

"Do you girls have any ideas of what we could name the baby?" Mom asked, trying valiantly to generate the same high interest level that we'd had with Rory's birth.

"I suppose if it's a girl we could name her Kristie," Kim suggested. "That's what we were going to name Ror if he'd been a girl."

"Do you hope it's a boy or a girl, Mom?" I asked her.

"Oh, I don't really care. It might be fun to get out the little dresses and pigtails again," Mom confided. "But if it's a boy, we'll have two girls and two boys. So that would be nice too."

"If it's a boy, his name should start with an R to go with Ror's and Dad's names," I surmised.

"The only trouble is that there aren't many good names that start with R," Kim went on.

"How about Rex?" asked Mom. "You remember that Dad was thinking pretty strongly about naming Rory Rex before he was born."

"No way," we chorused emphatically. "That sounds like a dog's name."

Mom laughed. "Well, you didn't like Rory's name at first either, and now it seems to fit him just right," she reminded us.

"Maybe Robbie will work," I said thoughtfully. "Rory and Robbie kind of has a nice ring to it."

"We'll see," answered Mom, as she parked the car in front of our house.

Dad was at his desk, reading, when we all trooped inside. Kim and I decided not to disturb him because we were uncertain what he would think about the baby or what we should say. We were afraid his reaction would be as funny as Mom's had been, and we didn't really want to deal with another encounter like that one. We were still trying to digest the information ourselves and adjust to the reality that in a few months our family would indeed grow from five to six.

"It's like Mom and Dad will almost have two separate generations of kids to deal with," Kim whispered, as the two of us closed the door to our bedroom in order to discuss the matter privately, just the two of us.

"And we'll probably miss most of their growing up," I added, "because we'll be in college or whatever by the time he or she is in kindergarten."

"Yeah. That's too bad," Kim agreed. "At least we'll get in on their babyhood though.

"Do you think it will be a boy or a girl?" I asked.

"I don't know," she replied. "It's interesting to think about either one really. I can't imagine having a brother other than Ror, but having three girls in the family and just one boy would be funny too."

"I guess we'll just wait and see," I told her. "I'm sure that once they're here, he or she will fit into the family perfectly, like Ror did after all those years of it being just you and me."

"Kim and Kon, it's getting late. Start getting ready for bed," Mom called from the other side of the door.

We put on our pajamas and went back into the living room to tell everyone good night. Dad and Rory were eating ice cream in the kitchen.

"And then I went to Miss Applewhite's class," Rory was saying. "She taught me some new chords, but I don't know how you would make them on the guitar yet. They're pretty hard."

"Really?" Dad asked. "Well, it sounds like you had a pretty full day of school."

"And you know something else?" Rory went on. "The girls say there's gonna be a baby in our house."

"That's what I hear," Dad replied. Then, turning to Mom, he added in a more subdued tone, "I suppose I should probably do a 'Train of Life' broadcast about that or something. What do you think?"

"Yeah, I guess that would be a good idea," she agreed.

"You mean you're gonna talk about the baby on the radio?" I asked.

I couldn't figure out why this baby warranted its own radio broadcast and what Dad would say to fill an entire half hour. But I was glad to hear they thought the baby was so special that they wanted to do a whole show about him or her.

"I'll ask Art and Eva if they can give me a slot sometime in the next couple months," Dad decided.

Art and Eva Nyberg lived only a few miles from us, and their program called "Train of Life," aired on our local radio station every Sunday morning. The broadcast featured songs, testimonies, and a brief message from God's word, given by Art. Every now and then, they would let our family have a guest appearance on the show, which gave us a lot of exposure in the area that we wouldn't have had otherwise.

A few weeks later, we all sat near the radio, listening with anticipation to hear what Dad had to say about our upcoming little brother or sister.

"Welcome to everyone out in radio land," Art began. "Today, Roland Hoffman is going to give us a few words about some things he would like to share with you at this time. So I would now like to turn the broadcast over to Roland Hoffman."

"Greetings to all our friends and neighbors listening to my voice over the airwaves this morning," Dad said. "I appreciate the opportunity to talk to you all about some things our family is facing."

I squirmed uncomfortably in my chair. So far, this was not turning out to be what I'd expected at all. Dad was being so solemn and mysterious. A baby should be a happy occasion, not something that was talked about with such sobriety.

What is Dad getting at? I wondered, but I decided to reserve judgment until I'd heard the whole thing.

"As most of you know," Dad was saying, "my wife, Karol, and I have three blind children. They are healthy and happy, and they have brought a lot of joy into our lives. Many of you have told us how you've been blessed by our music ministry. God has given our children some wonderful gifts, and we're glad they are using them for His glory. If it were not for our twin daughters, Karol and I wouldn't be born-again Christians today. I'm sure most of you are familiar with that story already. Our little boy, Rory, shows promise of becoming a great musician someday. We trust that God has a plan for all of these kids and that He will continue to show us what his purpose is for their lives as they grow to be responsible adults in control of their own lives.

"Recently, Karol and I have learned that we have another baby on the way. We realize that many of you are wondering how we could knowingly bring yet another blind child into the world. It is that question which I would like to try to respond to this morning. When Rory was born, we had no idea there would be anything wrong with his eyes. The doctors had assured us that all signs indicated any additional children we might have besides the girls should have perfect vision. They even encouraged us to have more children so that Kimmie and Konnie could be exposed to having sighted siblings. After we found out Rory was blind, we decided we wouldn't have any more children. Precautions were taken, but nothing in life is guaranteed. God had other ideas, and it is not up to us to question His ways. Instead, it's up to us to deal with the reality and not dwell on what ifs. It is a fact that another child will be born into this household, and our responsibility is to make the best of the situation and face it head-on rather than trying to deny or explain it away. You can't turn back the clock, and there's a reason for this, just like everything else that has happened to this family.

"We have been accused of quite a few things already in our lifetime, and I'm sure there's probably still more to come. We found out through the grapevine that there are some folks out there who believe we're using our children to get rich by displaying them in front of people to do their music and collect big sums of money. That isn't the case at all. Our singing is a ministry, and there is very little, if any, earthly gain involved. Sometimes it gets awfully tempting to just throw in the towel and call it quits, but we won't let ourselves do that because we believe with all our hearts that God has called us to serve him through our music."

Dad went on talking for several minutes longer, but I didn't hear much more of what he said. I was too busy trying to process everything I'd already heard. I had a funny feeling about it all but couldn't figure out quite why.

I soon realized though that I wasn't the only one who had mixed feelings about the broadcast. After it was over, none of us had a word to say. Even Mom and Dad seemed to want to avoid discussing it.

Finally, Rory piped up.

"How come there wasn't any music in that broadcast? There's usually a few songs to go along with the preaching."

"I guess Dad had too much to say and didn't have time for any songs," Kim answered.

Now that the ice was broken, I couldn't resist making a comment.

"But, Dad, it almost seemed like you were apologizing to everybody for having another baby."

"Yeah," Kim put in. "Why is it anybody else's business what you do?"

"It isn't really," Dad admitted. "But we just thought some people would have questions, and we figured we owed them some kind of explanation since we're in the public eye and everything."

"But babies are a good thing," I persisted. "I want to have kids someday, and I won't care if they're blind or not."

"Well, I'm sure we'd be a little sad if they were," Kim put in, "but even if the doctors tell us our kids might not be able to see, it wouldn't stop us from having any."

The room was silent for a long moment. I picked up my book from beside the chair and began running my fingers over the lines of text, although I wasn't really comprehending anything I read. Rory went over to the toy box, and Kim, who was sitting on the piano bench, started playing snippets of music on the keys.

"I was talking to somebody the other day," Mom said to Dad quietly. "This lady was going on and on about how terrible it was, us having another baby. After a while, I just wanted to slap her."

"The nerve of some people," Dad said with indignation. "In the first place, I'd sure like to know how all these people even found out about the baby already. I can't get over how fast things spread around this town."

"And the way this woman just kept at it, like we'd committed the worst sin or something," Mom went on. "What gives her the right to say anything? Her own kids are nothing to brag about. Two of them are stoned on drugs most of the time, and the other one is in jail more often than not. If anybody needs pity, it's her, not me or these kids. I'm proud of our family, and I'll put my kids up against hers any day of the week."

"That's right," Dad agreed. "I believe our kids are going to end up amounting to a lot more than some others we could name. Like I said on the broadcast, they're healthy and happy and they love God. What more could we ask?"

"Why, that's it," Mom assented. She was on a roll now. "What would some of these people expect us to do, have an abortion? I just don't get it. These kids are happy to be alive. If you asked them right now, all three of them would say they're glad they were born."

"I'm happy to be born," Rory chimed in, as he spun around in time with the song Kim was playing. No one was aware until then that he'd even heard any of the conversation.

"Out of the mouths of babes," Dad said, as he got up from his chair. "Well, I better get the rest of the chores done so we can make it to church on time."

After that, it was easier for all of us to talk about the baby more freely and with increasing excitement as the time drew near.

Arrival of Reed

"I wonder if it will be a Christmas baby," said Kim one day in December. She and I were home from school on our Christmas break, and we were hoping that the baby would be born well before we had to go back to Aberdeen after the first of the year.

"I hope so," I said. "Although that wouldn't really be fair to the baby I guess, not to have a day all his own."

"So you think it will be a boy?" Kim asked, noting my reference to the word *his*.

"Oh, I don't know. In a way, I guess I have been thinking of him as being a boy lately. It would be kind of neat for Ror to have a playmate. Don't you think?"

"He could play with a little sister just as well," Kim pointed out. "Maybe Mom will have twins again and we'll get one of each."

"I doubt that very seriously," I said. "The doctor would have said so by now. Just because Mom didn't know she was having twins back then doesn't mean it could happen again. I'm sure medical equipment has come a long way since we were born, and they're able to tell stuff like that a lot better now."

"Well, you never know," said Kim. "It's funny that Mom was actually hoping for twins when she was pregnant with Ror."

"Yeah. She said you and I kept each other entertained so much of the time that she thought we were less trouble than having just one baby would have been."

"Is there gonna be night school tonight?" Rory asked us hopefully, as he came into the room.

"No. It's too cold," Kim told him. "It was hard enough keeping the rooms heated during our regular school time today. Those little space heaters don't do a very good job when it gets this cold outside."

Kim and I had invented another pastime for ourselves and Rory, which we christened night school. It took place in the old house too, but only in the evenings. It was sort of like a mini version of Scouts or 4H or some other club-type gathering. During night school, we engaged in fun activities like making scrapbooks, going for walks, singing campfire songs, and telling ghost stories. Of course, Linda, Joey, and some other imaginary friends came along to add to the fun as well. The previous Halloween, we'd taken Rory trick-or-treating around the ranch to visit some of these make-believe friends, who all gave him candy and other surprises. Then we'd gone back to the old house for night school. This time, we'd converted it to a haunted house, complete with scary sounds and music playing in the background and unexpected smells and freaky textures to encounter at every turn. This was followed by a party where we bobbed for apples and ate popcorn balls made by Gram earlier that day.

"I hope the weather warms up soon," Rory lamented, "'cause I wanna go to night school again."

The weather didn't warm up much though. On Sunday, we were unable to make it to church, so Kim and I scurried around, turning the old house into a Sunday school for Rory, as we'd done several times before. There, we taught him all the Sunday school songs, had memory verses, told Bible stories, had quizzes to test Bible knowledge, and much more. Rory claimed he liked it even better than the real Sunday school at church because ours had more kids (albeit pretend ones), whereas he was often the only little boy in his class at the small church we attended in Lemmon.

"Plus, I don't learn as much at the one in town," Rory said, "'cause they just have the same old stories all the time that everybody already knows, and the verses are so easy."

Christmas came and went and still no baby. Kim and I were getting more impatient every day. Now that it had gone this far though, Mom said that he or she might as well wait until January 1 and maybe ours would be the first baby to be born in the new year in our community.

The baby though had other ideas. I woke up well before dawn on December 31 to hear Mom rattling around in the kitchen. I smelled shampoo and realized she must be washing her hair, of all things. A few minutes later, Mom came in to wake us up. I asked her what she was doing, and she said she couldn't sleep and that she thought today might be the big day.

Wide awake, Kim and I scrambled out of bed and got dressed swiftly. Mom, however, wasn't moving nearly as fast as we were. It was all she could do to get Rory dressed and hustle us all out to the van. Dad, on the other hand, actually seemed to be in a bit more of a hurry than usual for a change. He got us all to Lemmon almost as speedily as Mom normally would have done.

Mom let out a little groan a couple of times, but other than that, she stayed pretty quiet during the trip into town. Gramp was waiting on the front porch when we got there, and he helped Dad unload the things Mom had packed for our stay with our grandparents. Then Mom and Dad said a hasty good-bye and headed for Hettinger a half hour away, where Mom would be staying at the hospital for the next few days.

Kim and I were a little on edge and even snapped at our brother a few times that day.

"Ror, you're big enough to start eating your Cheerios with milk and sugar, like normal people do, instead of just having them plain all the time," I insisted. "Gramp, you can put milk on his cereal this time," I added, turning to our grandpa in a conspiratorial fashion.

"I don't want 'em that way," Rory complained.

But Gramp, not sure what to make of all our prattle, was pouring milk into Rory's bowl just like the rest of ours, much to the delight of Kim and me.

"There. It's made already," Kim said. "And you better eat it, Ror, or we'll do like we did with you when we wanted you to eat your pickle that time."

The pickle episode had taken place several weeks before, when Kim and I decided it was high time Rory tried the scrumptious morsel, which we had no doubt he would find to be delicious upon tasting it, just as we had. Gram had brought burgers home from the restaurant where she worked, and Rory insisted she take the pickles off his sandwich. Little did he know that I'd decided to hide my own pickles in my napkin, waiting for just the right moment when Kim and I could usher him into the bathroom, where we promptly locked the door and wrestled him to the floor. Once we had him securely pinned between us, Kim pried his mouth open while I jammed the pickle between his teeth.

I'm not particularly proud of that moment now, but Kim and I did feel righteously vindicated at the time, when Rory, upon carefully chewing and swallowing what we'd put into his mouth, announced that he liked pickles after all.

"No!" Rory begged now, as Kim's reminder of the incident brought back to his mind some not-so-pleasant memories, regardless of what the end result had been. "Don't put me in the bathroom again. I'll try my breakfast this way, but if I don't like it, you better leave me alone or I'll tell Gram."

"Oh, you'll like it," I predicted. "You liked the pickle, didn't you?"

Fortunately, Rory decided that he did indeed like his Cheerios with milk and sugar, so Kim and I tried to bring the point home to him rather vehemently that he should start trying new foods more often instead of claiming he didn't like something before he'd even sampled it.

After breakfast, Kim and I paced around restlessly, wishing Mom or Dad would call and give us an update on what was going on at the hospital. Gram tried to tell us it would likely be many hours before the baby was born, but we couldn't help but hope it would be much sooner than that.

Ever so slowly, the morning finally passed and turned into afternoon. Even Rory was so wound up that he refused to take his usual afternoon nap. Gram offered to play a game of Rummy with us, but Rory was being such a pest that it was hard to stay focused on what we were doing. At least that was our excuse.

When Gram left the room momentarily to get some food out of the freezer for supper that night, I leaned over and said to Rory in a dramatic whisper, "Ror, why don't you go in the bedroom and see how long it takes you to count to a thousand? Do you think you can do that?"

"Hmm," Rory replied thoughtfully. "Do I just count to one hundred, and then count to two hundred, and then keep going until I get to nine hundred and ninety-nine and a thousand?"

"That's right," Kim assured him. "Go ahead and give it a try, and you can come out when you make it all the way to a thousand. Okay?"

"Okay," Rory agreed happily, skipping off to the bedroom to give it his best shot.

In spite of myself, I did experience a twinge of guilt as he trustingly went off to do our bidding. But I tried not to think about it as we endeavored to get back to our card game.

About ten minutes later, Rory came out of the bedroom, tears streaming down his face. "I don't wanna count no more," he bawled loudly. "That's so boring. Why did you make me do it anyway? You just didn't want me around, right?"

Feeling thoroughly ashamed of myself now, I scooped him up and gave him a hug.

"I guess it was a dumb idea," I admitted. "But you did a good job anyway. How would you like to play cards with us now?"

Rory sniffled and said that he would.

"How far did you get anyway?" Kim couldn't resist asking him.

"Clear up to about three hundred and nineteen," he responded sullenly. "But then I started to forget where I left off and got all mixed up and it wasn't fun anymore."

"What in the world did you girls have him doing in there?" Gram asked sternly.

"Ror, why don't we quit our Rummy game for now, and we'll teach you to play Uno," I said loudly, hoping Gram would think I hadn't heard her question.

"Good idea," Kim chimed in hurriedly. "I bet you can do it. It's pretty easy. And now that you know how to read most of your letters and numbers, I'm sure you'll get the hang of it right away."

"Okay," Rory said doubtfully. "But you better not be trickin' me again."

"I'll get the cards," Kim said, heading for the middle drawer of the china cupboard, which we'd claimed for our own.

It was stuffed with gum, candy, balloons, and cards. She searched for the new ones that Mom had helped us put into Braille a few weeks earlier.

"Here they are," she announced, as she brought them over to the table. "Okay now, Ror, there are four colors in this game. Some cards are red, some green, others are blue, and the rest are yellow."

"But how will I know what color they are?" Rory asked in a puzzled tone.

"Easy. We Brailed a *Y* for yellow, *B* for blue, and so on," I replied.

Then Kim and I proceeded to explain the rules of the game to him. He listened attentively and showed he was understanding the concepts when we quizzed him along the way. After we were satisfied that he had a reasonably clear idea of how the game was played, we decided it was time to get started.

"Can you play with us too, Gramp?" I asked.

"Please, please," Rory begged. "It'll be a lot funner if you play along too."

"Oh, all right," Gramp consented reluctantly. "But I can't see why you need me to play. I never win anyway."

"You'll just have to try your best and be a good sport," Rory told him. "That's what the girls always say. Anyway, I'll help you if you get stuck."

Grandma and Grandpa Holdahl

Just then, the phone rang and we all jumped.

"Hurry, Gram! Get the phone," I shouted unnecessarily.

Gram had already picked it up before the second ring.

"Hello...Rolly...How is she? Oh my! That's great! A boy?" Gram was laughing and crying at the same time now. "What was that again? Reed Falon? Just a second. Let me write this down. He weighed how much?"

As I listened, I began to feel all tingly inside and almost bursting with excitement. It was really true. The baby was here.

And it was a boy. His name was Reed Falon, and he was our own baby brother.

"Ask when we can go see him," Kim urged.

It was obvious that she was feeling the same way as I was. Suddenly, all the uncertainty of whether this new baby would fit into our family and what it would be like had vanished into thin air.

Gram laughed. "Oh, the girls are wanting to know when they can see the baby. Really? You think Karol's up to it? Well, okay. If you're sure. We'll be there right after supper then."

"Cool!" my sister and I exclaimed joyously. "We get to see him tonight."

"I can't wait," I said fervently. "Just think. We'll get to hold him when he's only a few hours old."

"Oh, I don't think you'll be able to hold him yet," Gram corrected quickly, before we could get too carried away with our plans. "He's just a newborn, barely out of your mom's tummy. We need to be pretty careful with such tiny babies when they're that young."

"Well, let's hurry and eat so we can get to the hospital," Kim said, as she rapidly gathered up all the cards from the table to put them away.

"Hey, what about our game?" Rory asked indignantly.

"We don't have time now," I explained as I helped Kim pick up the cards. "We have a new little brother. That's a lot more important."

"You girls go ahead and play a hand or two with him," Gram chided. "You promised you would, and I still have to cook the food, you know. So there's plenty of time for a little Uno."

"Are you sure you want to play, Ror?" Kim asked him resignedly, certain that none of the rest of us would ever be able to concentrate on the game now.

"Of course," he stated without hesitation. "I don't really care that much about the baby anyway."

"Oh, yes you do," I contradicted knowingly. "You wait until you see him. You'll like him just fine then."

When we stood by Mom's hospital bed later that evening, I tried to be patient while Mom filled Gram in on details of the birth. She sounded exhausted but happy too. I broke in at the first opportunity. "Mom, where is he? Can we hold him?"

"Oh, I don't know," Mom said dubiously. "Let me call a nurse, and we'll see if she can bring him in."

"We'll be really, really careful," Kim promised. "Just let us hold him at least a few minutes, can't we?"

The nurse came in momentarily with the little bundle of joy, and much to our relief, Mom did relent and allowed us to hold our brother. I don't even remember which one of us got to go first. I guess we were just so happy Mom had said yes that we decided we'd better not argue about that. I do remember though how I felt when he was placed in my arms for the first time.

"I can't believe how little he is," I marveled. "Was Ror ever this small?"

"They sure do grow up in a hurry, don't they?" Kim agreed.

"You know what? I think we should try to appreciate his babyhood a lot more than we did Ror's," I concluded, as I explored his tiny fingers and nose and ears. "We were always so impatient for Ror to get big so we could play with him more and teach him and everything. But let's just let this one stay little for as long as we can."

"You'll spoil him if you do that," Dad pointed out.

"That's okay," Kim said. "They're only little once, so we might as well enjoy it for as long as we can."

"Ror, come over here and meet your new brother," I said.

Rory had been standing by, a quiet observer of this latest episode in his life. Hesitantly, he stepped forward and reached out his hand to touch his baby brother. Carefully, he found his forehead and touched his cheek.

"This is Reed," I told him, "your very own baby brother. What do you think of him?"

"Hi, Reed," Rory said in a hushed voice. Then he bent down and gave his little brother a kiss on the head, just as Kim and I had done with him so many times. "You're a pretty nice baby," he declared solemnly. "And you're gonna come live at our house soon."

"That's right," Mom said. "Just a couple more days and the baby and I will be able to go home."

"We should probably be heading that way now ourselves," Gramp put in.

"Yeah. Come on, you guys. Put on your coats and let's get ready to leave," Gram said.

"Already?" Kim protested. "We just got here."

"But your mom and the baby need their rest," Gram insisted. "They'll be back home before you know it, and then you'll get to see them every day."

"Until we have to go back to school you mean," I reminded her soberly.

"Well, you'll be home every weekend," Gramp said. "And you'll have your whole lives to get to know your little brother."

Dad decided to leave the hospital with us and followed behind in his own car. When we got back to Gramp and Gram's house, we all sat around and discussed the day's events further.

"What a great way to celebrate New Year's Eve," Gramp said enthusiastically.

"And just think. Every New Year's Eve from now on will be Reed's birthday," Kim added. "He'll get to have a big party every year."

"The whole world will be celebrating on his birthday," I agreed.

"What about my birthday?" Rory spoke up suddenly.

"Your birthday isn't until April, silly," I said, giving him a squeeze and then a tickle. "Don't worry. We'll do something special on your birthday too." I tickled him again and then told him the boogie monster was coming. Making my best boogie monster noises, I turned him upside down and began tickling him even more.

"Kim, help," Rory squealed, struggling free and rushing over to his other sister for safety.

Kim scooped him up, telling him she would help him find the perfect hiding place where they could be safe from the boogie monster. They started out on their quest, and I headed after them in hot pursuit.

"I guess we don't have to worry about the girls forgetting about Rory now that the baby's here," Dad observed with a chuckle.

"Why, no," Gram said emphatically. "Nobody will ever take Rory's place. I'm sure the girls will find plenty of room in their hearts to love both their brothers."

"That's for sure," Gramp agreed. "They'll both have their own special place. We love both girls, and now we'll have two boys to love."

"It's like it was meant to be," Gram said. "Now we have two of each."

"Well, there's no doubt about that," said Dad. "This is definitely just another part of God's plan for our family."

Standing on the Rock

"Gram, somebody's at the door," Kim shouted.

"I didn't even hear the doorbell," I said from the rocking chair, where I was giving seven-month-old Reed his bottle. "You were banging on the piano so loud that I'm not even sure how you heard it yourself."

"Hello there, stranger," Gram was saying in a very surprised tone as she opened the door and greeted the visitor.

"Milly," a somewhat familiar voice said, "so good to see you again."

It sounded a lot to me like my Uncle Rick, but it had been so long since I'd heard his voice that I couldn't be sure. Rick was my dad's younger brother, but we didn't get to see him often. It seemed he never stayed in one place very long, and he'd spent the past several years in California.

"Well, come on in," Gram invited warmly. "Rory, you might have to move out of the way so you don't get stepped on. And here's Kim at the piano. Kim, aren't you going to say hi to your uncle?"

"I'm just so surprised. I wasn't sure it was him," Kim responded.

"And aren't you getting to be quite the young lady," Rick noted. "The last time I saw you girls, you were barely knee high to a grasshopper. Well, that might be a slight exaggeration, but it's definitely been a long time."

"I'll just put an extra plate on," Gram said, as she headed toward the kitchen. "Supper will be ready as soon as Rolly and Karol get back from their meeting."

"You're sure growing up too, Rory," Rick noted, turning to my brother, who was sitting on the floor next to the piano, ice cream buckets in front of him and spoons (aka drumsticks) in hand. "How old are you getting to be these days?"

"Four," was the prompt answer. "Did you hear any of our music? Kim and I were just in the middle of playing some songs when you came in."

"I see that," said Uncle Rick. "Would it be all right if I sit and listen for a while?"

"Sure," Rory answered obligingly, always happy to have an audience. "There's a chair for you right by the door."

Uncle Rick took a seat and listened as Rory and Kim launched into another song. When it was over, Rick clapped his hands profusely and whistled with gusto as well.

"Wow, Kim! I just can't believe this! That's some of the best piano playing I've ever heard. And I'm not exaggerating. Last time I was home, you and Konnie were picking out a few chords on your organ, sure, but nothing like this. How did you manage to learn so much in just a few years?"

"Lots of practice, I guess," Kim replied.

"And did you like my drumming?" Rory asked hopefully.

"I certainly did," Uncle Rick told him. "Although I have to confess I was so engrossed in listening to the piano that I didn't pay as much attention to your drumming as I could have. You'll have to play another one so I can listen better. Actually, would you mind if I run out to the car real quick and grab my guitar first?"

"You play the guitar?" Rory asked in delight.

"Well, I'm rusty right now because I haven't had occasion to play it for a while."

"Uncle Rick is a great guitar picker," Kim told Rory, as our uncle went out to his car. "He can play all the licks on the Buck Owens records exactly like Don Rich does!"

"Yeah. Just wait till you hear him," I added from the other room. "Dad always wished Uncle Rick would have stuck around here and played in the band with us because we could never find anybody else nearly as good as he is.

"So how old are you now, Kim?" Uncle Rick asked when he got back with the guitar.

"Thirteen," she answered.

"I'm learning to play the guitar," Rory informed him. "Want me to show you?"

"Sounds like you're about as talented as your sister here," Uncle Rick commented. "Well, let's hear you drum a bit more first, and then you can show me how you play the guitar, okay?"

I listened enviously as the three of them jammed together. For the first time ever, I was eager for Reed to finish his bottle so that I could put him down and join all the fun. They were playing a bunch of old country songs that I hadn't thought about for a long time and others that I'd never heard too. After they'd finished one or two more, Rory put his ice cream buckets aside and went to fetch Grandpa's guitar from where it resided under the bed.

"I only know a few chords so far," he told his uncle. "So we have to play pretty much everything in the key of G for now. But maybe you can show me how to play more chords later on."

"I'll try my best," Uncle Rick replied, "although I have to tell you I've never seen a guitar played this way before. So you might need to show me a thing or two yourself first."

"It's a lot easier to play on my lap than how most people do it," Rory stated in no uncertain terms. "I wonder why everybody doesn't just do it like this."

Uncle Rick laughed. "Well, let's try 'Last Date' by Floyd Kramer. Do you know that one, Kim?"

"I think so," she said. "And if I don't, you just go ahead and get it started, and I'll figure it out as we go along."

At that moment, however, Mom and Dad arrived, so we all sat down to chicken fried steak, mashed potatoes and gravy, green beans with melted cheese on top, and fruit salad.

"It's so good to see you again, Rick," Mom said, as she dished up Rory's supper. "How long will you be able to stay this time?"

"Oh, I hadn't really thought about it yet," he answered. "I'm between jobs right now, so I don't have any deadlines or anything."

"That's good," said Mom. "You can stay as long as you want then. I know your folks will be anxious to see you too."

After supper, we played music late into the night. Kim and I stayed at the piano. I was at the high end and she at the low. Dad and Rick played their guitars, and Rory switched off between the pump organ, guitar, ice cream buckets, and harmonica.

"That's a kid of multi talents," Rick observed, as he watched his nephew. But his main focus still seemed to be in the piano. He just couldn't praise it enough, and Kim and I were quite flattered with all the attention.

When Mom and Dad finally decided it was time to pack up and travel the seven miles back out to the ranch, Rick followed behind in his car. He was planning to stay with our Grandma and Grandpa Hoffman in their home, right next to ours.

"But I probably won't get much sleep tonight," he told us. "I'm just too fired up about your incredible piano playing. I could've kept on going until dawn. I was having such a good time."

"Well, we can do it again tomorrow," I said. It was exhilarating to have a fellow musician—and one we'd always admired for his own talent—say such encouraging things about our playing.

Bright and early the next morning, we were back at it again full tilt. It just seemed that none of us could get enough of playing our music together. Having Uncle Rick picking his lead guitar added so much to the overall quality of each song. And Rory was having the time of his life finally being able to play music with us all day long rather than having his sisters grow weary of this activity after only an hour or two, as was normally the case.

Late that evening, after Mom had put Rory and Reed to bed for the night, we all sat around in the living room, talking about what a wonderful day it had been.

"You know, I've been thinking," Rick said seriously.

The rest of us stopped chattering and waited to hear what he was going to say. Rick cleared his throat and continued.

"I just can't get over how those girls play the piano. God has obviously given them a real gift, and it shouldn't be wasted."

"That's what we've said for years," Mom said.

"But they're using their talent to serve God," Dad added, "so it isn't being wasted."

"Oh, I know that," Rick acknowledged. "But what I'm saying is that this is too good to just be spent on some out-of-the-way churches in the middle of nowhere. Their music should be heard by thousands all over the nation, not just North and South Dakota."

I was sitting at the edge of my seat now, listening with anticipation to hear what Uncle Rick would say next. This was sounding more and more exciting by the minute.

"Something needs to be happening here," Rick said, "big time. And I mean right now. We shouldn't waste another minute without doing something major about all this."

Everyone was silent for a moment, and then Dad said, "Well, we're sure open to suggestions. Since the beginning, we've been expecting God to do something big with this ministry, but it just hasn't happened yet."

"That's what I mean," Rick answered, with a touch of frustration in his voice. "You've been waiting, and that's all you've been doing. You have to do whatever it takes to get this music off the ground. That's what needs to be going on."

There was another pause, and then Rick went on more calmly. "All I know is that I want to be here when it happens. I want to help make this dream a reality."

"You mean you're gonna stay here with us?" I asked in wonder. "You're not going back to California?"

"That's what I'm considering all right," Rick confirmed as he gave my shoulder a squeeze. "I think this could be huge if we all just put our heads together and figure out how to make it happen."

"You really think so?" Kim asked somewhat incredulously. "This sounds too good to be true." But Rick's enthusiasm was contagious, and we were all catching the bug.

"It doesn't have to be just a dream," Rick said with certainty. "God must want this ministry to go places or He would never have given you all the gifts that He has."

"Well, what should we do first?" Mom asked, ready to hear any brainstorming ideas that Rick might have up his sleeve.

"I think the first thing we need to do is record an album," Rick replied without hesitation. "That way, the recordings could be sold everywhere, and the music would get a lot of exposure."

"We didn't have very much luck the last time we tried that," Dad recalled soberly.

Several years earlier, before our brothers were born, Mom and Dad had made the long trip with Kim and me to Memphis, Tennessee, where we had planned to finally make our first record.

Dad had researched many studios, and we decided that in order to get a quality product, we'd need to go all the way to Tennessee, where many of the top-notch musicians resided.

Unfortunately, it seemed that this endeavor had turned out not to be part of God's plan for our lives. The place we'd selected was owned by an unscrupulous man who took our money and never gave us the completed project. Since we lived so far away and couldn't afford to keep going back there to straighten out the whole mess, we eventually had to accept defeat and press forward from there. That had been a time of bitter disappointment for all of us, and we weren't eager to repeat a similar experience any time soon.

"But you don't have to do it the way you did before," Rick insisted. "We can record the album close to home this time. We won't need any outside studio musicians. We can form our own band and play on the record ourselves."

"You mean you think we're good enough to play on a real record?" I asked breathlessly.

"No doubt about it," answered Rick with certainty. "All we need to do is find a drummer, and we'll have a full band right here."

"Who could we get to drum for us?" Mom wondered aloud.

After a few seconds, Dad spoke up again. "Why not ask Denny if he'd be interested?"

"Wow. That would be just like how it was when you had the country band a long time ago," I said excitedly. "It almost seems like a sign that this is really supposed to happen."

"I'll give them a call right now," Mom decided, as she picked up the receiver.

Mom must have been pretty convincing on the phone, because a half hour later Denny and his wife, Jane, were seated in our living room with the rest of us, making plans and dreaming a few dreams along the way.

"There's only one small problem I see with this plan so far," Dad interjected soberly.

"What do you mean?" Mom asked almost begrudgingly, not wanting the bubble to burst before it even had the chance to get off the ground.

"Where are the thousands of dollars we'd need for such a project going to come from?" he asked skeptically. "We sure don't have it, and I can't think of many people we know who have that kind of money laying around, just waiting to take a risk like this."

"Risk? What are you talking about?" Rick asked, his temper rising a bit. "There's no risk involved. It's as plain as the nose on my face that if this music just gets the right exposure in the right places, we'd get all our money back and then some."

Later that night, after everyone had gone home, Mom and Dad discussed the matter further amongst themselves. Kim and I were in bed by this time, but we still overheard the majority of what they were saying.

"Do you really think this is what we're supposed to do?" Mom questioned.

"Well, if we can just figure out a way to get the necessary funding, I don't see why not," Dad replied.

"But what if Rick jumps ship and leaves us high and dry right in the middle of everything?" Mom couldn't help asking. "Do you think he'll be able to stay put long enough to get the album done?"

"I don't know," Dad admitted. "But he sure seems sincere and ready to give it everything he's got. If this is really part of God's plan, who are we to stand in the way?"

The next evening, we all went over to Grandma Hoffman's house for supper, as was our regular routine. This gave Grandma and Grandpa a chance to see us on a daily basis and keep in touch with what was going on in our lives. We couldn't have imagined that even more surprises were in store for us as we sat around the table after the meal had been eaten.

"I have something I want to talk with you about," Grandma said, as she refilled my Kool-Aid glass. "Ricky has told me what you guys discussed last night, and I just want to let you know that if money is the only thing standing in the way of you recording this album, then I want to help you out."

"Oh, Mom, are you sure?" asked my own mother, hardly able to believe what she was hearing.

"Absolutely," Grandma answered without hesitation. "Pa and I have already come to an agreement on this. We would love to loan you whatever you need. No doubt you would be able to pay us back with the money you get from record sales later on. Why, this would be an answer to prayer. We've been praying for this to happen for years, and if Ricky is willing to stay home and be a part of this family, serving our Savior, that's just confirmation in my mind that this is what God wants you to do."

We all sat there speechless as what Grandma was saying began to sink in. The record really was going to become a reality after all. It wasn't just a dream.

"Wow, Mom. I just don't know what to say," Dad breathed finally. "If you're really willing to do this, I guess we better get cracking on this record right away."

"You'd surely better," Grandma agreed, dabbing at her eyes. "And to God be the glory."

Grandma and Grandpa Hoffman

I'll never forget what a happy time that was for our family. We were all so full of joy and just wanted to share it with the world.

"Why don't we have that dedication ceremony for little Reed one of these days real soon?" Mom suggested. "We've been talking about doing it for quite a while already, and it would be a great time to invite everybody out to the ranch and share the good news about our record with all of them."

"Good idea," Dad affirmed. "We could grill up some burgers and hot dogs and make it a picnic celebration."

There was an air of festivity a few days later, when a bunch of our family and friends gathered together out on our patio to witness the special occasion. Having our baby brother dedicated to the Lord seemed like just the right icing on the cake as a symbol of the wonderful things God had planned for us.

"This is all just so exciting," my nine-year-old cousin, Shawn, exclaimed jubilantly as she sat down beside me. "I can't believe you guys are really going to make a record."

"I know; I can hardly believe it myself," I responded.

"It would be so totally neat if your mom could be a part of it all too," Kim added from across the picnic table. "I just love to hear her sing."

Dad's sister, Diana, whom Kim and I had always affectionately referred to as our Aunt Deena, had actually been the first one in the family to learn to play the guitar, and her two brothers had quickly followed suit.

"Oh, I know Mom would love that so much," Shawn agreed wistfully. "But with her having my two little sisters and me to take care of, I'm not sure how it could work out. It's so much fun whenever I get to hear her sing with you guys though."

And that night proved to be no exception. After the pastor had asked God's blessing on little Reed's life and the rest of us in the family promised to do our best to help teach him in the ways of God, we all went into the house for another time of playing and singing more great music. Aunt Diana had her guitar too, and hearing her sing along with the rest of us really made everything feel so complete, and I wish that we'd thought to have our tape recorder going that evening, but I was hopeful that nights like that would become a much more common occurrence now that Rick had decided to move back home for good.

The decision was made to shoot for November as a target date for recording the album. We decided to call it "Standing on the Rock" and put a picture on the front cover that would portray all of us standing on a big rock that was located near our ranch.

"I think we should have a new name for the group too," Kim suggested. "Because Roland Hoffman and His Happy Household kind of sounds babyish to me now. Why don't we change it to something that sounds more professional?"

"Probably not a bad idea," Rick said, as the rest of us thought it over for a minute. "How about Roland Hoffman and the Believers?" he asked.

"That sounds perfect," Dad said after a moment's contemplation. "We can even use that song Dallas Holmes sings, 'Hey, I'm a Believer Now,' as our theme."

We all thought that was a marvelous idea and decided to begin every concert from that point on with our new theme song.

"We'll have to practice really hard between now and Thanksgiving if we want to be good enough to play on a record by then," I mused.

"Well, you'll have the rest of the summer," Mom said. "And after that, you guys will just have to be diligent about practicing every weekend when you get home from school."

And diligent we were. The rest of the summer went by in a flash. Once school had begun, Kim and I could hardly wait for Fridays to roll around so we could get back to our music. Sometimes Rick would come with Dad to bring us home from school, and that made the three-and-a-half-hour trip back to Lemmon go by much faster than it otherwise would have. All the way home, we'd talk about the record and the music ministry and lots of other fascinating topics. Rick was a deep thinker, and he and Dad would often get into interesting debates about God and how to interpret things in His Word. Before we knew it, we would be pulling up in front of Gramp and Gram's house, where our mom and grandparents would be waiting to hear all about everything that had happened at school that week. After supper, we'd head out to the ranch and would often jam together until bedtime.

Every Saturday night for the next several months, we musicians could all be found in the old house, which, besides being a school for Rory, had now been converted into a music studio as well. Mom and Jane, our drummer's wife, had been friends since childhood, so the two of them loved the chance to visit while we rehearsed. They always had a nice snack prepared for us to enjoy when each practice session ended.

Not surprisingly, Rory had to be right in the middle of all the excitement. Although it was usually the wee hours of the morning before we finished, he would sit in his assigned place and quietly listen to everything that went on until Mom buzzed him over the intercom system we'd installed and insist that he come home and get some sleep.

Sometimes we would begin our rehearsals before the drummer and his wife arrived. If this was the case, Rory would beg to be allowed to play on the big drum set until Denny got there. Fortunately, Denny was a good sport about letting a four-year-old pound on his drums when he wasn't around. Rory was always careful though and was in seventh heaven whenever he got to sit on Denny's stool and act like a real drummer.

"That kid does have the beat," Rick often commented.

It was pretty incredible to hear somebody who was smaller than the drum set actually carrying the rhythm and even getting in a few simple drum rolls now and then, using the cymbals and toms in addition to the basic floor tom and snare drum. But it didn't fully dawn on any of us until many years later just how remarkable this really was. At the time, we were all preoccupied in trying to make our music sound the best it could be for our upcoming record and simply took it for granted that, of course, Rory could keep a rhythm. He'd been doing it with ice cream buckets and spoons for years already and with his own portable voice-powered drum set before that.

The album included thirteen songs. Rory even had a short one of his own called "There's a New Little Baby in Our House." He also sang harmony along with Kim and me on another tune that was adapted by Dad from the Gaither's "I'm Something Special." Five of the selections were sung by Kim and me, another five were originals written and sung by Dad, and the final two were sung by Rick and Denny, respectively.

As the recording time drew near, our excitement mounted. At last, we were going to have an album of our own, just like other singers did. The thought of our music being played on radio stations all over the country was thrilling, to be sure.

In November, we headed to the studio in Hebron, North Dakota, as planned. One of the Tibor brothers, Harvey, was going to be our producer. The Tibor brothers were musicians in their own right, with a good following in our area.

I remember when I sat at the piano in the recording studio, preparing to get our initial take of the first song, which was one that Dad had written called "I Just Play Rhythm." Mom and Rory sat with Harvey in the engineering room while the rest of us were out in the studio, in front of our instruments.

"We're just going to do the music tracks for now," Harvey told us over the speaker. "Then later we'll come back and get the vocals. Rolly, you can go ahead and sing along for now just to keep the normal flow of the music, but then we'll redo your voice track later. Is everyone ready?"

We all said we were, and then Harvey turned on the reel-to-reel recorder and said, "I Just Play Rhythm, take one," and we were off. Our first official recording adventure was actually under way. I couldn't believe how good everything sounded over Harvey's recording equipment. The music was crisp and clear in our headphones, and each instrument could be distinctly heard. I was nervous about making a mistake, but that proved not to be a problem. We all ran through each song at least twice before accepting it as a final cut. If one of us goofed, Harvey was able to just punch in on the track where the slip-up occurred and let that person fix his mistake. Then he'd punch back out again and resume with the original recording. So it wasn't necessary for anyone to redo the entire song just because of one tiny error.

When it was time to do the vocal tracks, we were all amused at how Dad kept making strumming motions during his songs even though he wasn't holding the guitar.

"I'm just so used to always having a guitar whenever I sing that it doesn't seem right without it," he said.

Rory, of course, was entranced by all the technology surrounding him and by the fascinating things Harvey was able to do with his mixing board and other equipment. He wished Reed was old enough to come along and be part of all the excitement, but Gramp and Gram had kept his baby brother at home with them.

"I wonder if I'll be big enough to play on our next record," Rory mused. "Since we're gonna try to do one every year now, I'll be five years old by the time we're ready to do another one."

Mom laughed. "Well, that's still pretty young, but I'm sure we'll let you sing on the album again, if nothing else. Maybe you can even do two songs all by yourself next time."

"Can I do 'I'm Little But I'm Loud' on the next one?" Rory asked. "That's a regular, grown-up kind of song with three whole verses, and I really like it."

"We'll see," Mom told him. "Let's just take this one step at a time. Anyway, we'd better be quiet now so Harvey can concentrate on what he's doing."

We took two days to do the entire recording, and on the third day, we were all included in the process of mixing the music. We would give him our ideas or suggestions on how we wanted things to sound and how we'd like the instruments to be balanced with one another. Harvey's hands were constantly at work as each song played, adjusting volumes of solo instrument parts, or bringing up the lead vocals, or making countless other final touches to each track.

That was one of the most memorable and fun times I'd ever had up to that point in my young life. Everything looked so bright, and we couldn't wait to see what the future might hold for our family.

Christmas Program

"Look at this dinosaur," I said to Kim, as I pulled it out from where I had been rummaging at the bottom of the toy box, which sat in the corner of our bedroom. "I haven't thought of this toy in years."

"Yeah. I think he'll like that," agreed Kim. "Put it with the other stuff we picked out."

"Do you think this'll be enough gifts?" I asked her while I examined the collection of items on the bed that we'd selected to present to Rory after our upcoming Christmas program.

"Should be," Kim decided. "I can't wait to give all this to Ror tomorrow night, especially this UFO top. He's gonna love the noise it makes when it spins."

"Wonder if Ror even knows what a top is?" I mused. "I don't think he's ever spun one before.

"Well, we better make sure he does know what it is and maybe even try to get him to thinking about how much fun it would be if he had one," said Kim.

"What are we gonna use for wrapping paper?" I asked.

"Probably just rip a few pages out of some of those catalogs that are stored in the old house," Kim said nonchalantly. "The pages are so smooth they'll feel just like wrapping paper to Ror."

"Good idea. That way we won't have to bug Mom to wrap it for us or get us any paper. 'Cause then she'd just ask all kinds of questions about what we're up to."

That night at Grandma Hoffman's, while we waited for supper to get on the table, Kim and I asked Rory if he knew what a top was. He said he'd heard of them but didn't know how they worked.

"They're really neat!" Kim told him enthusiastically. "Some of the bigger kind have this little thing on top that you keep pulling and pushing up and down, and that makes it spin around faster and faster on its little stand."

"Oh," Rory said but without much interest.

"And some of them even make noise when they spin," I put in hopefully.

To our relief, this made Rory perk up right away. "They do?" he asked. "I wish I could have one someday."

"Yeah, that would be cool, wouldn't it?" Kim agreed. "But you probably won't get one any time soon. I think they might be kind of expensive."

"Oh shoot," said Rory disappointedly. "Well, maybe I can start saving my own money for one then."

"Do you remember all your songs for the Christmas program?" I asked him without thinking. I regretted my carelessness immediately and hoped nobody else had heard what I said.

"Of course," said Rory, as though insulted that there could be any doubt. "I only have three to do anyway."

"Christmas program?" asked Uncle Rick from the couch where he was flipping through a magazine. "What program is that?"

"Oh, nothing," I replied evasively. "Just a little deal we're having for Ror as part of our playschool in the old house."

"Really? That sounds like fun. Are other people allowed to attend? I'd like to see it when the time comes."

Fortunately, Kim and I were saved from making a reply by Grandma telling us to "Come and get it." We all crowded around the table, and I figured the topic was closed for the time being. But no such luck.

"I hear Kim and Konnie are putting together a Christmas program in the old house," Rick announced to the others at the table. "I said they need to inform us when it's going to be held so we can watch it."

"That's a good idea," Mom exclaimed. "I'll call Gramp and Gram, and we can get the whole crew to come see you guys. That way, you'll have a regular crowd out in the audience."

Suddenly, the food in my mouth seemed dry and hard to swallow. I gulped some Kool-Aid to wash it down. Things were getting out of hand in a hurry.

"Well, we don't know exactly when it's gonna be yet or anything," Kim said vaguely. "But if you want, we'll try to remember to tell you when we're gonna have it."

"You be sure to do that," Dad said. "We all want to be there."

"That's right," Grandma added. "I'd like to come too."

I was surprised Rory didn't pipe up and assure everyone that the program was indeed scheduled for the following day. He didn't spill the beans though, and I was grateful.

My relief was short-lived, however. The next morning, Rory asked what time we were having the program.

Mom overheard him and said, "Oh, so it's going to be today?"

"Yup," Rory replied excitedly. "And I'm doing three whole songs all by myself."

"Good for you," Mom enthused. Then, turning to Kim and me, she advised, "Try to plan your program for late this afternoon if you can so Gramp and Gram will be able to get back to town afterward before it gets too late."

"Okay," we answered soberly.

So that was that. It was going to happen, and everybody was going to be there.

Right after breakfast, Kim and I rushed off to the old house in a panic in order to discuss what, if anything, could be done.

"What are we gonna do?" I moaned melodramatically. "It will never work to have everybody there."

"I know," Kim agreed. "They'll all think it's stupid. I mean, if we would have known anybody wanted to come, we could have made it better and more exciting for an audience to see. But now we don't have enough time to redo any of it."

"Yeah, and what will they think when all they'll mostly hear is a bunch of kids singing on a tape?" I asked ruefully. Kim and I had spent a lot of time the day before, making crowd noise and applause by using two tape-recorders and dubbing our voices several times from one to the other in order to create the audio effect of having a whole bunch of people in the audience. We'd done the same thing with the music—recopying ourselves singing to it so that it would seem to Rory as though many children were involved in the program rather than it being just the three of us.

Kim sighed. "Well, I suppose you and I can get up in front of the mic and act like little kids and sing along with the tape so at least they'll have something to watch. But they're still going to think it's pretty dumb."

"Maybe we can also ask Ror some questions about the Christmas story at the very end or something so he'll have more to do in the program too," I suggested. "But what about the gift-giving thing afterward? That's gonna seem totally ridiculous, that we just dug some old stuff out of our toy box and wrapped it in catalogs."

We both sat there silently for several moments. Then Kim declared in a matter-of-fact tone, "Well, there's nothing we can do about it now, so let's just make the best of it. We're not going to ruin this for Ror at the last minute, so let's just do everything like we planned and not worry about it."

"I guess that's our only choice," I admitted. "In that case, we better start getting ready. Let's see. How many chairs will we need to round up? If both sets of grandparents come, and Mom and Dad, and Uncle Rick, plus the three of us makes ten 'cause Reed can just sit on people's laps. Do you think the room is big enough to fit that many?"

"We'll figure out something," she decided. "Come on. Let's get busy."

Although time had been dragging for the past several days in anticipation of the program, it now sped along much too quickly to suit us. Nevertheless, when 4:00 p.m. rolled around, we had finished with all our last-minute preparations and were waiting serenely as our guests began to arrive.

Finally, Kim cleared her throat and stepped up to the microphone.

"Greetings, ladies and gentlemen. Welcome to our program this evening. It's wonderful to have so many of you with us today. We have a very special program planned for you all, and we hope you will enjoy it as much as we liked putting it together for you. To get us started, let's all stand up tall and sing along to a familiar Christmas tune: 'Jingle Bells.' But before we begin, I'd like all of our students to come on up here to the front please."

Rory and I walked forward and joined Kim at the microphone. She pressed the play button on the recorder that was hooked up to also be broadcast through the amplifier, and the tape began. It started out with a few minutes of crowd noises and the sounds of many children clearing their throats and getting situated. Excited whispers could be heard coming through the speaker, which normally would have added a festive air to the occasion. But Kim and I were a little embarrassed by it all and just tried our best to ignore the recording, which we'd put so much effort into making only the day before.

Rory though was already entranced by this special moment in his life. Reaching over to where I was standing, he asked, "Linda, where are you at?"

Quickly, I knelt and whispered back in a very subdued version of Linda, "I'm right here, Ror."

"What's wrong? Aren't you excited?" Rory wanted to know.

Normally, Linda would have been screaming her head off at the mere prospect of the Christmas program. He couldn't figure out why she was being so standoffish now that the moment had arrived.

I knew I wasn't doing justice to Linda's character, so I took a deep breath and decided to simply attempt to forget about the fact that we had a real audience and instead put my whole heart into the event for Rory's benefit.

"Yeah. I'm just a little nervous," Linda told her classmate. "But I'll get over it if you promise to sing real loud so I won't mess up the words. Okay?"

"All right," Rory agreed. "But I'm sure you know 'Jingle Bells.' It's easy."

Linda sang with her usual vigor and even began stamping her feet in time with the music. I could hear engaged titters from our audience, and I started to realize that maybe people wouldn't see this as being quite as absurd as Kim and I had envisioned. After all, whenever our family had concerts anywhere, Rory was always the hit of the entire evening with his cuteness and jokes. So maybe if Kim and I could capitalize on similar qualities this evening, we might be able to use such childlike antics to our advantage, in order to get the people watching us involved in what was going on. Besides, Dad always said that if you didn't act nervous or uncertain, most of the time, people would never know the difference. So I could only hope that would prove to be true in this instance as well.

When the song ended, everyone clapped and cheered loudly. Bolstered by such a positive response, the master of ceremonies went on with much more enthusiasm than she'd had before.

"Thank you very much. You all sounded marvelous on that first number. And weren't the children wonderful?" She waited for more applause before continuing. "Yes, we're very proud of our students this year, and we think you will be too when you hear the great program they have in store for you. Our first solo this evening will be sung by Rory Hoffman. The rest of you can be seated, but Rory, you might as well stay where you are and do your song for us right now. Ladies and gentlemen, here's Rory with a tune called 'Mr. Snowman.'"

Everyone clapped for Rory while the piano intro began. Rory, feeling perfectly at ease as he always did in front of people, cleared his throat dramatically and started to sing. Of course, everyone loved it, and afterward, the emcee announced the next item on the agenda.

"Now we invite you to all just sit back and relax for a few moments while we present some audio scenes for you of the very first Christmas."

Kim and I had selected a few clips from our Bible in Living Sound cassettes, which dramatized all the great Bible stories. We'd divided the sound-clips into three five-minute segments that would be interspersed throughout the program. Everyone was very quiet and attentive while the tape was playing. We'd been dubious about whether it would hold their attention, but our concern was unfounded. This first part of the story depicted the wise men analyzing dates and scriptures and coming up with the conclusion that a Messiah would be born at any time.

After the segment had ended, the emcee told everyone that next up would be the children's choir with "It Came Upon a Midnight Clear." The original plan for this song had been to merely let the tape recorder run while Kim and I would stay seated in the audience with Rory. We weren't at all sure of many of the lyrics and had simply taped the song from a children's Christmas record. Now though, we realized it would be kind of silly to just sit there and play the tape, especially when our audience had already sat through five minutes of purely auditory stimuli. So the two of us hurriedly conferred and decided to get up in front and be part of the children's choir. Since we didn't know all the words, we just incorporated this into part of our act, pretending we were mischievous kids who were misbehaving and not singing nicely as we should have been doing. I had thought far enough ahead to put a whole wad of bubblegum in my mouth just prior to the song, so in between mumbling through the words, I would pop bubbles loudly and turn my head hurriedly this way and that as an extremely hyper child might do. Kim was doing her best imitation of a kid singing opera and was adlibbing extra little notes here and there for effect between the actual melody lines.

To our surprise, the grown-ups seemed to appreciate this song as much as the previous one that Rory had sung. We even heard a few whistles mixed in with the applause, which we knew must have come from Dad and Uncle Rick. All the same, I breathed a sigh of relief when the song had ended and was more than happy to turn things back over to my little brother again.

"Thank you, children," said the emcee, as I noisily blew bubbles all the way back to my chair. "And now we have another song from our star pupil, Rory Hoffman. At this time, he's going to sing a lively little number entitled 'I Can Hardly Wait till Christmas.'"

This song was as well received as the others had been. Then everyone stood up and sang "Away in a Manger" together, at which point it was time for the second audio segment of the Christmas story to be played. That one dealt with the shepherds seeing the star in the sky and then the angels proclaiming, "Glory to God in the highest, and on earth, peace, good will toward men." Then it was time for the children's choir again with "Winter Wonderland." Fortunately, we knew more of the words this time, so it wasn't necessary to add as much extraneous distraction.

When that song had ended, Joey (aka Kim) stood up and sang "Frosty the Snowman" in his shy but sweet way. Then the emcee informed everyone that we were going to slow things down a bit for the final two selections.

"Rory is going to come up here next and do a very important song that will remind everyone of the true meaning of Christmas, which should never be forgotten. After that, we'll have our final segment of the Christmas story, and then I would like everyone to stand and we'll all close with 'Silent Night.' But be sure to stick around afterward, as the children will be opening some gifts from their teachers."

So Rory sang 'C is for the Christ Child,' in which the word *Christmas* was spelled with each letter having a special meaning to commemorate this most significant of holidays.

C is for the Christ child, born upon that day;
H for herald angels in the night.
R for our redeemer,
I for Israel,
And *S* is for the star that shone so bright.
T is for three wise men,
They had traveled far.
M is for the manger where He lay.
A is all he stands for,
S means shepherds came,
And that's why there's a Christmas Day.

When the song had ended, it was followed by sounds of Mary and Joseph in the stable after the miraculous birth. Then the shepherds came and presented their gifts to the holy child. As the story ended, the three of us sat on the piano bench at the front of the room for a short, informal time of reflection before the program came to a close.

"Rory, what is the most important thing about Christmas?" Miss Green asked him quietly.

"That Jesus was born," Rory replied unhesitatingly.

"Correct," Miss Green told him. "And why did Jesus come to this earth?"

"To die for our sins," was his prompt answer.

A few weeks earlier, Rory had come to a saving knowledge of Jesus Christ. Kim and I had been trying to explain to him a little bit about what it meant to be a child of God, but he wanted to learn more about it from Dad. So we'd gone into the kitchen, where our parents were talking while Mom fed the baby. Rory asked Dad what it meant to be a Christian, and Dad told him that as soon as Mom had finished giving Reed his breakfast, we'd all go into the living room and talk to him about it.

That day, Rory had asked Jesus to come into his heart and be his Savior. He understood that all of us are sinners and that we needed to repent and believe that God would forgive us for the things we had done wrong.

"Do you know why Jesus had to come to earth as a baby and die on the cross?" I asked him now as everyone listened to our conversation.

"'Cause he had to grow up like an ordinary person, but he was perfect, so he took our punishment for us. That way, we could go to heaven and be with Him forever."

"Very good," I said, wiping a tear from my eye as Kim played the beginning notes of "Silent Night." We hadn't rehearsed this talk ahead of time, and I was touched and grateful to see how much Rory understood at such a young age.

Everyone stood and sang along with the well-loved tune that had such a stirring message that would be sung through time immemorial. When the final notes were played and the last line was repeated ("Sleep in heavenly peace"), the emcee thanked everyone for coming and told them to be sure to join us again next year for another marvelous program to commemorate the season.

"Now is it time for our presents?" Rory asked hopefully.

"It certainly is," said Miss Green. "They're all stacked right over here on this table."

While Rory's teachers showed him where his gifts were located, background noise was provided from the tape player to create the effect of other students opening their gifts as well. Rory found the smallest package first, which had been deliberately placed closest to where he sat at the table. He was so anxious to open it that I'm sure he didn't even notice the unconventional wrapping paper.

"What's this?" he asked, as he withdrew a plastic figure that he couldn't immediately identify.

"That's a dinosaur, Ror," Linda told him exuberantly. "You know, we studied about those in science a few weeks ago."

"Oh yeah," Rory acknowledged. "They're the really huge animals that we think got all extinct after the flood."

"And here's another gift to your left," Miss Green said.

Rory took his second package and opened it eagerly.

"Hey, this is some kind of musical instrument," he said excitedly. "I can hear a C chord play when I rattle the box."

"Let me help you open it," Linda shouted with glee, as she jerked the package away from him and threw the lid off in her jubilation.

"Hey, Linda, give that back!" Rory exclaimed indignantly, as he grabbed the box away from her. "You open your own stuff."

"This is two musical instruments in one," Miss Green told him. "See. This side is a little drum. There's even a stick here that goes along with it. So you won't have to use ice cream buckets and spoons anymore."

"And if you turn it over, the other side is a xylophone," Miss Cavin said, demonstrating how the different notes were played by tapping the stick across the notes.

"Cool!" Rory said, as he tried it himself. "I wish it had more than three notes, but it's still pretty good for being just a toy."

"And you have one more present, Ror," said the ever-at-hand Linda. "Right here." She scooted the biggest package over to him with anticipation.

Rory took it from her and examined his final gift more carefully than he had the others before opening it, as though wanting to really appreciate this last gift for as long as possible.

"Well, open it," said Linda impatiently, reaching toward the package.

Quickly, Rory moved it out of her grasp and deliberated over the item even longer just to spite her.

"Well, hurry, Rory," Miss Green finally admonished. "It's almost time to go home."

Rory folded the paper back and examined the contents inside. "This looks interesting," he declared. "But what do you do with it?"

"It's a top, Ror!" Linda said enthusiastically.

"Really?" Rory asked in amazement. "The girls and I were just talking about tops yesterday."

"You stand it on the table like this," Miss Green instructed. "Then you keep pulling and pushing on this little deal up here, and that's what makes it spin."

"Wow! It even makes noise!" Rory shouted unbelievingly. "This is one of those really special tops!"

"It's a UFO top," Linda told him. "It sounds just like a real spaceship when it spins."

"I can't believe I got one of these! This is really something!" Rory said, as he clutched his gift and turned around to where the adults were gathered. "Mom, look at this! My own UFO top! I think this is the best present I ever got!"

Kim and I had been so caught up in showing Rory all of his presents that we'd forgotten about the grown-ups observing the whole affair.

Mom blew her nose and said rather hoarsely, "Wow, Ror! That is a nice gift, isn't it?"

"Are you gettin' a cold, Mom?" Rory asked concernedly. "You sound kinda funny."

"She just really, really liked your program, as we all did," Dad told him.

"In fact," Mom spoke up again, "I'm going to phone Ruby right now and set up a time where you guys can do this all again for the folks in the nursing home."

"What?" I asked in disbelief. "We can't do this crazy stuff in front of all those people."

"Sure you can," Mom insisted. "They would just love it, wouldn't they, Rolly?"

"No question about it," Dad agreed fervently. "They'd be on the edge of their seats like we were, loving every bit of it. I can just see them now, singing along with all the songs and just having the best time ever."

"And they'd get such a kick out of how you girls act like little kids and change your voices and everything," Mom went on.

"That's a great idea," Rick affirmed. "Then I could come along and see the whole thing again myself."

"Well, I guess we could probably do most of it," I decided hesitantly. "But maybe we'd just leave out the Christmas story tape."

"Are you kidding? That's the most important part," Dad told us. "Besides, it would remind those old people of way back when, sitting around their radios and listening to all those great old-time shows."

"And they won't be able to get over the part where you ask Ror those questions at the end either," Mom added. "That was really special."

"We just came up with that idea today," Kim said as we all put on our coats. "Anyway, we're sure glad you liked the program."

"We didn't know you all were going to come," I admitted, "but it made everything more realistic and fun this way."

The tape player clicked off, and the room suddenly grew quiet without the extra background noise.

"I guess the other kids and teachers have all gone home," Kim said. "We better leave before they lock up the school for the night."

"I don't think Joey got to see my UFO top," Rory lamented. "Is it okay if I bring it back to school tomorrow so I can show him?"

"Of course," I answered. "We're sure glad you liked all of your presents so much. And just think. In a few more days, you'll be getting even more presents, when Christmas gets here!"

"And we might even get the demo of our album in the mail before our break is over," Kim said hopefully. "Then it really would be the best Christmas vacation ever."

Changes and Choices

A lot of that Christmas vacation was spent in practicing for our second album. Although it was true that our first one wasn't even out yet, our momentum was going strong, and we wanted to keep at it while the inspiration was flowing. Besides, since we had begun, we were going to try to put out a new product every year if possible, so we knew there was no time to waste. Uncle Rick had come up with the title of *Cross Country*, which we all agreed was the perfect name for several reasons. Our music was about Christ, as denoted by the word *cross* and it was a cross between country and gospel.

"Plus, we're hoping to someday travel 'cross the whole country with our music," Kim added.

Rick had also put his artistic creativity to good use by designing an album cover that displayed a cross in each corner. We'd even gone a step further and composed an instrumental that would be the title track on the album. This song featured the different instruments coming in one at a time until the whole band was going full steam. We couldn't wait to start performing it as an introduction at our future concerts.

Uncle Rick had also written a new song entitled "Running from the Call," which we were planning to put on the *Cross Country* recording. It had a unique chord structure that wasn't typical of the style of music we normally played, and we were eager to give it a try. Denny had chosen one of his favorites called "Outlaw's Prayer" to do on the upcoming project as well, and it was agreed to let Rory do two songs this time instead of only one. We decided on "I'm Little, But I'm Loud," and an original by the Lundstroms called "Bundle of Joy," which would be dedicated to his little brother. The balance of the new record would be comprised of original selections by Dad and others sung by Kim and me.

"I love that thing Rick does on his mandolin for 'My Jesus Makes a Way,'" Kim said to me, as we headed to the old house for another practice session. "It really adds to the song."

"I know. And I wonder how he ever came up with that neat guitar sound on 'Try a Little Kindness'? I bet nobody will be able to figure that out when they hear it."

"He sure does have a lot of good ideas," Kim agreed fervently.

And that night was no exception. "I've been thinking about your song, Rolly, 'Something Changed Me Inside,'" Rick said thoughtfully, as we all sat down at our instruments. "What if we slow it down a little bit and incorporate a smoother rhythm—something like this." He strummed through a few lines to demonstrate.

"Hmm," I don't know," Dad said. "It sure sounds different that way. Might take some getting used to."

"I believe you'll like it once you get the hang of it," Rick went on. "Then I was also thinking that we could put in a few fancy breaks and chord changes in the chorus—something like this." He started to sing. "Now people say I'm crazy." F, C, D went the guitar. "I'm giving up my music"—F, G, C—Playing in those honkytonks and singin' in those bars. How do you like it?"

"I think it's really cool that way," Kim told him enthusiastically. "Let's all do it together and see how it sounds."

We were all in high spirits as we trooped back home late that night. It had been a very productive few hours, and we were keyed up about having made so much headway in one evening. To add to our excitement even more, the next day was Christmas Eve.

That Christmas was a very memorable one for Kim and me. Our *Standing on the Rock* demo still hadn't arrived, but there was a sense of anticipation in the air, which added to the overall festive mood of the holidays. On Christmas Eve, everyone, including all the grandparents, gathered in our living room to open presents, as was our tradition. For Kim and me, the highlights of the gift giving that year were surprisingly provided by Uncle Rick. Even though he had no previous experience shopping for fourteen-year-old nieces, he seemed to know exactly what we would most enjoy.

"What on earth is this?" Kim asked in a puzzled tone, as she removed a long plastic object made of connected little blocks from the package.

"It's called a snake," Rick replied. "You can make all kinds of interesting stuff with this thing, believe it or not."

"Hmm. Like what?" I asked curiously.

"Just watch this," Rick said, taking the snake away from Kim and tinkering with it for a few moments. "There. See what I did?" He placed the object in my hands, but it no longer resembled the long, thin snake it had been at first. Instead, it now looked like a cross.

"Wow. Look what he did with this," I said to Kim, as I showed her how it had been transformed.

"Hey, how did you do that?" asked Kim, quite intrigued. "I wanna try."

"Wait a minute. Let me show you something else," Rick said. "This is pretty far out."

He worked with the snake some more, and that time, it turned into a round ball, of all things.

"Hey, that's neat! So I guess you can make all sorts of stuff out of it," I said excitedly.

"I just love puzzle-type things like this," Kim cried, reaching for the snake eagerly. "I'm gonna keep practicing until I'll be able to make that ball in thirty seconds or less soon."

"That wouldn't surprise me at all," Rick affirmed. "But there's another present here that I think you're going to like even more."

To our delight, Rick's prediction proved to be correct. His second gift to us was a Simon Deluxe. It contained twelve colors rather than the four that were normally found on a typical Simon game. Each colored button made a different musical note, so we were able to tell which one was flashing. And instead of only one or two games, the deluxe version included a grand total of eight, each having many different levels and permutations.

Kim and I were enchanted as Rick patiently explained to us how each game was played and what all the different knobs and buttons did. He'd obviously done his homework ahead of time. We were completely oblivious to everything else that was going on around us except for the large racket made by Reed, who was having the time of his life kicking and rolling around in the huge pile of wrapping paper. We had to shout in order to be heard above all the commotion he was making, but other than that, we just ignored it and concentrated on what our uncle was saying.

"Now this next one is a two-player game, so you'll both be able to do it at the same time. One of you works with these four colors at the top, and the other uses the ones at the bottom. The colors in the middle will be flashing sequentially, and whenever they stop, you both get to see which of you has the fastest reflexes and is quick enough to hit the appropriate next color on your row first."

"So pretty much the same concept as hot potato or musical chairs," I surmised.

"I guess that's true," Rick agreed.

He played the game with us a couple of times to demonstrate how it worked, and then he showed us another one.

"This next game is kind of like twenty questions, where you have to figure out which three colors the Simon is thinking of by trying guesses and using process of elimination."

"That sounds like fun," I said with interest.

"And then, of course, there's your typical Simon game, where it keeps adding one more color each time to test how much your memory can retain. Plus, there's a chain reaction-type game, where the two of you kind of invent your own Simon by copying what the other person does and then adding your own color."

"Boy, this is going to be so fun!" Kim exulted. "It will make our trips to Aberdeen go a whole lot faster. That's for sure."

"Well, I'm really glad you like it so much," Rick told us. "I was hoping you would."

"Girls, it's getting late," Mom put in. "I know you could stay up all night and play with that thing, but we'll have another big day tomorrow."

"And we'll get to have our fancy dinner with turkey and dressing, and potatoes and gravy, and pie, and all kinds of yummy stuff," Rory added from where he was playing with his new motorcar at the other side of the room.

It always amazed us how he was tuned in to what everyone else was doing and talking about, even while being engrossed with his own activities.

"Oh yes, we'll have our Christmas dinner," Gram assured him with a laugh. "Well, we should be getting on home, Stan. It's late."

The rest of our Christmas vacation sped past before we knew it. As the time drew near for Kim and me to return to school, our anxiety increased because it looked like we wouldn't get the demo before we left for school after all. If that proved to be the case, we'd have to wait until an upcoming weekend to hear how it had turned out, and that would seem like forever.

When the dreaded day arrived though, to our immense relief, the weather was so stormy that Mom and Dad decided the trip back to Aberdeen would need to be postponed.

"We might as well keep the girls home the rest of the week," Mom declared, "because tomorrow will already be Wednesday, and even if we are able to make it out of here by then, we'd be going after them again in just a couple more days."

"Yay!" Kim and I shouted joyously. "That means we might get to hear the demo right away when it comes."

Much to our delight, this proved to be the case. The roads were still pretty snow-packed the following day, and our postal service decided not to risk sending the mailman our way just yet. However, Mom and Dad had driven in worse weather than this, so Dad plowed Mom out enough to make it possible for her to go to town and see if there might be any mail waiting for us at the post office.

Sure enough, our album had arrived. Mom phoned us from Gram's house to give us the exciting news, and we all agreed then and there that the thing to do was to invite Jane and Denny and both sets of grandparents to join us that evening so we could all listen to the finished product together for the first time.

Kim and I could hardly wait for evening to arrive. Neither could anyone else, apparently, for we were all gathered in the living room next to our stereo long before dusk.

"This first song is one that I wrote many years ago," Dad said by way of explanation to the grandparents. "You probably won't recognize it though because I haven't sung it for a long time. It's a country tune called 'I Just Play Rhythm.'"

"I think I remember that one," Gramp put in. "Didn't you do it sometimes with your country band way back when? It talks about your brother playing lead guitar but you just play rhythm or something like that, right?"

"That's the one," Dad confirmed. "We decided to dig out a couple of my old country songs to begin each side of the record. Anyway, here it is."

Of course, being the devoted grandparents they were, everyone oohed and aahed after each song in turn, claiming they only got better with each passing melody.

"This has always been one of my favorites," whispered Grandma Hoffman, as the opening notes of "Through it All" began to play. "It has such a good message, and you girls sound just like angels when you sing it."

"Now this last number on side one is called 'Rusty Old Halo,'" Dad said when we'd reached the sixth tune. "Denny does this one."

"I didn't know Denny could sing," said Gram in surprise.

"Yeah. He really came out of the woodwork for this album," Jane told her proudly. "He even sings harmony with Rolly on one of the songs you'll hear later."

"I'll be darned," said Gramp. "I can't wait to hear it."

"And I want you to listen really close to the piano on this one," Dad said. "Kim is playing, and you aren't gonna believe what she does on the last chorus."

Everyone sat on the edge of their seats, absorbing the music and appreciating Denny's vocal talents, which none of them had heard before. They all jumped when Kim did a quick piano run near the end, from the bottom to the top of the keyboard.

"Wow! I didn't know you could do that, Kim!" Gramp exclaimed. "That sounded just like Jerry Lee Lewis!"

"Back that up and play it again, Rolly," Mom enthused. Then, turning to our audience, she expounded further. "Yeah. We were sure surprised when she came out with that. She'd never done anything like it before, but doesn't it sound neat right there?"

"It sure does," Gram agreed. "Did that take a lot of practice, Kim?"

"It's not too hard once you get the hang of it," Kim told her.

"I guess she really wanted to make Denny's song special," Mom added. "And wait until you hear the last song on side two. That's Rick's, and Konnie does something on there you won't want to miss either."

"Well, this is sure something," Gramp said, after Dad had played the last part of Denny's song again and then went to flip the recording over to the other side. "I just can't believe you guys finally have your record after all these years. And it's such a good one too!"

"And they'll only get better from here," I predicted boastfully. "You should hear all the new ideas we're cooking up for the second one already."

"You're working on number two so soon?" Gram asked incredulously.

"Strike while the iron is hot." Rick laughed.

"You still awake, Pa?" asked Dad of Grandpa Hoffman from where he was nodding off in the corner. "This next one's for you."

Grandma gave him a nudge and told him to pay attention.

"This is called 'Daddy's Gonna Hear His Songs Again,'" Dad explained. "If you listen carefully, you should hear snatches of some of your favorite old songs."

He started the music, and we all listened as his voice on the record proclaimed, "Daddy's gonna hear his songs again, the ones that he used to sing when he was just a kid. We'd gather 'round his favorite chair, we'd play his songs and sing while Daddy rocked, tapped his foot, and grinned."

After a couple more measures had elapsed, Grandpa perked up and observed happily, "That sounds like 'Oklahoma Hills.'"

"It sure does," Grandma agreed. "That's really great how you all were able to put in the different songs that way."

After the second refrain, this time, it was Grandpa Holdahl who noticed the second old favorite hidden within the main song. "That's 'You Are My Sunshine.' I don't know how you guys come up with all these ideas, but it really sounds nice."

The praise and compliments continued all the way to the final song entitled "Why I Didn't Stay."

"Now this is the song that Rick wrote," Mom reminded everybody. "Listen to the violins in the background."

"That sounds like a whole orchestra," Gram said in astonishment after the first few notes began. "Where on earth did you get all those instruments from?"

I laughed. "That's just me, Gram. I'm using one of the instrument voices on our electric piano that sounds like strings. So I play the bass notes with my left hand and the violins with my right."

"Gosh. That sounds pretty," Gramp told me. "I haven't heard you play like that before either."

"Isn't it beautiful though?" Grandma Hoffman agreed. "I never heard anything like it."

"That's what we all thought," Mom praised me further. "It's pretty neat how God worked it out so one of the girls really added a special touch to Denny's song and the other one did the same thing for Rick's."

"That's really great," said Gram. "I could just sit here and listen to the whole record all over again."

And we promptly did just that. It seemed none of us could quite get over the fact that this album was, indeed, a reality.

It was mutually agreed that we should start booking ourselves now rather than waiting for churches to call us. We believed that playing in city halls, high school gyms, and other auditoriums would encourage more unchurched people to attend our concerts. Since we wanted to start doing the shows on Friday and Saturday nights, we reasoned that people from all different churches would be able to attend. Mom and Dad also planned to take our album all over North and South Dakota to as many radio stations as they could in order to ask the DJs if they could give our music some air play.

As things turned out though, the next couple of months were very difficult. Most of the many station managers that Mom and Dad talked to seemed reluctant to play our record because we were largely unknown and not part of their official playlist. Our concerts weren't nearly as well attended as we'd hoped either. In fact, our audiences had usually been bigger before, when we were playing in churches. Our family was in charge of doing all the advertising too, which was an additional expense on top of the normal costs, such as gasoline, meals, and sometimes hotel costs for the entire band as well as general wear and tear on the van and musical equipment. We had so much gear to bring along that it was necessary to purchase a trailer that was pulled behind the van. Every Friday, after bringing us home from Aberdeen, we would all practice for our second record. Then, early the next morning, Dad and Rick would move everything from the old house into the trailer and we'd take off for wherever we were scheduled to be that night. We usually had to bring our own piano because, unlike churches, most of the places where we were now performing didn't have one. It was heavy and cumbersome to load and unload every week. The drums, amplifiers, and other equipment also took a lot of time and effort to unload, set up, and then load back into the trailer again after the concerts, not to mention needing to be put back into the old house when we got home.

After months of this rigorous routine, Jane and Denny, in particular, were starting to have second thoughts about the whole thing. Jane had always been a homebody, and it was stressful for her to pack up every weekend and travel the hundreds of miles with the rest of us to our destination for such little gain. Finally, it was decided that all of us would get together at their home one evening so we could try to find out what their intentions were in order to know how to proceed. Sadly, by that point, nothing they shared with us was really very surprising.

"Even if your dreams do come true and the ministry gets to be full time, I just couldn't hack all the traveling involved," Jane admitted. "I hoped I would be able to, but it's just harder than I thought it would be."

"There just isn't an easy answer," Denny continued. "Things don't seem to be going anywhere right now, but like Janie said, even if they were, that would present its own problems."

"We couldn't just pick up and leave our jobs and our horses and the folks," Jane put in. She was dabbing at her eyes and sniffling, so we knew this wasn't any easier for them to say than it was for us to hear.

"But what are we supposed to do without a drummer?" Mom asked. "Especially now, when we're right in the middle of practicing for the second album? We won't be able to find a new drummer right away, much less teach him everything you've all been working on, Denny."

"There was a long silence. Then Dad questioned further in a soft tone, "Why didn't you both say something sooner if this is what you've been thinking?"

"This is exactly why," Jane said. "Because we realized the fix we'd be putting you in and we knew how disappointed you'd be. We just didn't know how to back out without hurting everyone's feelings."

"You guys have been our good friends for years," Denny went on. "We sure don't want that to end now."

There was another long silence. Then Dad spoke up again.

"Well, if that's the way it has to be, let's just have a word of prayer for now and leave each other in love, trusting that God will work out all the details and help us get through this trial just like the others we've had to face."

Mom blew her nose and gave Jane a hug. Then we all held hands and said a heartfelt prayer that God would show us what to do next and that there would be no hard feelings between any of us.

On the way home that night, I soberly contemplated what Jane and Denny had said and what this would mean for our family and our music. Everyone else must have had similar thoughts because the trip was very somber and quiet. At last, Uncle Rick decided to comment. "Well, that sure puts a clinker in everything, doesn't it?"

"We can't give up," Dad replied firmly, as though he were convincing himself along with the rest of us. "We'll just have to start looking around for another drummer."

"I'll be your drummer," Rory put in suddenly. As usual, he'd been tuned in to everything that was going on.

The rest of us sat there, speechless, as we tried to take in this announcement.

"You're way too young yet, Ror," Mom told him sadly.

"But I already know all the songs and the beats that Denny uses on every one," Rory insisted. "Sometimes when we practice, I get to play Denny's drums until he gets there, and I do pretty good, don't I, Dad? Tell Mom I'm big enough to be your drummer."

"You do a pretty good job for a kid your age, but in order to play on a record, you have to do a whole lot of practicing, and I don't think you're quite up to that," Dad responded gently.

"Hold on a minute," interjected Uncle Rick. "Let's give this some thought. Rory is usually right there the whole time we're practicing, and he does have good rhythm. Besides, it isn't like we have a lot of choice at this point."

"With a little practice, we might be surprised at what all he could do," Kim added.

"But he doesn't have a drum set," I reminded them. "And he won't be able to use Denny's anymore."

"We'd just have to buy him his own if we're actually going to consider going this route," Dad said. "I suppose if we had to, we could always postpone the recording of the next album until he's ready."

"Oh, I don't want to postpone anything," Rick hurried to voice his opinion on that score. "Let's just hope he'll be ready when the time comes."

"I think you guys are expecting an awful lot of a four-year-old," Mom told us doubtfully.

"He'll be five by then," I corrected her, as though this fact made a world of difference. "Five and a half even."

"Big deal," Mom retorted a little sarcastically. "Well, I haven't heard him on Denny's drum set, but if you all think he might be up to it, I suppose we can give it a try and see how it works out. Just don't expect too much too soon."

This advice was hard to follow though. We already had a picture in our minds of how this second album was supposed to sound, and none of us, including Rory himself, wanted to give up that dream. We were all so proud of him when he sat behind his new little red drum set for the first time. I'm sure that Mom, who takes pictures of everything, still has photos of that momentous occasion. It was almost bigger than he was, and the cymbals were hard for him to reach, even though several catalogs had been placed on his stool to boost him up higher. It frustrated him at first that he wasn't able to hit all the drums at the right time and make things sound just the way Denny had, but he was determined to stick with it.

Our intensive practice schedule didn't slow down a bit after Rory took over as our drummer. In fact, it picked up momentum. Since it was no longer necessary to plan ahead in order that Denny would know when to drive out to our place to rehearse, we grabbed extra time whenever we could. We wanted to give Rory as much opportunity as possible to learn the songs, and he would never turn down a chance to play music. Even when the practice sessions were difficult, Rory was always up for more and didn't lose his enthusiasm.

"Ror, you forgot to use your ride cymbal on the chorus," I reminded him. "Why don't we back up and try that again so he gets used to going to the ride as soon as the verse is done?"

"And try to stay as steady as you can, Ror," Kim added. "You sped up a little bit last time.

One of the hardest techniques for Rory to master seemed to be the cross stick, which we referred to as the rim shot. It just didn't have the same firm sound that it had when Denny did it. We tried not to be too fussy about it, but even Dad and Uncle Rick seemed to think he could get the hang of it if he just kept at it. Dad tried to show him how to lay his hand so that he could hit the rim of the drum, but then it was hard for Rory to move his hand again in time to go to a full snare beat whenever the rim shot portion of the song had ended. Finally, Dad decided that the best solution for now might be to just buy Rory a wood block, which he could hit instead of the rim of the snare drum.

The months continued to pass by, but little progress was being made with promotion of our first album or audience growth. Kim and I were beginning to sense tension in the family, but we didn't want to think about it or face what that might mean. One evening, though, Mom made a strange announcement.

"Your dad and I are going to leave you girls with your brothers for a couple hours tonight while we go over to Grandma Hoffman's for a while. Okay?"

"What are you going to do there?" Kim wanted to know. "Can't we come too?"

"No. I think it will be best if you girls stay home," Mom replied. "We're just going to talk to your Uncle Rick about a few things."

Neither of us responded right away. We had already gleaned inklings of what this conversation might be like, and we were sobered at the thought. Even though we were afraid it wouldn't be pleasant, however, we still wanted to be part of the conversation, if we could. We felt that even though we were only fourteen, we should have the right to get a true picture of whatever went on with Roland Hoffman and the Believers. We didn't want to be given a glossed-over version of events after the fact. Besides, Uncle Rick was part of the family.

"Maybe you could turn on the intercom so we can listen over here to what's happening," I suggested.

Our parents had purchased some intercoms which they'd placed around the ranch to facilitate communication. There was one at Grandma's house, one at ours, another at the old house, and also one in Dad's shop where he worked on the farm equipment. They were generally used for practical purposes such as Grandma telling everybody to "Come and get it" whenever it was suppertime. Now though, I figured they might come in handy for occasions like this as well.

Mom seemed to understand how we were feeling and gave my idea some consideration. "We'll see," she relented. "I'll probably turn it on for a few minutes at least, just so you can get the basic gist of the conversation."

Time dragged by at a snail's pace after that. We were dreading what might happen but were also anxious to get it over with and find out where things stood. At last, the moment arrived. Our parents kissed Rory and Reed good night and then started for Grandma Hoffman's house. Kim and I stood by the intercom, waiting for Mom to turn it on at her end so we could adjust the volume and get everything tuned in just right. We wanted to be able to hear what they discussed as clearly as possible.

"I wonder if she forgot," Kim said after what seemed like an eternity.

Just then, however, a crackling noise began to come out of the speaker, and we could hear the sound of the intercom at Grandma's being moved to a better location. At first, there was the obligatory small talk, but it was obvious that everyone wanted to just get down to the matter at hand as quickly as possible.

"Well, Rick," Dad began, "we know you haven't been very happy with the way things are going lately, and we just wanted to get a handle on what you're thinking and try to get to the bottom of whatever it is that's going on in your head."

Uncle Rick didn't answer right away. When he did, his voice was so subdued that Kim and I were forced to put our ears right next to the intercom, in order to hear what he was saying.

"I'm sure you can probably figure it out," he said. "You aren't dummies."

"You feel like the ministry isn't moving fast enough for you and you want out," Mom replied bluntly, cutting right to the chase. "Is that it?"

There was another long pause.

"Pretty much I guess," he admitted dejectedly. "I just feel so frustrated and don't know what to do about it. They aren't playing our music on the radio, and nobody's coming to our shows either. We go through all that work and time and practice, and for what? It all just seems so hopeless."

"Oh, it isn't that bad," Mom corrected him. "You're exaggerating. The Lemmon radio station is playing our records, and a couple others are starting to play it too. And I wouldn't exactly say that nobody comes to our concerts. The people who do show up always leave feeling blessed."

"I don't believe it's hopeless either," Dad continued. "We just have to give it time and learn how to promote ourselves. Hardly anybody even realizes we have a record out yet. Maybe we need to start going back to the churches so more people will find out what we're doing now."

"No, I'm not interested in going that route," Rick said determinedly.

"But why not, Ricky?" Grandma put in with tears in her voice. "Aren't you interested in serving God anymore?"

Rick sighed. "It isn't that so much. I guess maybe I just don't feel worthy or strong enough to stick with it. I'm just restless. You know me, always wanting to see what's on the other side of the fence and not be tied down. I thought it would improve in time if I toughed it out, but I've never been a patient guy." He laughed self-consciously. "We just don't have that professional sound since Denny left. Not to belittle Rory's talents or anything. The kid is great. He's phenomenal even for his age. But it's just not a tight sound anymore."

"You have to start somewhere though," Dad told him. "If we wait until we're perfect to start serving God, none of us would ever do anything for Him."

"That makes sense too," Rick conceded. "And who knows? Maybe in a few years I'll be back. You can never tell."

"But you just can't keep coming and going like that, Rick," Mom said. "Do you realize how devastated the girls will be when they hear you're pulling out?"

"I know, and I'm not proud of it. That probably bothers me more than anything else about this whole deal, disappointing Kim and Konnie. But what can you do? I gave it my best shot. I just don't have it in me anymore, and I'm not going to pretend that I do."

Tears slid silently down my face as I listened to what they were saying. I didn't want to believe it, but I knew I had to. Our Uncle Rick was really going to leave again, just when we'd gotten to know and trust him. We certainly had never thought he would do anything like that to us. It didn't make any sense.

Kim and I sat quietly, the matter weighing on us so heavily that we didn't even feel like discussing it with one another. What on earth was going to happen with our music now that both Rick and Denny would be gone? Memories of only a few months earlier flooded my mind: the wonderful Christmas vacation we'd had with that program in the old house, and the great presents Uncle Rick had given us, and how we'd gathered so excitedly to listen to our record for the first time. Could it all be coming to an end so suddenly, before it had really even begun?

Rory, the Drummer

"All right now. Let's go through that again," Miss Applewhite (also known as Kim) said patiently to her prize pupil.

Rory was trying valiantly to learn the fine art of opening and closing the hi-hat with his foot and hitting it with his stick at just the right rhythm all while keeping the core bass-snare beat going with his other foot and hand at the same time. Nothing to it, right? Think again.

"I can't do it," Rory said forlornly. "I know how it's supposed to sound, 'cause I've heard Denny do it." He attempted the rhythm once more but to no avail. "I just can't get all my hands and feet working together at the same time like I'm supposed to," he declared.

"Of course you can," Miss Applewhite told him in no uncertain terms. "You just have to keep working at it. Let's start out very slowly so you can have more time to concentrate on each step of the process."

So Rory, trooper that he was, gave it another try.

"Hey, I think I'm gettin' it," he exclaimed excitedly. "Listen to this! I'm really doin' it!"

"You certainly are," Miss Applewhite agreed in a matter-of-fact tone. "Now just gradually speed up a little more if you can."

Rory tripped up a bit when he attempted this, but once he knew it could be done, his confidence was bolstered to the point where he was determined to be master of the hi-hat and not let it get the best of him any longer.

"There you go," praised Miss Applewhite. "You're getting the hang of it. Now I'll play along on the piano, and remember, when I get to the end of the verse, you do that fancy roll we talked about and then do the chorus with the ride cymbal. Okay?"

"Okay," Rory agreed hesitantly. "I'll see if I can."

"Excellent job," Miss Applewhite told him when they'd done a verse and chorus successfully. "Actually though, I have an even better idea."

"Tell it to me tomorrow. I'm gettin' kinda tired," Rory said. "Besides, I don't wanna miss supper."

"Oh, I won't let you miss supper," Miss Applewhite assured him. "This will be simple. Instead of hitting the snare drum on the verses, let's find out how it sounds using the rim shot."

"No. That will be too hard," Rory complained. "I just learned how to do the rim shot a few days ago, but I won't be able to think about how to do that plus the hi-hat all at the same time."

"Let's just give it a try," Miss Applewhite insisted. "You thought you'd never be able to do the rim shot either, and now look at you. You don't even need the wood block anymore. So don't give up on something before you've even attempted it. That's not being a very good sport."

Rory sighed loudly. "I don't wanna do this," he muttered, even as his arms and legs were already beginning the rhythm.

Within a couple of minutes, Miss Applewhite's high expectations were again fulfilled.

"That's wonderful, Rory! I knew you could do it! Now let's just see if we can vary the rhythm a little bit."

"No!" Rory rebelled vehemently this time. "I bet you couldn't even do some of this stuff. I don't wanna learn any more things right now."

"Rory," said Miss Applewhite sternly, "what kind of way is that to talk to your teacher?"

"I'm goin' home," said Rory determinedly, as he got up from his stool and headed for the door. "Mom says she's makin' fish and fried macaroni for supper, and I don't wanna be late."

"Rory, you come back here right now. I haven't dismissed you yet," Miss Applewhite called after him indignantly, reaching out her hand in an endeavor to catch him before he could get away.

Rory, however, was too quick for her. He leaped from her grasp just in time and ran out the door. His teacher was left behind with only his beanie in her hand, which she had snatched from his head in her effort to stop his escape.

Right after supper, we were back at it again, having our usual weekend practice session with Dad. Fortunately, Rory's enthusiasm for playing music had already returned by that point. This was probably mostly due to the fact that he knew that Dad's presence would keep things from getting too out of hand.

Tonight would be the first time we'd practiced together as a band since Uncle Rick's departure, and Kim and I weren't really looking forward to it. Rick had done a lot of the musical arrangements and had come up with most of the unique ideas. What would we do now without that input, not to mention without a lead guitar to add fancy licks and improve upon the melody lines of our songs? We knew we'd have to just accept the fact that this second album was destined not to be as good as the first one had been, but taking so many steps backward after all the progress we'd made was very difficult.

The atmosphere that evening was much more somber and far less energetic than was typical for our Saturday night sessions. Usually, we would have burst into a spontaneous mini jam session before getting down to business, but we didn't have the heart for that this evening. Instead, we soberly took our places in front of our instruments and waited for the new order of procedure to take effect, whatever that might be. Finally, Dad strummed his guitar a couple of times and said in what sounded to me like a falsely enthusiastic tone, "Well, first on the list is our 'Cross Country' instrumental. What do you suppose we should do with that one?"

My sister and I sat there silently for several moments. Then Kim spoke up.

"I think we should just get rid of it," was her blunt response. "It won't sound nearly as good without Uncle Rick's lead guitar, and I don't think Ror is quite steady enough yet to be able to do the beginning intro all on his own, like Denny did."

None of us could dispute what she said, so Dad resignedly agreed that she was probably right.

"Even if we take that one out though, we still have more songs than most albums do," he reminded us, wanting to put the best light possible on the situation.

This time though, it was my turn to put the damper on it.

"But, of course, now we won't have Rick's and Denny's songs, either," I said unhappily.

"Well, maybe we can come up with something else to take their place," Dad suggested. But that prospect wasn't a pleasant one this late in the game either.

Rory was the only person who didn't seem to be very affected by Uncle Rick's absence. He did an impressive drum roll and crashed around on his cymbals until Dad finally told him to tone it down a bit.

"Dad, I know how to do a good hi-hat beat now," Rory told him proudly. "Just listen to this." And he proceeded to show Dad his latest achievement.

"Wow! How did you learn that all of a sudden?"

"I dunno," Rory replied. "I just kept workin' at it, and pretty soon, I got the hang of it."

"Miss Applewhite helped you, didn't she?" Kim hinted knowingly, deciding it was only fair to give credit where credit was due.

"No. Not really," insisted Rory. "She just kept buggin' me until I finally got mad and went home. She even grabbed my beanie. I wonder where it is now."

"I think she brought it home and put it on the table," answered Kim hurriedly and then quickly changed the subject. "Dad, I've been thinking about something I could do on the keyboard for 'Try a Little Kindness' since Uncle Rick isn't here to do that nifty guitar part anymore."

I swallowed hard, trying not to think about the incredible guitar accompaniment that Rick had come up with to embellish the song. We would just have to make do with what we had left. Kim was fiddling with the buttons and slides on the electric keyboard where she sat.

"I wonder what would happen if I used a lot of violins on the intro with a little sustain added in," she said thoughtfully, adjusting the sound a bit more while she spoke.

In fact, it didn't sound bad at all. Different from what the effect had been before, naturally but definitely worth listening to and expounding upon in its own right.

"I'll play the piano at the lower end, so those high violins will stick out more," I reasoned. "And why don't we try to slow down the ending, like this." I demonstrated what I was thinking, and the others agreed that it was a good idea.

We went over the song again, and as we did, I concentrated on putting as much variety into my piano playing as I could since we no longer had the lead guitar to fill in extra notes. I observed that some of the energy and excitement which had been lacking before now seemed to be returning somewhat. Maybe, just maybe, with God's help, we could pull this off after all.

We rehearsed the song a couple more times and noted that it kept getting better with each successive attempt.

So far so good, I had to admit to myself.

Now if we could just keep the ideas flowing in a similar fashion for the rest of the night, we'd have it made. I figured that was probably wishful thinking though. What we'd accomplished already that night was more than we'd dared to hope for.

"Let's do 'Lord, Hear My Prayer' next," Dad suggested.

Kim and I switched instruments, and Dad began to sing. He stopped midway through the chorus though.

"I just got a brainstorm. I wonder what it would sound like if we did it more like this."

We started again, only this time Dad's voice had a new timbre and he was using a different style of singing. He changed the melody slightly as well, and I had to confess that I liked the revised version. It apparently inspired Kim too because she was playing differently than she had been before.

"Sounds really good, Kim," Dad praised her. "How did you come up with that?"

Kim told him that she'd recently learned the slurring technique she'd chosen from listening to one of Mickey Gilley's records.

"Well, however you're doing it, keep it up. It really adds to the song."

"What's next?" I asked eagerly.

It was hard to believe that we were actually anticipating each song instead of dreading it. God was certainly giving us an extra measure of creativity that night. It was impossible to ignore the fact that He must really want us to go forward with our plans in spite of everything.

"I think we'll do 'I'm Little, But I'm Loud' next. How does that sound? Are you ready to give that a try, Ror?"

"Sure," Rory obliged without hesitation. "I know I won't have to sing and drum at the same time for the record, but I should still practice it that way so I'll be able to do it at the concerts, right?"

"Not a bad idea," Dad agreed. "Let's give it a whirl."

I recalled with irony the first time Kim and I had broached the question to our parents of whether we could be allowed to play and sing at the same time. We had been way more than twice Rory's age. But I decided it best to refrain from reminding anybody of that fact right now.

Rory, of course, did a great job. I couldn't help but wish that Uncle Rick was there to hear how well we were managing this evening. I was so proud of my little brother as he ran through the song without a hitch.

The rest of the practice session that night went just as well as the first part had. It was decided that we'd even get Mom involved in the action by asking her to play her tambourine on a couple of the tunes. Kim and I thought of a different-sounding beat for Rory to do on the verses of one of our songs, which would add a unique flavor. The chorus was played with a 4/4 rhythm while the verses would now be done in more of a 2/4 pattern. When we'd gone through all of the songs, Dad suddenly had yet another brainstorm.

"I just got to thinking. You know that song Denny was going to do, 'Outlaw's Prayer'?"

"Yeah, what about it?" we asked in unison.

"Well, instead of that, how about I do the story out of Grandma's scrapbook about the school teacher? I'll just read the story, and you girls can play some nice background music. I think that would be a good way to close out the album."

"Good idea," I affirmed eagerly. "That will probably end up being one of people's favorites."

"And you could even close out our concerts with that same song," Kim added. "It would be a good lead-in for how you usually like to end the program, explaining to people about becoming a Christian and what that means and everything."

We couldn't wait to tell Mom all about how productive our evening had been. She was very happy to hear that everything had gone so well, and it gave us all a much-needed boost to carry us through until the time came for recording our second album.

The big day finally arrived, and we felt well-prepared for what was to come. I think that even more than the final product, what we were looking forward to most at that moment was showing off Rory's talents to Harvey, the recording engineer who had produced our first project and would be doing the same for the new one.

Harvey was very professional about it though and simply treated him like one of the guys. The only time he deviated from this pattern was when he'd finally had enough of Rory's big sisters' constant little criticisms and corrections of their brother's drumming.

"Ror, you were a little late coming in with that new beat after the chorus. Try it again."

"Ror, you're dragging a little bit. Be sure to listen to the rest of us and stay right with the rhythm."

"Don't forget that fancy roll before we head into the chorus, Ror."

"For Pete's sake, you girls! The kid is only, what, five years old? Give him a break, all right?" Harvey's exasperated voice came through the speaker into the room where we were recording.

Then we heard input from Mom too. "That's right Kim/Kon," she said, referring to us in the single-name-combination she often used when reprimanding us both. "He doesn't have to do everything one hundred percent perfect." Then in a lower tone, she added for Harvey's benefit, "We all forget he's just a kid most of the time. I'm glad you told them to lighten up a little."

Kim and I realized it would do no good to point out that the only reason we expected so much of Rory was that we knew he was always capable of delivering whatever we requested of him. Instead, we just made certain that our directives to Rory were not spoken into the microphone after this incident, in order that Harvey would not be able to hear us.

Our second album caused just as much stir for our family and friends as the first one had. This was likely due to the fact that everyone was curious about how a five-year-old could possibly be good enough to drum on a record. When the demo finally arrived in the mail, everyone once again gathered in our living room to listen to it together. Even though our grandparents had heard Rory drumming a few times at our recent concerts, they were amazed by the great job he had done. Kim and I couldn't help but take pride in the fact that we had taught him many of the skills that he was now demonstrating on each song, but we knew our responsibility was far from over. In fact, it was just beginning.

Our work was indeed cut out for us as we began making plans for the third album, which would be called *Country Gospel Blend*. This time, Rory wouldn't be able to just copy the basic rhythms that Denny had already laid down for him before leaving the group. It would be completely up to us to assist Rory in creating and cultivating his own drumming style and try to come up with interesting and unique new ideas to give each song a special touch.

Even little Reed was going to sing on this third album. He would be nearly three by then, which we thought was high time that he begin developing his own musical talents. He was growing up to be quite a charming little boy. Reed was never in a bad mood. Even when his asthma was acting up and his breathing became labored, this didn't slow him down any. He never complained about anything and was always happy and carefree. It was impossible to imagine that there had ever been a time when he wasn't an essential part of the family.

In spite of the age difference, Reed was Rory's constant companion and playmate when Kim and I were at school. Mom often made the comment that just as God had given Kim and me each other, He sure knew what He was doing when He gave Rory a little brother to play with and love too. They looked out for one another and stuck together, just as Kim and I always had. Rory enjoyed having someone closer to his own age to interact with now, and Reed certainly looked up to and admired his big brother as well.

One day, when Rory was playing our little organ and trying to record some songs he had learned, Reed was making a bunch of racket in the background and distracting his brother. Rather than get mad at him though, Rory just calmly suggested to Reed that it was time for his nap and that he should go and notify Mom of this. Reed dutifully went in search of his mother, and when he found her, he obediently did as Rory had instructed.

"Ror says I'm supposed to remind you that it's time for my nap now," he informed her, "but I don't wanna take my nap!" he protested tearfully at the end of his little monologue.

Nevertheless, Mom hid her amusement and told him that it was, indeed, getting close to his nap time and then proceeded to put him to bed.

Even at a young age, Reed was always thinking and usually had a witty comment ready for any occasion. Once, when Mom told him to put away his toys, he replied innocently with the logic, "I wanna take turns like you say we should. I took the toys out, so now you put them away."

Unlike the rest of us, Reed had a mop of curly hair that was so cute and adorable that Mom found it hard to have it cut. Whenever anyone asked him where he got his curly hair, his matter-of-fact response was, "God gave it to me," as though wondering what could be more obvious.

Our parents helped Kim and me to purchase a synthesizer that year, and we loved it immediately. We were able to position it in such a way that whichever of us was not on the piano could reach over and play the synthesizer with our right hand, while still doing the bass notes with our left. The control panel had buttons similar to those on a calculator, with a different instrument sound for every two-digit combination from eleven through ninety-nine.

"This is going to give our music so much more variety!" Kim exclaimed joyfully.

"I can't wait to give it a try," I agreed with fervor. "Now we'll have so many instruments to choose from that we might have to start Brailling up a song list before each program so we can remember what we're doing for each one."

From that point on, each time we had a booking, one of us would take her turn at the Brailler, putting two sheets of paper in at once so that both of us would have a copy. Then Mom would read off the song titles that we'd all chosen for that particular program while we took notes.

We also had another reason to be joyful that spring. It was looking more and more likely that Kim and I might be able to begin attending high school in Lemmon the following year. An IEP (individual education plan) meeting had been scheduled at the school in Aberdeen to discuss the matter. Many blind students were being mainstreamed into their own communities, and we reasoned that we should be allowed to do the same. For the past two years, we had already been attending a couple of classes at a local public junior high school in Aberdeen just to get our feet wet, as it were.

"We'll just leave it in God's hands," Dad said. "We've been praying about this for several years already, and we believe our prayers are being answered. Now we'll just trust in Him to work out all the details."

Passage of Time

"Camp is coming up really soon," Kim said. "Are you excited about going, Ror?"

"I think so," said Rory after a moment's contemplation. "I've never been to camp before, so I'm not sure if I'll like it or not."

"It will be fun," I assured him. "Besides, Kim and I will be there with you, so that should help you not to feel too scared or lonesome."

Fortunately, my prediction proved to be correct. As the youngest camper, Rory was a hit with everyone and was spoiled by all. A classmate of mine and Kim's from the school in Aberdeen who was also at camp that year was just old enough to take Rory under his wing and teach him the ropes of life at camp.

"Did you all have fun?" Mom asked at the end of the week, as she and Dad loaded the suitcases into the station wagon for the trip back home.

"I liked it," Rory told her. "I'm glad the girls were there with me though."

"They do some things a lot differently now," Kim said. "We hardly even saw our actual counselor. The girls who were supposedly in charge of us most of the time were called counselors in training, or CITs, and they were just teenagers like we are."

"That sounds a little strange," Dad commented. "A setup like that might work for younger kids but not for girls your age."

"I guess they just figured people who can't see are all pretty helpless," I decided. "You'd think they should know better at a camp specifically for blind people though."

"At least they put us with the two other campers our age so the four of us got to hang out together," Kim went on. "And after a while, the CITs pretty much left us alone."

"What all did you do there?" asked Mom.

"Oh, just the usual. Horseback riding, swimming, crafts, paddleboats, and stuff like that."

"And I got to be in a talent show," Rory spoke up. "My very first one."

"Really? How did you do?" Mom wanted to know.

"Well, it wasn't really a contest," I explained. "But if you go by the amount of applause and cheering that went on after the song, I think you could safely say he would have won."

"And I didn't even have any instruments with me," Rory added. "The girls and I just stood up there and sang 'How Do I Know? The Bible Tells Me So.'"

"And they had Bible quizzes every day," Kim put in. "But after a few days, they told Kon and me we couldn't participate anymore because we knew so many of the answers."

"That's because we listened to those 'Your Story Hour' tapes so many times," I said. "I wish we could get that program on a radio station around here. They act out the best stories ever."

"I heard there's a new Christian radio station in Bismarck now," Dad said, "but it's FM, and I don't know if it will have good enough reception for us to get it from home or not."

"It would sure be nice to be able to listen to Christian music and programs whenever we wanted to," Kim said wistfully. "I hope we can pick up the station when the time comes."

That fall marked the beginning of tenth grade for Kim and me. Our first year in public school was exciting but also difficult in some ways. We didn't really make any close friends. Many of the students were nice enough, but they were already well established in their own circles. Being on the shy side, it was easier for Kim and me to stick with one another rather than reach out more to the other kids. We didn't live with these students as we had at the school in Aberdeen, so there wasn't as much chance to get to know them individually. There were also far more of them here than had been the case at our other school, which we found to be a little overwhelming. Because we lived on a ranch and didn't have our own car as many of them did, it wasn't as easy to get to some of the activities in town as it would have been otherwise.

Even so, it was great to be home and to be able to spend more time developing our music ministry. Dad had recently purchased two new Ovation guitars just in time for our third album. Rory in particular was enthralled with both of them, especially the twelve-string, which none of us had ever heard before.

"It sounds so rich and full," Kim said when Dad strummed it for the first time.

"I bet the chords are harder to hold though, aren't they, Dad, since you have twelve strings to press instead of just six?" I wanted to know.

"Well, I can always help him figure out different ways to make the chords," Rory volunteered. "I'm sure he'll get used to it."

As had become our tradition, we were planning to record our third album in November. This one would once again feature ten songs, five of which had been written by Dad. We had decided to try a studio in Bismarck for this project, which Dad had heard good things about while researching possible options in the Dakotas.

Although he was not yet quite three… Reed would be singing on the record too. It was funny to think that he had even beaten his older brother into the studio. Rory hadn't been able to make his first recording until the age of four.

"I just hope Reed will sing when he's supposed to," Rory said to Dave, our new recording engineer, when we arrived at the studio. "Sometimes we drag him all over the place to our concerts and put him in front of a microphone and the kid just sits there and won't say a thing. So finally we just started leaving him with Gramp and Gram."

Dave laughed. "Well, let's hope he'll do better than that for this album," he chuckled. "What will Reed be singing?"

"We didn't think it would be a good idea to give him a whole song to do by himself this time," Rory answered sagely. "So he only has a couple lines on one of Dad's called 'Our Little Boys.'"

"That's still pretty remarkable for such a young fellow though," Dave pointed out.

"Yeah, and he's been singing better lately so I think he'll do a good job," Rory said reassuringly. "Anyway, I told him he needs to do his best or I'd pull his hair like the girls did to me when I was little. But that was a long time ago. I'm six now, so I hardly ever mess up anymore."

"I see," Dave said soberly. "Well, let's get started then and maybe we'll save your little brother's songs for tomorrow. Does that sound like a plan?"

"Sure," said Rory. "That will give him time to see how it's done."

As it turned out, Reed came down with a sore throat that day. Mom kept pumping Chloroseptic spray into him though, and we were all relieved that he was able to do his little part when the time came. He still has memories of that first recording experience, listening to everything that was going on and being allowed to play with Mom's tambourine when not in use.

The next few days were enjoyable for all of us. It was good to get back into the studio, and we couldn't deny that we were improving with each successive recording we'd made up to that point. Our audience numbers had continued to grow steadily throughout the Dakotas and surrounding states. As long as progress was being made, we had learned to wait for God's timing and not get ahead of where He was leading.

Rory would be officially starting first grade in the fall, so it was kind of sad to see our make-believe schooldays in the old house drawing to a close. Mom and Dad had decided to wait until he was seven to put him in school, just as they had with Kim and me. They knew he would have no trouble catching up to his peers because of all the preparation he'd already had at home. The officials, however, weren't so sure. They insisted that Rory be tested by the state before he started school so they would know where to place him in the system. Rory didn't mind taking the test though. In fact, he was looking forward to it.

"So why don't you tell Lovette what you thought of your testing?" I asked Rory on the day after he'd taken the exam. He and I were sitting outside in our hammock, making a cassette letter for my pen pal in Canada.

"It was easy, of course," Rory answered without hesitation. "So now I won't have to go to school in Aberdeen like the girls did because I showed everybody I could already read and write Braille and work math problems on the abacus and everything."

"He tested at a third-grade level or higher in every subject area," I went on proudly.

"Everybody was so surprised, except Kim and me of course. We'd been working with him for so many years in our playschool that we were sure his scores would be high. So I think people are finally starting to feel pretty confident now that he should have no trouble succeeding in public school.

"They tested Kim and me too, and we're right on target gradewise and above average in most of the subjects."

Rory hopped down and scampered away as I continued tapping my letter. A few minutes later, I paused for breath as Rory passed by on his way to the swings. "Did you tell her we're getting a new motor home soon?" he asked me.

"No, not yet," I replied. "Go ahead and tell her about it."

"Well," Rory said obligingly, "we've been lookin' all over, and it's fun checking them out. Mom and Dad let us kids go inside and explore them all, and there was this one that had a nice table you could fold down and it would make into a bed. It was pretty cool. A lot of them are out of our price range, but Dad says we should be able to find a good one eventually. It will be so nice to have if we start doing our music full time like we've always wanted to."

That November once again found our family in the recording studio. The name we had given this album was *Country for the Lord*, which was also the title track, written by Dad. I took particular pride in this project, as I was able to incorporate so many of the techniques I'd been learning lately from the Keith Green and other recordings. We proudly used our new keyboard synthesizer on every song. It gave our music much more variety, as we were able to use so many different instrument voices. No longer were we limited only to the piano and violin sounds that our original electric keyboard provided. Because of the synthesizer, this latest project would contain the additional sounds of flutes, chimes, trumpets, and a lot more.

One of Rory's solos, "God Likes People," was a song Kim had recorded from the Gospel Greats radio program. Rory had outgrown his first drum set, so he was excited to be using his brand-new drums on this fourth album. He was getting to be quite a remarkable drummer, coming up with lots of unique ideas all on his own and even suggestions for the rest of us to implement as well.

Little Reed was given an entire song to do by himself on this latest project. He sang all three verses of "Jesus Loves Me" and did a great job. Kim and I had matured to the point that we didn't make him redo the part where he ad-libbed an extra note at the beginning or the part where he deliberately sang a word staccato fashion in the middle of the third verse. We could appreciate the cuteness of these foibles and didn't expect perfection. If Rory had tried similar stunts just a couple of years earlier though, he never would have heard the last of it from us.

Contrary to the pattern we'd set of recording every fall, however, we weren't able to make a fifth album the following year. Our booking calendar was busier, so there wasn't as much time to rehearse songs for a new record. Also, there were just so many other things going on, what with Kim and me graduating from high school and making our college preparations. I had chosen to attend the college in Dickinson, and Kim would be going to Trinity, In Ellendale, both in North Dakota. It was a little sad thinking about not only the separation from home but also the separation from each other. Kim and I had never been apart for more than a day or so in our entire eighteen years, and we were now embarking on our own lives. Things would never be quite the same again. Plus we would also be away from home and family and would no longer have the day-to-day interaction with our parents and little brothers. It was hard to imagine.

Learning and Growing

"Looks like all the mail is for you this time," Marlene, my roommate, announced, as she dropped the load on my end of the long desk where we occasionally sat to do our homework. "Here's a tape from Kim and another letter from your boyfriend. And I think you got another care package from your mom too."

"Wow. I guess this is my lucky day," I said as I tried to decide what I should open first. I quickly slid the letter into a drawer, saving it for a time to read when Marlene wasn't around. I was glad that my optacon allowed me to read printed material independently.

I picked up the tape from Kim but then decided to lay it aside for the time being as well, since I had a class coming up in a few minutes. The two of us had already visited each other's colleges and met each other's friends. So whenever she shared all her news, I was able to visualize where she was and who she was referring to when she talked about her classmates. I was always a little envious as I listened to the recordings she made of her chapel services and other social functions. Everyone was so on fire for God, which was an aspect of college life that I didn't have. However, I was, for the most part, very happy with the school I had chosen, and I had peace in knowing that I was right where God wanted me.

Quickly opening the box from Mom before it was time for class, I pulled out a bag of chips; the Braille labeler I had forgotten at home; a cassette tape; and, last but certainly not least, safely tucked away in a corner was the spending money I had requested. A little wave of homesickness assailed me as I thought of the family back home. I had missed seeing them the last weekend because I'd decided to visit Marlene's home instead. And that weekend, I had promised my friend, Bev, that I would stick around to help babysit her three kids for several hours on Saturday and do the special music at her church the following day. It was rare that I stayed at school three weeks in a row, but I was determined that I would make it home the next weekend if Debbie was planning a trip to Lemmon. Otherwise, I figured that either Mom or Dad would be willing to come and get me. It was only an hour-and-a-half jaunt, after all, which was nothing when compared with the many hours they had spent on the road, making the weekly trip to the school in Aberdeen.

Curious as to what was on the tape Mom had sent, I quickly put it into the recorder to find out before heading for class. To my delight, I heard the voices of my two little brothers speaking into the microphone.

"Hi, Kim and Kon," Rory was saying. "We're making you both a copy of this tape because neither one of you has been home for a while, so we thought we'd fill you in on the news."

Reluctantly, I stopped the tape for the time being and picked up my cane and backpack. I would have to hurry if I was going to make it to class on time.

"Over here, Konnie; I saved a seat for you," a friend of mine called out as I entered the classroom." Kelly lived a couple doors down from me in the dorm, and we had been happy to discover that we both had scheduled this class for the same time slot.

"I picked up Reba Mcentire's latest tape today," she told me as I took out my Braille slate and paper for taking notes. "It has some really good songs. Feel like doing some jamming after class?"

"Sure, why not? Do you mind if we stop off at the bookstore first though? I'm trying to get all my cassette books ordered for next semester, and I need to pick up a couple that my tape library doesn't have, so I can send them a copy to hopefully get recorded by the time I need them."

"Sure, not a problem," Kelly responded.

An hour later, I grabbed Kelly's elbow and we headed for the bookstore. Sometimes people tended to want to take my arm when trying to lead me somewhere, but my friends had soon learned that it was easier for me to discern what was ahead and feel the upcoming terrain or whether there might be steps approaching if they walked in front and let me follow behind them. I couldn't help remembering how uncomfortable some of them had felt at the beginning of the year when they had guided me somewhere, though.

"Everybody is staring at us," they'd said in embarrassment. "People are so rude!"

I was a little surprised by this revelation. I had never really realized or thought about the fact that people were probably often staring at me. I was kind of glad I couldn't see the stares, and felt mortified to be the cause of my friends' discomfort.

After it happened a number of times, I asked my sister if she had encountered anything similar at her college. She confirmed that the same thing had, in fact, been an issue for her, as well. When we went home that weekend, we questioned Mom about it.

"Do people sometimes stare at us, like when we're walking somewhere or whatever?" I inquired.

"Well, I suppose they do sometimes," Mom replied offhandedly, as if it didn't matter in the least. "Why do you ask?"

"Oh, we just wondered, because our friends have mentioned it, and we wanted to know why you never said anything about it."

"I guess it just never came up," Mom answered.

"Doesn't it bother you when they do that?" Kim asked.

"I don't even notice anymore," Mom answered. "People just automatically look at things that are a little new or unusual. I do it, myself, when I see something different that catches my attention. People are just curious, and I figure why not let them watch, if they want to? They might learn something."

Her explanation made a lot of sense to me. I hadn't thought of it in quite that way before, and I was glad that my parents had such wisdom and insight. I couldn't do anything about people staring, so there was no use in letting it get to me. I told my friends that it was just a natural reaction from people who didn't know me, and eventually the stares began to matter less and less to all of us.

When I got back to my room, I put my headphones on so as not to disturb Marlene in her studies and turned on the tape from my brothers. I couldn't help smiling as I listened to their lively little voices telling me about their trips to the park with Gramp and how things were going for them in school.

Reed had started kindergarten that year, and he said there were lots of neat toys to play with in his classroom.

"I like all my teachers too, but my favorite one is Mrs. Seim," he claimed emphatically. "She's so much fun, and I'm sure glad I'll have her every year, 'cause Mom told her she better not even think about quitting until Ror and me are all graduated from high school."

Mrs. Seim had been a little nervous at first about taking the reins all by herself as my brothers' aide, but since Kim and I had already given them a head start in our play school, we knew she had nothing to worry about and would do a great job. She'd already begun teaching herself Braille and had needed only a very few pointers from Kim and me along the way. One of the main requirements of her job would be putting the boys' assignments into Braille and then transcribing the completed homework back into print for their teachers to correct.

"Some time when you guys are home for a long break or something, you should come and spend a whole day with us at school so you can see what our classes are like and meet our teachers and all that," Reed suggested. As I listened, I thought he had a great idea and made a mental note to be sure to do that very thing at my earliest opportunity.

"We're practicing pretty much every night for our new album," Rory went on. "Reed knows the words to all his songs now, and Dad has learned most of the chords in 'Mommy's Boys.' I have to keep reminding him of where they go though or he gets pretty goofed up. You guys better not skip any more Saturday practices, or we'll never be ready by November."

I wiped a tear from my eye as I continued to listen. They didn't need to convince me that I was overdue for a trip back home. I also realized that what Rory said was true. If we wanted to be ready to make our fifth album in November, these last few weeks would be crucial. We'd done a lot of practicing during the summer months, but, of course, there was still a lot of last-minute fine-tuning to be done on each of the songs. Rory was getting to be quite the little guitar player already, and we were even considering letting him do a bit of acoustic lead on a couple of the songs.

We were really excited about this most recent project for several reasons. It would be called *Up with Families*, and three of the songs on the album had been written by Kim. "She's the Mother of Kids" was an upbeat song about all the things moms do for their children on a daily basis. "God Is on My Side" encouraged people to remember that we can make it through anything with God on our side. "Mommy's Boys" featured Rory and Reed singing a humorous tune about what it was like for Mom to have two little boys to raise. Mom had asked Kim if she would try to write just such a song to compliment the one Dad was singing called "Daddy's Girls," on which Kim and I changed our voices like little kids and talked about some of the things dads experience as their daughters are growing up.

"I'm startin' to save keychains," Reed was saying on the tape now. "So if you find any good ones, get them for me. I'll show you my collection when you come home. I found about fourteen of them connected together one day in Gram's candy drawer, so I asked her if I could keep them because they weren't being used for anything. She said I could, and now other people are starting to give me more. It's pretty cool. And, oh yeah, I learned this new knock-knock joke—"

"Don't get started with your jokes or we'll be here all day," his brother interrupted. "If there's enough room on here, why don't we try to copy one of the story tapes we acted out?"

Reed agreed that this was a good idea, so Rory began rummaging around on the headboard, where many of their cassettes were stored. Kim and I marveled at how he and Reed were always able to locate exactly which one they were looking for without using any labeling system. They kept their tapes in certain locations or just remembered what sort of cassette a particular thing was recorded on, which they found by touch.

"These stories might not be quite as good as the ones you girls made yet," Reed was saying, "but we have some already that are pretty long, and we use the same sound-effect tapes that you had when you were little and everything. I think I'm going to start recording some effects of my own though, 'cause I can think of a lot more sounds that you guys don't have, and I know of a bunch that I could do myself or copy from other tapes or TV shows and stuff like that.

"Oh, and guess what else. I'm starting to learn how to play the drums now. I'll have to remember to show you when you come home. Once I get really good at it, I can be the full-time drummer, and Ror can play the guitar and other stuff."

Always up to something. Never a dull moment, I mused to myself as I listened. I couldn't wait to get home to see how Reed could drum and find out the new chords Rory was learning on the guitar.

As things turned out, our fifth recording project was destined to be the last one that we would do together as a family. It was also my last time in a typical recording studio. The engineer/producer, Dave, was quite familiar with our work by now and contributed several creative ideas to our songs.

"Why don't we use some chimes and xylophone voices from one of my own keyboards on this song?" he suggested at one point.

We were working on "I Wish That I Had Prayed," which Dad had written about his own testimony. It talked of the night he came to know the Lord in a personal way, when Grandma's prayers were finally answered.

He got out the keyboard, and I played around with the sounds he'd mentioned and liked what I heard.

"I think that's a good idea," I told him. "How do the rest of you like it?"

"Sounds good to me," Kim affirmed. "Don't you think so, Dad?"

Dad agreed that the new voices added a nice touch to the music, and so did Rory.

"Not quite as good as my guitar solo would have been, but still pretty good," was his verdict.

"Are you learning to play the guitar, Rory?" Dave asked with interest.

"Yeah, and I had a part all worked up for this song, but then we decided I shouldn't play it because I wouldn't be able to do it during our concerts since I'd be too busy drumming," Rory replied. "If you want, I'll show it to you when we take our next break."

And so he did. Dave said it was a nice solo but expressed concern at the unusual way Rory was playing.

"I'm afraid he's going to start running into problems later on down the road if he doesn't begin to conform to the conventional way a guitar is typically played," he told Mom and Dad.

"Well, we can always cross that bridge if we come to it, but seems to be working right now," Dad said. "I guess we'll just see what happens."

Dave brought in a couple extra musicians to play violin and steel and bass guitar on a few of the songs. Dad agreed to let him do this, reasoning that at some point in the not-too-distant future, Rory would likely be playing all of these instruments himself and would eventually be able to duplicate the songs exactly while performing on stage. Dave also had Rory play along with a drum machine on "God Is on My Side" to help him stay as steady as possible on the speedy tune. Rory had never used such a gadget before, but he adapted quickly, and we all agreed that it was a good decision.

Since we spent very long days in the studio, Dave brought in some pizza and ice cream for supper one evening, just as he had done the year before. That way, we were able to just stay right there and finish up what we were doing. Reed was the only person who didn't partake in spite of his sisters' chiding. He didn't have much of a sweet tooth and declined dessert more often than not.

Reed was showing more interest in what was going on in the studio, and when he wasn't listening to his story tapes, he was absorbing everything we were doing. Although Dave threatened to throw him and Rory out once when they were horsing around while we were trying to do the final mix down, they sat quietly most of the time, fascinated by all the technology and how it was used to make a professional album.

Looking back now, it's easy to see that Dave exhibited a great amount of patience where we all were concerned. I'm sure he was never asked to produce an album like ours before or since, for which he was probably rather grateful. Not only did he have to put up with a nine-year-old drummer and a five-year-old tag-along, but he was also required to endure the numerous suggestions and critiquing of two know-it-all teenagers, namely Kim and myself. He took it all in stride for the most part though and listened to our ideas and comments with respect and good humor, even when he disagreed with our opinions.

As we drove home from Bismarck after the final day in the studio, we all agreed that that project was our best effort up to now.

"I sure wish we had really good microphones to use on stage like the ones Dave has in the studio," Rory lamented. "You don't have to be right up on them like you do with ours."

"I know," Kim affirmed. "It actually sounds better if you back away from them a little."

"And I really like how he recorded the piano in stereo this time, using two mics instead of one," Rory went on. "I bet Harvey wouldn't have been able to do that because he doesn't have as many tracks on his machine."

I had to smile at the thought of such observations coming from a child of his age. "I can't wait till it's all mastered," I said enthusiastically.

It was a happy time in our lives. We were glad to have gotten back into the studio again, especially after the extended length of time between our last two projects. Our booking calendar was becoming busier, and we were looking forward to traveling around the country in our new motor home as our music ministry continued to expand.

Unfortunately, it only took a few short months to prove to us once again that change is always right around the corner and is often quite unexpected. I still remember vividly when the phone rang one evening in early spring. I picked up the receiver, and as soon as I heard Mom's voice, I knew something wasn't right.

"Hi, hon. Is anybody there with you right now?" she asked.

"No. Marlene is out of town. Why? What's wrong?"

"We have some bad news, I'm afraid. Are any of your other friends around? Somebody should be with you."

My heart dropped to my stomach as I wondered what on earth had happened. I didn't even want to contemplate the possibilities. Taking a deep breath, I forced myself to be calm and try to think of an appropriate response.

"Well, I'm sure I could get a hold of somebody. What's up though?"

"It's about Grandma Hoffman," Mom answered.

"Oh no. You mean…?" But my voice trailed off, unable to finish the thought.

"She passed away this morning," Mom confirmed. "She went after the mail and brought ours over, just like always, and we visited for quite a while before she went back home."

Mom seemed unable to continue until I prompted her through my own tears, "What happened then?"

"Well, your dad went over there just a few minutes later, on his way back from doing the chores, and she was just sitting in her chair by the table, like she was reading her mail or something. She was slumped over though, so he beeped me on the intercom, and of course, I came right away, but she was already gone."

Gradually, the reality of Mom's words was starting to sink in. "But how can that be, Mom?" I denied. "She wasn't even sick or anything."

"I know," Mom agreed. "It must have been her heart, but it seems like she was just sitting there peacefully and Jesus told her it was time to go home."

I reached for another Kleenex.

"Are you okay, Kon?" Mom asked.

"I guess so," I told her in a quavering voice.

But of course, I wasn't okay at all.

"I'll put Dad on for a minute," Mom said. "But then you call Debbie or somebody right away so you don't have to be alone. Love you."

"I love you too." I sobbed, wishing I was home right then. I found out later that they would have come to get me if I'd asked, but the next day was Thursday, so I figured I could get through one more day before the weekend.

"Well, I sure didn't think this was part of the plan," Dad said when he got on the line. "There's still so much that was supposed to come to pass yet, you know, before her time came."

I sniffled, realizing it was now my turn to try to offer some comfort.

"I guess she'll be seeing it all from up there instead," I commented tearfully.

Dad sighed. "The minute I saw her all bent over like that, I said, 'Not today, Mom. This can't be the day.' But I guess God had other ideas."

I swiped at my eyes again, but to no avail.

"At least she went quickly and in her own house, just the way she always said she wanted to," I reminded him.

But inwardly, I was wondering how we'd ever get along without our steadfast prayer warrior. Ever since her own children were small, Grandma had spent hours in prayer for them every day, and that commitment extended to her grandchildren as well. She was a constant support and never gave up believing in our ministry no matter how things might look on the outside.

"That's true," Dad admitted, although the thought didn't help either of us to feel any better right then.

"Well, I guess I'll let you go," he said after a pause. "But keep your chin up and try to remember that no doubt she's having the time of her life right now. I hope she'll be able to look down on us here on earth every now and then, and I know she'll continue to hold us up in prayer to her heavenly Father, just like she always has."

His words made me smile through my tears. "And just think. Now she'll be able to talk to Him face to face," I said in awe at the thought of it.

The next few days passed in a blur. Before I knew it, the funeral was over, and we were expected to resume our normal routines and get on with our lives, almost as though nothing had happened. But of course, that was much easier said than done. It was still hard to believe that Grandma was actually gone, and I wondered if I would ever really get used to the idea.

Life did go on though.

Almost before I realized it had happened, my third year of college was drawing to a close. I was really beginning to understand what older people meant when they commented on how quickly time flew by. I could hardly believe that I had only one more year of college left and then it would be time to embark on a life of my own. It was exciting to contemplate but also a little scary too. There were so many decisions and things to consider. I didn't yet feel ready to move far away from my family. My brothers were still so young, and I hoped to be nearby to witness their growing-up years. Also, if God wanted our family to have a full-time music ministry, this would be impossible if we were all scattered hither and yon. Even so, I knew I wanted to be a teacher, and it might be necessary for me to go wherever I could find a job.

"Well, you girls still have a year to figure this all out, so no need worrying too much about the future right now," was Dad's advice. "A lot can happen in a year."

Teaching Experience

My desk was in the very front row where Mr. Haakedahl couldn't possibly miss me. The way I saw it, he'd been trying his best to ignore my existence for the past week, ever since my "teaching experience" class had begun. I realized I was going to have to take some sort of stand or I'd be overlooked entirely. This class was a prerequisite for anybody pursuing a teaching degree, and if I didn't perform at a satisfactory level here, I knew I wouldn't even be considered for a student-teaching position later on. Mr. Haakedahl was the one I'd be dealing with when it came time for doing my actual student-teaching, so a precedent needed to be set that would guide any future communication between us.

My face grew hot with resentment when I realized that there was only one other person left in the room besides me, as everyone else had already been assigned to the perspective elementary schools in the area where they would be working for the rest of the quarter. I raised my hand and cleared my throat loudly as my instructor walked past me to the back of the room, where the one remaining student sat, waiting for her assignment.

"I think Konnie was trying to say something," the girl put in quickly before he could begin speaking to her.

I was grateful for her intervention and wondered briefly how she knew my name since we hadn't met before. But then, I'd gotten used to the fact that a lot of people knew who I was even though I'd never met them. It just comes along with the package when there is something that makes you different from those around you.

Seemingly taken aback, Mr. Haakedahl turned around hurriedly, as though noticing me for the first time. I forced myself to stay poised and speak calmly, though what I really felt like doing was shedding a few tears of humiliation.

"I was just wondering where I was going to be helping out. I haven't received any assignment yet," I reminded him.

"Oh, that," he replied as though it were a simple oversight of little consequence. Then he proceeded to pace around the room, shuffling papers as he did so. Finally, he came to a dead halt in front of me and said dismissively, "I'll just send you along with Heather here."

Fighting panic, I tried to decide quickly how to respond to this. I didn't want to be "sent with Heather" as though I were some sort of afterthought. The solution he'd come up with wasn't fair to either of us. She likely didn't relish the thought of me tagging along with her any more than I did. If someone were partnering with me, I knew that that person would get all the focus while I was stuck in a corner somewhere, doing menial tasks that wouldn't prepare me at all for teaching in the real world.

Trying to remain respectful, I pointed out that I thought it would work out better if I were assigned to my own classroom, just as every other student had been given.

"That isn't an option," he informed me, in no uncertain terms. "You can go with Heather tomorrow if you want to, and if that turns out to be too challenging for you, we can talk about having you opt out of the class."

Shaking with anger now, I figured I'd better drop the matter temporarily, before things escalated any further and poor Heather was caught in the middle somewhere. I bit my lower lip until it almost started to bleed in order to keep my composure while I listened to the instructions he was giving Heather about the location of the school and the name of the teacher, etc.

Heather and I left the room together, and she patted my shoulder sympathetically as we turned down the hall.

"Sorry that didn't quite go the way you wanted," she said.

"Well, it wasn't your fault," I assured her. "It's just frustrating to not even be given the chance to prove myself. You know?"

"I can certainly imagine," she empathized. "Maybe once he sees you in action…"

But I knew that wasn't going to happen. Mr. Haakedahl was already biased against me and would surely have already talked to the elementary teacher by the time I met her the following day.

Heather must have seen the doubtful look on my face. "There has to be something we can do to get through to him," she persisted.

I was touched that she was taking such an interest. "Well, thanks for your concern anyway," I told her. "I appreciate that a lot."

"Just let me know if you can think of anything I might do to help the situation," she offered generously. "I'd be happy to do whatever I could."

I gave her a wan smile. "In that case, would you mind walking to the school with me so I can familiarize myself with the route before tomorrow morning?"

"Not a problem," she responded quickly. "We can go right now if you want."

"It's just not fair!" I exclaimed with extreme irritation as we continued down the corridor. "I don't get why he's so insistent that I have a partner! I mean, what would happen if you were ever to get sick or something? Does he think I'd just stay behind too? If so, he better guess again!"

We walked on in silence for another moment or two, when Heather suddenly coughed rather obnoxiously and began rummaging around in her purse for a Kleenex.

"This is a pretty strange coincidence," she mused after vigorously blowing her nose, "but it isn't completely out of the question that I might have to leave you in the lurch tomorrow. I've been coming down with this bug since yesterday, and it seems to be getting worse practically by the minute."

"That's too bad," I said, trying to sound properly concerned, though my heart was starting to beat just a little faster.

"Not a big deal," she said as we went out the front entrance of the building and onto the sidewalk. "Whenever I get a cold, it just seems to drag on and on. I usually don't let them get me down too much, but I hear that it's supposed to be below freezing and snowy tomorrow, so I might not want to risk going out into the weather and all."

"That's understandable," I said soberly, although I was finding it very hard to keep a smile off my face. "Well, if you aren't able to go, don't worry about me. The school is only a few blocks from here, so I should be able to make it there without any difficulty once I know the way."

And that proved to be the case. The rest of the week went by in a blur, and Friday came before I knew it. My friend, Debbie, from Lemmon was planning a trip home that weekend, so I was going to ride with her. Since it was also Thanksgiving break, Kim and I would both be home for a couple extra days, and we had a concert scheduled for Sunday. Performing our music together as a family was even more enjoyable now that Rory was playing several different instruments. This also meant that Reed had been promoted to drummer, which was an extra bonus.

Debbie took the bag I was carrying and put it into the trunk while I walked around to the front of the car and settled myself in the front seat.

"So how is your teaching experience going?" she asked with curiosity as she got in beside me and started the engine.

"Oh, fine," I replied. I still had a hard time believing that the little scheme Heather and I concocted had actually succeeded.

"I heard from the grapevine that you are already getting to do way more work with the kids than any of the rest of us," Debbie remarked a little enviously. "How on earth did you manage that?"

"It was pretty amazing how God worked everything out," I told her. "At first, it didn't look like I was going to get to do the class at all."

"I could tell that good old Travis Haakedahl wasn't very comfortable having you there," Debbie acknowledged. "That's why I was so surprised when I heard how well everything seemed to be going for you."

"You and me both." I smiled. "We didn't get started on very good footing. That's for sure."

"So what turned everything around for you?" Debbie wondered.

"It was kind of funny really," I replied. "I couldn't have done it without Heather's help though. That's the girl Haakedahl partnered me with."

"You got to work with a partner?" Debbie questioned.

"That's what he wanted to happen, but it didn't turn out that way fortunately," I told her.

"You didn't want a partner?" she asked in surprise. "I'd think that would make things easier for you."

"It would have. Too easy," I explained. "None of the rest of you worked as a team, and I didn't want him to be able to claim later on down the road that I required a lot of extra help."

"Makes sense I suppose," Debbie affirmed. "I hadn't thought of it like that before."

"So I was trying to object to his plan as politely as I could, but he wasn't having any of it." I went on with the story. "Fortunately, Heather took my side though."

"Really? What did she say?"

"It wasn't so much what she said. It's what we *did*," I corrected with a little giggle.

Debbie waited a bit and then said impatiently, "Well, don't keep me in suspense. What did you do?"

"It was really pretty simple. Heather had already been coming down with a bad cold, so when she didn't show up the next day, I just assumed she was sick and took off without her."

"Yeah right," Debbie laughed. "This is starting to sound a little fishy if you ask me."

"What do you mean?" I asked innocently. "It was a perfectly plausible story."

"Is that what Haakedahl thought?" Debbie wanted to know.

I shrugged. "I have no idea. But by the time he found out, it was too late for him to do anything about it, and I had made my point by then regardless."

"So wasn't the teacher surprised when you showed up without your partner?" she asked.

"Yeah, she was pretty befuddled at first, but I just explained that Heather wasn't able to come with me and asked what she wanted me to do to help out."

"And did she put you to work right away?"

I opened my can of Pepsi and took a few swallows before answering. "That was the beauty of the whole thing!" I exclaimed happily. "She just stood there and stammered around nervously for a minute or so, and then, finally, she asked me what I thought I could handle. I told her I wanted her to expect me to do anything that she would require of any other college student she was given. But she still seemed a little flustered and at a loss, so I basically had to take charge of the situation and give her a few pointers on the type of things she might let me do."

Debbie considered that for a second. "Wow! So you pretty much got to set your own agenda. Must be nice."

"It was. I just jumped in and got to start working directly with the kids right away instead of doing all this busy work that most of the rest of you had to waste your time on at first."

"So what did Mr. Haakedahl say when he finally figured out what happened?" Debbie wanted to know.

"That's the best part," I told her excitedly. "So Mr. Haakedahl is on his rounds, and he shows up near the end of the class period, and I'm sitting at this table with all these little kids around me, reading to them from one of the print Braille books I'd fortunately thought to bring along. They were all quite fascinated with it, of course, and asking me lots of questions and everything. I guess it must have been pretty obvious to him how comfortable I usually am around children because he just said, 'Good job,' as I was walking out the door, and that was that."

"So did he assign Heather to a different teacher then or what?" Debbie asked curiously.

"I'm not sure. He must have," I replied. "I haven't seen Heather since then. But when I got to the school the next day, the teacher's attitude had totally changed. Right away, she put me to work helping this little girl with some math problems, and the rest, as they say, is history."

"Good for you," Debbie praised. "I'm glad everything turned out so well. And like you said, it should be a lot easier now to get people to believe you can do this."

"I hope so," I said. "But if nothing else, at least now I feel more confident that I can win if put to the test."

Debbie turned up the heater in her car another notch. "And how is your sister faring at Trinity? Is she having to deal with similar kinds of issues there?"

"At the beginning, she was," I said. "They didn't even want to let her enter the education program at first. The National Federation of the Blind had to get involved, and they sent her a bunch of literature about blind teachers working in the public school system, so she had tangible proof for all of her skeptical professors."

"And did that do the trick?" Debbie asked.

"For the most part, it did," I told her. "They've pretty much accepted her ever since then."

"That's good," Debbie said as she turned on the radio.

We listened to the music playing in the background for a few minutes, and then she asked, "So how about your brothers? What are they up to these days?"

"Reed tells me he just wrote his first song. Can you believe it? I guess it has six verses, no less."

"Wow. I'm sure you can't wait to hear it," she responded.

"And Rory is keeping busy too, of course." I went on. "He's enjoying playing in the school band and is really getting to be pretty good on the saxophone these days, if I do say so myself."

"I'm not surprised," Debbie said. "What made him choose sax as his band instrument rather than guitar or drums or something like that?"

"Not sure," I admitted. "Probably because it would have been hard for him to be a drummer in a marching band and he wouldn't get to use the whole drum kit like he's used to having. As for the guitar, he's likely afraid his teachers would try to make him learn to play it the right way, if you know what I mean. He sure doesn't want to unlearn everything he's already figured out and start from scratch."

"I can see why," said Debbie. "Not when he can already outplay most anybody around."

During his fourth-grade year, several music class periods had been devoted to letting the students try out many of the school's musical instruments, in order to decide what they might want to play in the school band the following year. Rory had chosen to try a horn of some kind, but he found it quite difficult to pick which one he liked best. He checked out the flute, clarinet, sax, trumpet, and trombone and had fun exploring the shapes of each one. For some reason, he couldn't make the flute sing at all though, and he hadn't heard of anyone who played country music on the clarinet, so those two were ruled out fairly quickly. Rory preferred bigger horns, and his teacher, Miss Heggerfield, thought that he should pursue the trumpet, which was her favorite and thus would have probably been easier for her to teach him. Rory really liked the sound of the trumpet and was able to make a few notes right away, but again, he wasn't able to think of many country songs that employed that particular instrument.

"I think the main reason he chose sax instead of some other horn is that he's heard Boots Randolph play, so he knows it can be used for country music," I told Debbie. "I'm sure he remembers when Kim and I played it a little bit in junior high too, and he's heard it on our grandpa's polka tapes, so he was already pretty familiar with how it could be played."

"I see," Debbie replied. "And didn't I hear something about him taking up the banjo lately too?"

"That's another interesting story. Our family did a joint concert awhile back with this bluegrass band, and one of the musicians let Rory hold and try to play his banjo. He even said he had another one that he'd give to Rory if he promised to learn to hold it the proper way and play it correctly."

Debbie laughed. "Well, that seems to be relative, isn't it?"

"That's what Rory thought." I smiled. "But this guy claimed there just wasn't any way to play it the way Rory was used to because of how you have to do the finger rolls in a certain order with all those fingerpicks. So, anyway, the man happened to be in the area a few months later, and he even went so far as to come out to the house in order to try to give Rory a longer demonstration to see how he would catch on. But Rory just kept insisting that he would be able to do a whole lot better if he could be allowed to flip it around and lay it on his lap. So, long story short, suffice it to say that he never got the offered banjo."

"Bummer," Debbie said sympathetically. "But wait a minute. I was sure somebody had told me not long ago that they'd seen him playing banjo somewhere recently."

"Probably so. He was fascinated enough after that guy's visit to want to learn more about the banjo, so he borrowed one from Mom's cousin shortly thereafter and proceeded to work with it on his own."

"Figures," Debbie said in amusement.

"And now that he has his own lead guitar too, he's all set," I added. "Although he's always looking for something new to play, so I'm sure it won't be long until he has added even more instruments to his arsenal."

When we pulled up in front of Gramp and Gram's house awhile later, I opened my purse and located the place in my wallet where I kept ten-dollar bills. Handing one to Debbie to help out with the cost of gas, I thanked her for the ride and told her that my dad would bring me over to her house on Sunday for the trip back to college.

"Sounds good," she replied. "Looks like your grandpa and brothers are playing out here in the front yard. They're heading this way now."

"Hi, Kon. I'll take your bags," Gramp said as he gave me a warm hug. "Wow. It seems like you have a ton of stuff in here. You'll only be home for a few days, you know."

"Yeah, but I have quite a bit of homework to do this weekend, so that's why I had to bring home so much junk," I replied as I scooped Reed up and reached to hug Rory with my other arm.

"I get to sing a solo for the school Christmas program," Rory informed me as we made our way to the house. "'Oh Holy Night.'"

"Wow, really?" I asked. "That's a pretty hard song for a twelve-year-old, don't you think?"

I felt the shrug of his shoulders under my arm. "I dunno. Evidently, Miss Heggerfield doesn't think so."

"You made it," Dad said from the front door, which he held open for us while we entered the house. "I'm glad the snow held off until you got here."

"Hi, hon," Mom called as she came to join us in the entryway. After embracing me, she stood back to peer at me more closely. "Where did you get that big bump on your forehead?" she asked in concern.

I put my hand up there to examine the spot. "I'm not sure. It probably happened when I accidentally hit the corner of my bookshelf while I was running from another room to get to my phone before it stopped ringing."

"And you have a big black-and-blue mark on your arm too," she observed as she held it up to inspect further. "You need to be more careful."

"You should know by now that I'm always getting little bumps and bruises like that. It's no big deal," I said, trying to dodge away from her scrutiny. "Most of the time, I can't even remember where they come from. They probably look a lot worse than they feel."

To my relief, Gram came in from the kitchen just then. "Well, hello, Kon," she said as she put her arms around me. "How was your week at school?"

"It was pretty eventful," I admitted, and proceeded to recount the entire teaching adventure again for my family.

They all seemed to enjoy the tale at least as much as Debbie had. One of my brothers was on my lap, and the other one was squeezed in beside me on the rocking chair. Gram kept coming in from the kitchen where she was preparing one of her usual scrumptious suppers in order to hear what I was saying amidst the sizzling frying pan and clanking dishes.

"I bet he was sure surprised when he found out that other girl didn't go to the school with you," Dad said from the couch next to where I was sitting.

"We should wait until Kim gets home so she doesn't miss all this," Mom said as she began to set silverware and plates at the table.

"I already told her everything on the phone last night," I assured her.

Just then, Gramp got up from the chair by the window and stepped over to the door.

"There she is now," he announced as he went out to greet my sister.

After everyone had said their hellos and I'd finished my story, we all sat around the table and began to dig in.

"Why don't you tell your sisters about the paper you were supposed to write in school this past week, Reed?" suggested Mom a few minutes later. "You won't believe this, girls."

"Yeah. I couldn't think of nothin' to write." Reed sounded more than a little upset with himself. "I was the only one in the class who never came up with anything."

This was surprising news. Even at his young age, Reed was already very conscientious about his grades and always seemed to have more than enough creativity on hand for any situation that might arise.

"Wow. It must have been a hard assignment," Kim said sympathetically.

"No, it wasn't," Rory contradicted. "All he was supposed to do is talk about something that made him unhappy. And he couldn't even think of one thing."

I smiled, thinking how much this sounded like little Reed, who hardly ever had a bad day. "I'm sure your teacher was pretty surprised," I commented.

"I guess so," said Reed. "But I just don't get what a kid should have to be unhappy about if nothin' much really goes wrong for them or anything. I think it was a dumb assignment."

"I hope that's always your outlook on life," Dad put in. "That's a pretty good testimony, I'd say."

Mom scooped another helping of mashed potatoes onto my plate. "So you girls are planning to do your student teaching here in Lemmon this spring, right?" she asked.

"I should be able to," I told her. "A lot of my classmates will be student teaching in their own hometowns. But I'm not sure how that will work for Kim since her college is so much farther away."

"Yeah, I doubt that my supervisor would be willing to drive that far to check on my performance," Kim said.

"There's a house for rent right across from the Lemmon elementary school, which would be the perfect location for you two," Mom mused. "That's why I was asking, so I could try to reserve it for you if that's what you were planning to do."

"I wonder if we could work out some sort of arrangement between our two colleges so that Mr. Haakedahl could just check on both of us and then report back to Trinity," I speculated thoughtfully.

"It's worth looking into," Kim agreed. "That house Mom found seems like it would be an ideal situation."

"Well, that was a pretty delicious supper, Gram," I told her as I put down my fork and stood up from the table.

"And just think, tomorrow's Thanksgiving, so we'll have even more yummy food then," Rory added happily.

"Well, I suppose we better be getting on home if you guys want to get some practicing in yet tonight," said Dad as he handed me my coat.

"I can't wait to hear the new song you wrote, Reed," Kim said. "What's it called again?"

"'He Rose from the Dead,'" Reed answered. "I'll show it to ya when we get home."

"We'll see you guys tomorrow," Gramp said as he walked with us to the door.

"Yeah! Turkey and dressing!" Rory exclaimed joyously as he thought of what the next day held in store. "It just doesn't get much better than that."

Concerts and Recordings

On our way out to the ranch that evening, the four of us siblings burst into spontaneous singing as we often did. It was nice to have a fourth part to our harmony now that Reed was old enough to chime in. Two of our favorites were "Operator" and "Bad Connection," which we put together into one medley because both had a central theme that talked about getting Jesus on your telephone line. We usually managed to work in an old hymn or two as well, which always reminded us of Grandma Hoffman, who had so much enjoyed hearing us sing the great classics like "Amazing Grace" or "What a Friend We Have in Jesus."

"Reed, take your inhaler," Kim commanded as an audible wheeze came through on the final note of "Inside Out," a tune originally sung by Londa Lundstrom.

"Oh, don't be so picky. A wheeze now and then doesn't hurt anything," Reed complained. But he dutifully took it out of his pocket and did as he was told.

He was usually able to keep his asthma under control with his inhaler and the occasional use of his breathing machine, although late-night trips to the emergency room weren't unheard of either. Reed never fussed about it though, even when his breathing became labored. We fervently hoped he would grow out of the asthma someday and that the more severe occurrences would become a thing of the past.

"Home again, home again," Dad chanted as we turned into our front yard.

We all piled out, and everyone went in various directions. Dad took the van to the car shed while Mom went inside the house and checked for messages on the answering machine. Kim was inspecting the corner stash in the living room to see whether any mail had come for her in the past week, and Reed started for his own room to catch the last few minutes of one of his favorite radio programs. Rory was on his way to what had formerly been Grandma Hoffman's house and was now our music studio. I was sure Grandma would have wanted us to use it for that very purpose since she was now living in a heavenly mansion and no longer needed her earthly dwelling.

I lugged all of the paraphernalia I'd brought home into our house, dumped it at the foot of the bed where Kim and I slept, and then went to see what Reed was up to. "Adventures in Odyssey" was just ending as I entered his room.

"Why do you bother to listen to that if you're only going to catch the tail end?" I wanted to know.

"That's better than nothing," he pointed out. "And besides, another good show is coming on right away, so there."

"What program is that?" I inquired.

"It's a really funny one! I just discovered it. You need to stay in here and listen to at least part of it. I'm sure it's the weirdest talk show that you've ever heard of."

I groaned. "Leave it to you to ferret out the strangest thing out there."

"Just wait 'til you hear it. This guy, Mischke, reports on some of the craziest news stories he can find and then usually adds his own concocted details or makes little songs or skits about them. Sometimes he'll take phone calls all about the story or makes prank calls himself. It's so cool!"

"Hmm. So are you implying that your radio programs are more important than your dear sisters coming home for the weekend?" I needled him further.

"Well, you're in here with me right now, aren't you?" Reed reasoned, always having a comeback for any argument. "So it isn't like I'm not spending time with you or anything."

"That's only because I took the initiative to hunt you down," I retorted. "Otherwise, you'd just hermitize in here the whole time and we'd never get to see you."

"You wouldn't let that happen, so why worry about it? Anyway, wanna look at my keychain collection real quick, before the next show comes on?"

I reached over and discovered that he'd added several new ones since the last time I'd inspected them.

"If you keep this up, you won't have room to sleep in here by the time you're a teenager because your key chains will be taking up all the space." I laughed.

"If it starts getting that big, I can just stand it up on end," Reed assured me. "See how I have them all hooked together so handily?"

"I guess I know what we can get you for Christmas from now on: just a few key chains," I suggested.

"Don't bother. I get enough of them during the rest of the year from everybody else," Reed told me.

"Speaking of Christmas, I suppose you still remember what you got every year since you were two?" I questioned, just to be sure his memory wasn't beginning to fail him, now that he had almost reached the ripe old age of nine.

"Of course," he said indignantly. "Why would I forget a thing like that? I remember all my birthday presents too." And to prove it, he proceeded to list them for me in chronological order by year, even remembering who each gift was from.

"I sure don't understand how you can get such good grades in school when your brain is so full of all this extraneous stuff," I said. "I've never heard of anyone else who knows the table of contents of their favorite books by heart or anybody who can recite a half dozen story records word for word just from listening to them so often."

"It isn't hard," Reed replied. "I remember nifty little details without even trying."

Just then, Kim opened the door and announced that Rory had called us over the intercom to say that everything was hooked up and ready to go.

"I guess you'll have to miss your show after all," I said in a mournful tone. "It's time to practice."

"Well, if I have to miss it, playing music is the best reason," said Reed.

We all trooped over to the music studio, and Reed found his newly acquired position behind the drum set while Kim and I took our places in front of the piano and keyboards. As Kim did some fancy warm-up trills on the piano, Reed began showing off the new drum rolls his brother had taught him and I added to the overall effect of the din with a helicopter sound from the synthesizer on my right hand, while playing an impressive bass accompaniment with the left. Rory now knew almost as much as Dad did about where the myriads of wires and cords belonged, so the two of them were scurrying to get everything plugged in and ready to go. He was also a pro on our mixing board already and could tell you exactly what each of the dozens of buttons did and how they should be adjusted so we'd all sound our best.

Finally, Rory picked up his lead guitar and asked, "Well, should we get this show on the road?"

"Okay. Don't keep us in suspense any longer, Reed," Kim said. "Let's hear your song now."

Reed cleared his throat dramatically, and then the boys began to play the new song that Reed had just composed, with Dad joining in on the guitar. Kim and I were so engrossed in listening that we didn't think to accompany them on our piano and keyboards as we normally would have done. I was amazed at the good chord structure and the rhythmic flow of the lyrics. It would have been a fine first attempt for any songwriter but was especially so when considering it had come from a child of his age.

Kim and I cheered enthusiastically when the song was finished.

"I can't believe it," I marveled. "It has so many words that you have to be listening really close to catch them all."

"Yeah. It's just like you're telling a story or something," Kim agreed. "Do it again, Reed."

Reed happily obliged and repeated the tune, all six verses worth.

"I think you'll have to be our main songwriter from now on. Since you're getting started so early in life, you'll be writing phenomenal stuff by the time you're twenty," I noted.

"This one is already pretty phenomenal if you ask me," added Kim. "You'll have to do it on Sunday for sure."

"And, Ror, you should get with the program soon or you'll be left in the dust." I chided my other brother good-naturedly. "Do you realize that you're now the only member of the band who hasn't written any songs?"

"Well, I can play more instruments than all of you put together, so that should count for something," Rory pointed out. "I guess I'm just more into figuring out melodies than trying to come up with ideas for lyrics."

"Excuses, excuses," Kim said.

And that was all I needed to hear. Her remark had brought a song of the same title to mind, about all the funny excuses people come up with for not going to church, and I played the beginning bars on my keyboard. The rest of the clan joined in right away, as though it had been rehearsed.

Afterward, we went through some of the songs for Sunday's program. Rory's skill on the guitar was constantly improving and expanding. Already, he could play at least as well as our Uncle Rick had, which was hard to imagine because Rick had always been at the top of our list of musicians. We would never have believed we could find anyone else with the same talent, much less such a person turning out to be our own little brother.

Kim and I had Brailled two copies of the song list so we would know what was coming up and could switch instruments with each other whenever the upcoming song warranted the change. Our brothers, of course, had the song list memorized and scoffed at our inability to do likewise.

"Looks like next up is your saxophone number, Ror," I said as I consulted the list.

Rory began putting his horn together. "Too bad I can't convince Dad to do any old-time stuff on stage," he lamented. "You guys should hear what I've been doing over here lately, since we bought our new recording equipment. I've been makin' all kinds of old-time music, and it sounds really neat."

"Go ahead and show them a couple tunes," Dad encouraged. "It's not too bad for a bunch of waltzes and polkas, especially when you consider that Rory is playing all the instruments himself."

"Not to mention also doing all the recording and mixing too," Reed added.

"Well, Gramp has been wanting me to make a tape for him of me playing all his favorites, so I figured this would be as good a time as any to learn how to run all the sound equipment and kill two birds with one stone," Rory reasoned. He laid his horn aside and went over to find a song he could share with us. "I don't have the final mix done on all of these yet," he told us, "but I'm getting there." He turned on the machine, and the next thing we heard sounded just like a full band playing the old, familiar melodies we'd known ever since our childhood visits to Gramp and Gram's home.

"Wow, Ror! This is too good to just keep to yourself. You should be selling it or something," I told him.

"Is that really you playing all those instruments, Ror?" Kim asked incredulously.

Rory laughed. "Who else do you know around here who can play old-time music?"

"You have a point there," she acknowledged. "I just can't get over how good it sounds though."

"And the quality is great too," I continued. "I'm sure people would have a hard time believing this was the first effort of a twelve-year-old engineer."

"Seriously, Ror, if you keep this up, we wouldn't even need to go to Bismarck to do our albums anymore," Kim went on excitedly. "We could just do them right here at home."

"Yeah," I said, catching her enthusiasm. "That would make things a whole lot easier for everybody because we could just work on it little by little as we had the time rather than having to get it all done within a couple of days."

"That would be so much better, especially now that Kon and I are gone so much of the time," Kim said.

Mom and Dad had mentioned to us more than once that they thought it would be nice if Kim and I would do a recording composed solely of songs written by the two of us. At first, we hadn't been able to imagine how such a thing would be possible when we didn't even have enough songs written yet to fill an album. Now that Rory was making the whole endeavor seem so much more feasible, however, I was sure we would be motivated to work on some new material for the record.

Rory played a couple more songs for us from his first recording project, and then we got back down to business. He was beginning to come up with creative ideas of his own for unique chord progressions and catchy rhythms, and it was easy to picture him someday being the leader of our group or having a band of his own that would go far beyond anything we were capable of doing.

We were all up bright and early a couple days later and ready to leave for the concert that was scheduled for that evening. Dad had loaded our equipment into the trailer the night before, so everything was ready to go. I grabbed the novel I was currently reading and settled myself in the backseat. Kim was right behind with her stereo and tape case. The cassettes she played for us on these trips consisted mostly of songs she had recorded from the Christian radio station in Bismarck. She turned on the player now, just as Rory and Reed climbed in.

"Gee, Kim, I think you could have picked a better time for making that one," Reed commented. "Sounds like the reception was terrible that day."

"But wait!" Rory cried in exaggerated amazement. "Kim, rewind that, would you? Listen to this, everybody. She actually finished a whole song. The ending isn't cut off or anything. How did that ever happen? I wonder. And wow! Hold on a minute. The next song even starts at the beginning instead of right in the middle someplace."

"She might be getting pretty good at this in her old age," Reed conceded grudgingly. "Now if only there weren't so much static in the background."

To my brothers' dismay, the hopes they had of hearing subsequent songs played in their entirety were not realized. Nevertheless, we all enjoyed the music Kim provided, even if the high standards set by Rory and Reed weren't completely met.

"I think I'm gonna learn that one to start doing at our concerts," Kim told us as an upbeat number proclaimed that it won't be old Buddha sitting on the throne. "I could tell our audiences how I go out witnessing to people at my college and about some of the odd answers that are given when we ask how they know they're going to heaven. That would fit in perfectly with this song, don't you think?"

"Yeah, that's a good idea," I told her.

"Play it again," Rory requested. "I was too busy listening to all the music and not paying any attention to the lyrics."

"It was talking all about how there's only one way to God and that none of the other leaders of false religions are going to be the ones sitting on the throne," I explained. "You mean you didn't hear any of that?"

"You should know by now that I don't usually hear the words until I've listened to a song several times and have a good idea of what all the instruments are doing," Rory reminded me. "That's just the way I'm wired. I'm almost always drawn to the chord structures and stuff like that first whenever I hear a new song."

"Weird. Well, I guess maybe that's the mark of a great musician."

"Anybody in the mood for a salted nut roll?" Dad called out. "I have a couple extra up here."

"This early in the morning? Not I," Reed answered.

"You wouldn't take him up on the offer regardless of the time of day," Rory pointed out. "You never eat candy."

"I bet you guys never realized that candy bar manufacturers have to put instructions on the wrappers, telling you how to open them," Kim declared.

"No, I hadn't heard that. Where did you glean that little tidbit of information?" I wanted to know.

"Oh, some of my friends at college were teasing me about how I just rip them open any old way, and I asked them what they meant. They were all surprised that I didn't know there was a correct way to open the things. So then they had to enlighten me, and I guess there's this line with arrows or something on every wrapper showing you just where to tear, and the words *tear here* are even written for you just in case you still don't know what to do.

"Oh, Kim, that can't be true," I protested dubiously.

"Yes, it is," she insisted. "Just ask anybody. And not only that, but apparently, practically all food containers and boxes are the same way."

"What on earth?" Rory said in amazement. "Sometimes it seems like poor-sighted people can't figure out anything for themselves."

"No kidding," I concurred. "It's really starting to dawn on me just how insecure some people are. Like, if I'm at a social function with somebody who has never been there before, they're always looking around at everybody else so they don't do anything that might be construed as being different or out of place."

"I know what you mean," Kim agreed. "Like, it would be the worst thing ever if anyone teased them or had to correct them or anything. And yet they usually won't ask anyone for advice or help either because that would be admitting they aren't sure of themselves, which would never do."

"And thinking everything is such a huge deal, like waiting to see which fork they should use first and dumb stuff like that," I went on. "I mean, just think how unfun our lives would be if the four of us were always worrying about those kinds of things. We wouldn't want to even get out of bed in the morning."

"That's for sure," Kim said. "Now I see why some people just don't get how we're able to function without sight. They're so dependent on all their visual cues."

"And even when they are given instructions, they won't follow them unless someone else does it first," I observed further.

"Just last week, I was at a meeting, and when the guy said 'Meeting adjourned,' I stood up to go, and my college friend grabbed my arm and whispered frantically that nobody else was leaving yet. Everybody was afraid to make the first move, so finally, the chairman had to say, 'You're dismissed,' and even then, the girl next to me wouldn't budge until she had seen that somebody else was leaving the room ahead of her."

"Dr. Dobson was talking about the same type of thing on those 'Preparing for Adolescence' tapes that Kim played for me," Rory mused. "He said he was at a meeting one time and nobody acted like they wanted any coffee when they were asked until finally it was James Dobson's turn and he went over and got some. So after that, most everybody else who came after him went and got coffee too."

Reed had burst into laughter at these revelations and thus was unable to make his usual witty comments. When he had calmed down sufficiently, though, he didn't hesitate to contribute his two cents to the conversation.

"I just recently discovered that most doors in public places have signs that tell you whether you should push or pull to open the door so people know how to get in and out of wherever they are."

"Funny." I grinned. "And the other day at the cafeteria, Shelley was stunned when I opened my own milk carton. She said she'd never noticed the little lines that are easy to feel on the part where it should be opened. Until then, I had always thought that was how everybody figured out which end was which."

Just then, Dad pulled over and brought the van to a grinding halt.

"What's wrong?" Rory questioned.

"Flat tire, I'm afraid," Dad replied as he got out of the van to replace it.

"Why does something always have to happen to put us behind schedule no matter what?" Mom wondered aloud.

In spite of this setback, however, we knew we had to be prepared to begin the concert when 7:00 p.m. rolled around, and I breathed a sigh of relief several hours later when, once again, we'd managed to get everything ready just in time.

While the rest of us were stressing over setting last-minute volume levels, plugging everything in correctly, re-teaching Dad some guitar chords he had forgotten, and wondering why the amplifier was making an obnoxious buzzing noise, Reed took his place behind the drums and began doing his best to lighten the mood. He started a rousing beat and began singing with gusto.

"All I want for Christmas is my upper plate…"

"Oh, Reed, can't you get into the Christmas spirit any better than that?" I moaned when the song was over.

"You didn't like that one?" he asked innocently. "Well then, how about this? I just heard it on the radio last week for the first time ever. I had to memorize it right then and there because I couldn't find a tape recorder anywhere handy and I knew I'd probably never hear it again."

And with that, he launched into the tune, which was sung to the melody of "Jingle Bells."

> Rust and smoke, the heater's broke, the door just blew away.
> I light a match to see the dash, and then I start to pray.
> The frame is bent; the muffler went; the radio, it's okay.
> Oh, what fun it is to drive this rusty Chevrolet.

All of us began playing along with the catchy melody in spite of ourselves, and afterward, Kim asked him to do a repeat performance because she hadn't been able to catch all the words the first time around.

"You guys, people are starting to come in," Mom cautioned in an undertone.

Undaunted though, Reed began the song for the second time, only to be interrupted by a sneeze, followed by another, followed by six more. He never did a halfway job when it came to sneezing.

Of course, this reminded all of us of a tune we'd composed spur of the moment at one of our previous concerts when the same thing had happened, and we all began the fast-tempo country song called "I Feel a Sneeze Coming On."

There were a few titters when we reached the conclusion, and I remembered Mom's warning that we had an audience. People must really be wondering what they were in for. To my chagrin, my sister only made matters worse by deciding that this would be a good time to sing "I am Slowly Going Crazy, But They Haven't Got Me Locked Up Yet," which was sung to the tune of "Battle Hymn of the Republic."

After that, I quickly whispered a directive to my youngest brother, telling him to do his version of "Achy Breaky Heart," which had Christian lyrics. It was always a hit with folks, and I hoped it might help to set people's minds at ease to the fact that perhaps we weren't completely insane after all.

> Let Jesus heal your heart, your achy-breaky heart.
> He's the one that really understands.
> He will heal your heart, your achy-breaky heart,
> He's the only man I know who can.

As more people began entering the church building, Kim and I decided to do a few tunes on the piano with me at the high end and her at the low. Dad helped Rory and Reed to find a seat in the front row and then went to help Mom set up the record table in the back. This promised to be a good evening. Even though the concert wasn't officially underway as yet, people were already engaged in the music we played and were applauding after each song. Having such an enthusiastic response greatly helped to boost our spirits and reduce the tension we'd been under earlier as we'd hurriedly attempted to get everything organized before it was time to begin.

After Kim and I had ended our third duet, the pastor walked to the microphone and gave everyone a warm welcome. He then introduced our family enthusiastically, and Dad came back up to the front with Rory and Reed while I went to the keyboard and synthesizer and began making the appropriate adjustments for the first song. Dad began with the opening bars of "I've Got a Whole Lot of Things to Sing About," and we were off to a rousing start.

Afterward, Kim and I switched places so that she would be on the keyboards while I played the piano. Unfortunately, we bonked heads with each other in passing, but I quickly tried to cover the awkward moment with humor by saying into the microphone, "Now you can see why Kim and I decided to attend different colleges."

Everyone seemed to enjoy this joke so much that I wondered briefly whether perhaps we should try to incorporate the accident as part of our regular concert routine.

Then Kim began telling people about the next song, which was one of the old standbys that she and I still did on occasion: "One Day at a Time."

"Living life one day at a time is a philosophy that our family has adopted for about as long as I can remember," she was saying. "Konnie and I attended school two hundred miles away from home for the first nine years of our education, but Mom and Dad came to take us home every weekend during that time. When they first started making that long trip though, they didn't know they'd have to be doing it for nine years. They just took it one day at a time, not thinking ahead to the possibility that it would mean driving two hundred and seventy thousand miles. Sometimes we need to just step out on faith and trust God, even though we might not understand exactly how he'll supply the needs."

"And another thing we've learned over the years," Dad put in, "is to never give up. If you know you're right about something, don't let anybody try to talk you out of it, no matter how things might look on the outside. When there's something you know you should be doing for the Lord, you can't let anything stop you. If we want to wait until we've got all the answers and have every detail figured out, none of us would ever be able to serve Him. Just keep putting one foot in front of the other, and He'll show you the next step along the way."

When the song had ended, Rory did an upbeat tune that was named "Please Don't Advertise." The lyrics stated that if we aren't living what we preach, we shouldn't go out of our way to advertise the fact that we're Christians. It was usually well received by the audience, and that night was no exception.

Next, it was Dad's turn. He said he would be doing a song he had written called "Sing a Song for Jesus."

"Whenever I get discouraged, I try to remember that somebody is probably sitting in their car somewhere with their tape deck going, listening to me sing all about this new life that God has given me. Then I realize I need to shape up my attitude and try to live out what I'm preaching, like Rory was talking about earlier. So I get out my old guitar, and before long, things start looking a whole lot better."

When Dad had finished singing, Rory said, "This next one is called 'U-Haul Trailer,' and it talks all about the fact that we shouldn't be so focused on material things because when it's our time to leave this earth, we won't be able to take any of that junk with us anyhow. So we should be generous with what we have, which actually brings up an interesting point. It didn't cost any of you a dime to get in here tonight, did it? If anybody had to pay anything, speak up now because I don't see any raised hands out there."

Rory waited for the laughter to die down before continuing. "Well, that's good because I have news for you. You're going to have to pay to get out."

There was more laughter.

Rory chuckled and went on. "Well, anyway, I think they're going to be taking the offering in a few minutes, so just remember what I said. God does love a cheerful giver, but I'm sure he would also accept from a grouch."

Rory started to sing, and after the offering had been taken, Dad announced it was time for the youngest member of the family to have a turn.

"Well, it's about time," was Reed's assessment. "And now, ladies and gentlemen, the moment you've all been waiting for." He punctuated his remark with a crescendoing drum roll that ended with a loud symbol crash. "It's none other than Reed F. Hoffman, here to sing for you about the fact that I just don't care."

Amid the puzzled laughter that followed this comment, the lively song began, on the topic of not caring what people thought of Reed praising God in his own way. By the time the song had ended, people were tapping their feet and clapping along with the music.

"Thanks very much," Reed said graciously. "And now I think it's time to turn you over to my sister for this next number."

"Well, that's a hard act to follow," I said. "I guess I'll just try my best. This song is called 'I Love My Jesus,' and it pretty much speaks for itself, so I think we'll get right to it without further ado."

"I just wanted to say a few words before you get started, Konnie," Dad interjected. "We don't always need to make a big show of our love for the Lord. A lot of times, it can just be the little things or the stand we might take in our own quiet way that has the most influence. A good example of what I mean happened not too long ago, as a matter of fact, on Konnie's twenty-first birthday. Some of her friends had planned an evening out on the town for her, now that she was officially old enough to go out and party. But she just told them she would rather spend a quiet evening in the dorm. I think that probably made more of a statement than anything else she might have said. And the fact that she didn't cave into the peer pressure and go along just to save face says a lot too. When her mom and I heard about that, it was just one of those moments that made us proud. Okay. Go ahead, Konnie."

Until then, it hadn't occurred to me that what I'd seen as being such an insignificant event in my life would make an impression on anyone. I realized anew that we don't always know when our day-to-day behavior might be impacting people.

After we had done a few more songs, it was time for Dad to bring things to a close.

"We're going to slow things down a bit as we wrap up here tonight," he said. "This is a song we learned about a year ago called 'I've Never Been This Homesick Before.'" There was a catch in his voice as he began to reminisce about Grandma Hoffman and told how she had always kept us in her prayers and was likely still doing so from up in heaven. "She can talk to God face to face now," he said, "and I'm sure she hasn't forgotten about us down here but is interceding on our behalf every day. We all miss her so much, but we'll see her again someday, and that's such a comfort, knowing that this life is only the beginning and that the best is yet to come."

Even after the concert had ended, I was still reflecting on what Dad had said about Grandma, and I hoped she had been allowed to peek down on us as we sang our songs and that we were making her proud.

Loading and unloading the equipment took even longer then than it had back when Rick and Denny were with us to help out. We had accumulated a lot more of it since then, and our parents were very grateful for the times when a few thoughtful people would stick around after the concerts to lend a hand. Even so, the job wasn't an easy one, and often, folks were careless in their handling of the heavy amplifiers and instruments. Sometimes Dad would encounter a tangled jumble of cords and cables when he opened the trailer after unhitching it from the van when we got home. He didn't intend to look a gift horse in the mouth, however, because the help was certainly appreciated.

Kim and I were glad that our Christmas vacations began in time for us to be able to attend our brothers' school Christmas program that year. They would usually tape the ones we had to miss, but we much preferred to be there in person whenever possible.

We all arrived at the gymnasium early on the night of the program so we could be sure to get good seats. Of course, the highlight of the evening was when Rory did his solo, "O Holy Night." A hush fell over the audience when he began to sing, and a little tingle went up my spine as he hit the high note near the end just perfectly, in a loud, clear voice. The room erupted when he had finished as the people stood to express their appreciation. It was a memorable moment, to be sure.

When the program had ended, Pam Seim, our brothers' aide, was the first person to express her congratulations.

"Great job, Rory," she said as she walked up and gave him a big hug. "I think I even saw a little tear in your dad's eye when you got that standing ovation. And, Reed, you were just awesome too!" she continued, turning to my youngest brother. "I'm so proud of you both."

"Well, hi, you two," she went on as she came over to where Kim and I were sitting. "Wasn't this just great? I'm so glad you got to be here tonight."

"Yeah, I'm sure glad we didn't have to miss it," I answered sincerely.

"So how's college treating you guys? This must be your last year already, if I'm not mistaken."

"That's right," Kim said. "And you might actually be seeing a lot more of us this spring if we get to do our student teaching here in Lemmon."

"That would be a blast. We could pester each other again, just like old times," Mrs. Seim replied with a chuckle.

We all laughed and reached for our coats. It had been a fun evening, and there was a lot to look forward to in the months ahead.

The new recording project that Kim and I began working on would feature five songs written by her and five by me. The first song was entitled "Sisters," which Kim had written about the two of us. It would be followed by one of mine, and so on. I had composed my first song a few months earlier, which I'd named "My Humble Prayer." In it, I asked the ever-provoking question that most of us have probably wanted to know at one time or another: "Is it your will, God, or is it mine?" Once I'd gotten started, lyrics were beginning to come more easily to my mind, until I had only a couple more songs to write for the album's completion.

When all was said and done, Rory was playing a grand total of eight instruments on the recording, including mandolin, violin, recorder, lead guitar, rhythm guitar, saxophone, drums, and bass guitar. We were amazed and humbled by the fact that our thirteen-year-old brother was not only the chief instrumentalist on the album but the recording engineer and vocal accompanist too. His voice was just beginning to change, so he had to switch from singing high harmonies to low by the time the album was finished.

The project was not without its challenges, of course. During one of my songs, "New Doors," Rory came down with a bad case of the flu. He was so ill that he couldn't even partake of one of his favorite specialties that Mom had prepared for supper that night: fish and fried macaroni. For Rory not to indulge at mealtimes was a rare occurrence indeed. Nevertheless, that very evening, the immense dedication he already had toward music was made very evident when he managed to drag himself back over to the music studio in spite of feeling far less than optimal. I was heading to college the next day, and we didn't want to forget the arrangements we had worked up, so Rory insisted on finishing his guitar and drum parts for the song before calling it quits for the night.

What was even worse than the stomach virus though was the bad ear infection Rory contracted, one of the very few he's ever had. The thing that bothered him even more than the pain was the fact that it affected his pitch in one ear. He was trying to record one of Kim's songs and had to keep turning his good ear toward the music and attempt to block out the distorted notes coming from his other side.

It wasn't until many years later that we found out just how worried he had been about this incident in his life. Never having had an infection so severe before, he didn't know what the long-term effects might be and couldn't think of anything worse than having his hearing damaged in such a way. Fortunately, the problem did eventually fade as the infection started to heal, but even to this day, some of the higher frequencies are gone in that ear. Still, as things turned out, it wasn't nearly as bad as it could have been, and for that we were all quite thankful.

When we listened to our finished product a couple months later, it was apparent to us how much God had obviously been at work, helping us at each step along the way. The recording was a completely homegrown project, and the three of us siblings were the only ones who had a hand in it. Even Dad hadn't been able to help much except to give Rory a bit of technical advice every now and then. The more contemporary genre of music was not Dad's cup of tea, and many of the chords we were playing were ones he'd never heard of before. But he and Mom were behind us all the way, as usual, praising each of the attempts Kim and I were making at composing songs and giving us the moral support we needed when times got tough.

"Side By Side Back To Back"
Roland Hoffman and The Believers
featuring Kim and Ronnie
Christian Contemporary Country

Rory's polka tape was also doing well. Mom had taken a few of the finished copies to our local Ben Franklin store in Lemmon, and they had actually sold out rather quickly and were in need of more. A radio station in Dickinson that featured that type of music every Sunday was even giving it some airplay, of all things. The rest of us couldn't get over the fact that it was the old-time music that was gaining notoriety, and all played by a thirteen-year-old, which just added to the irony.

As Kim and I had hoped, an arrangement was made between our two colleges that would allow Kim to do her student teaching with me in Lemmon, so we began to make plans to move into the house that Mom had found for us. As things turned out, I was assigned to work in Mrs. Thorn's third-grade class, which meant that Reed would be one of my students. Kim was going to teach in Miss Podoll's fourth-grade room next door.

Mr. Haakedahl had undergone a complete change of heart since my teaching experience class the previous semester. Surprisingly enough, he was one of my biggest fans and was staunchly in my camp when it came to convincing people that I would be a great teacher someday. I appreciated the turnaround on his part more than I could say, especially since he was giving me his full support before I'd even begun my student teaching and was willing to supervise my sister as well. I knew it was just another one of God's blessings and a confirmation that He really does care about all aspects of our lives.

Rory and Reed Visit

"Okay, kids. Today, we're going to begin a unit on our five senses. Do any of you know what they are?"

"Dominick."

"Jessica."

Several children's voices rang out, but those two always seemed to stick out above the rest. I had instructed the students to say their names rather than raise their hand so I would know which ones I should call on.

"Dominick, Dominick," the precocious boy kept repeating eagerly, until I finally smiled and gave in.

"Dominick, what do you think?" I questioned him.

"The five senses…well, I know seeing and hearing," he responded enthusiastically.

"Very good. Does anyone else know the others?"

"Those were the ones I was gonna say," Jessica replied indignantly.

"What about you, Bekah? Can you tell us what any of our other senses are besides sight and hearing?"

Bekah didn't normally speak up unless asked, but she usually new the right answers. "Tasting?" she questioned shyly.

"Very good," I affirmed. "And then there's also smelling and touching. Those are the five senses. We'll be talking more about these in the next couple of weeks and doing some fun activities to learn why they're so important and to find out what it would be like if we didn't have them."

"You and me only have four senses," Reed declared, forgetting to state his name first.

"That's right, but remember to say who you are and wait for me to call on you," I reminded him.

"But you already know who I am," he pointed out sagely.

Rather than make a big deal of the situation right then, I decided to just handle it that evening when he and Rory would be coming over to our house for supper. I was determined that Reed not be treated any differently from the rest of the kids. In fact, to my way of thinking, he should be expected to provide a good example for them.

The remainder of the lesson passed quickly as I asked my students if they could name some of the things Reed and I did to make up for not being able to use all of our senses. They were eager to give me their input, since most of them were already quite familiar with many of the adaptive techniques that Reed used in his everyday life.

"Well, that's about all the time we have left for our science lesson today," I said finally as I opened my Braille watch. "But we'll continue this discussion tomorrow, and maybe you can be thinking of some ways people adapt when they can't hear. But for now, I want everybody to take out the spelling quiz I gave you this morning and pass your paper to the person behind you. So each of you should end up with somebody else's paper. Do you all understand?"

When they answered in the affirmative, I went on.

"I'm going to spell each word aloud, so you'll all have to be good listeners and see if the word is written correctly on the paper you have. If the word is not written the way it should be, draw a circle around it."

I spent the next few moments answering questions and clarifying my instructions, and then we got down to business. Since Reed's test was written in Braille, I graded that one myself. When all of the words had been corrected, I asked each child in turn to tell me whose paper he had and how many circles were drawn on the paper. My hope was that having each child's score read aloud would motivate the kids to try even harder the next time around, not to mention having the obvious advantage of enabling me to grade the papers without any help from the aide that my college had hired to help Kim and me with our student teaching.

I had tried to politely explain to Mr. Haakedahl that an assistant would not be needed and might actually be detrimental when it came time to find a real job next fall. But the college insisted they wanted to do everything possible to help Kim and me to succeed in our goal of becoming teachers, so it was hard to refuse their generous offer of paying for a helper to come in and work with us. Instead, we decided to take a less aggressive approach. We would simply try to give our aide so little work to do that hopefully it wouldn't take long for everybody to realize that hiring somebody to help us hadn't really been necessary.

After taking down each child's grade on my Brailler, we were finished for the day. "Don't forget your math books," I directed as everybody gathered their belongings. "I expect you all to have those subtraction problems finished by tomorrow. And remember, if there's a zero in the middle of the top number, you'll probably have to skip over the tens and borrow from the hundreds."

"And if we do that," Jessica added loudly, "we need to cross out the zero in the tens and put a nine there instead."

"Very good," I praised, grateful that what I'd been trying to drill into their heads earlier that afternoon had taken root. "And why do we have to put a nine?"

"Uh…I'm not sure," she replied uncertainly.

"Because when we take from the hundreds, that's ninety more than we meant to borrow, so we need to add that to our tens," I reminded her. "If any of you have trouble, I'll be happy to help you out in the morning before you turn in your papers."

After the last child had left, Reed waited patiently for me by the door while I made sure I had everything I would need to take home with me in order to prepare for the school day ahead. Satisfied that all was in order, I heaved my backpack over my shoulder and grabbed my Brailler with one hand and my cane in the other.

"You'll have to follow along behind me this time, Reed, because my hands are full," I told him.

"That's okay. I know how to get to your house from here by myself," he replied.

"That might be true, but I still want you to walk behind me because there's a street to cross."

"I'm not a baby," he complained indignantly. "I'm sure I can listen for cars as good as you can. And there's never that much traffic in a town this size anyway."

"Well, even so, it doesn't hurt to be on the safe side. Now hurry up because this backpack and Brailler are getting pretty heavy."

I was grateful that at least I didn't have to climb down two flights of stairs with all my paraphernalia as I had done in college. I smiled as I remembered how my classmates would quickly dodge out of my way when they saw me in a hurry to get somewhere, fearful that they were about to get clobbered with a Braille book, or tape recorder, or whatever else I might be carrying at the time.

"Wait up!" a familiar voice called as Reed and I turned onto the sidewalk that led to the house. It was my student, Jessica. She had begun dropping in for a visit occasionally, especially whenever she heard that her friend, Reed, might be coming over too.

"Hi, Jessica. Come on in. I think Kim and Rory are already here. So you kids just make yourselves at home while I get supper started."

I knew Kim wouldn't be of much help in the kitchen that night, because she was busy preparing for the Bible study that she would be leading later on that evening. She had actually begun two studies since moving into that house: one for ladies and another for teens. Needless to say, she hadn't wasted any time in putting some of the skills she'd learned at Trinity Bible College to good use.

"You aren't gonna do tater hash again, are you, Kon?" Rory jibed from the other room as I set about rattling pots and pans and rummaging in the refrigerator.

"Oh, hush. You aren't ever going to let me live that one down, are you? I'll have you know we're doing our faithful standby of hot dogs and macaroni and cheese because I don't have time for anything more elaborate tonight."

"Whew. That's a relief," Reed put in, to my chagrin.

"What's tater hash?" Jessica wanted to know. "I never heard of it."

"You aren't missing anything. Trust me," Rory assured her. "It's one of Konnie's originals."

"Yeah," Reed chimed in. "It was supposed to be tater tots, but something went a little wrong and it turned into this mushy stuff that wasn't very appetizing at all."

"Some of it was burnt, and some wasn't quite cooked enough," Rory added. "Thus the name tater hash. We helped her come up with what to call it. Isn't that creative?"

Jessica laughed as I tried unsuccessfully to defend myself. "Well I'm sure it was because I was trying to make too much at one time since I was cooking for a lot more people than I normally do," I explained.

Just then, the phone rang, and I snatched it up, glad to get a few moments reprieve from my brothers' ribbing.

"Um...Kon, you better get out here," Rory called after a few minutes. "The water is boiling over."

I quickly brought my phone conversation to a close and went back to the stove, where I turned down the heat. Jessica joined me and watched with interest as I stirred the macaroni and took it over to the sink to drain.

"Miss Hoffman, I think you're the funnest teacher I ever had," she exclaimed spontaneously.

"That's nice of you to say," I smiled, deciding that it wasn't the time to point out the fact that *funnest* wasn't a word.

"She's just saying that so you'll give her a good math grade," Reed speculated jokingly.

"I know she wouldn't give me one if I didn't deserve to have a good grade," Jessica answered as I finished measuring out the milk and then cut a stick of butter in half. "Can I help you with anything, Miss Hoffman?"

"There isn't really much left that needs to be done right now," I told her as I dumped everything into the pot.

"How can you tell when the food is ready if you can't see it?" she asked with curiosity.

"Well, as we were talking about in our science class today, there's usually different ways to do things if we're missing one of our senses. Like right now, I could tell when I stirred the macaroni that it was soft enough and it was time to pour out the water."

"She could also set a timer but never bothers. That would make things too easy," Rory noted with a touch of sarcasm.

"That's what my watch is for," I shot back at him. "And, anyway, with a lot of foods, you can also tell by how the food smells when it gets done."

"Or there's always the smoke detector method," Reed pointed out. "When the alarm goes off, you know supper's ready."

Jessica laughed again. "You guys are so funny," she said. "But I guess cooking isn't really that much different for you than it is for anybody else."

"Some of our teachers wanted to make it pretty complicated, but it sure doesn't have to be," Kim told her as she closed her notebook and put the volume of the Braille Bible she'd been reading back on the bookshelf. "Reed, do you want to help me set the table tonight?"

"Not if there's a bunch of crumbs on it like there was the last time," Reed answered.

"But why bother to clean the table when it's just going to get dirty again?" Rory questioned with mock sincerity.

"Ha-ha," Jessica giggled. "Well, I wish I could stay, but I told my mom I'd be home by five, so I better get going before she starts to worry about me. And, Reed, don't forget that you promised to play with me at recess tomorrow."

With that, she said her good-byes and headed for the door just as the phone rang again.

"If that's my mom, tell her I'm on my way," Jessica called, slamming the door behind her as she ran out.

"I'll get it this time," Kim said, before I had a chance to protest.

She was usually anxious to be the first one to answer the phone lately because she'd recently begun dating a guy she had met in college and was always hoping the call might be from him.

Kim took the phone into the bedroom and closed the door behind her while I dished up the macaroni and told my brothers to have a seat at the table.

The room grew surprisingly quiet while the simple meal was being consumed. "I can't believe you guys haven't had anything insulting to say about my supper this time!" I exclaimed incredulously as I began filling the sink with water to start the pots soaking.

"Give us time. It hasn't digested yet," Rory retorted blandly. "And by the way, what's for dessert?"

"Well, I think there's still a couple ice cream bars in the 'fridge," I told him.

"Good. I'll have both of them because I'm sure Reed doesn't want any, do you, Reed?"

"Nope. I'll just have seconds on macaroni instead," Reed said.

The boys had just finished eating and I was clearing the table to start washing dishes when Kim came back out to the kitchen and hung up the phone. Rory and Reed had retired to the living room, where they turned on the TV to see if any of their favorite game shows were on.

"So how is Scott doing?" I asked her.

"That wasn't him. It was a prospective job offer," she announced a bit smugly. "It seems there's this four-year-old boy in a little town called Dillon, Montana, who's blind, and they're looking for a teacher for him."

"How on earth did they ever get your name?" I asked curiously.

"I guess they're members of the National Federation of the Blind, and Fred Schroeder told them about me."

"Interesting. So if you hadn't had all that trouble at the beginning of your college career and gotten to know Fred because of it, he probably never would have thought of recommending you," I mused.

"Yeah. It's funny the way stuff like that works out sometimes," she agreed. "Anyway, they're going to call me again in a few days with more specifics, but for now, they basically just wanted to know if I would even be interested."

"And you said yes?" I questioned her.

"Yep. I didn't think it would hurt to check it out, and there will still be plenty of time to change my mind later on if I want to. But I'm sure not going to say no to a possible job offer so soon. I mean, I haven't even graduated from college yet."

"That's true. And it would be an easy job too, just pretty much doing the same type of thing we've already been through with Ror and Reed," I surmised.

"Exactly. Well, I better make sure everything's ready for my Bible study. People will be starting to show up any minute now."

"And do we have everything planned for our get-together tomorrow night?" I questioned her.

"I think so. We're just going to be flexible and see who all shows up. Mom said she'll drop off Taboo and Scattergories for us to use when she comes to pick up the boys."

"Knock, knock," came Mom's voice at that very moment. "Anybody home?"

"We just got done with supper," Rory told her.

"Oh, too bad I missed it," Mom said. "I don't suppose there are any leftovers."

"Nope. They finished the last of it. Did you remember to bring those games?" I asked.

"Of course. When was the last time I forgot something?"

We had to admit that it didn't happen very often. Mom was used to juggling and keeping track of a whole lot of things at the same time.

"Speaking of games, there's this new card game that Kim's gonna show us on Saturday that she says we'll really like," Reed told her.

"Is it another one she made up?" Mom inquired with amusement.

"I hope so because she never wins those," Rory piped up.

We said our farewells, and then I prepared to spend the evening working on my autobiography. I plopped down on the bed and took out my word processor. My brothers had only recently succeeded in convincing me to take a look at the computers they had been given for their schoolwork. Until then, I just didn't see much point in computers and felt that a typewriter did the job just as well. But I had to admit that it was pretty cool to be able to hear the built-in speech synthesizer telling me what I was typing, which made checking my work a lot easier. I was also discovering how to move text from one place to another, which was certainly a lot better than retyping the whole page each time I wanted to change something.

Writing my life story and getting it published was certainly taking a whole lot longer than I had at first envisioned. I was learning, however, that God's plan is always best, and I wasn't going to question His timing.

Life Marches On

The next year proved to be a busy one. Kim had accepted the teaching position in Montana, and I had decided to pursue a Master's degree in special education from Minot State University in North Dakota. As my time there drew to a close, I began to think about where I might want to do my student teaching in the spring. When the South Dakota president of the National Federation of the Blind contacted me about a possible opportunity at Ellsworth Airforce Base near Rapid City, I jumped at the chance.

After completing the student teaching required for my special ed degree, I moved into a new apartment in the heart of Rapid. I hoped to build a clientele of piano students that summer, and maybe get a tutoring business going as well. I figured that living in the middle of town would be the best location for getting the maximum number of potential students.

Of course, Kim and I also made it a point to spend a good portion of the summer break with our family. Mom and Dad came to pick me up one day near the beginning of June, and Kim was planning to arrive by bus the following morning.

I showed Rory and Reed around my new apartment, and then we all piled into the van for the trip home.

"So what have you guys been up to lately?" I asked the boys as I opened a bag of chips and passed it back for them to take some.

"We went fishing with Gramp again yesterday," Reed told me through a mouthful of crunching. This had been one of their favorite activities, ever since my brothers were very small.

"Oh my. I hope it wasn't as eventful as your last fishing excursion was," I commented dubiously.

I couldn't help but smile though as I recalled the phone conversation in which my brothers informed me about their previous fishing trip. Gramp had tried to teach Rory how to cast the line, but for some reason, things hadn't gone exactly the way they were supposed to.

"Somehow, I got the arm movement wrong or was a little too aggressive or something and the thing got caught in some bushes," Rory had told me.

I could just picture him trying feverishly to undo the damage and only making it worse in the process.

"It was hilarious," Reed had said as they'd related the incident to me. "Only Gramp didn't think so. He must have spent a half hour or more trying to undo the wreckage. He said some words I haven't heard him say before, and me and Ror were trying not to laugh because we knew how upset he was, but it was so hard not to!"

"You guys think everything's funny," I replied, "especially when you aren't the ones having to rectify things."

"That's what makes it so funny," Rory had replied.

As we neared the outskirts of Rapid City, I was eager to hear about their latest fishing adventure. "You should have been there. It was pretty darn funny," Rory said.

"Gramp's nephew, Larry, came along this time"—Reed took up the tale—"and he just about had a fit over how much potted meat and crackers Ror and I could go through in one sitting. 'For Pete's sake!' Larry had said. 'Of all the great things you could have brought along for a picnic lunch, why on earth did you have to pick something as disgusting as potted meat and crackers?'"

"He just couldn't get over it." Rory laughed. "So, of course, Reed and me had to eat more than ever just to hear him get riled up about it."

"We got pretty stuffed. That's for sure," Reed put in. "Larry said he wasted more time helping Gramp fix all our crackers than he got to spend actually doing any fishing."

"But the best part was that we caught thirty-six crappies that day, which was our record," Rory went on with the story. "So I tried to point out to him that crappies obviously must love the stuff, too, and were attracted to the smell."

"Sheesh, you guys," I said in amusement. "I'm sure he didn't buy that one for a single moment."

"Not a bit of it," Rory concurred. "But it was certainly fun getting a reaction out of him and hearing all his choice comments about my little theory."

"They're probably better left to the imagination though," Reed chimed in as we all laughed some more.

"I must say, that's a lot of crappies though," I noted. "Did you at least invite Larry to supper that night as payment for all the crackers he made for you guys?"

"Of course," Reed answered. "Gram fried up the fish real yummy like she always does, and there wasn't a morsel left by the time we all got done."

Not surprisingly, Rory headed straight for the piano the minute we got home. He always had an instrument of some kind close at hand. No matter where he happened to be in the house, there was a guitar or harmonica or some other musical gismo within easy reach of wherever he was sitting. More often than not, he was tinkering away with some melody or other, even while in the midst of a conversation, game, or whatever else might be going on at any given time. Multitasking was no big deal for him.

As I skimmed through a Braille magazine, I was listening with one ear to what Rory was playing. It didn't take me long to notice that some of the chords he was coming up with were ones I'd never tried or even thought of. I put my magazine aside and gave him my full attention. With sudden clarity, I became aware for the first time that my brother's ability on the piano had surpassed my own.

I still remember that moment with mixed feelings because it marked a turning point of sorts for me. Never again would I be looked up to and admired by him in quite the same way. The rewarding days of imparting my musical knowledge to him and showing him something he hadn't known before were fast coming to an end. Sad as this was, I couldn't help but have an overwhelming sense of pride at his accomplishments. To think that not only was he already able to play the piano better than I could but that he'd also achieved such a level of mastery on so many other instruments as well and at such a young age was humbling to say the least.

"Hey, Ror, how did you come up with that chord, anyway?" I asked after he had played the final notes.

"Oh, Mr. Shimke, my music teacher, always has these jazz demo tapes laying around on his desk, so whenever I'd get to class early, I would listen to them for a few minutes while I waited for him to show up. Finally, I just asked him if I could start making my own copies of some of the stuff. It's really pretty cool music."

"Really?" I asked a little doubtfully. "So you're starting to like jazz now?"

"Some of it is pretty nifty," Rory replied. "But don't worry. I still like country as much as ever."

"And you like your new music teacher?" I asked.

"Yep, but he really makes me work hard," answered Rory as he continued to play a catchy tune on the keys. "Even though I could play all the songs the school band needs to learn without any trouble, he wants me to understand the theory and concepts behind the written musical notation. So rather than letting me just play by ear, he reads the sheet music to me and I have to figure out how the song goes that way."

"Wow. That sounds pretty cumbersome. I'm surprised he wants to take all that extra time. He must really think it's important that you learn the skill."

"And it will be good to know," Rory assured me. "I kind of like the challenge in a way, although it can be a real pain sometimes to go through such a tedious process when I know that all I'd have to do is listen to the song one time and I'd have it down."

"Wouldn't it be easier to just order the music in Braille?" I questioned.

"I never learned Braille music very well, and it's so much different from print that I still wouldn't have much understanding of the musical staff and whatnot."

"So let me see if I have this straight," I said. "First, he reads a couple measures to you or dictates them on to a tape. Then you have to interpret that and translate it into what it should sound like, and then you have to memorize what he just said and put it with everything that came before."

"That's pretty much it," he affirmed.

"Yikes. Not too many people could put all that together, I'm sure. But it's working out okay for you?"

"Oh yeah. Not a problem. Just takes forever is all."

"Well, I guess it's a good exercise in patience and brain power if nothing else," I told him. "Should help keep you on your toes."

We were all eager for the next day to come, when Kim would join us. Things never seemed quite complete whenever one of us was missing. Everyone always took great pains to save any big news to share until we were all present, and this time was no exception.

Our brothers wasted no time upon her arrival, in showing us the latest addition they'd made to the band.

Rory reached behind the chair he'd been sitting in and brought out a couple of instruments, one of which he gave to Reed. "Are you ready?" he asked.

"Sure. Anytime," answered Reed. "I'll take the lead, and you can do harmony."

So Rory counted off a couple bars, and they began to play "O When the Saints."

The sound was a unique one that I hadn't heard before. "What are those things?" Kim and I asked in unison when the song had finished.

Rory handed it over so I could check it out. "Hmm. I still can't tell," I remarked as I explored its shape further. "Must be some kind of horn, but it's so small and light that it almost looks like a toy."

"Exactly," Rory said.

And Reed burst into laughter.

"What do you mean?" Kim asked in puzzlement.

"It is a toy, and it is a horn," Rory replied. "Or, to put it another way, it's a toy horn."

"Where did you get them from?" Kim questioned.

"Mom and Dad just happened to see one at a Best Buy in Bismarck. So they brought it home, and I liked it so much that they got another one for Reed the next time they made a trip there."

"So these really are just meant to be toys?" I asked in amazement. "That's sure not how you make them sound."

"You can say that again," Kim declared. "I really do think you should play a couple songs on them at every concert. People will love the way you can make practically anything sound like a real instrument."

"They're battery operated. So that's what gives them the extra volume," Reed said. "But, yeah, we thought we'd give it a try at our next program and see how people like it. 'Twill be something different, at any rate."

"And speaking of something different," Rory continued, "Reed oughta show you what we came up with to do whenever you girls can't be here for some of our concerts."

"Yeah. Nobody will hardly even realize when you're gone," Reed added gleefully. "Just listen to this."

And with that, he marched over to where Rory's keyboard was sitting and began switching buttons.

"You've never liked playing the keyboard much before this," I couldn't resist pointing out to him. "Surely you aren't as good as Kim and I are already."

"Maybe not," Reed admitted. "But I can do something that you've never done. Or even Ror either, for that matter."

"Yikes. After a build-up like that, I can't wait to hear it. And it had better be good," Kim told him in no uncertain terms.

"Don't worry. It will be," Reed assured her. And with that, he proceeded to demonstrate how he could play the bass notes with his left hand and drums on his right.

"Cool. I didn't know you could get a keyboard with drums programmed into it like that," Kim said.

"Granted, they aren't the most realistic-sounding drums in the world," Rory noted, "but at least we'll have a fuller sound than if we had to do without one or the other."

"See. This key is the snare drum, and next to it is the floor tom, and over here is the crash cymbal, and so forth," Reed explained. "So I'll just have to train my fingers to do the work now instead of all my limbs. Not nearly as much fun as banging away on a real drum kit, but you can't have everything, I guess."

"So how did you ever come up with this idea?" I asked.

"We were trying to think of something besides just singing to tracks," Rory put in. "Because you know I had made several of those to use as accompaniment, but it's always been hard for Dad to follow something prerecorded like that. And besides, doing a completely live performance is always better anyway."

"Pretty nifty," Kim acknowledged. "Even if it means Kon and I won't be as sorely missed anymore when we aren't able to join you."

"Isn't it hard to think about playing all the bass notes with one hand while you keep a steady rhythm going with the other all at once?" I had to ask.

"Course not. What do you take me for? I even manage to get a few pretty nifty rolls in there besides," responded my youngest brother.

"And Reed has even started playing a little bass guitar," Rory said. "I mean on the actual real guitar, not just the keyboard."

"Very little," Reed clarified. "I mean, I'm not nearly good enough to play it in the band, but I'm learning a couple progressions on it anyway."

"Boy, what we miss when we don't come home for a couple months," I remarked.

"Yeah, really," Kim agreed. So do you play it backward and upside-down like Ror does?"

"Sure. That's the best way," Reed informed her unhesitatingly. "And besides, Ror's the one teachin' me, so what choice do I have?"

"And how did all this come about?" I asked curiously.

"Well, you know that high school girl, Christie, who says I'm her idol?" Rory began.

"Oh please!" Kim guffawed. "If this story is going to be all about someone singing your accolades, I'm not sure I want to hear it."

"Don't worry. She's too old for me. And besides, I haven't even heard whether she's a good cook or not," Rory stated matter-of-factly, as though that ended all debate on the subject.

"At any rate, she and Angie wanted to know if I would play the piano for some songs they were doing for the school talent show, including one they wrote together."

"Really? I didn't know Angie had written any songs," Kim said with interest.

Our cousins, Angie and Donell, had been playing guitar for about a year, and the two sisters could often be found singing their favorite country songs together.

"Yep. And it's not a bad song either," Rory replied. "Anyway, they also asked the drummer and bass player from the high school jazz band to play with them too, but the bass guy couldn't play by ear at all. So somehow, Reed got drafted to do it even though he barely knows his way around a bass guitar himself."

"At least I can hear the right notes and know when I goof up," Reed said.

"So after the talent show went off so well," Rory continued, "Mom and Aunt Diana started thinking it would be cool if the four of us cousins formed a little group of our own and tried to get a few places here and there to play together. So that will be another fun little outlet for doing music."

"Never a dull moment," I said. "Be sure to record it for us so Kim and I will be able to hear what you all sound like."

We all sat silently for a moment, until Reed noted that apparently the time had come for the infamous seven-minute lull that nearly every conversation experiences.

"Well, let it never be said that we succumb to your average statistics," Kim replied hastily. "Anybody up for a monopoly game?"

"I really wish we could find a computer version that would work on our word processors or something," I lamented as I located the correct box from the shelf and began distributing the Braille money to everybody. "It would sure beat having to dig out this board game every time, and things would go so much faster too."

"But then you have to consider that the game would also go a lot faster if Reed wasn't constantly making us mortgage and unmortgage all his stuff every couple of turns," Kim pointed out. "If we ever do get a computer version, Reed, we're electing you to run it for us in retribution for all the things you made us poor bankers go through."

"That wouldn't bother me any," Reed said cheerfully. "It would be great not having to wait around for you girls anymore. Then I can just do my own mortgaging and unmortgaging in peace and nobody could say anything about it."

"I wouldn't go that far," I hastened to assure him. "You would still be in for plenty of ridicule each time you tried to make one of your crazy deals with us. Never fear."

"Oh, I have no doubt. But if you think that's going to stop me, you have another thing coming," Reed retorted.

"Yeah. Since when has Reed ever let common sense get in the way of his predetermined strategy?" Rory put in.

"Exactly," Reed concurred, undaunted by our teasing. "So without further ado, let the fun begin."

New Horizons

The family band was going through a quiet phase, and Rory, a high school freshman already, was becoming somewhat restless and eager for more to be happening on the music scene than what he was currently experiencing. So when some friends of the family asked if he would like to join their gospel singing group as a piano player, he agreed without hesitation.

"How are things going with the new band you joined?" I asked him over the phone one evening, after he'd been playing with them for a month or so.

"Oh, you know me. I never turn down a chance to play music," Rory replied diplomatically. "But what a motley crew we are, if I do say so myself," he added with a smile in his voice.

"Well, let's hear all the details," I insisted. "To begin with, you could refresh my memory on who all is in the group."

"There's Larry and Darlene, of course, and we can't forget Gramma Olson, as she calls herself, who asks me every time we meet if I recognize her voice."

"I remember her." I giggled. "She used to do the same thing with Kim and me."

"And then there's good old Robert, who tends to mumble a lot and is kind of deaf but at least can hear good enough to play guitar if the amps are loud enough and there's nothing else going on," Rory continued.

I chuckled again. "And did it take you long to learn all the songs?" I wanted to know.

"Nah. They're quite similar. So once you have the basic melody down, you can pretty much go from there."

"Larry writes the songs, and Darlene plays drums, right?" I inquired.

"Uh-huh. She's the first woman I've known who can play drums. Sometimes she gets a little confused as to where the down beat of a measure is, but, hey, no biggie, right? Larry has a cool sound system too. Probably way more than we'll ever need or know how to operate, but it's there if we want it."

"Alrighty then," I said. "And do you go out to eat afterward? I know that for a growing boy such as yourself, food is a big issue in your world."

"Oh, we usually just bring along a few cheese sandwiches or something simple like that in order to conserve resources. But who's complaining? It's something to do, and I like being able to go with them to different churches in the area and play music."

Anyway, that's about all I have to report. Do you want to talk to Mom?"

"She and I chatted a couple days ago, and not much has happened since then," I replied. "Especially not anything that could top the news I gave her last time."

A few days earlier, I had announced my wedding engagement to Bob Ellis, a man from the little church I attended. I had introduced him to my parents some weeks prior to this, and they were very favorably impressed. We were planning a September wedding, (only six months away) and Mom had already offered to help with all the arrangements. She was always in her element when coordinating gatherings and other functions, so Bob and I were more than happy to let her work her magic with very little interference from us. I had heard so many horror stories from perspective brides who were totally stressed before their weddings, trying to sort out all the little details of the preparations, and I was grateful not to be one of them.

"It's probably just as well that you don't talk to her; she's pretty hoarse right now," Rory told me in exasperation. "She's been on the phone so much lately that she completely lost her voice for a while. The whole state must know you're getting married by now. I would suggest that when you bring Bob home this weekend, you come straight to the ranch and don't stop in Lemmon at all, unless you want to be bombarded by dozens of curious spectators."

"I don't think Gramp and Gram would forgive us if we didn't stop at their house on the way home." I laughed. "Besides, I think Gram is already planning lunch for everybody, so we wouldn't want to miss that. I guess we'll just have to take the risk."

As I suspected, Gramp and Gram were almost as anxious to meet Bob as Mom and Dad had been. I found out from Kim later that Gramp kept going over to the window every few minutes to make sure he'd be on hand the minute we drove up.

Upon our arrival, I tried my best to take the focus off my fiancé as much as possible, so as not to make him unduly nervous.

"I have a new Chipmunk tape for you guys that I think you'll really enjoy," I told my brothers as I dug the item out of my ever-overflowing purse.

"Cool! Let's hear it right now," Reed said as he grabbed it out of my hand. "It's so fun to put their music on slow speed to see how it sounded before they turned into chipmunks."

"You'll have to go into the bedroom if you want to listen to Chipmunk music so the rest of us can visit," Mom informed them.

"But wait a minute," I was quick to interject, not wanting them to disappear so soon. "I haven't had a Kojak update yet."

"He's doing good," Rory said.

"Kojak is a dog," I explained to Bob. "He technically belongs to our uncle, but whenever Rory and Reed are in town, they insist on keeping Kojak with them most of the time."

"I always had a dog as a boy," Bob said. "Is this your first one?"

"Our first dog, but not our first pet," Reed told him. "Our teacher, Mrs. Seim, gave us two Siamese kittens a few years ago, and we also had a little bird named Sammy, until he died."

"And that's a story in itself," I put in, glad for the opportunity to prolong the topic. "They had to give poor Sammy a funeral and everything when he passed away."

"Of course," Rory said. "Why should he deserve any less? Grandpa dug a grave for him right out in the yard, and then we said a few words before letting him rest in peace, just like they do at a real funeral."

"The only ironic touch to the whole ceremony was that the circus was in town, so we could hear all this lively carnival music playing in the background during such a sad and serious event," Reed informed him with a chuckle.

Just then, a loud chirping could be heard from a cage over on the end table.

"Wait a minute. Did Sammy come back to life or what?" Bob wanted to know.

"Don't worry. That's just his replacement: Petey," Rory assured him.

"Okay. You guys can sit up to the table," Grandma announced at that moment. "We're ready to eat."

As I suspected, the conversation at the dinner table turned inevitably to Bob. But at least we had survived the initial appraisal, so I hoped it would be easier sailing from there.

"We've started house hunting already," I said at the first sign of a lull in the chatter. "The one we're leaning toward has five bedrooms, so there would be plenty of room for an office for each of us and guest rooms for when you all come to visit."

"I'm not sure how Bob would feel about us descending on you guys all at one time," Kim quipped.

"I wouldn't have a problem with it," he stated quickly.

"I see he's trying to butter up his future in-laws already," teased Mom.

"Don't speak too soon, Bob. It just might happen," Rory warned him.

After we had finished eating the delicious potato soup Gram had prepared, we took my fiancé out to the ranch. Bob drove behind Mom and Dad's van as they guided the way.

As we made the last turn onto the road that led to my parents' home, he commented on how beautiful everything looked. "Those rows of trees give such a unique touch to the whole place," he noted. "And all the buildings are kept up so well too. Nothing is the least bit run down."

"My dad takes a lot of pride in keeping everything shipshape," I told him. "He wants to be the best steward he can of the land that God has given him. I'm sure he'll be happy to give you the grand tour whenever you want."

I had hoped that Rory and Reed would be on their best behavior as Bob joined us for supper that evening, but no such luck. In fact, they seemed to be showing off even more than normal for our guest's benefit. Reed's jokes were cornier than usual, at least to me, and Rory was no better.

"I bet nobody sitting at this table right now can tell me why the Romans had to close their coliseum," Reed declared matter of factly at one point.

"Well, please, don't keep us in suspense," Kim shot back with a touch of sarcasm.

"Why, it was because the lions were eating all the prophets, of course," he replied, not missing a beat.

Everybody groaned, but Reed continued without any letup. "And furthermore, are you all aware of the fact that it takes a mayonnaise jar two years to float from Boston to Dublin?"

"We are now," I answered sardonically. "And how we ever could have managed without that bit of useless trivia, I'll never know."

"That's why I'm here, to keep you in constant supply," Reed told me unhesitatingly.

Just then, Rory let out a very loud belch, and I covered my face with my hands in dismay.

"Excuse the pigs. The hogs are passing by," Dad commented dryly as Mom reprimanded her oldest son rather sternly.

"Hey, I'm famous for my belches," Rory said defensively, "and I figure we might as well let Bob know what he's in for right away, while there's still time for him to back out."

"Besides, that was nothing compared to the belch that stampeded the cattle," Reed pointed out.

Bob almost choked on his food at this revelation. "What's that?" he asked unbelievingly.

"Well, if you really must know—" Rory began in a dramatic voice.

"I'm sure he doesn't care that much," I cut in hopefully.

"Oh, you're wrong there." Bob was quick to correct me. "This sounds like something I have to hear."

"Okay then. This is how it happened," Rory said triumphantly, in his best storyteller's voice. "We were on our way home one day, and I let out one of my masterful belches right there in the car. It sounded something like this—"

"Ror, we don't need any more of your sound effects," broke in Mom before he could demonstrate further.

"Gee, that's no fun," Rory said mournfully. "But anyway, of course, Mom had a fit and told me to quit doing that and for me to at least wait until I was outside if I had to act that way."

"And this isn't made up. It actually happened," Mom interjected, lest there be any doubt.

"So being the obedient son that I usually am," Rory continued, "I did just that. I waited until I'd gotten out of the car, and then I let loose again. Dad had just finished weaning the calves, so all of the cattle were a little on edge as it was. I guess they'd never heard a sound like that before, and it made them a tad nervous, to say the least."

"That's putting it rather mildly, don't you think?" Reed asked. "They only managed to tear down a section of fence is all," he added gleefully.

"So now Dad begs me to go in the house every time I feel the urge to let one fly," Rory finished the tale with a flourish.

Bob had burst into laughter about halfway through the telling and was finding it difficult to contain himself enough to hear how the monologue ended.

"I think this story has been embellished somewhat over the years," I added hurriedly.

But my comment was ignored by one and all. Bob had been eagerly engrossed in every detail of the bizarre event, and my face was growing hotter by the second.

"All right. Time to change the subject," Dad said finally. "This isn't exactly the best topic for dinner conversation."

I tried to relax a little and convince myself that maybe my brothers' antics had actually helped to put my fiancé at ease. I was relieved to find that he seemed to be taking everything in stride so far, and I dared to hope that he would soon come to love my family just as I did.

Turning Points

After everyone had eaten their fill of Mom's delicious roast beef and potatoes and gravy, we all wandered out to the living room to visit some more.

"This house used to be a whole lot smaller before Dad got the addition built," I remarked as I settled myself on the couch beside my fiancé.

"You did all this yourself, Rolly?" Bob asked, impressed.

"Every bit of it," Dad replied.

"It took a very long time," Mom added. "But it sure is nice now that it's finally done."

"There just never seemed to be enough hours in the day," Dad went on. "Between farm work and the music ministry and everything else we had going on, the building project was on a backburner and just had to be squeezed in during a few hours here and there."

"We'd dreamed about it and wanted to do it for years, ever since the girls were small," Mom added. "Then, when we finally had the resources to get the ball rolling, it was still such a slow process every step along the way."

"But it's completed now," Rory put in. "And that means that Reed and I don't have to share a bedroom anymore, which is really great considering how small those rooms were and how big I am."

"It's pretty ironic that it finally gets done after Kon and I leave home," Kim put in. "But at least now there's plenty of room whenever we come for a visit."

"Dad even has his own little room for an office now so he can study the Bible and do other stuff without a lot of interruptions," said Reed.

"Very nice," Bob remarked. "I'm looking forward to getting a tour of the whole ranch at some point before we head back to Rapid."

"We'll have to show you our motor home too," Reed said. "We've had it since I was about six."

"Has it been that long?" Kim asked in surprise. "That's a half dozen years ago already. It sure doesn't seem like it. I can remember the day we first got it as clear as can be."

"Me too," Rory said. "We were all waiting for them at Gramp and Gram's house that day, and when they got there with the new rig, we picked up Art and Eva too and took it for a spin."

"But Reed was so young then," Mom put in. "Do you really remember when we first brought it home, Reed?"

"He has a brain like a steel trap," Dad reminded her.

"Especially when it comes to the obscure and irrelevant," Rory noted.

"Of course I remember," Reed said, ignoring his brother's jibe. "For one thing, Grandma Hoffman was with us that day too. That's actually one of the last memories I have of her. We were all so excited, and for our first jaunt, we decided to go to Hettinger for supper."

"You're right," Mom agreed. "I had forgotten we did that, but now it's all coming back to me. That was a special time, wasn't it?"

"I bet it was," Bob agreed. "So tell me more about the RV. What is it like?"

"You'll see it tomorrow, but we really like it," Rory replied. "It's partitioned off, so it can be divided into two separate rooms if we want."

"And there's a couch near the front that folds out into a big bed," Reed went on with the description. "And then in the back part, there are two bench-type seats that also make into beds for Kim and Kon, with two bunk beds above them where Ror and I sleep."

"Sounds nice," Bob enthused. "I can tell that you all really like it a lot."

"The only bad thing is that we haven't gotten to use it nearly as much as we would like," Dad said. "Most of the singing engagements we've had lately weren't that far from home. What we're really hoping for is to start getting some tours that would keep us on the road for several days or even weeks at a time eventually."

There was a brief pause in the conversation, and then Mom broke it by announcing in a very serious voice, "Well, Konnie, maybe now would be a good time to dig out that big questionnaire for Bob to fill out. What do you think?"

"Questionnaire?" Bob asked dubiously. "I don't recall Konnie mentioning anything about this."

"She didn't? Konnie, you're slipping. How could you have forgotten to tell him about something as important as this?" Mom inquired in a surprised tone.

I was picking up on the teasing note in her voice, so I decided I might as well let this one go without any intervention on my part. I had learned at supper when I was beaten, so there was no use trying to change the inevitable.

"What questionnaire are we talking about here?" Bob asked warily, still completely oblivious to the fact that this was all just a big joke in progress.

"Well, I always told the girls that whenever they were to get really serious about a guy, I would have this big survey for him with a hundred questions on it for you to answer. We can't let them marry just anybody, you know. We need to find out all about you first: your background, and whether there's any criminal activity in your history, and things like that."

This revelation was met by complete silence on Bob's part, and Mom pressed on further.

"So are you ready to fill out something like that? I know it's short notice and everything…"

Bob let out a big sigh. "Uh…sure. I guess I could…if you really want me to."

At that, we all burst into laughter, and Mom hastened to assure him that she was just kidding and that he wouldn't really be expected to fill out any such form.

"You should see the relief on Bob's face right now," Dad told me laughingly.

"Says quite a bit for Bob, if you ask me, that he would actually have been willing to do such a thing," Kim noted.

"I should say," Mom agreed. "I never thought he'd go along with it so easily. I think that alone means you're a keeper, Bob, as far as I'm concerned."

"Well, I'm glad to hear it," Bob said. "But I must say it's good to know there isn't really a questionnaire after all."

We continued to talk far into the night as Bob and my family got to know each other better. It was still hard for me to believe that in just a few short months, my life would change forever. As the following weeks came and went, I tried to get the most out of every moment that passed, for I realized that our family dynamics would never again be quite the same after I had become someone's wife.

My wedding day arrived almost before I knew it. Bob had moved into the new house we'd bought just a few days prior, and my parents would move my things in while the two of us were away on our honeymoon at Yellowstone National Park.

As I began to prepare for the ceremony, my mind whirled with thoughts of the future and fond memories from my past. I donned my mom's wedding dress, which I had decided to wear for this most special of occasions. Kim had written a poem about why the dress meant so much to me, which I would proudly display at the wedding reception.

> It may be yellow, it may be torn,
> But on this special day it's worn
> With pride, for not so long ago
> My mother wore it all aglow.
> That day in '66 was when
> This dress was worn, and now again.
> It will adorn a bride whose love
> Can only come from God above.
> It isn't really very old,
> For Mother treasured it like gold
> In 1970, one dark day,
> Tornado winds snatched it away.
> Four days later, when it was found,
> It lay in shambles on the ground.
> She lovingly packed it away,
> Assuming it was there to stay.
> But now that I have found the one,
> This dress's role is far from done.
> I begged for Mom to take it out,
> But she was sure beyond a doubt
> That it would not be fit for me

To wear for all of you to see.
We washed and scrubbed it carefully,
And God has made it white as can be.
This dress has really seen it all,
From happy days to tragic falls.
It has withstood the good and bad
And come out strong like Mom and Dad.
It is my prayer that Bob and I
Can share this strength as time goes by.

We had decided to hold the wedding in Lemmon, since that was where a lot of my relatives and friends of the family still resided. Pastor Tim from our church in Rapid City had graciously agreed to officiate, and many of our friends from there would be traveling to Lemmon to celebrate the day with us. I was eagerly anticipating the ceremony to come because I knew that Mom had planned a very special and unique wedding just for me, complete with a few surprises. It wasn't often that a bride was surprised at her own wedding, but that was just another reason I knew it would be a day I'd always remember.

The day was everything I hoped it would be and more. I was glad Mom had thought to give me some Kleenex ahead of time because I had to wipe my eyes at several points throughout the proceedings. Kim had written a song just for the moment, and she hadn't even practiced it during the rehearsal because she wanted me to hear it for the first time at that moment. I was glad the wedding was being videoed so I could listen to it again later and not have to worry so much about keeping my composure. She and Rory had recorded all of the musical accompaniments ahead of time, and Kim told me later that she had put vocals on the tape too in case her voice faltered while she was trying to sing.

Rory and Reed performed a duet entitled "What a Difference You Made in My Life," and my friend, Laura, and her husband,

Jim, sang a song called "It Takes Three." Mom and Dad also recited a touching poem about putting God in the center of our marriage. I found it all to be very memorable and knew I would relive every part of it again in the days ahead.

Shortly after returning from our honeymoon, a visit from my parents was expected. Mom had kept the wedding gifts with her, and she was going to bring them along so we could all sort through them together. My new husband's eye for precision came to the forefront as he critiqued every inch of our new home in preparation for our guests' arrival. I figured this was a result of all the military inspections he'd undergone, but I wasn't accustomed to having my house so thoroughly scrutinized.

"Don't you think we should clean off those shelves a little?" he asked me. "They seem kind of cluttered to me."

"But that's what shelves are for: to put stuff on," I pointed out. "I'm sure Mom and Dad won't mind."

Bob was insistent that things be in perfect order for our company, however, so I decided to bite my tongue and reminded myself that he would likely be a great help to me whenever it came time for a major house cleaning, which was a quality a lot of brides would envy.

My brothers and grandparents came along with Mom and Dad, and just as we'd hoped, there was plenty of room for everyone. I was anxious to open and see all the wedding gifts we had received, so I was glad that we didn't waste much time in getting right to the task at hand.

"This card is from somebody I don't recognize," Mom told me as she opened another envelope. "The name sounds familiar, but I can't place who it is: Travis Haakedahl."

"Really?" I asked incredulously. "That's the man from Dickinson State who supervised me during my student teaching days. To think he's still keeping tabs on me after all this time. I wonder how he even found out I was getting married."

"That sure is something he would remember you on your special day and take the time to write a note and everything," Mom agreed.

She went on to read his sentiments, which expressed pleasure in having gotten to know me and best wishes for my future. It was remarkable to think about how much our opinions of each other had changed since our first meeting, and I was filled with gratitude for how well everything had turned out in the end.

"Here's something pretty special from your friend, Barb," Mom went on. "It looks like a wall-hanging of some sort, with words in Braille that she sewed on with beads."

"Oh, cool! It spells out the thirteenth chapter of First Corinthians," I noted as I examined the cloth. "What a unique idea."

When we'd gone through the rest of the gifts, Bob and I decided to give my family the grand tour of our house so they could see how we were already putting all the space to good use.

After a while, I wandered into the front room to find my youngest brother sitting at the piano. "What do you know these days, Reed?" I asked him.

"It takes a pretty big dog to weigh a ton," he replied.

"I mean other than that," I clarified.

"Well, I know it takes an even bigger one to whip him," Reed answered.

"Fine," I said with a sigh. "Would you like anything to drink?"

"Why, certainly. But not if I have to decide what it is."

"Okay then. If you can't make a decision, you're getting Pepsi. So you might as well say Pepsi, in that case."

"That's what you think," Reed retorted. "I refuse to say any such thing."

I poured his glass and instructed him not to drink it in one gulp as he normally did, which he promptly ignored. Then he hit the button on his talking watch and observed that it was getting rather close to suppertime.

"What are we havin'?" he wanted to know.

"I hadn't even thought about it yet," I said. "Maybe we'll go out somewhere. But your watch really sounds like it could use a new battery at some point in the near future."

"Why get in a hurry to spend my hard-earned dollars when I don't have to?" Reed asked. "You know perfectly well that I won't do a thing about it until it has completely given up the ghost."

"I guess some things never change," I mused as I began to unload the dishwasher. "By the way, Ror tells me you've started to experiment on the Dobro lately."

"Yeah, I'm just using Uncle Rick's right now, but I might end up buying one of my own if I like it," said Reed.

"I can't wait to hear it," I said. "And I assume you're playing clarinet in the school band again this year?"

"Yep. And I'm even starting to learn some of that jazz stuff I know you love so much," he quipped.

"Wonderful. I thought it was bad enough when Ror started delving into that genre. Seriously though, isn't it hard to play a wind instrument when you have asthma?"

"Nah. A little horn like that doesn't take much air."

"Well, you'd better be careful. You know what happened the week of my wedding. You had the worst bout yet," I reminded him.

It had been easy to tell how worried Mom and Dad were when they'd explained to me afterward what happened. They'd had to rush Reed to the emergency room in the middle of the night, and he hadn't even been able to get into the car by himself. He just kept saying that he couldn't get enough air, and Dad was afraid he was going to lose consciousness completely before they got to the hospital. Mom said she just felt so helpless, especially when they could see that even his breathing machine wasn't doing him any good.

"Yeah, I have to say that that last episode even had me a little concerned," Reed admitted. "But you know what I hated the most about the whole experience?"

"No. Tell me," I replied.

"Why, it was the fact that I had to miss a whole day of school, wasting my time in a boring hospital room with an oxygen mask on for hours on end."

"Whatever." I groaned. "If that's the worst of it, I'd say you got by pretty lucky, even though it had to mean the end of your flawless school attendance record for the year."

"But, hey, at least I'm not likely to ever forget the occasion of your wedding with a memory like that to go along with it," Reed said with a laugh.

During the months that followed, I continued to keep in close touch with my siblings. Maintaining that connection with them was as important to me as it had ever been, and I didn't want any of them to think that I would be less interested in their lives because I was married.

Kim's life had recently taken an exciting turn. She had begun dating a pastor in Dillon who was introduced to her by mutual friends. The two of them had actually known each other for some time but had recently gotten better acquainted on a more personal level. He sounded like a really nice guy, and I was eager for Kim to bring him home so we could all meet him.

Rory was continuing to experiment with jazz, and when Kim and I remained skeptical about this turn of events, he tried to convince us that it wasn't any different than the music we'd all grown up on whenever we'd listened to our kiddie records as children.

"Most of that Disney music on our story records is jazz," he pointed out. "And even many of the Christmas songs you love so much have a lot of jazz foundations too."

"Yeah. That big band stuff is okay," Kim conceded. "But some of those songs you've been playing lately sound like just a bunch of random chords to me."

"Well, true musicians can appreciate the fact that it's actually way more than that," Rory insisted. "I mean, it's the complexity of the whole thing that has me so intrigued."

"I guess I'm not a true musician then," Kim answered derisively, "because I don't think I'll ever find it the least bit intriguing."

"By the way, have I told you that I haven't had any more asthma attacks since the fateful week of your wedding?" Reed questioned.

"Really? Wow. It would sure be nice if you were finally outgrowing it," I said. "You've never gone nearly this long without any spells."

"So do you think you're over it completely?" Kim asked in wonder.

"Oh, I still have some allergies and sniffles and whatnot. But I just take my inhaler once or twice a day and I'm good to go," he replied.

"Cool! That sure is a blessing," I said happily.

I was surprised at how quickly my life had settled down into a peaceful routine after my marriage. Of course, there were the usual adjustments that all new couples must make as they adapt to living with one another. However, Bob and I had spent so much time with each other before our wedding that life didn't seem much different from what it had been then. We enjoyed watching movies together in the evenings, taking walks, or sometimes playing cards.

Unfortunately, all of us were about to be confronted with the sad fact that life can often turn from calm and tranquil to frightening and tragic in the blink of an eye.

Attack from Satan

That summer day in the middle of June started out like any other morning. At least that's what everyone thought. None of us could have imagined how differently it would end.

Dad woke up to the noise of his two sons arguing ferociously about whose turn it was to have the TV remote. He and Mom had recently gotten a satellite system put in, which meant there were a lot more channels to watch than had previously been the case. Unfortunately, this also meant there were more choices to argue over. Rory usually preferred game shows while Reed liked the Western channel the best, especially when he was able to hook up his tape recorder in time to catch all of the various sound effects.

"You know it's my day to have the remote," Rory pointed out, trying to get his brother to see reason.

But Reed was having none of it. "You had the remote yesterday," he lashed out defensively. "And it was actually even my day to have it."

"That's because you handed it over willingly since the Westerns were all reruns," Rory reminded him rationally with a not-so-patient sigh.

"Exactly!" Reed said, as though his brother had made his point for him. "And that's why I should get it today."

"Reed, you're not even trying to be logical!" Rory claimed in utter exasperation now. "Just because you don't mind game shows when your channel has reruns doesn't mean you should get to have the remote whenever there's a Western you want to see."

"All right, you hooligans. What's going on out here?" came Dad's groggy voice from the bedroom doorway. "Don't you know there are people in this house still trying to get some sleep?"

"But Ror won't give me the remote, and he had it two days in a row already!" Reed told him in a very offended manner.

"So that gives you guys the right to make enough racket to raise the dead, is that it?" Dad wanted to know.

"Reed refuses to understand that just because he doesn't like reruns, that shouldn't mean he gets to watch his shows whenever they're on," Rory grumbled.

"Well, neither one of you are getting the TV for now," Dad decided. "There's no reason to be squabbling over something like this. You should be smart enough by now to know how to sort out these things without getting so bent out of shape about it. There oughta be plenty of time in the day for you both to watch some shows you like."

"Hey, you guys, what's all the commotion out here?" Mom asked sleepily as she entered the room.

"I'm going out to the field," Dad informed her as he hurriedly made his exit.

"You two should know better than to be making so much noise so early in the morning," Mom chided the boys. "Especially when you know Dad hasn't been feeling so good lately. He needs all the rest he can get."

Even though Dad hadn't come right out and said anything to her about it, Mom could see clearly that he hadn't been himself for several weeks already. His skin had taken on a grayish pallor, and he was moving more slowly than normal. At a recent singing engagement they'd had, Mom noticed that he was just dragging along, taking twice as much time to unload the equipment as was normally the case. When the concert had ended, he was pretty much done in, and she'd ended up doing most of the loading of the equipment herself, with only minimal help from Dad, which definitely wasn't like him.

Fortunately, Rory and Reed were much better behaved for the remainder of the day. Dad didn't make it home for lunch and just barely got back from the field in time to tell them good night before they went to bed.

Mom awakened much later to find Dad sitting in the recliner, looking terrible. It was then that he finally told her he wasn't feeling the greatest and that he'd been having chest pain.

The ringing of the phone startled me to alert attention. I'd been sleeping, but getting a call at such a late hour didn't bode well, and it was enough to bring me fully awake immediately.

It was Kim on the other end of the line, and her voice sounded frantic. "Something's wrong with Dad!" she said. "I just got off the phone with him, and he didn't sound normal at all."

"What do you mean?" I asked impatiently. I couldn't remember a time when Dad had been so sick that he would actually let it show.

"He was just sounding all mumbly, and I could hardly hear him or understand anything he was saying," Kim clarified further.

I could tell she was trying hard to stay in control, but that was precisely what had me so worried.

"Why was he even calling?" I wanted to know.

Dad wasn't usually the one to initiate phone calls, especially if he was feeling under the weather.

"It wasn't him who called," Kim tried to clarify. "It was Mom. I mean, she's the one I talked to at first, and then she put Dad on."

"Well, what was she calling about?" I snapped, starting to run out of patience myself.

"Dad, of course!" Kim replied brusquely. "What else?"

I took a deep breath and attempted to regroup as best I could. Bob was awake by this time and was asking me what was going on, but I couldn't stop to talk to him right then.

"So what exactly did Mom say?" I asked in a quieter tone, hoping that would help Kim to explain things more coherently.

"She just wanted us to pray," came her tremulous answer. "But you know it has to be pretty bad for her to call in the middle of the night like that. I guess Dad hasn't been doing well for quite a while, but he never said anything, and of course, Mom didn't want us to worry. So that's why she didn't call until now. But he's having pain in his chest."

I lay there with the receiver to my ear, almost not believing what I was hearing. Maybe it was just a bad dream after all. But even as the hopeful thought crossed my mind, I knew it was only wishful thinking.

Although my stomach had dropped at Kim's revelation, I knew I'd have to keep my composure if I had any hope at all of getting the facts straight.

"So did you tell them to get to a doctor?" I asked calmly.

"Of course. But I'm sure you know how successful I was. Dad just kept saying that he was going to wait it out and that now wasn't the time to admit defeat, and on and on."

I clenched my teeth and my hands balled into fists. It was frustrating to be so far away and to feel so helpless.

"What I actually told them to do was to call an ambulance," Kim continued. "But Mom just said that Dad wouldn't hear of going to a hospital. You know how much he has always hated to rely on doctors."

"Well, I would have hoped that in an emergency situation like this, he'd rethink that philosophy a little," I said with extreme irritation. "That's it! I'm going to call them myself and try to talk some sense into them."

I disconnected the call, knowing Kim would understand, and dialed Mom and Dad.

Mom picked up right away, and I could tell she'd been crying. I cut right to the chase and demanded an update. Later, I experienced a twinge of regret at being so short with them at such a critical time, but at the moment, I was too worked up to do anything but try to get them to seek some medical attention immediately.

It didn't take me long to figure out that Mom was so flustered by Kim and me telling her to do one thing and Dad saying another that it was difficult for her to think straight. So I decided I'd better get the ball rolling myself. I hung up the phone once more, and this time, I called information to get the number for the ambulance.

My hands trembled as I dialed the number the operator had given me. Time was going by at a snail's pace, and things weren't happening nearly fast enough to satisfy me. Each ring of the phone seemed like an eternity, but I'm sure that in reality, it was answered within seconds.

The nurse I talked to was very courteous and professional, but to my utter disbelief, she informed me that they couldn't send an ambulance out to the ranch without anyone's permission. She must have sensed how very annoyed I was to hear that, because she was gracious enough to add that she would give Mom and Dad a call and see if she could convince them to heed the seriousness of the situation.

Apparently, what she said to my parents must have had some effect because when I talked to Mom again a few minutes later, she told me they were getting ready to leave for the hospital.

"Dad has to put some bales in the feeder for the bulls first since we don't know how long we'll be gone," she said, "but then we'll be on our way."

"What on earth is he thinking?" I almost shouted. "This isn't any time to be worrying about the cattle, of all things!"

But I knew my anger wasn't helping matters, so I tried to focus on the fact that if nothing else, at least they'd finally decided to go to Hettinger, where the hospital was located.

I quickly phoned Kim to keep her posted. She sounded slightly better than when I'd talked to her earlier, and I figured out why when she told me that she had asked her fiancé, John, to come over. I was glad she had somebody to be with her during this crisis. Even though I still hadn't been able to clue Bob in much, except for a brief summary, I was grateful that I didn't have to be alone. I figured Bob was getting the gist of what was going on by listening in to my telephone conversations.

"That nurse must have really read them the riot act," I said to Kim with a little laugh. But we both knew the situation was far from humorous. "I guess she told them Dad was probably about to have a fatal heart attack, which scared them enough to get moving."

"I'm still a little surprised that Dad actually agreed to go," Kim mused. "You know how stubborn he can be."

"Well, it sounds like he finally consented more for Mom's sake than anything else," I told her. "He knew how awful she would feel if anything happened that could've been avoided if he'd gotten the proper medical attention."

As Hoffman luck would have it, they had a flat tire on their way into Lemmon to drop the boys off with our grandparents. Dad himself must have been pretty worried at that point, because he actually told Mom to just keep driving on the rim rather than take the time to change the tire.

Gramp was standing outside as they pulled up in front of their house. "Now what-the-sam-hill is going on?" he wanted to know. "I heard you coming from two blocks away!"

Hurriedly, they notified him about the flat tire, and Gramp insisted that he was taking them the twenty-five miles to the hospital in Hettinger himself.

I lay awake the rest of that night, wondering what was going on and how Dad was doing. My mind kept reliving the special memories I had growing up. I recalled the countless late-night talks Dad had shared with Kim and me after he'd read us our bedtime story. Dad liked to read us all of the wonderful books he had enjoyed as a boy, so we got to hear such great classics as *White Fang* and *The Black Stallion*. After he'd read a chapter and was about to say good night, either Kim or I would invariably detain him with a question or two. Usually, our discussions turned to things of the Lord, such as what the Bible meant when it said that God could be everywhere at once or how it was possible that He had no beginning.

I also recollected the hikes we'd taken, especially the eventful one in which the weather had suddenly gotten very warm and both Kim and I had passed out from the heat. I thought about the many sermons we'd listened to during our trips back and forth from Aberdeen; and about riding with Dad on the tractor while he did his work; and of course, the multitude of times we had played our music together as a family. I refused to let myself think of all the things that might go wrong and just kept thanking God that He was with Dad right then and for giving us a measure of peace as we went through the trial.

It turned out that Dad needed to have angioplasty done the next morning, so he was moved to the hospital in Bismarck, which had the facilities to carry out such an operation. Kim and I were on pins and needles as we waited impatiently to hear how everything had gone. Fortunately, Mom called both of us as soon as the procedure was over because she knew we wouldn't want to wait a minute longer than necessary for the news.

"Everything went okay," she informed me. "He's just resting now."

A wave of relief flooded through me. I hadn't realized until that moment just how much tension I had been under. Suddenly, all the anxiety that I'd been trying so hard to keep at bay threatened to surface as I thought about just how serious it all was and how grateful I was that everything had turned out all right.

"Did you remember what today is?" Mom was asking me.

I scrubbed at my eyes and determined not to let my emotions get the best of me. After all, the worst was over, so it wasn't the time to get all weepy. I knew Dad wasn't out of the woods yet, but he had gotten through that far, so there was no reason to worry needlessly.

"That's right! It's Dad's birthday, isn't it?" I realized with a sniffle. I had thought about the fact that it was coming the day before, but of course, after what had happened, it was the furthest thing from my mind.

"Well, you know your dad. He never remembers things like that anyway. So of course, he hadn't even thought of it until I reminded him," Mom said with a trembling laugh.

"Dad sure does know how to have eventful birthdays," I remarked sardonically. "As if the tornado that happened back when wasn't a big enough present, now he has to try to top it with something like this." I grabbed another Kleenex and wiped my nose.

"But you know what he said when I told him what day it was?" Mom went on. "He says there's no way Satan is going to get away with trying to kill him off at the young age of fifty-four. Now he's determined to stick around for at least another fifty-four more years, which means he isn't even going to consider checking out until he's a hundred and eight."

The thought made me smile through my tears. It sounded just like something Dad would say, and I was glad to hear that his willpower and sense of humor were still intact, even in such a critical time.

Mom continued to keep Kim and me updated on Dad's progress for the next couple of days. Even though he was sleeping a lot of the time, we still wished with all our hearts that we were there with them. The two of us were chatting on the phone and lamenting that fact to each other one evening when Kim suddenly had an idea.

"Why don't we go there?" she asked.

"Where?" I questioned, wondering if she was really saying what I thought she was suggesting.

"To Bismarck. Why don't you and I both catch a bus and give them a surprise they won't forget?"

I had to think about that a minute. "Hmm. Mom said she thought they would be letting Dad go home on Sunday. Isn't that Father's Day? That would sure be a cool gift for Dad, wouldn't it?"

"That's what I was thinking," Kim said.

"Do you suppose they would be up to having the extra company right now though?" I had to ask.

"Well, it would only be us, so they wouldn't have to go to a lot of extra trouble," Kim reasoned. "And one good thing about us going right to Bismarck where they are is that hopefully it would all work out so that we'd be able to just go home with them from there and they wouldn't have to make any extra trips to pick us up from a bus depot or anything."

"That's assuming everything goes according to plan," I pointed out, trying rather unsuccessfully to play devil's advocate. "You know that schedules aren't always the most reliable where buses and doctors are concerned."

Even as I raised the objection, though, I had to admit that I was becoming excited about the possibility of surprising Mom and Dad and of being able to be with them and know firsthand how Dad's recovery was progressing.

"Well, before we get our hopes up too high, let's find out what the bus schedules are and then get back to each other," Kim said. "That way we'll know if this scheme will even be at all feasible."

So that's what we did. I was annoyed to find out that for some reason, the route I would need to take to get to Bismarck went all the way through Billings, which was quite a distance out of the way. But the bright side was that it meant that I would be able to join up with Kim at that point and we could travel the rest of the way into Bismarck together.

"Let's do it!" I said eagerly to Kim when we were once more on the phone with one another. Once we'd gone that far in our planning, I couldn't bear the thought of not carrying things to fruition.

"Don't you think we better tell somebody at the other end though, just in case anything were to go awry?" Kim inquired.

"I doubt anything would go wrong but probably not a bad idea," I conceded, although I hated giving up the thought of surprising everybody. "If we told Gramp and Gram, though, they'd just worry about all the stuff that might go wrong. More than likely, they'd try to chase us down before we even got halfway to Bismarck."

"True," Kim admitted. "Let's just tell Ror and Reed then," she decided after mulling it over for another moment. "We'll just explain that they'll need to keep it to themselves unless they haven't heard anything from us by a certain time."

Now that we had all the logistics ironed out, the only thing left to do was to pack our bags. Or so I thought. Bob, on the other hand, wasn't so sure.

"How will you get to the hospital once you reach Bismarck?" he wanted to know.

"Just hunt down a pay phone and call a cab," I said reasonably. I wasn't used to having to explain myself like that but realized that I was a married woman and would have to take my husband's viewpoint into account.

"I don't know...seems kind of iffy to me," Bob was saying. "I won't stand in your way if you really want to do this, but be sure to call me as soon as you get there."

"Oh, I will. Don't worry," I assured him, relieved and grateful that he hadn't raised any real objections.

The journey began without incident. Our buses were right on schedule, and we were able to meet up with each other in Billings without any trouble. Kim was supposed to have gotten there ahead of me, so I just asked the person at the desk if she had seen anybody else arrive with a white cane.

"Does she look a whole lot like you?" the lady asked. "If so, she's right over here. Just follow my voice."

Kim and I spent our time on the bus talking, reading, and listening to tapes. My mind kept wandering to the scene that awaited us at our destination, and my thoughts would then leap to the weeks and months ahead. I wondered what the long-term effects of the ordeal would be for Dad and whether he would continue to have serious heart problems and need to be carefully monitored. I knew a lifestyle like that would be quite hard for such an independent person to get used to. Working on the ranch required a lot of physical activity, and I wasn't sure he'd be able to continue to handle all of the responsibilities that such a life entailed.

And that didn't even touch on the more personal aspects. Rory and Reed were still so young, and they definitely needed to have Dad around for many years to come, as did the rest of us. Would we be able to convince him of the importance of taking life a little easier?

All at once, I stopped my runaway imagination midstream and gave myself a mental shake. Our family had never been one to borrow trouble, so I was determined not to change that pattern now. Everything had always worked out for us before, as long as we put our trust in God, and there was no reason to assume that wouldn't be the case. We just needed to keep our focus on Him and take life as it came. I wasn't going to dwell on what-ifs any longer because I knew that God had everything well in hand.

Surprise Trip for Father's Day

"I'm thinking we better call the hospital at our next stop to be sure Mom and Dad haven't left there yet," Kim suggested at one point as the bus continued on its journey. "It's already almost ten, and a lot of times, they'll try to get people dismissed before noon."

"Not a bad idea," I replied. "In fact, it appears that we're slowing down right now. Run in real quick and do that. I'll save your seat."

"Yikes. It's a good thing I called ahead," Kim told me as she made her way back to where I was sitting a few minutes later. "Mom and Dad had just finished filling out the last of the paperwork, so I explained the situation to the nurse and asked if they could be detained awhile longer until we got there."

"Wow. Was she agreeable to doing that?" I asked.

"Once she heard the whole story of how you and I wanted to surprise them and everything, she was more than happy to cooperate. She said they would just keep Dad around until after lunch, and I told her we were sure to be there by that time. So let's just hope this bus doesn't break down or anything before then."

When we arrived in Bismarck, we waited in line to get our luggage. I told one of our fellow passengers what our suitcases looked like and explained that they also had name tags that should make them easily identifiable.

"Hmm," I don't see them anywhere," the lady commented in a bewildered tone after several minutes had passed. "It looks like everything has already been claimed, and I didn't see anything like what you described."

"Oh, dear. It looks like we might have just hit our first snag," Kim remarked.

We had come so far by that point though that a trifling matter such as lost luggage didn't really seem like a big deal.

After questioning the people at the reception desk, it was finally ascertained that our luggage was still at our previous stop in Dickinson.

"I wonder how that happened," I said. "They usually keep it right under the bus we're on."

"I bet somebody probably became confused when I got off to make that call," Kim conjectured. "They must have thought we were stopping there and took out our luggage. That's the only thing I can think of."

We were both aware that regardless of how the mix-up occurred, it would be necessary for Mom and Dad to go back to Dickinson to pick up our luggage before heading home. This would delay things considerably, but we couldn't do anything about it at that juncture.

"Is there a payphone anywhere nearby?" I asked the woman at the desk.

"Certainly. Right this way," she responded.

I rummaged around in my overcrowded purse until I located some spare change. After obtaining the number from directory assistance for a local cab company, I dialed and told the dispatch person that my sister and I were both blind and were in need of a taxi at the bus depot.

"We'd better go out front so we'll be easy for the driver to spot," Kim said.

I picked up my bag and followed her to the curb. We were only there a minute when we heard a car pull up and come to a stop right where we were standing. We doubted it could already be our cab.

"Well, if it isn't Kimmie and Konnie," a vaguely familiar voice called out. "What in the world are you girls doing here?"

My mind was whirling as I tried to identify the woman who was speaking. Her voice sounded a lot like Mom's good friend, Jane, the wife of the drummer who had played on our first album. Then, suddenly, everything clicked. I realized it must be her sister.

"Judy," I asked, "is that you?"

"It sure is," she replied. "I've come to pick up two sisters who are wanting a taxi."

"You mean you're the cab driver?" Kim asked in disbelief.

"That's right," Judy replied as she stepped out of the car and loaded our carry-on bags into the trunk. "Where are you girls headed?"

Kim and I settled ourselves in the backseat and explained what had happened and that we were on our way to the hospital to see Dad.

"Oh, I'm so sorry to hear that about Rolly," Judy said sympathetically. "He always seems to be the picture of health whenever I run into him."

"Yeah, he normally is," Kim said. "That's why this has caught us all so off-guard."

"And are your parents expecting you?" Judy questioned further.

"No. We're surprising them," I replied, unable to disguise the gleeful note in my voice.

"Oh, boy, and I get to be part of it," Judy said, almost as excited as we were.

"Yeah. This is working out so well," I commented. "To have somebody we know as our cab driver, of all things."

"No kidding," Kim affirmed. "Now you'll be able to help us find exactly where Dad's room is and everything. They're sure going to wonder when they see you with us."

"Maybe I'll just try to stay hidden in the background until they get over the initial shock of seeing you guys standing there," Judy said. "I sure wouldn't want to do anything to set your dad's progress back any."

Upon our arrival at the hospital, the receptionist gave us Dad's room number and pointed out the way to Judy. A couple of the nurses greeted us warmly when they guessed who we were as we neared Dad's doorway. "The whole crew must be in on this little conspiracy," Judy whispered to us, "if all the secret winks and smiles are any indication."

With that, Judy stood back and quietly directed us to the correct room. We found the open door, and Kim knocked loudly as we walked in.

"Is anybody here?" I called out in a voice that had begun to tremble slightly. "Happy Father's Day."

Mom whirled around and then stopped in her tracks. "Well, my word! Rolly, you have company, and you're not going to believe who it is."

"I heard the voice, but I thought my ears must be playing tricks on me," Dad said, turning to get a better look.

"How on earth did you guys get here?" Mom was asking with a warm embrace.

Kim and I were too choked up by this time to answer, but Judy, not able to resist any longer, had joined us in the room.

"Well, I'll be!" Mom exclaimed. "Rolly, look who's here with the girls."

Everybody started talking at once, and Kim and I hurried over to the bed where Dad was finishing his lunch. He grasped our hands, and the strong clasp was reassuring. I had to keep wiping at my eyes as I reveled in the fact that we were really here.

"Well, I have to run because I'm still on duty," Judy said a few minutes later. "But it sure was great to witness this reunion."

"I'll go with you out to the cab and grab their suitcases," Mom offered.

"Uh…that brings up an interesting little detail that we should mention," Kim said. "Our suitcases are still in Dickinson."

We went on to explain what had happened and were relieved that Mom and Dad didn't seem upset at all.

"At least we know where they are," Mom pointed out. "It won't be a big deal for us to stop there and pick them up."

"Well, Rolly, you'd better get well soon if you know what's good for you," Judy said as she prepared to leave.

"Oh, I'm working on it," Dad assured her. "Next time you see me, I'll be fit as a fiddle."

"I was wondering why the nurses started acting so funny," Mom mused. "They kept hem-hawing around, taking forever to find the correct forms for us to fill out. And then, once we finally had them, they claimed they'd accidentally given us the wrong ones and that some of the others we'd done earlier had gotten misplaced and made us fill out the dumb things all over again and then said we might as well stick around until after lunch…"

"I was almost ready to threaten a lawsuit if they couldn't get with the program any better than that," Dad added. "Now it finally all makes sense why they kept delaying us so much."

Kim and I laughed. "I guess it's a good thing we got here when we did," I said, "or you'd have left without us."

"That's for sure," Mom agreed as she absently brushed some of my hair back from my face. "I'm just so glad you guys got here without any trouble. You don't know how much this means to us. What a surprise! I still can't get over it."

We were all energized as we made the trip home that afternoon. Most people would probably never have guessed that one of us had recently undergone heart surgery, another one had endured several nights on a cot in a hospital room, and the other two of us had spent the previous night and several hours thereafter on a crowded bus.

Of course, Gramp and Gram were as surprised to see Kim and me as Mom and Dad had been. Gramp kept reiterating that we shouldn't have taken the trip without letting any of them know, which only served to make us glad we hadn't. Rory and Reed sat smugly by since they'd been aware of the whole plan all along.

Suddenly, the phone jangled above the din of our chatter, and when Gram picked it up, she said it was for me and handed over the receiver.

"Oops. I think I might be in trouble," I whispered to the room at large as I put the phone to my ear.

Sure enough, it was my husband, trying hard but not quite succeeding in keeping the panicked tone out of his voice.

"Why didn't you call me?" he asked reproachfully.

"We just got here," I said lamely. But I knew that wasn't going to cut it, so decided I'd better own up. "I know I said I'd call when we got to Bismarck though," I acknowledged. "Sorry about that."

No response.

"And then we had some additional delays with our luggage and I just completely forgot," I went on apologetically. "I guess I'm just not used to being accountable to somebody else now. I'll have to rectify that, won't I?"

"Well, I just never thought you'd forget to keep me posted, so I was really starting to worry," he said in a hurt tone.

"I'll do better next time," I promised. Then I tried to lighten the mood a little by adding, "It's a good thing you didn't call a few minutes earlier because you would have had Gramp and Gram really upset."

He chuckled at that, and we ended the call amicably enough. I resolved to be more considerate of his feelings after that because I knew I would have appreciated an update from him if the tables had been turned.

As the following days passed, Dad continued to make marked progress in his recovery and was already beginning to explore alternative medical options for the future that would include a more natural approach, allowing him to take as little medication as possible.

Less than a week after Dad's return from the hospital, a big storm blew in and destroyed many of the trees that he had planted so painstakingly. Things were in quite a state of disarray around the ranch because of this occurrence, so Bob and John came out to the ranch for a couple of days to help Dad run cattle and clean up the debris. These were jobs that Dad wasn't quite up to doing himself yet, after the ordeal he'd just gone through, and he was grateful for the help. My husband and Kim's fiancé came away from the experience with an appreciation of the hard physical labor that being a rancher entailed, but they were more than willing to do what they could to be of assistance.

It also afforded the two prospective brothers-in-law a great opportunity to become better acquainted and for all of us to get to know John more. He found his new future family to be a little overwhelming at first, but he was gracious to everyone and was willing to take part in any activity that was suggested, much to our brothers' delight. It didn't take them long to discover that he knew several card games and had a lot of patience and endurance when it came to said games, probably because he was as eager as they to come out the winner and not give up without a fight.

It felt good to have all of us together, including new husbands and fiancés. Dad was getting better too, and we definitely had a lot to be thankful for. Of that there was no doubt.

Christmas Rabbit, Burned Eggs, and a Spaghetti dinner

It was Kim and John's first Christmas as newlyweds, and we were all gathered in Mom and Dad's living room. Soon after their marriage, John had accepted a position as pastor of a small church in Thompson Falls, Montana. Although this meant that Kim was even farther from home, they were happy in their new life together.

"Well, that was another super Christmas," was Grandpa's verdict. "Seems they just get better every year."

"Doesn't it though?" said Mom as she began gathering up discarded wrapping paper and boxes from the floor. "I think Kim and Kon came up with the best gifts for everybody, once again."

"That's for sure," Gram agreed. "You girls really know how to put your heads together and find things we'll enjoy and get lots of use out of."

"The ideas are just there when we need them," I said. "We were having a little trouble thinking of something that you would like, Gram, until I got that cassette catalogue in the mail that listed that scented bubble bath."

"Well, that was just perfect for me," Gram affirmed. "You know how much I look forward to my bath every night."

"And John and I just happened to see those Louis L'Amour tapes in a gas station on our way to Thompson Falls," Kim added. "We figured Ror and Reed would like them and were hoping they weren't ones that you already had. Are they?"

"Nope. These are definitely stories we haven't heard before," Reed assured her. "Should come in handy for something to listen to on our travels."

"And Dad likes those westerns so much too," Mom added. "Helps keep him awake on all the long drives."

"Although that could be a dangerous proposition," Rory pointed out. "Dad has been known to get so caught up in the story that he misses his turn-offs and we wind up in parts unknown."

"He'd just claim to be taking the scenic route if that happened," said Reed. "Although, I must say, having a bunch of blind people as passengers, I'm not sure how much good a scenic route does anyone."

I reached for the traditional box of chocolate-covered cherries that Mom usually presented to us each year. "Anybody wanna split a cherry with me?" I questioned. "I don't really feel like eating the whole thing."

"Um…I wouldn't recommend trying to split one," Rory cautioned.

"What's the big deal?" I wanted to know. "All you do is just divide it like anything else, and then…" My voice trailed off as I suddenly found my hands engulfed in sticky goo.

"Watch out, Kon! It's getting on the carpet!" Mom cried as she ran for the kitchen for a wet towel.

"You were saying?" Rory asked gleefully. "What just happened, my dear sister?"

"That was just an extra messy one," I stated defiantly. "It would've worked fine if I had just—"

"In that case, maybe you should try again with another one," Reed interrupted hopefully.

"I'm not even in the mood for cherries anymore," I decided as I scrubbed feverishly at my candy-laden fingers. "I wasn't that hungry to begin with, which is why I only wanted half."

"Uh-huh. Nice try," Kim said.

"I sure love this here newspaper you girls got for me," Gramp remarked as he flipped through the pages. "How on earth did you ever find it?"

"That was the strangest thing," I told him. "I was up late one night listening to the radio and just heard this commercial by chance about getting a copy of a famous newspaper from the exact day of a person's birth, no matter how long ago. So I figured that would be something kind of unique and special for you to have."

"I should say," he replied. "We'll have to hang it up somewhere."

"Well, my coffee will definitely get used," John said. "You know what a coffee drinker I am."

"I really like the book you gave me too," Bob said from behind his camera, where he had been taking pictures of the evening's proceedings. "I got a chance to look it over a little already, and the plot line grabbed my attention right away."

"I think what you got Mom and Dad will be used more than anything else though," Rory surmised. "Probably not necessarily by them, but the rest of us will certainly make use of it."

"Well, hopefully, Mom and Dad might slow down enough to enjoy it every now and then too," I said. We had gotten them a porch swing similar to the one that Bob and I had recently set up on our own deck in Rapid City.

"Oh yeah. We're sure to try it out sooner or later, even though it may have to wait for the weather to warm up a little," Dad said with a laugh.

"It seems funny actually having a tree this year instead of the Christmas rabbit," Mom observed as she looked around at all the sparkling lights.

"Yeah. What a faithful standby that old rabbit was for all those years," Rory mourned.

"What's that?" John asked, sounding more than a little confused.

"You never heard of a Christmas rabbit?" Reed questioned jokingly.

"'Fraid not," John replied. "Maybe you had better clue me in."

"It was our own unique tradition," Reed lamented. "We had this actual real rabbit that our uncle had shot and stuffed way back in the day, and Mom had it all dressed up in Christmas garb and decorated so pretty, with gifts piled all around. And now you'll never get to see it."

"Too bad," John replied. "Sounds intriguing."

"Next time you stop at our house, give me a reminder and we'll be happy to show it to you," Bob suggested.

"So...you and Konnie own it now? How did that transpire?" John wanted to know.

Rory laughed. "I'll give you fair warning, John. Trying to connect all the dots in this family can sometimes be a daunting task," he notified his new brother-in-law.

"Oh, I've already become well acquainted with that fact," John responded.

"Anyway, to answer your question," Rory continued, "it ended up at Konnie's house because her husband was so enthralled with it that he begged us to let him take possession of it himself."

"And to think that his wife was embarrassed to even let him see such a prize at first," Reed said in dismay.

"I'm not sure that that's exactly how it happened, but close enough I guess," I conceded.

"If you ask me, it's good to finally be rid of the thing," Kim added dryly.

Gram stealthily handed me one of her delicious popcorn balls, and I tried to munch quietly so my siblings wouldn't notice that I was eating after having just claimed I wasn't hungry.

"So what have you two been doing to keep yourselves occupied during the Christmas break?" I asked my brothers.

"Oh, we ran across some of your old diary tapes and have found them to be quite fascinating," Rory answered.

Surprisingly, his comment didn't evoke the response in me that I would have expected. At the time Kim and I had recorded the tapes, I would've been beyond mortified if our diary had been discovered, but I was only amused at the thought. What a difference a few years could make.

Kim must have had a similar reaction, for she laughed and wanted to know what section the boys were listening to.

"It's all about when you guys were at the school in Aberdeen," Reed explained. "Pretty interesting to hear what dorm life was like and things of that nature since that's a part of your history that we wouldn't have known much about otherwise."

"Which reminds me," Rory piped up sardonically, "the lady from Grand Forks came by a few weeks ago, and you'll never guess what she had up her sleeve this time."

"I give up. What happened?" I asked eagerly.

Whenever the specialized teacher for the visually impaired made one of her periodic trips from the North Dakota School for the Blind to check up on how Rory and Reed were doing, they usually came away from the experience with at least one entertaining anecdote to share with the rest of us.

"The latest thing she's come up with is that she suddenly decided that it's of utmost importance that I navigate the lunch room completely independently," Rory replied. "Even though I've been surviving the noon break all these years just fine without any trouble, apparently we can't leave well enough alone."

"That's because she needs to keep thinking of new things to work on with you guys or she'd probably be out of a job," Kim reasoned with a touch of sarcasm.

"Up until now, I'd always just go with friends or else some of the cafeteria staff would help me find a table. But since that won't do any longer, she devised this method where I was supposed to use my cane with one hand and balance a full tray of food in the other. You can imagine how easy that was, attempting to maneuver an unwieldy cane while picking up a tray of food."

"Yikes. So was she finally forced to come up with an alternative plan?" I asked.

"You're so intuitive," Rory answered a little derisively. "What we tried next was a method by which, after getting my tray filled, I had to set it down on the end of the counter, where you go through the line, and then turn sideways so that the tray was now on my left side, grab the back of the tray with my left hand and support the front of the tray against my hip while using my cane with the right hand, find a table, and somehow negotiate putting my cane down and set this full tray of food on the table that was now beside me rather than in front of me."

Kim and I couldn't help laughing at the little scenario, but inside, I was also seething a bit at his plight. It reminded me of some of the unpleasant experiences I'd had myself with people wanting to make things far more difficult and complicated for me than was necessary.

"Sheesh," Kim was saying. "Really makes you wonder if these people even stop to weigh the practical value of going through an exercise like that against all the obvious disadvantages."

"Anyway," Rory went on, "that little idea worked about as well as you might expect it would, so what they finally settled on was to put a reserved sign at the end of the very first table in order for me to hold a tray with both hands and not need to use my cane for such a short distance. But, of course, all that's going to accomplish is to isolate me from everybody else because they'll see the big 'this is where the blind guy sits' sign, and you know that high schoolers are going to think they're way too cool to purposely sit at that table."

Neither Kim nor I could refute what he said, so we didn't bother to tell him that his suspicions were probably groundless. "Well, hopefully, it won't take them long to realize it's a dumb idea and go back to the way things were before," I offered.

"But, hey, at least we've graduated from making tuna salad sandwiches," Reed, ever the optimist, spoke up cheerily.

"I beg to differ," Rory corrected him. "That was before the egg fiasco occurred. We'll probably be demoted way back to making cheese and crackers after that little episode."

"Hmm. This sounds like an incident worth relating as well," Kim hinted curiously.

"Oh, you know she always wants us to do a little experimenting in the kitchen when she comes," Reed said. "So this particular day, Ror was assigned to make a nice breakfast of scrambled eggs with cheese and sausage mixed in. The whole works, yum. But, alas, he had to ruin it."

"How could you do such a thing, Ror?" I asked in a mockingly reproachful voice.

Rory sighed and launched into the tale. "We were in the high school home ec room, and I was trying to ask her how I'd know when the food was cooked enough because I'd never done it before and didn't know what to be aware of. She just kept saying I'd be able to tell by the firmness of the texture under my spatula when the eggs were ready. Only I couldn't tell because, number one, with the meat and onions and all the other ingredients in there, it was hard to figure out what was what. And number two, I hadn't used a spatula before, so I didn't know how anything felt with that implement. So finally, I just decided 'the heck with this,' and I set to making the toast or pouring the juice or something. I was just frustrated enough to not care and figured if it burnt, I guess it was done. And that's exactly what happened. She finally said that I'd better tend to my eggs, and they were definitely more than done, to say the least."

"It's funny that she wouldn't have given you some additional tips along the way," Kim mused. "I've always found a long, wooden spoon to be a lot easier to use than a spatula."

"Sometimes I'll even go so far as to quickly touch the food I'm cooking with my fingertips to see how done it is," I added. But I'm sure all the specialized teachers out there, plus the sanitation department and maybe even the world at large, would have a few conniption fits if they ever found out I did that. I can just picture their shock at all the germs I was spreading around and assuming I was about to accidentally set myself on fire or something."

Rory chuckled at that before continuing with his story. "And to make matters worse, as I was trying to pile the stuff onto the plates without burning myself on the pan, a blob of it fell off the spatula onto the burner, which was still quite hot. And that started one heck of a smoke. I have no idea how the rest of the home ec classes survived in there the rest of the day because that entire hallway smelled of a rather tragic experience."

"Oh no," I said sympathetically, although I had to smile at the pictures he had conjured up in my mind. "Now you're probably more determined than ever to find a wife who is willing to do all the cooking."

"However, on a more cheerful note, I have some exciting news to relate," Reed claimed vibrantly. "And it's even good news at that. I wrote another song!"

"Wow! That is exciting, to be sure!" I exclaimed. "This is the first one you've written since 'He Rose from the Dead,' is it not?"

"Indeed, it is," Reed concurred. "So that means that in another five years or so, I should have a third song ready to go."

"Well, as long as they're all good, I suppose we'll let you get away with being a slacker for a few years between each one," I relented.

"What's it called?" Kim inquired.

"'Church Pews Aren't for Sleeping,'" he replied. "It says that if you're gonna bother going to church, you'd better listen to what the preacher says."

"It sounds like a good one," I surmised. "You'll have to be sure to play it for us tomorrow."

"Speaking of new songs," Kim remarked, "I keep meaning to ask you both how you like the new music teachers."

"Oh, they're great!" Rory replied enthusiastically. "The husband teaches junior high, and she does the high school."

"She seems to be taking Lemmon High to some new heights. Pun intended," Reed noted.

"Really? In what way?" Kim asked curiously.

"I'm finding out our school band has a lot more potential than I suspected," Rory said. "I was pretty skeptical about some of the stuff she wanted us to try, but the students are sure rising to the challenge so far. I'm actually quite impressed."

"Cool. It's pretty nifty that you'll have such an excellent music program to finish out your high school career," I mused.

"For sure," Rory replied. "We're all fired up and ready to go places, if you know what I mean. She's already talking about sending me to All-State Jazz Band in the spring! So now we just need to hope I'm able to pass the audition."

"And how does that process work exactly?" Kim wanted to know.

"They'll send me some sheet music with things I'll need to be able to do, and I'll then play it on tape and send it back to them. It might have some exercises like playing a twelve-bar blues in three or four different keys, for example. Or they might give me a lead sheet with some chords on it for me to read down and play."

"But how will you be able to do that?" Kim and I asked in unison.

"Mrs. Raber will probably play the notated stuff for me on the piano or something, and the rest she'll likely just dictate for me to memorize. It shouldn't be a very big deal."

"I'm glad you don't think so. It seems pretty tedious to me."

"Oh, not nearly as much as if I actually end up making the audition. So I might as well get used to it now. You know I've always been up for a good challenge."

"Well, wife," John interjected, "do you suppose it's about time to head over to the other trailer?"

"I reckon so," Kim consented as she reached for her coat. "It's getting pretty late."

"Be sure you have the right sister now," Rory cautioned. "She might be hard to identify when she's all bundled up and everything."

This had been a running joke in the family ever since John had almost mistaken me for Kim during their wedding rehearsal. I was sure Rory and Reed wouldn't let him forget that slip-up for many years to come.

The next few months proved to be busy ones for Rory. Shortly after the Christmas break ended, he was asked to join some of his classmates in performing for a Valentine's Day spaghetti dinner that the youth group of the Lutheran church was hosting.

"Who all will be performing?" Rory asked. "I assume a few of you guys from the Lutheran church who have been playing together some already?"

"Yep," Jarid replied. "Brant is playing drums, Josh on bass and vocals, and me as sort of the utility guy, doing acoustic or bass or vocals or whatever needs filling in. And since you're the best musician in the whole school, we were hoping that maybe you could help us out on lead guitar and perhaps some piano."

"Hmm. Sounds like a pretty good conglomeration to me," Rory mused. Where do you rehearse?"

"Oh, we try to get the church basement or else just jam at each other's houses if that doesn't work out. A couple of times, we were able to get the school music room. So, basically, wherever we can find a spot."

"Well, how about if I join you during your next practice session and see what I think? Then I can let you know whether I want to belong to this outfit or not," Rory quipped.

"Fair enough." Jarid laughed. "But we sure hope you'll say yes."

After listening to the band, Rory decided they were reasonably good but woefully lacking in musical equipment, at least compared to what he was used to.

"You guys would be welcome to take a look at my digs sometime," he offered. "We have a lot of PA equipment and stuff out there."

"Never thought of that," Jarid answered. "I'd imagine you'd have pretty good facilities, being in a family band and everything."

"And in the meantime, we should probably try to come up with a list of at least a half dozen or so more songs to go along with the ones you guys already know. That should be enough to get us through the Valentine's dinner. Don't you think?"

"Should be," Josh replied. "Let's get on it right away so we'll hopefully have enough time to have them somewhat worked up for our next rehearsal."

"So what say we try to meet at my place next time around?" Rory suggested. "I'll make sure it's okay with the folks, but I don't see them having a problem with it. It would also mean me not having to worry about arranging transportation to the rehearsal either."

"Sounds like a plan," Jarid agreed. "Now all we have to do is set the date."

A few days later found them all gathered at the Hoffman's music trailer.

"Wow! This is so cool!" Josh exclaimed enthusiastically as he got his first look around. "Just take a gander at this big sound board over here. Think of all the great effects we should be able to get out of something like that."

"By the way, I think Mom put Dr. Pepper or something in the fridge in case anybody gets thirsty. Just help yourself," Rory told them.

"Oh, that sounds good. Thanks," Jarid replied as he walked over to investigate.

"And to think, there are even enough microphones here to go around for a change," Josh commented. "What a concept."

"Hmm. I'm finding some interesting stuff in here, but no Dr. Pepper so far," Jarid announced as he stuck his head further inside the refrigerator for a better look. What's this? It looks like some sort of cow antibiotics."

"Yeah. You never know what you might come across in there. But the pop should be someplace. Maybe way in the back," Rory conjectured.

"You have a lot of equipment around here," Josh noted. "I'm not even sure what half this stuff is supposed to do."

"Did Brant come out with you guys or what?" Rory asked suddenly. "I haven't heard a word from him since you got here."

"Yeah. I'm just writing down some impressions real quick," Brant said distractedly from where he was scribbling some notes over in the corner. "Looks like the drums are already situated, so I'm ready to roll whenever you are."

A few minutes later, they launched into a familiar country tune, and afterward, the general consensus was that it didn't sound half bad.

"Why don't we get really brave and try something like 'Hold My Hand?'" Jarid suggested after running through several songs they all knew fairly well. "You've heard that one, haven't you, Rory?"

"Oh sure. Never played it before, but I've heard it plenty of times."

When the song had ended, the four of them cheered themselves resoundingly.

"Hey, we actually kinda sound like a real band!" Jarid said. "Whaddaya know about that?"

Musical Adventures

The group unanimously agreed to continue meeting at the Hoffman ranch for their future practice sessions. After discovering the great setup that was available to them in the music trailer, it was an easy choice to make. The fact that Mom always had the refrigerator well-stocked with pop and an assortment of goodies for the crew to snack on didn't hurt a bit either. More often than not, she invited them to stay for supper, where they got to partake of such marvelous delights as her huge taco salad haystacks or her grilled, stuffed cheeseburgers that were so thick you could hardly get your mouth around them.

When I made a trip home that spring, Rory was brimming with news for me.

"Now I finally get to hear all about the fantastic Valentine's Day performance," I said happily as I found a comfortable position in the rocking chair under my blanket and prepared for a nice, long chat with my brothers. "You've already given me the highlights, but now I want the whole scoop on everything that led up to it and what all has taken place since then. So just start at the beginning, and don't leave anything out."

"Okay. I'll try my best," said Rory as he absently strummed through a few jazz riffs on the guitar he held.

"Of course, you have me here to fill in anything he forgets," Reed pointed out. "So I have no doubt that between my stellar memory and your countless questions, nothing will get missed."

"The only problem being that I could get through the story much faster and more coherently without all the interruptions," Rory countered. "But I know that isn't going to happen, so I'm resigned to the inevitable."

"Well that's good, because you know you can't teach an old dog new tricks this late in the game," I retorted emphatically. "So to start with, you could refresh my memory on how the group was formed. You guys are calling yourselves the Lampheads now, correct?"

"That's right. Don't ask me how we got the name. I mean, you could ask if you really feel the need to know, but the facts aren't all that exciting."

"Well you know me. I'm always curious nevertheless," I reminded him.

"Mrs. Raber, our music teacher, was telling about when she was having an insult fight with her five-year-old nephew one time, and at some point, he blurted out, 'Lamp head!' Don't know how he came up with that, but we got to thinking that it has a nice ring to it. Wouldn't you agree?"

I laughed. "That's one way to come up with a name for a new band," I hedged. "So, Reed, I guess this means that we now know you aren't the only one who has hurled supposed insults that weren't the least bit offensive."

"Yeah. So take them apples, you old pencil!" Reed declared vehemently as a time many years before was brought to mind when Reed's ability to name-call had lacked the skill he now possessed. Back then, any random noun he could recollect at a moment's notice would work just as well as another, to his way of thinking.

"Getting sidetracked already I see," Rory noted. "I believe that sets a new record for how quickly we became distracted from the main topic."

"Oh, never mind that. So what made you guys decide to start looking for other venues to perform?" I questioned, trying to get the discussion back on course before it wandered too far adrift, as was so often the case.

"We just wanted to keep a good thing going," Rory replied. "We were all having so much fun hanging out and playing all the popular country tunes of the day and figured that we shouldn't let our talent go to waste."

"It didn't take them long to get an audience either," Reed put in. "I think it was only your second or third practice session when all those cheerleaders showed up, wasn't it?"

"Who's telling this story anyway?" Rory asked mildly.

"It's a good thing Reed is here," I said. "You hadn't mentioned any cheerleaders before. Can't wait to hear the details on that one!"

"Some of them were gathering at one of their houses a few miles from here to do some baking for a fundraiser, and they stopped by to see if Mom had a mixer or something that they could borrow. They came back a couple hours later to return it, and we were still hard at work, running through our set. We heard a car drive up, and then Jarid said he could see all these silhouettes running through the yard, and the next thing we knew, they had come in and made themselves at home on the couch while we finished up 'Hold My Hand' by Hootie and the Blowfish."

"Wouldn't you know they had to make their appearance during one of your more difficult numbers," I noted.

"But everything went fine," he assured me quickly. "And as luck would have it, our next song was Garth Brooks' 'The Dance,' which, as you know, is one of the sappiest songs of all time."

"Wow. So were the other guys nervous to have all those girls watching and listening in?" I asked.

"Are you kidding? I think we all could have levitated off the ground if we'd wanted to. I'm pretty sure that's when we all realized we were destined for more together as a band than just a one-time event."

"So I take it the cheerleaders liked what they heard. Would that be a safe assumption?" I smiled.

"That's an understatement," Rory confirmed. "I guess every one of the girls had tears in their eyes by the time the song ended. I'm sure it will be remembered as the unquestioned highlight of our rehearsals."

"Cool," I had to admit. "It's no wonder you hadn't any inclination to quit after the Valentine's Day dinner. Especially after you saw what a resounding success it was."

"And we've grown in number since then too," Rory informed me. "We now have Matt Barnes on guitar, and we figured we should have a girl singer in there somewhere, so we asked Shanna to help out with vocals and keys sometimes. It's been nice getting to know the others in the band better too. I hadn't really hung out with any of them after school hours until now."

"You know Jarid pretty well, don't you?" I asked. "I seem to remember you guys playing together quite a bit at recess on the barrel of fun when you were little kids and always competing for the highest grades and stuff, even way back then."

Rory laughed. "Yeah. We liked to compare and see who had gotten a better score on the spelling tests and whatnot, and sometimes Shanna would have to get into the act too, so the three of us were neck and neck a lot of times. I also knew Josh pretty well back then, but we sorta drifted apart as we got older and had less in common."

"And don't forget Mic," Reed reminded him.

"Oh yeah. We can't leave out our loyal roadie," Rory agreed. "Of course, I've known him ever since we were wee tots playing together while all you big people were having your weekly Bible study. He's always around too, helping to set up the equipment and critiquing our music and everything. He seems to never be without an abundance of pithy comments to offer from the couch whenever we play."

Now it was my turn to chuckle. "Well, every band needs a peanut gallery to keep things in perspective," I reasoned.

"Anyway, I just hadn't really thought of all the side benefits of playing music, which is fun enough just in itself. But it's also turning out to be a great avenue for making new friends."

"I bet you'll never guess which of Ror's awesome talents the other band members find most impressive," Reed piped up.

"You know, I have so many that it's hard to pick just one favorite," Rory put in before his brother could elaborate further. "But one skill I know they greatly admire is my ability to identify people's phone numbers just by hearing the pitch of the dial tones."

"Funny. How on earth was that talent ever discovered?" I asked.

"Oh, Barnsey was just calling his house to say he was running late or something, and he had the phone receiver far enough away from his ear that I was able to hear what numbers were being dialed and promptly rattled them off, to the amazement of one and all."

"Ah, quit showing off, Hoffman," Matt had said after making his call. "You just happened to know my phone number is all."

"No way. How do you do that, Rory?" asked Jarid incredulously as he grabbed the handset away from Matt and began punching out random numbers. "Okay, dude. What did I just dial?" he quizzed.

"And, of course, I was able to identify all of the numbers perfectly without a hitch," Rory said triumphantly as he continued relating the tale to me.

"But that wasn't the talent I was referring to," Reed went on. "I'm talking about the times you and Shanna demonstrate your wonderful belching prowess."

I burst into laughter at this revelation in spite of myself. "Of all things!" I retorted, trying to sound offended at the very thought. "So are you telling me that you actually have a cohort in Shanna?"

"Oh, I don't think she holds a candle to me, of course," Rory said. "But she really isn't half bad at all, especially considering that she's a girl and everything."

"The two of them even belched their way through an entire rendition of 'The Star-Spangled Banner' into the microphones at one point," Reed said in delight.

"That's totally disgusting, you guys," I said, even as I resisted the urge to ask whether anyone had thought to record the momentous event.

Just then, Mom showed up bearing Pepsi and munchies, so our conversation was temporarily put on hold since eating always took first priority for both of my brothers.

"We're really coming along as a band though," Rory finally went on through a mouthful of Doritos topped with chili dip. "When I listen back to the tape of the dinner, I can hear the progress we've made in just a few months. Josh has come a long way on the bass, and Matt's already improved a lot with his guitar solos too. Of course, we also have more people now, so that's definitely a plus."

"Try playing the five note after the one on the bass if you could, Josh, rather than just sticking with the root," Rory had suggested during one of their earlier jam sessions. "Like this." He demonstrated what he was talking about, and Josh was quick to catch on.

"There you go," Rory encouraged. Then he went on to give Matt a few pointers on taking the lead part when it came time for his solo on "Me and You."

"I can help you figure out the parts note for note if you'd like, until you get the hang of it," he offered.

"Sure, I'd be game for that," Matt replied. "I don't have much experience yet at playing my own improvs, so anything to make us sound better is a good idea as far as I'm concerned."

Everybody had to agree that in addition to accompanying their playing, Rory would be able to teach the rest of them a lot in the days ahead as well.

"You better not forget to tell her about that nifty men's choir song you did for music contest," Reed reminded his brother at the first sign of a lull in our conversation.

"Yeah. That was pretty incredible," Rory agreed. "There were eight of us guys in the choral group, and I was the lead singer. The song we did was an old spiritual called 'Down by the Riverside.'"

"I've heard of that one before," I commented.

"This is a really cool arrangement," Rory said. "In fact, we have a recording of it somewhere. Why don't you go hunt it down, Reed, while I tell the story?"

"I know right where it is, so 'twill only take me a minute to get it," Reed answered.

"Anyway, we decided to rehearse outside on the steps, and there was this huge crowd gathered around listening by the time the song was over. And then when the time came to do the song in front of the judges, word had gotten around, and the room where we were to perform was totally packed. I mean, not even standing room only. Kids were sitting on top of desks and everything else. The judges said they figured what they were about to hear would be pretty good before we even started because they hadn't seen the room nearly that full all day."

"Wow. I wish I could've been there," I said wistfully.

"So we went through the song, and there was this thunderous applause, and we got a one plus, which is the highest score possible."

"And then they had to do the song all over again when they got out into the hall for everybody who was waiting out there who hadn't been able to get into the room to hear it the first time around," Reed put in.

"Yeah. It was crazy," Rory added. "A lot of people were waiting there just because they'd overheard all the cheering and whatnot from within and were curious to see what the hubbub was about."

"Okay. So now I want to hear the recording," I said. "Hurry and find it, Reed."

After listening to the song, I had to agree that they'd done an excellent job, and I insisted that Reed play it for me a second time.

"By the way, have I told you that I did, in fact, make the all-state audition for jazz band this year?" Rory asked when the song had finished.

"No, you didn't! How could you have forgotten something like that?" I chided him.

"I actually passed in both guitar and piano, but they're putting me on guitar since there aren't as many of those. And I even got placed in the top band out of the four that will be there."

"And to think, Kim and I weren't even sure how you were going to get past the first hurdle," I recalled with irony. "So what exactly is the difference between contest and All-State anyway?" I wondered aloud.

Rory thought about that for a minute. "I guess the simplest way to explain it is that the schools are collaborating together at All-State and contest is where each school is competing for the highest scores. So, of course, there are a lot more people from each district at contest, whereas All-State is a bit more selective and difficult to attain, which is why I never really aspired to go to All-State until now."

"So are you nervous about it at all?" I questioned.

"A little, this being my first time and everything," he answered honestly. "But Barnes is going to come along as my guide, so I'll have him there to read charts for me and help outline chords and such if I need it, which will really come in handy while I'm learning the ropes."

"I can't wait to hear all about it when the time comes," I said as I smothered a yawn. "But for now, I think it's about time to retire for the evening, at least for old fogeys like me."

"You'd better wake up all rested and refreshed," Rory warned, "because as soon as I get up tomorrow, sometime after ten, I plan to trounce you very soundly at a game of Rack-O or Skip-Bo or whatever other poison you decide to pick."

"That's what you think," Reed contradicted him. "I fully intend to do the trouncing myself."

"That remains to be seen. I might just surprise you both," I said, trying to sound properly convincing. "But in the meantime, I'll be experiencing sweet victory in my dreams, so that will surely help to prepare me for anything the morning might bring."

Rory's first experience with All-State was everything he hoped it would be and more. The event was held at Northern State College in Aberdeen. All of the clinicians brought in to teach the classes were professional jazz musicians, and it was the first time Rory had worked with people of that caliber. He was impressed to hear such a large group of students playing together and was amazed to discover just how professional a bunch of high schoolers from the good old state of South Dakota could really sound.

The music chosen was by far the most complex that Rory had ever played up to that point. He realized that he would be stretched to the limit of his comfort zone and then some. The event took place over a three-day period, which wasn't much time to learn the approximately half dozen songs that would be required, so his work was definitely cut out for him.

Dennis Diblasio was the name of the instructor to which Rory was assigned. He had played sax with jazz greats like Maynard Ferguson, and to say that Rory was quite impressed by this would be an understatement. Willie Thomas, a first-rate trumpet player, was another clinician Rory got to know pretty well while he was there.

Rory came away from this experience with an even greater appreciation for jazz and was already looking forward to doing it all again the following year. After seeing how well he had done and how much he had enjoyed the event, his music teacher, Mrs. Raber, began discussing with him the possibility of attending international music camp the following summer. Needless to say, he was very interested in the prospect. It would be a weeklong affair that would take place at the Peace Gardens. Many Canadians would also be in attendance, and there were usually some people there from places like Sweden and Australia as well.

Before school let out for the year, another group of Rory's classmates had formed a Christian contemporary band called World Detour. Some of the members were also in the Lampheads, so it was only natural that Rory found himself as part of this new endeavor too. The group played for vacation Bible schools and other functions in the area and performed songs from Newsboys, Third Day, and many more.

All of these additional opportunities afforded Rory the chance to get to know the other guys in the group even better. Sometimes he would stay overnight with Matt if the band was scheduled to leave for a performance early the following morning. On other days, he would hang out at Brant's house when they would practice there. Rory was very intrigued with the Cakewalk software that Brant had on his computer. It was a program that was used to record, edit, and mix music and was Rory's first exposure to midi files and how they could be used to create songs, which he found to be very fascinating. The utility was later destined to become Sonar, which Rory still uses to this day for music production.

The summer went by very quickly for Rory, and the time for the international music camp was upon him almost before he realized it. It was being paid for by the music boosters, and he was very grateful to have such a show of support from the community. Jarid would be accompanying Rory as his guide and chart reader, and both of them knew that it would be an experience they'd never forget.

The event stepped things up another few notches for Rory in the world of jazz. He'd be playing with some of the best high school musicians in the nation. It was a daunting prospect but thrilling to consider at the same time.

Auditions were held on the first day, which determined the placement level of every participant. Each student was then assigned to a band, where he would play during the rest of the week.

"Well, you got into one of the top bands," Jarid remarked as he and Rory left the room where the auditions had been held. "Can't do much better than that."

"Yeah, I suppose," Rory agreed halfheartedly. "I was a little disappointed that I didn't make the honor band, but this is international, after all, so I know we're dealing with a lot of talent here."

Honor band was where the best of the best students would have the opportunity to spend an hour each day away from their regular band and would get to perform together as a separate unit.

"I was somewhat surprised you didn't make it though, to tell you the truth," Jarid admitted. "Especially when I saw all the positive feedback you were getting."

"I just hope it isn't a matter of them thinking I wouldn't be up to learning all the songs or something like that," Rory speculated. "They probably figure there's no way I'd be able to master all those extra tunes in only four days of rehearsals."

"Now that you mention it though, learning that much when the band only meets for an hour each day would be pretty challenging," Jarid pointed out.

"Well, if that is the reason, I sure wish they'd just address the issue with me directly and not make assumptions," Rory replied in frustration.

Jeff Jarvis, the regular band instructor to which Rory was assigned, soon discovered, to his amazement, that Rory was picking up on the material by ear even faster than his peers were able to do with their sheet music. The appropriate channels were apparently notified of this fact because the following day, Rory was told to report for honor band.

Rory was overjoyed at the turn of events, even though it meant that he would have one less day than the rest of the band members to master the material. The music arrangements they were using were not scored for high school students. Instead, the honor band would be expected to perform from professional big band charts, such as a Sammy Nestico tune arranged for the Count Basie band.

Scott Prebys from the University of Mary in Bismarck, ND, was the honor band instructor. It didn't take him long to begin recruiting Rory for his college, even though graduation from high school was still a year away.

In addition to the band rehearsals, the students at the music camp had lessons with the clinicians. Rory and other guitarists met together for classes each day with Bob Peske, also from the University of Mary.

Mr. Peske was also very impressed with Rory's skills and offered to give him private lessons in the evenings in order to help him with the honor band charts. Some of the chords Rory would be expected to play were new to him, and Peske had to admit that he wouldn't be of much help when it came to giving Rory suggestions on how to hold them.

"Just play them for me and I'll figure out the rest," Rory told him.

So that's what they did. Peske would let him hear how the chords were supposed to sound, and then it was up to Rory to find the best fingering for each note.

When he wasn't in class, Rory and Jarid could often be found playing guitar and singing out on the grounds. Rory took advantage of the breaks in the rigorous schedule to play some of his favorite country tunes and current chart-breaking hits. Within minutes, a group of kids was usually gathered around, listening and singing along.

"Wanna do that song of yours, Jarid?" Rory asked at one point after they'd concluded one of Allan Jackson's number-one tunes.

"You mean 'Hold My Ham'? Sure. Why not? Go ahead and give me the opening bars."

And with that, they launched into the parody of "Hold my Hand" that Jarid had composed.

> With a little roast
> And some tender ham,
> We'll walk around the kitchen,
> We'll rise above the Spam.
> With a little beef
> And some pork 'n' beans
> We'll feed the world together,
> We'll feed 'em by the hand.
> 'Cause I got a ham for you,
> And I wanna cook with you.
> Yesterday I saw you standin' there
> Your meat was burned, your cheese was green.
> No spoon had touched your pears.
> I said get up
> And let me see you fry.
> We'll make a ham together.
> Fry the ham awhile.
> 'Cause I got a ham for you, (I got a ham for you)
> And I wanna cook with you (won't you let me cook with you)
> Hold my ham (want you to hold my ham)
> Hold my ham (I'll take you to a place where you can eat)
> Hold my ham (any meat you wanna eat 'cause)
> I wanna make you the best ham, the best ham I can.

They went through another verse and chorus and were met with resounding applause and cheers when the song had finished.

"Wow! That's terrific! Totally far out, you guys!"

"You should really do that for the grand finale talent show," someone suggested.

That idea caught on like wildfire. "Yes, definitely. You need to! That is bound to be the hit of the whole evening!"

Jarid laughed a little self-consciously. "Well, they probably wouldn't let me since I'm not even officially a student at the camp or anything."

"Oh, I'm sure that could be worked out. The rules for the talent show are pretty flexible."

"Really? So we can do any style of music we want?" Rory asked with interest.

"Oh yeah. It isn't restricted to just jazz or anything."

"And we can put together our own combo with anybody we choose?" Rory questioned further.

"Yep. Hey, could I be in your group, Rory? I've sung 'Hold My Hand' along with the radio dozens of times, so I know it by heart."

They all started to make their plans right then and there. Each group was allowed to perform two songs, so they decided on "Take the A Train" for their first selection, which was more typical of the jazz style at the music camp, but all agreed that "Hold my Ham" would be a fun way to add variety and round things out.

Rory's musical knowledge grew exponentially that week. He was exposed to so many new concepts, and even the ones with which he was already familiar were greatly expounded upon. He was eagerly looking forward to hearing the faculty concert at the end of the week and wasn't disappointed. It was a very impressive performance, and the honor band was given the privilege of opening for them. Rory was beyond thrilled to be presented with the outstanding instrumentalist award that night, which also meant that he would be able to attend the camp free of charge the following year.

The talent show for the students was held on the last day. Mom and Dad were there to see it, along with the other parents.

There were probably about a thousand people in the audience all-told, which was by far the largest crowd for which Rory had ever performed. But he was too keyed up to be nervous. When it came time for "Hold my Ham," they executed what they'd been practicing flawlessly and brought the tune to a rousing conclusion.

> See, I was bastin'
> 'Cause it was a bastin' time.
> Then I thought about your lunch meats,
> I thought about that crap.
> And I stood up
> And then I threw it out.
> I don't wanna eat none of your lunch meats,
> Don't wanna eat none of your fries, no.
> 'Cause I got a ham for you (I got a ham for you)
> And I wanna cook with you, (Oh, won't you let me cook with you, yeah)
> Hold my ham (want you to hold my ham)
> Hold my ham (I'll make for you some leg of lamb)
> Hold my ham (Maybe we can't feed the world, but)
> I wanna make you the best ham, the best ham I can!

The song was a smashing success, and the group received the biggest standing ovation of the evening, with the possible exception of the jazz combo Rory also played in at the end of the show. He was even given a big solo in this final set, which was especially noteworthy, considering how reluctant the honor band staff had been to have him on the team initially.

"Kind of ironic, isn't it?" Rory said with a chuckle when he related the exciting events to Kim and me on the phone a few days later. "To think that a ridiculous song like 'Hold my Ham' would make us the talk of the whole music camp. I guess just because it's such a popular song and the version we did was so comical."

"Plus the lyrics being original and I'm sure you guys were some of the best musicians," Kim surmised. "You must have been pretty elated after all that."

"Yeah, it was a spectacular ending to an incredible week. That's for sure," Rory replied. "I mean, I'm utterly and thoroughly hooked on jazz now, never to return. And that's putting it mildly. There's no going back for me anymore."

"Wonderful!" I said with a grimace. "Well I suppose it was destined to happen anyway."

"This experience has pretty much busted down the doors that had only been creaking open bit by bit until now. All I had before this was some programs on public radio and those tapes I borrowed from Mr. Shimke. But now there's a whole new world open to me, and I fully intend to explore it to the utmost."

Climbing the Ladder

The music department at Lemmon High that year was more active than it had been in anyone's memory. They took a band tour to San Francisco that summer and even chartered a bus for the event. Rory sampled oysters on the half shell for the first time while on the trip but told us he didn't like them at all, a very rare occurrence, indeed, for someone who enjoyed trying new foods as much as he did. The group also went through a World War II submarine while they were there and visited Alcatraz Prison, where Rory got a picture of himself behind bars and obtained a tape of sound effects from the facilities, which his brother greatly appreciated.

Reed was now a freshman in high school and was already spreading his wings in the music department there. Mrs. Raber had decided she'd like to put a rhythm section with the jazz choir and asked Reed if he would be willing to accompany them on the bass guitar.

"Nah. I don't think so," Reed said. "I haven't played the bass guitar all that much yet, and when I do, it's only been country music."

"Well, there's no time like the present to start learning," his music teacher pointed out. "You have a great ear, just like your brother, and I'm sure you'd catch on without any trouble if you gave it half a chance."

"Oh, I don't know," Reed protested further. "I'm just not good enough to play jazz."

"You might be surprised," Mrs. Raber contradicted him. "Just give it a try. That's all I ask. You're the only bass player available, and I know you'll do a great job if you set your mind to it."

Reed hesitated. "Okay. I guess I'll take a stab at it and see what happens, if you really want me to," he agreed reluctantly.

To no one's surprise except perhaps his own, once he got the hang of it, Reed became very proficient at the job and played bass not only for the jazz choir but for the pep band and jazz band throughout his entire high school career and beyond.

The Lampheads again provided the live music for the Valentine's Sweetheart Banquet that year and had already been asked to play for an upcoming high school dance, for which they were more than happy to oblige.

Kim and John were expecting a baby in early April, and, of course, this announcement had caused quite a stir among family and friends. I was beside myself at the prospect of becoming an aunt and didn't know how I'd ever be able to wait so long for the big day to arrive.

In March, Bob and I learned that a baby would be joining our family as well. I would have been happy to put the event on hold for a while longer since I knew it would bring many more changes and new responsibilities into our lives. It didn't take long, however, for excitement and anticipation to become the overriding emotions as I thought of what the future held in store.

Of course, Bob's parents were also thrilled at the expected arrival of their first grandchild. They didn't waste any time in sending us a congratulation gift consisting of a new camcorder. We knew we'd be expected to take lots of footage in the days ahead, but that was just fine with my photography-loving husband.

Because of their poor health and the distance involved, his family hadn't been able to make it to our wedding, but we had made the trip to Mississippi a couple times since then. I was welcomed into their family immediately and felt right at home with them from the start. Zane and Shelia treated me just like a daughter, and Mike was a wonderful brother. I knew I was very blessed to have such kind and loving in-laws.

Bob had retired from the air force after putting in his ten years and found a job working in the collections department of a finance agency that was located very near our home. The two of us had begun attending a church that was a lot bigger than what we were used to, but it didn't take us long to decide that we wanted to become members. Shortly thereafter, Bob began helping out as substitute Sunday school teacher, and I was asked to serve on the worship team, which was responsible for overseeing the music program.

"We really like our new church, but it's hard trying to navigate and learn my way around in such a crowd," I confided to my siblings at one point. "I usually just let Bob guide me, and since none of the people knew me before I was married, I've noticed that they tend to see us as an inseparable unit. A lot of them assume that only Bob knows how to help me and seem afraid that they'll do or say something wrong whenever they're around me."

"I know what you mean," Kim sympathized. "Sometimes, when I'm with John, people seem to address their comments mainly to him and avoid talking to me directly if they can help it. And they don't offer to drive me places or read written information to me and whatnot, like they did when I was single."

"I find it pretty ironic when people get so offended by how other people look at them or treat them or whatever," I mused, "always reading so much into facial expressions or things that are said or not said. And yet, people who don't know me very well are almost always hesitant around me, and I'd be pretty miserable if I took everything so personally and was holding a grudge all the time."

"Have you guys ever noticed that blindness seems to get the credit for everything, good or bad?" Rory asked. "Like if a blind guy is super neat and organized, people will conclude that it's because he can't see and naturally remembers precise details or what have you. And then there's the blind person who's a slob, and everybody assumes that all people who can't see are that way and can't be expected to do any better."

"Hmm. I never quite thought of it that way, but I'd have to say you're right," I acknowledged.

"Speaking of false perceptions," Kim smiled, "the other day, this lady noticed that I was pregnant and came up and started gushing on and on about what a big help our child would be to me and that my life was going to be so much easier after the baby was born."

I laughed outright at that. "At least she wasn't questioning your ability to raise a child, as I'm sure some will," I pointed out. "And besides, if you're able to survive all the extra work that this new addition will bring, like its babyhood and the toddler stage and the preschool years, just for starters, maybe there will eventually be some truth in what she says."

"But I'm not having this baby so that I can have a built-in slave at my disposal," she scoffed. "I mean, even though I don't plan to let the kid get away with not doing his fair share of chores, it won't be any different than what other kids are expected to do."

"Well, we might ask them to do things that most parents wouldn't require," I reasoned, "like reading mail occasionally or showing us where something is, but that doesn't mean they'll have to do more than their friends. Just maybe some different tasks is all."

"So what do you guys think about Kon's big news?" Kim asked our brothers curiously.

"I don't know what we're ever gonna do with two babies around here," Reed said skeptically. "I think she should've waited a few years so we could get used to yours for a while first."

"Well, that would've been fine with me," I said, "but, apparently, God had other ideas. And anyway, you'll have six whole months after Kim's baby is born before mine comes along, so that should give you plenty of time to adjust."

"And it will be so nice for the two cousins to be so close in age. Don't you think?" Kim added.

"There's gonna be babies all over the place underfoot," Rory speculated. "We won't be able to go anywhere without worrying we're gonna trod upon one of them."

"And not to mention all the fussing and carrying on that we'll have to put up with," Reed concurred.

"What are you talking about?" I cried in an exaggeratedly offended tone. "We're going to be such good mothers that our babies won't cause any hubbub at all. You're not even gonna know they're around most of the time."

Our brothers remained dubious, but I was certain they'd come around eventually.

"Anyway, how is life at school these days, you guys?" Kim wanted to know.

"Fine," Reed told her. "You knew that we got chosen as the official pep band for the SD State Class A boys' basketball championships, didn't you?"

"Yeah. Pretty incredible," Kim commented.

"There are just a lot of really good musicians in our class this year," Rory explained. "Josh played bass; and Reed is one of the drummers; and, of course, I'm playing guitar, which is pretty unique for a pep band. So that's probably another reason we got selected."

"And the Rabers have concocted this new plan," Reed continued enthusiastically. "They've decided we're going to do an annual jazz dinner theater that will give us a chance to shine and have our own concert for a change, just the jazz band and jazz choir."

"We're going to go all out too," Rory piped up. "Not only will our patrons be treated to an entire evening of jazz, but they'll get a mighty fine prime rib dinner as well. And all the proceeds from ticket sales will go to the music boosters."

"Wow. That sure sounds like a neat idea," I said fervently.

"Have the girls heard about Jazz Fest yet?" Reed asked his brother.

"I'm not sure if I filled them in on that or not," Rory admitted. "That's where high schools from all over got together, both jazz bands and show choirs. I won the Outstanding Soloist Award and got a nice, big trophy and had my picture taken with Lenny Pickett and so on. Any of that ring a bell?"

"Yeah, I remember you did tell us about that," Kim recalled. "He's a regular on the David Letterman show and plays great saxophone, right?"

"And you even got to perform with him and everything," I recollected further.

"Yep, that's it," Rory said. "It was held at the University of Mary in Bismarck. They certainly do have a fine music program at that school. Still can't make up my mind whether I want to go there or to Northern in the fall. When I went to All-State this year, it seemed like every time we had a break, either Dr. LaFave or Patnode or somebody else from Northern was trying to recruit me to go to college in Aberdeen next year. Kept asking if I'd decided on a school yet and invited me to come and listen to their jazz bands and all this. But I still don't know what I'm gonna wind up doing."

"Well, I'm sure you'll have it figured out when the time comes," I said confidently. "Either one would be more than adequate."

"Absolutely. I know I could learn a lot about playing sax from Mr. Patnode, and everybody else there at Northern would be good too. So I'll probably end up going that route since they're less expensive."

"But getting back to All-State," Reed hinted, "you should tell them about that little incident you had with that instructor of yours."

"Yeah, that was pretty wild," Rory agreed. "We were in this small group setting, and the great Willie Thomas was there, teaching us about the basics of improv. Let's just say there were some lesser students in the class who were having a hard time catching on. So you can about imagine how bored I was because I've been way beyond all that rudimentary stuff for ages already."

I chuckled. "Wonder why they even put you in a class like that to begin with."

"No idea. But anyway, he told us we would only be allowed to use two notes for our entire solo. Like C and D, for example. We could use whatever rhythm we wanted, but the whole thing could only consist of those two notes. Then, after we did that for a while, he let us use three notes, and then four, and you get the picture."

"Yikes. I can see why that would get quite tedious pretty quickly for somebody like you," Kim sympathized.

"You ain't kiddin'!" Rory exclaimed vehemently. "I guess the point was to teach them which notes would work with what chords, and it forces you to think more rhythmically than melodically, but it sure wasn't very fun. I just got bored stiff with it and finally lost patience and started embellishing a little."

Rory downed the last of his Pepsi and then went on. "So Mr. Thomas stops what he's doing and says to me, 'Okay there, Rory. You want a challenge, do you?' So I assured him that I'd love a challenge, and then he and I got into this cutting competition, where he would play a phrase and then I would have to repeat it. At first, they were just one-bar licks, and then, in the second chorus, we would do two-bar licks, and so on."

"How long were you able to keep that up?" Kim asked eagerly.

"Oh, I was able to hold my own for quite a while, but I finally succumbed when he started throwing this bizarre stuff at me out of left field that I'd never heard of before! I don't even know how to describe it to you."

(Rory learned in college much later that what the instructor had been "throwing at him" was nothing less than some four-bar octatonic phrases using a diminished scale.)

"Yikes! So were you properly humbled?" I questioned teasingly.

"It taught me a few things all right," he admitted. "I got a glimpse of just how much there still is out there, musically speaking, that I don't have a clue about. And it was also probably good for the other students to see what's possible for a high schooler to accomplish if he sets his mind to it. But, gosh, I'm finding out there's a whole other world out there that I don't understand yet. And I wanna learn about it now more than ever."

As the weeks passed and Kim's due date drew ever nearer, we could hardly contain our excitement. The big day turned out to be April 11. Kim had called to notify us that she and John were on their way to the hospital, and needless to say, Mom and I were on pins and needles as we waited for reports. We wished fervently that we were there with her, but because of the distance, we didn't want to plan a trip there until we were sure we'd be seeing a baby. The two of us, along with my grandparents, were planning to go to Montana just as soon as we could after the birth, however.

As luck would have it, April 11 was also the day of the regional music contest, in which both Rory and Reed were participating. Mom was coming along as one of the chaperones, but her mind was elsewhere for most of the day.

"I'll need to get hold of a payphone or something as soon as we get there so I can see how Kim is doing," she fretted.

"I'm sure everything is going just fine," Shanna assured her.

"Does she know what she's having?" asked Tiffany, one of the other students.

"I'm certain it will be either a boy or a girl," Reed surmised dryly.

"They wanted to be surprised," Mom replied, deciding to ignore her son's remark. "I just hope she's doing okay. This is our first grandbaby, you know."

"How exciting!" Mrs. Raber enthused. "No doubt the doctor has everything well under control."

"I don't think Mom's in much better shape than Kim is," Rory observed with a wry grin. "She might need more chaperoning than the rest of us today."

And Grandma, as it happened, wasn't much better than Mom or me. She called me several times, asking if I'd heard anything and worried about the fact that nearly an hour had passed with no news.

"You know how stubborn babies can be." I tried to assuage her fears. "It sometimes takes quite awhile for them to be born, especially when it's the first one."

"Yeah, I'm sure you're right," she assented unconvincingly. "I just wish somebody would call and let us know."

Which they did, eventually. I'll never forget when I heard my new little niece cry for the first time. Kayla Rae Bojkovsky. What a big name for such a tiny person. But I knew she'd grow into her name all too quickly and that we needed to appreciate every moment of her babyhood while she was still small.

In the meantime, however, Rory had a couple months of school to finish before graduation. Of course, we would all be there for the ceremony and were anticipating the time even more when we learned that Lemmon High would also be performing the popular musical "Bye Bye Birdie" while we were home.

My brothers were both in the pit band—Rory on guitar and Reed on bass, along with Tiffany on flute, Mr. Raber playing drums, and Mrs. Raber on piano. There were three performances, and all were well attended.

"It's a good thing you guys weren't here for the first performance though," Rory told Kim and me. "The volume on my guitar was turned down so low that you couldn't hear me at all. I think Mrs. Raber was a little nervous because the mics that the actors wore didn't work very well, so she sort of overcompensated."

"And lest you think he exaggerate," Reed put in with a laugh, "Ror was literally turned so low that he finally started playing in a completely different key than the rest of the band, and nobody even knew the difference."

"Why did you do that, Ror?" asked Kim in amusement.

"I wanted to have a convincing case when I told Mrs. Raber that I needed to be a little louder," he replied.

Rory must have made his point because the instrument balance sounded great when Kim and I heard it the next day. Everyone did a fine job, and we offered our sincere congratulations afterward.

"Well, that little endeavor will also add a tidy sum to the music department's funds," Reed noted with satisfaction. "We've been needing new choir robes for a long time, so I'm sure that's where some of the money will go."

"And selling tickets for only ten dollars each was more than reasonable for such a unique event," Kim affirmed. "It isn't every day that an opportunity like this comes to Lemmon."

"The Rabers sure do have a lot of interesting new ideas," I agreed. "It's cool to see all the recognition Lemmon High is getting now. Pretty impressive for a town this size."

"I think it's a combination of great musicians and great teachers," Rory said. "But as far as I'm concerned, it's about time that the music department gets noticed more. Usually, it's the sports programs getting all the glory."

"Very true," I acknowledged. "And just think, there's still the international music camp to look forward to this summer."

"I know. Can't wait," he responded with anticipation. "And this time, I'll be able to attend both guitar week and jazz week since I won that free scholarship last year."

Rory's graduation from high school was a time of reflecting on the past but mainly of excitement as he looked toward the future. Of course, Mom hosted a reception afterward, and many attended to extend their congratulations and wish him well in the days ahead.

International music camp took place in July, and Rory was notified right away upon entering the auditions for guitar week that he would be one of the very few floating students. This meant that he would not be assigned to a particular instructor but would have the freedom to explore the various classes and learn as much as he could from all of them. One of the teachers would focus on the more finger-style classical approach while another might emphasize jazz and a third would specialize in rock, etc.

Rory chose to spend most of his time with Bob Peske, the jazz professor from the University of Mary. The class would be performing a song called "Sister Sadie," the arrangement of which consisted of approximately ten guitars playing simultaneously. As usual, Rory picked up on the diminished licks or bebop riffs or whatever Peske happened to be teaching way before his peers, so he was told he could just accompany or back up whatever the class was doing.

Bob Peske again spent a lot of time with Rory one on one that year, and he asked if Rory would be interested in learning a rendition of "Spain" by Chick Corea. This was a very complex and intense fusion jazz number, which was made even more so by the fact that Mr. Peske had worked up a version with a 6/8 time signature.

"Basically took me all week to learn the thing," Rory told us later. "But I got it down eventually. So well, in fact, that it was decided we would get to play it during the faculty performance. Just Bob Peske and me, doing our own little duet together. And, of course, he had to go into this big spiel beforehand, giving our audience the whole scoop on how I had never heard of the song before that week and so on. So they found that pretty amazing."

"Cool. And how did the talent show go?" I asked eagerly.

"Oh, you should've been there. This time Barnsey was my guide for the week, and he brought his guitar with him. You know, he's getting to be a darn good player, if I do say so myself, and he pretty much got to participate in everything just like one of the gang since he was there with me for the entire time. The two of us would sit out on the grass or at the picnic tables and play country tunes to our heart's content, and there'd always be this big crowd gathered around whenever we got started."

"So you had a pretty big following from the beginning, way before the talent contest," I remarked.

"You got it," he concurred. "We were pretty much the stars of the whole event by then because people were diggin' all the Allan Jackson and Diamond Rio hits we did and thought it was so neat to hear me play all the hot licks just like on the albums. So, of course, we had to do a couple of those tunes for the show."

"I bet Matt was beside himself to have so many people all agog like that." Kim laughed.

"Oh yeah. I don't think he was expecting anything like the reaction we got. To have just come along as my guide and ending up being up front like that. And being treated like we're heroes of the whole place was kind of overwhelming actually. But anyway, suffice it to say we pretty much stole the show without really even trying. But it was sure a heck of a lot of fun."

"I imagine quite a few people remembered you from last year," Reed guessed.

"Oh, sure. I had a bunch of friends immediately, so that's always nice too. Just felt like I belonged right away."

"Well, it certainly sounds as though it will be another memory you won't ever forget," Kim said. "And I'm sure there will be lots more to come."

"I imagine we'll make a few memories when we do the Texas tour together next month," I said in anticipation.

All of us were looking forward to the upcoming trip through Texas that had been scheduled. A guy from there who had come to Lemmon to help with vacation Bible school the previous summer had fallen in love with Rory and Reed's music and, after learning about our family's ministry, had offered to try to book some concerts for us in that area. It was just the type of thing we had dreamed about for so long. We'd finally be able to put our motor home to good use, sharing our songs with a part of the country that we hadn't been to before.

"That's right in the middle of the Bible belt too," Dad noted. "I'm sure those people will really go for the type of music we play."

"And if it catches on, we'll probably be invited back and become more well-known in the area," I conjectured.

"Wouldn't it be cool if we were picked up by the Southern Baptist circuit or something and could just start traveling around the country full time?" Mom added hopefully.

"Well, it's going to get harder for all of us to coordinate schedules and whatnot now that we have husbands and kids to think of," Kim cautioned. "So this could actually be one of the last times we all get to play together."

"Don't talk that way," Mom admonished. "God can work out all those details if our music ministry is supposed to be part of the plan."

"Well, if nothing else, this trip should give us a good taste of what life on the road would be like," Rory said. "Of course, Konnie's kid won't be born yet, but Kayla will be along, so that should make things interesting."

"It won't be any trouble at all to have Kayla along," Mom predicted. "We'll just make a nice little bed for her in the bathtub, and she'll be snug as a bug back there."

"And we'll get to see Milo and Faye again, after all these years," Dad reminded us. "That alone would be worth the trip down south."

"We might even have to see if Rick would want to come along," Mom mused.

Our Uncle Rick was back in Lemmon, and we were sure he would love to make the trip with us to see his brother, Milo, who lived in Oklahoma, and to once again hear us play our music. It would almost be like old times, except maybe even better.

Texas, Here We Come

"So are you guys ready to get this show on the road, or what?" I asked my brothers as I climbed into the motor home, suitcase in tow, and reached to close the door behind me.

"What are you talking about?" Rory asked. "We've had all kinds of excitement already, and you're only just now joining the fun."

"Oh really? What did we miss?" Kim inquired, continuing to rummage around in her overflowing diaper bag for some unknown and, as yet, elusive item.

"Oh, we've had car trouble already, believe it or not," Reed was quick to inform us. "Or I should say motor home trouble, to be more precise."

"Sheesh. Off to a good start," Kim noted dryly. "Couldn't even have waited until we were officially underway. It wasn't the generator again, was it?"

"Surprisingly no, not this time," answered Rory. "Good thing too because I wouldn't have relished the ride without any air-conditioning. I'm not sure what it was exactly, but at least we made it here to Rapid in time for our concert."

"That's good," I said in relief. "It wouldn't have made a very favorable impression if you had been late. I've only been attending this church a few months, you know."

"Well, if anything goes awry, at least you'll be gone for the next couple of weeks," Rory soothed, "which means that your poor husband will have to survive any embarrassment caused by tonight's performance without you."

"Thanks for those comforting words," I said as I took my whimpering niece from where she was squashed between her mother and the huge diaper bag that Kim was still desperately sorting through.

"Glad to help," Rory replied without a hitch.

"Here it is! Finally!" Kim said triumphantly as she retrieved the hidden treasure she sought from deep within the diaper bag. "Ror, why don't you actually make yourself useful and put this in the player for me?"

"Pardon me?" Rory said indignantly. "May I remind you who has already done the sound check and tuned the instruments and helped Dad brush up on last-minute things to remember? And all the while you guys were here at Konnie's house, relaxing, yet you dare to question my usefulness? Something seems very wrong with this picture."

"Oh, just be quiet and take this, won't you? The stereo sitting right there next to you."

"What on earth! This tape is all sticky!" Rory exclaimed as he grabbed for what she held out to him. "You really want to put that into the stereo?"

"Then she wonders why her boom box has seen its better days," I mused under my breath.

"It's no big deal," Kim insisted calmly. "Some of Kayla's juice must've spilled on it is all. I'm sure none got on the inside, so it should play just fine."

"Oh boy," Reed sighed. "This is going well already."

"Here. If you wanna play the thing, do it yourself," Rory decided. "I wash my hands of the whole affair, literally. Hand me a baby wipe, if you don't mind."

"I imagine the wipes are probably in her tape case," Reed surmised. "Makes about as much sense as putting her music in with all the neonate paraphernalia."

"When you're a mother, you learn to be flexible," Kim replied sagely. "It's not as though I have the luxury of bringing tons of suitcases when there's eight of us crowded into this one vehicle."

Just then, there was a knock on the motor home's screen door and Gramp called out, "Hello, you guys. I see you're not at the church yet."

"Nope. Just waiting for Mom and Dad to finish loading the girls' suitcases and everything into the trailer," Rory said. "But Dad and Rick and I have already been there and set everything up, so the majority of the prep work is already done."

"Did you and Gram just get here?" Kim inquired as they came on board and took a seat on the couch.

"Just a few minutes ago," Gram replied as she took Kayla from my arms without so much as a by your leave.

"We didn't want to miss the chance to see our great-granddaughter," Gramp put in, leaning over to peer at her and give her a little kiss on the head.

Kim and my brothers went to the back and began messing around with the stereo while I stayed up front and thumbed through the book I'd brought along as my grandparents showered attention on Kayla.

"Look at this," Gram said as she held something out to the baby. "See that? Look there."

Something seemed a bit odd about the way Gram was acting, and I understood what it was when I heard her murmuring in an undertone to Gramp. "Stanley, watch this."

And Gramp responding quietly yet fervently, "I'll be darned. She sees it."

"Why, sure she does," Gram affirmed tremulously, as though she'd never doubted it.

Next, I heard Gramp taking out his handkerchief and blowing his nose, and I could tell that Gram was dabbing at her eyes too. "There you go, babe. Just reach out and take it," she said with a sniffle, albeit a happy sniffle.

I realized they'd been assessing Kayla's vision and were marveling in gratitude at the fact that she did, indeed, have sight after all. It suddenly dawned on me just how worried they must have been about this. Several things interested me about this fact, although it was difficult to articulate them or know what any of it signified. First off, I found it noteworthy in some way that they hadn't mentioned their fears to Kim or me. Secondly, there was the irony that Kim as Kayla's own mother had harbored no such fears herself. Not that she was naïve or in denial. That wasn't it at all. We both knew that the possibility existed that our children could be blind since the cause of our eye problem had never been diagnosed to anyone's satisfaction. It had simply never been in our nature to borrow trouble or agonize in advance over things that would probably never happen. It was almost amusing in a sad sort of way to contemplate the many times our well-meaning family and friends had felt undue sorrow and regret when they'd seen us run into something or worry on our behalf about challenges we faced when we ourselves hardly gave such things a second thought.

I recalled what Kim's good friend had told me when we had gone to Montana to visit my sister shortly after Kayla's birth. This friend had been with Kim when Kayla was born and had somehow reached the conclusion that God had told her He was going to heal Kim's eyes at the moment of the baby's birth so that the first sight Kim would see would be that of her precious daughter. When this hadn't happened, the friend was brokenhearted. And all the while, oblivious to the whole thing, Kim was just thrilled to be a new mom and happy to have the ordeal of giving birth behind her.

This was just one of many similar episodes we'd experienced through the years. Sometimes, complete strangers would come up to us, overwrought over our lack of vision, and insist on praying for our healing right then and there. Not that we didn't appreciate their good intensions or believe in the power of prayer, but it was sometimes hard not to be annoyed when we knew there were probably many other less visible but more urgent needs all around us that were being completely overlooked.

Mom and Dad joined us then, and we headed for the church. I was filled with anticipation at what the next couple weeks held in store. That night would be the first in a series of programs we would be doing together as a family, something that was becoming less frequent with each year that passed. In the morning, we would leave for Texas, where we would be performing during the Sunday and Wednesday night services at various churches. There would be quite a bit of down time, and we wished that more bookings had been scheduled but figured we had to start somewhere, and maybe it would be enough to make people in that area aware of our ministry and hopefully ask us back.

"Do you have all those sixteenth notes on your hi-hat mastered by now, Reed?" I wanted to know.

"Of course. Need you ask such a thing?" Reed said indignantly. "Anyway, you'll soon find out for yourself because we're doing 'Someday' tonight. Figured in a church the size of yours, there's bound to be a few folks in the crowd who will appreciate hearing some Michael W. Smith."

We had prepared two set lists for the days ahead. One had a more laid-back, traditional flavor for our audiences that were on the conservative side. The other list of songs was more energetic and better suited for the younger generation. We'd decided to put "Someday" on this second list, which was a contemporary number that Rory had played with World Detour. This meant having to teach Dad a couple new chords and worrying about whether or not Reed would be able to maintain the very fast, steady pattern on the drums that the song required, but we were confident he could pull it off.

"And you have my song all worked up and ready to go on your steel, Ror?" Kim asked.

"As ready as I'll ever be," Rory replied. "You know, I hate to admit it, but I'm afraid the steel guitar is one instrument at which I'm never going to excel. If I'd only thought ahead of time, I never would've put out the investment."

"But why are you giving up on it so easily?" asked Kim in surprise. "And how could you have known before even giving it a try? Besides, every good country band should have a steel guitar."

"That's just it. I couldn't be sure until I actually had one," Rory said. "But I figured it would be a challenge since the pedals and levers need to be in the front, which meant I wouldn't be able to turn it around and play it backward like I do everything else."

Kim and I both burst out laughing at the sincere way in which he made this seemingly absurd statement.

"Well, it sounded plenty good enough to me when I heard it a few weeks ago," I encouraged. In fact, it had brought tears to my eyes at how well he was doing after having only had the new instrument for such a short period of time.

Reed did, in fact, do a marvelous job on his drums that night, and Rory's steel guitar sounded even better than I'd remembered.

"I'm sure glad they were finally able to locate some sticks for me to use instead of those brushes," Reed said happily.

"Why didn't Dad just get yours out of the trailer?" Kim asked.

"They were buried somewhere, and he didn't want to unload a bunch of stuff just for that," Reed replied. "But all's well that ends well. I just wanted to use actual drumsticks since we were playing in a big enough building for a change. I hate putting towels on the snare drum or having to use brushes the whole time. Drums weren't meant to be smothered."

Playing together again after such a long time and still managing to maintain a quality performance after having had only limited practice made us more eager than ever to begin our tour. We started our journey bright and early the next morning, and as soon as Kim had her daughter safely tucked into the bathtub, she suggested we siblings play a game of rummy.

"That depends," Reed said noncommittally. "Are the cards going to be all bent and sticky from residing in your diaper bag?"

"And won't it be a little challenging trying to play cards in a moving vehicle without a table?" Rory added further.

"Oh, quit complaining, would ya?" Kim asked in disgust, as she began handing out the cards.

We managed to make it through several hands, albeit with periodic interruptions so my sister could check on Kayla.

"Hey, I have an idea," Rory said. "Why don't we play that new Monopoly game you guys have for the computer? That should work a whole lot better in a situation like this than playing cards does."

"Before we do, however," Reed put in, "I feel the need to make a proclamation at this juncture." He cleared his throat dramatically and announced, "I do believe that Nebraska is officially the smelliest state we've traveled through to date."

"I can't argue with you there," Rory had to agree. "Even with all the windows closed, that manure has a way of permeating quite potently."

"Kim, does Kayla need to be changed?" I asked none too subtly.

"What are you trying to say?" she asked in a very offended manner.

"Just a question," I pointed out innocently.

"At least she hasn't spit up yet," Reed commented.

"Not that we know of anyway," Rory corrected. "She's probably waiting until my pocket is near at hand like she did when I held her for the first time."

"You guys are mean," Kim said. "She's being good as gold back there, and look how you treat her!"

As if to prove her mother wrong, Kayla chose that moment to let out a loud squall, which made Kim jump up and rushed to the bathtub to see what was wrong.

"I think we're stopping here someplace for lunch," Mom called. "So you guys can start gathering your stuff together."

"Kim's the only one who needs to drag a lot of junk around with her everywhere," Rory told her. "The rest of us don't have any neonates to worry about."

"Don't forget about my neonate," I reminded him. "In fact, it just kicked in protest. Must've heard what you said."

"Well, yours doesn't count yet because you haven't yet reached the stage where you have to carry around a lot of junk for it."

"Reed, you go with your Uncle Rick, and Ror can take Dad's arm," Mom directed. "You girls follow behind me."

We filed inside, at which point my mother felt compelled to launch into our infamous restaurant story, this time for the benefit of our Uncle Rick, who'd been staying pretty quiet for most of the trip thus far.

"So Konnie is sitting at this table along with some of the other kids from the school for the blind, and she's trying to decide what to order. She just starts naming things off, without realizing that the waitress is standing there all the while, taking down her order. First she said, 'Maybe I'll have some pancakes. But French toast sounds good too. I haven't had waffles for a long time either,' and just kept listing different possibilities like that."

"Oh no. I think I have an idea of what's coming," Rick said.

"Yeah. You wouldn't believe the pile of plates the lady brought back with her," Mom went on. "I couldn't get over it when Konnie told us. There were pancakes, French toast, waffles, sausage, bacon, hash browns, eggs, an omelet—you name it!"

"Pretty dumb waitress if you ask me, to just stand there and not confirm anything," Rory observed. "She was obviously rather gun shy around blind people or something."

"Well, looks like they don't have any Braille menus here, so I'll start going over everything with you all," Mom said. "Can everybody hear me?"

"I'd be able to hear you a lot better if Kayla wasn't bawling in my ear," Rory complained. The babe in question had been whimpering and whining for the past several minutes, and the volume level of her cries was becoming more pronounced with each second that passed.

"They have biscuits and gravy—" Mom began.

"Oh, I bet Ror would love some of that," Reed said.

"Or not!" Rory exclaimed vehemently. "I think it will be a mighty long time before I wish to indulge in said items. My memories of what passed for them on the school lunch menu are still far too vivid in my mind!"

"I don't remember them being particularly terrible when I was in high school," Kim said as she jiggled her daughter up and down in an attempt to quiet her.

"The biscuits must have gotten a lot worse since then," Reed replied. "Didn't Ror tell you about the speech he wrote in protest?"

"No, I don't remember anything about that," I said. "How long ago was this?"

"Oh, a couple years I guess," Rory answered. "It was for my speech class. We were supposed to write a persuasive speech, and mine sure must've been that, if nothing else. I don't even know what grade I got on it anymore, but of much greater importance is the fact that they never again served biscuits and gravy for lunch!"

"How did you pull that one off?" I wanted to know. "Did the cooks get hold of your speech somehow or what?"

Rory laughed. "No. What happened is that for some reason or other, the principal, Mr. Maxon, was in the class and heard what I said. Anyway, all I know is we never had them since."

"Wow. So what made these biscuits so horrible anyway?" Kim questioned.

"They were just tasteless, pasty biscuits, and the gravy was so watery that it ran right off them. Yuck."

"So now we just have that same less-than-appetizing gravy with mashed potatoes instead," Reed put in. "But at least that's a slight improvement."

Mom proceeded to read the menu, and then we all sat around impatiently, waiting for the waitress to come and take our order.

"If I'd have known she was going to take so long, I could've fed Kayla beforehand," Kim grumbled.

"Maybe the waitress is related to Cassandra," Reed speculated.

"You think? In that case, we better sing the song for her. Perhaps that would roust her out," suggested Rory.

"Who's Cassandra?" I wondered aloud.

"A girl on the school bus that we always had to wait for each and every morning," Reed answered. "Ror and I finally decided that she deserved a song of her very own to commemorate that very annoying habit of hers. It goes something like this."

And without further preamble, he and Rory began the tune that sounded a lot like "Sink the Bismarck." The lyrics, however, were obviously the "Ode to Cassandra."

> Cassandra is a little girl who never seems to run.
> She thinks that she can take her time, but waitin' isn't fun.
> Nobody really likes it 'cause she always makes us late.
> We have to get to school on time; we can't afford to wait.

"And then there's the chorus," Reed explained quickly before the next lines commenced.

> Hurry up, Cassandra, 'cause you're holdin' up the bus.
> We have to go, or else the teachers will be mad at us.
> Cassandra, come a-runnin' and we'll turn this bus around.
> We're on our way to school, and we're headed straight for town.

I cleared my throat self-consciously, as I suddenly became aware of the fact that the restaurant seemed a whole lot quieter than it had before the song began.

"Hey, even Kayla likes it," Rory observed happily. "Let's hurry up and do verse two before she starts up again."

We've left that girl so many times, you'd think that she would learn.
But each and every time we do, she doesn't show concern.
We've warned her time and time again that she must be prepared.
The way she creeps up to the bus, you'd swear she was impaired.

"Okay. Thanks, but you don't need to do the chorus again," I cut in quickly as they concluded the second verse.

"But there's more," Reed insisted. "We wouldn't want to deprive you of the last part."

One day we pulled up to her house with not much time to spare.
But when we knocked upon the door, we found she wasn't there.
It doesn't pay to stop there just to find she's still in bed,
If she can't get aboard on time, she'll have to walk, instead.

"You guys, the waitress is standing here, waiting to take our order," Mom informed them as their performance drew to a close.

"Oh, didn't mean to keep you waiting," Rory said, although he didn't sound nearly as mortified as I felt.

"Not a problem. It was...interesting to listen to," the girl replied politely.

We told her what we wanted and then proceeded with our lively chatter. Dad and Uncle Rick began discussing what had gone wrong with the motor home the day before and conjecturing on the likelihood of its reoccurrence. Kayla had started fussing again, and Mom was trying to make the case for letting her have some juice, but Kim was insistent that this would interfere with her nursing schedule. Rory and Reed were conversing amongst themselves about the latest songs on the country charts, and I was just taking it all in while enjoying my turn at holding my little niece, cranky though she was.

Our banter continued after the food arrived, and as our appetites wound down, we all began handing off our leftovers to Rory, as was our customary routine. He never had any difficulty packing away his own meal in addition to "samples" of whatever might be available from the rest of the table.

"Ror, I'll give you ten bucks if you'll march around the restaurant with my bread bowl on your head," Mom dared her son at one point in the conversation.

"Make it twenty dollars and you've got yourself a deal," Rory replied without a hiccup.

"Will you really?" Mom asked doubtfully. I believe it was then that she realized she would probably be elected as the "lucky" person who got to accompany Rory on his march.

"Sure. Why not?" Rory said, sounding more eager by the minute.

"You must be pretty hard up for cash these days, Ror," Kim guessed.

"No. I just think it would be fun to imagine all the stares, especially since I know I will likely never meet any of these people again," Rory said as he stood up and pushed back his chair. "Well, Mother, what are you waiting for? Hand over the bowl."

I pretended rather unsuccessfully to be uninterested in the antics of my strange relatives as they made a trip around the room and then came back to our table. That would've been an ideal time to make our exit as far as I was concerned, but Dad never hurried at mealtime, and that day was definitely no exception. He hadn't even started on dessert yet.

"I betchya Kayla would like some of this ice cream," Dad theorized hopefully as the whining continued from the youngest member of the family.

Not bothering to ask Kim's permission, he put a little on the end of the spoon and brought it to the baby's lips. She smacked eagerly and quieted down immediately.

"Mmm…nim-nim," she cooed happily. Then, a moment later, more forcefully, she cried, "Nim-nim!"

"You want more?" Dad asked. "You like that nim-nim. Huh?"

Kim didn't protest, evidently as happy as the rest of us to hear her daughter's fretting subside. Kayla ate a couple more bites of the ice cream and proclaimed, "Nim-nim," after each one.

"That's her first word, isn't it, Kim?" I asked proudly.

"Well, if you can call it that, I think it is," Kim affirmed. "And only four months old at that! What a smart child I have. Wouldn't you agree, Reed?"

"I reserve comment until I've seen just a bit more proof," Reed told her.

When Dad had finished, we trooped back out to the motor home and resumed our journey. As we traveled south, the day grew ever hotter and Kayla continued to become more restless and uncomfortable.

"Kim, would you please do something with your kid?" Rory finally asked in exasperation.

"She has a tummy ache," Kim informed him as she patted the baby's back.

"Oh, Mr. Burp, Burp, Mr. Goofy Burp, please come out of the baby," she crooned as she rocked back and forth on the seat.

"I think your skill at composing songs is quickly going downhill," Reed told his sister.

"That's not an original song, I'll have you know," Kim retorted. "Barney does it."

"And who is Barney?"

"You don't know who Barney is?" Kim asked in disbelief. "The purple dinosaur, of course!"

"Oh yes. Of course. Why did I not know that?" Reed taunted a bit sarcastically. "And you're telling me that this Barney fellow sings about burping and you actually let your neonate listen?"

"Well, the song is really called 'Mr. Sun,' but I just thought I'd adapt it a little for our current situation," Kim explained. "See, you learn to be very flexible when you're a mom."

"If you say so," Reed hedged.

The day wore on, and poor Kayla didn't get much better. When we stopped at a hotel for the night, Kim put on the tape for her that consisted of rainforest sounds, which she claimed always did the trick when nothing else would quiet her down. But no such luck that evening.

"You sure don't need to resort to pinching your offspring in order to get her to cry anymore," Rory observed.

When Kayla was first born, Kim had done just that when she'd called from the hospital to give her brothers the news of Kayla's birth. She had wanted them to hear what the baby sounded like, but Kayla just lay there quietly, not cooperating at all. Kim finally gave her arm a little pinch to get some sound out of her. "Otherwise, I couldn't have proved I'd even had a baby at all," she'd explained.

"This traveling lifestyle is all new to her, and she doesn't know what to think of it, yet," Kim said in frustration.

"Well, tomorrow is another day, and I'm sure things will be better," I predicted optimistically.

Sometimes, not knowing the future is definitely a blessing.

Just the Beginning

"Where are we?" Kim asked as our motor home decreased in speed, indicating that we'd entered a new town.

The day had been a long one. We were thankful that at least our unreliable generator was still holding its own, but Kayla had been out of sorts for most of the day, and our nerves were somewhat frazzled.

"Just a little place in Oklahoma," Dad replied. "Trying to find somewhere to eat supper, and then I think we'll call it a night. It's getting pretty late already."

"Man, there sure are a lot of cars around here," Mom remarked. "There must be some kind of big convention going on or something."

The waiter at the restaurant where we stopped confirmed Mom's assumption when she asked about getting a room. "If you don't have any reserved already, there's no way you're going to get one now," he told her. "I'm afraid you'll have to drive on a little longer. Norman isn't too terribly far though. Hopefully they'd have something there."

Mom concealed her disappointment and thanked him for his help. We'd all been looking forward to retiring for the evening, but it looked as if we'd have to hold out a bit longer.

Deciding to make the best of it, we siblings prepared to play out our current Monopoly game to the bitter end upon re-entering the motor home, even though it was already pretty much a foregone conclusion that Rory had won again, as usual.

Afterward, we thought about what else we might do to occupy ourselves until we'd made it to Norman. "You guys don't have time to start another game now," Mom informed us. "We're just outside of Norman—"

Her words trailed off as the motor home suddenly slowed and then veered.

"What the—?" Rick began.

"Look out, Rolly. There's a semi," Mom cautioned unnecessarily.

We ground to a stop, and silence reigned for at least ten whole seconds.

"Now what's wrong?" I wanted to know.

"Oh, Rolly, what are we ever gonna do now?" Mom asked. "Kids, start praying. We're right in the middle of a bridge."

"It's a good thing you were able to coast her over to the side before she ran out of steam altogether," said Uncle Rick.

"Well, Rick, I suppose we better try to get underneath and figure out what's going on," Dad suggested as he unbuckled his seatbelt.

"How are you gonna do that?" Mom questioned. The railing is so close that there's barely enough room for you to squeeze out the door. And when you're under there, your legs would be sticking right out in all that traffic."

"Semis are going past every few seconds," Rick noted further. "Seems to me like a good way to get a limb chopped off."

"Well, we can't just sit here all night. That's for sure," Dad pointed out. "Gotta do what ya gotta do."

The two of them disembarked and began their investigation. Every time a truck went past, the whole bridge shook. This caused my brothers no end of amusement, much to my annoyance.

"Do you guys always have to find humor in the most stressful of circumstances?" I asked indignantly.

"Are you kidding? This is more fun than being at Six Flags," Reed exclaimed. "because we're actually in real peril, so that's even better than a roller coaster."

I hoped Reed could sense the glare I gave him, as it expressed my sentiments much better than words ever could. Just to be sure though, I accompanied it with a drawn-out, longsuffering sigh for good measure.

"Breaker, breaker one nine," Mom was saying from up front. I heard the crackle of the CB radio, which I'd forgotten was even there, and I realized Mom must be putting out a distress call.

"Is anybody listening out there?" she inquired frantically. "We're in quite a mess here and we need some help. Can anyone hear me at all?"

She waited a few seconds and then repeated her plea for assistance.

"Our vehicle died on a bridge right outside of Norman, and my husband and brother-in-law are out there trying to find out what the problem is. Semis are going by like nuts, and we're pulling a trailer full of musical equipment behind us. We're traveling with our four kids, who are all blind, and we're from the Dakotas, so we don't know of anyone that can help us. Is anybody out there?"

"No response.

"We really need some help here," Mom said desperately into the receiver. Our daughter's baby is with us and isn't doing very well at all. I think she's probably getting dehydrated from all this heat."

Still no answer was forthcoming. So Mom turned things up another notch.

"My other daughter is six months pregnant," Mom continued into the microphone, "and one of my sons has asthma. The other one has high blood pressure. Please, isn't anyone listening?"

"Gosh. We are in dire straits, aren't we?" Rory asked dolefully. "I could almost start weeping myself just listening to such a woeful tale."

"Ror, be quiet!" Kim hissed. "People aren't going to take this seriously at all if they hear your commentary in the background."

"You folks needing some assistance?" came a crackling voice with a slow Southern drawl.

"Oh, thank God," Mom breathed a heartfelt sigh of relief. The trucker who had responded said he'd be more than happy to call the sheriff's department for us, who would contact a towing company and get us out of our precarious predicament just as soon as possible.

"You people have enough food with you?" he asked in concern.

"Oh yes. Thank you. Especially since we have help on the way. There's more than enough food around here for us to snack on until they get here. But thanks so much for asking and for everything you've done."

"Well, I'm glad to hear it," the man replied. "In that case, would you mind whipping up a big batch of biscuits and gravy? If so, I'll be right over."

Rory groaned at the thought, but the rest of us couldn't help but laugh at how the request had come so unexpectedly out of nowhere.

"I'm afraid that's one thing I've never made before," Mom told him. "But you'd be welcome to whatever we have on hand."

The tow truck finally arrived at about midnight and pulled us right up to the garage in Norman where we were to have our vehicle repaired. An emergency mechanic was called, but none of us was surprised to learn that the repair job would need to wait until morning.

"We'll need to jack it up and put it on a lift and everything," the man explained. "Sorry I can't do anything more tonight."

"That's okay," Dad assured him. "We'll just stay right here for the night, and that way it will be ready as soon as your doors open."

"I would be happy to take the rest of your family to a motel if you'd like," the man offered generously.

"Oh, would you?" Mom asked in relief. "That would be so nice!"

Unfortunately, finding a vacancy proved to be much more difficult than any of us had counted on. The big convention that was going on in the town nearby had apparently drawn quite a crowd.

After finally managing to secure a room in a town about twenty miles away, we were confronted with another problem. The mechanic was kind enough to be willing to make the trip, but his car was very small.

"You mean there isn't going to be enough room for Kayla's car seat?" Kim asked. "I don't like that idea at all."

"I'm sure Kayla will fare a whole lot better than I will in a four-passenger car," Rory pointed out unequivocally. He was over six feet tall and wasn't relishing the thought of being in such cramped quarters for the length of time it would take to get to our destination, along with all the luggage, five other adults, and a screeching niece besides. Kayla had never done so much traveling before, and her feeding schedule and daily routine were coming unraveled, much to her great dislike.

But manage we did—somehow. Kayla never let up for the entire drive, and having to sit on laps and suitcases with more piled on top wasn't exactly anybody's cup of tea. I'm sure the man who had volunteered his services was regretting having done so before we even left the city limits.

The motel, when we finally located it, turned out to be yet another big disappointment. There was only one room available, and it was the grungiest we had ever encountered. Reed later described it on a creative writing assignment he did as being "in the state of a poorly run POW camp." The floor was so coated with dirt that Mom was reluctant to set anything down. Working out the sleeping arrangements seemed like a huge hurdle, as it was nearly four thirty in the morning. Somehow, Rory ended up in the most precarious spot, a saggy couch that was too short for him by far, which meant that his head and feet were way up on top of the arm rests while his body sank way down almost to the floor.

Kayla screeched for another hour, rainforest tape notwithstanding. Nothing we tried would comfort the poor thing, and we were afraid that her cries could be heard throughout the building, as the walls were quite thin.

"Do we really have to endure listening to those sounds again?" Reed asked as Kim turned up the volume on the tape player in an attempt to cover Kayla's cries.

"Now you know how we felt when you insisted on hearing that one tape of ghost sounds all the time when you were little," Kim reminded him.

"I wish we would've just stayed in the motor home," I fretted fervently. But we all knew it was far too late to do anything about that now. We would just have to wait until the next morning, when Dad and Uncle Rick came in the motor home to pick us up.

The mood was somber as we once again prepared to get underway the following day. Kayla was dead to the world by this time, so things seemed almost too quiet by comparison. Once we were all situated, Dad hesitated before starting the engine.

"Well, what's the plan for today, Lord?" he prayed with a touch of skepticism in his voice. "Things haven't been going the greatest so far, at least not according to anything we're able to understand."

"I think we should take a family vote before we do anything else," Mom declared, "to see whether we should even go on or just head for home."

I was a little taken aback to see such discouragement from my parents. They weren't usually ready to admit to defeat, regardless of circumstances or how disheartened they became. I realized it was likely partially due to the fact that we were all drained and overtired from lack of sleep and probably also exacerbated by the fact that we'd had such high hopes for this trip. It was disconcerting though and made me question my own resolve as to whether or not it was wise to continue on in spite of the obstacles.

"We've come this far. I don't see much point in turning back now," was Rory's verdict.

"That's what I was thinking," Reed concurred.

"I guess it really should be up to the rest of you to decide since you have more at stake," I reasoned. "Continuing onward is okay with me, but Kim's the one with the baby to worry about, and you guys have to think about all the logistics and expenses and whatnot."

No one had anything to say for a minute. Then Kim finally cleared her throat and got the ball rolling by saying, "Well, Kayla's been quiet so far today. I'm thinking she'll probably start adjusting to life on the road any time now."

"What about you, Rick?" Mom asked. "I'm sure you would never have come along if you'd known what kind of craziness you'd be going through."

"No, I don't mind going on," he said. "Things can't get much worse than being under a vehicle on a bridge with semis going past, so I figure it should be easy sailing from here on out."

"What do you think, Rolly?" Mom asked.

"Well, we know that the Hoffman luck hasn't changed any," he observed dryly. "It would sure be nice if just once, things could go as they're supposed to. But I reckon it doesn't pay to give up this far in the game."

"We can go ahead if that's what you all want to do," Mom acquiesced. "I'm just feeling so rumdum right now that it's hard to even think straight."

"After you've gotten some good, hot food in your belly and had a nice, long nap, you'll be good as new again," Rory predicted.

Dad turned the key in the ignition, and Kayla suddenly came back to life with a vengeance.

"Oh dear," Reed said worriedly. "I bet that's enough to give Kim second thoughts about this whole thing already."

"Poor Kayla is just casting her vote," I conjectured. "And she's upset because we didn't bother to ask for her opinion."

"Yeah. That works," Rory affirmed hurriedly. "But even so, I don't think it would hurt to hunt down some nim-nim or something as a token of our remorse for having left her out of the discussion."

Fortunately, the rest of our trip was pretty tame by comparison. We were struck by how hot and humid it was when we finally reached our destination, and it turned out that most of the places where we played were small and not equipped with air-conditioning. I was glad to be able to sit on a piano bench during the concerts because the likelihood of my passing out otherwise would have been pretty high.

Charlie, the man who had gotten the bookings for us, was planning to tape one of our performances, and he told us it would be a high-quality recording since he was going to do it directly from the mixing board.

"The only problem is that then you won't hear the drums at all," Reed said. The building is small enough that the drums haven't been miked, but that means they aren't going to come through the sound system and won't show up on the tape."

Charlie seemed a little unsure about this but said he would look into the matter. The show that evening turned out pretty well, and we were looking forward to getting a copy. When we tried to play it later, however, we were filled with dismay.

"Well, looks like he took your advice, Reed," Rory said with a touch of irony.

"That he certainly did not," Reed insisted emphatically. "What he did do I'll never know, but the drums are definitely loud and clear."

"You can say that again," Kim put in. "That's all you can hear!"

"How could that happen?" Dad asked in puzzlement. "It's like the other instruments aren't even there."

"I doubt we'll ever know the answer to that," I said. "And this also means we won't have anything to remember this trip by."

"Oh, I don't think there's any fear that this trip will go unremembered," Reed assured me a bit sarcastically.

"One old guy came up to me afterward and was all in a dither about the Michael W. Smith song I did," Rory commented. "Said I was on a slippery slope to going secular, among other things."

We all chuckled at that, but there was some underlying annoyance there along with the humor.

"Not sure how he makes that leap, but it isn't as if playing your music for unchurched people would be a bad thing anyway," Kim said.

"Sometimes it seems like Christians are the hardest people to please," I agreed in frustration. "They have all these standards and expectations that you're supposed to live by, which differ from church to church, and they sometimes seem the most reluctant to express their appreciation."

"And you have to be so careful not to offend people or give anybody the wrong idea," Rory added. "You don't dare have too much fun or you'll be accused of not being humble or spiritual enough, and if you're good at what you do, people say you're not giving God enough credit or that it's all for show or you're in it for the wrong reasons, etc. I say the heck with all that. I'm just gonna do what I do and be happy and serve God as best as I can and not worry too much about what people might think."

"You'd go crazy otherwise," I said, "just getting so many mixed messages thrown at you all the time."

"So what's on the agenda for tomorrow, Mom?" Kim asked.

"Oh, not too much really," Mom replied. "Charlie asked if we'd be willing to put on a little concert for some nursing home folks in the afternoon, but that's about it."

"Maybe that would be a good time to try our little piano experiment," Reed piped up. "The girls and Ror already know it can be done with three people, but now we must try it with all four of us."

The piano experiment involved all of us standing in front of the piano and then a couple of us switching places every few measures so that by the time the song ended, we had each played every part of the keyboard. The end result wasn't the smoothest production known to mankind, but our audiences seemed to enjoy it all the same.

One of the highlights of our trip was getting to spend time with Uncle Milo and Aunt Faye on our way back home. Their kids were all grown, but we were still fortunate enough to get the opportunity to visit with them briefly as well. Beverly and Donna were a few years older than Kim and me, and Dusty was exactly our age. We weren't able to see our Oklahoma relatives very often, so were always grateful whenever we got the chance.

We stayed with Milo and Faye for several days, and Aunt Faye was a good hostess. She set about making a fine breakfast for us on our first morning there, and Mom felt obliged to clue her in to the fact of how much food our crew could consume.

"Just so you know, Rory and Reed can really pack it in when it comes to eating," Mom informed her with a smile, as she helped to get things ready. "I figured I should warn you about that because it sometimes takes people by surprise."

"Oh, well, in that case, I'd better go grab a few things from the grocery store right now," Faye hastened to say. "I wouldn't want them to go hungry."

"We're growing boys, so that gives us a good excuse," Rory said. "But one good thing is that we aren't the least bit picky. As long as you aren't planning to make any biscuits and gravy, we'll be good to go."

"That's for sure," Reed put in. "Masticating our comestibles is one of our most favorite ways to pass the time."

"There goes Reed, the professor, talking again," said Aunt Faye. "I'm beginning to think your vocabulary contains more words than there are in the dictionary."

"Not quite," Reed laughed. "But 'tis a worthy goal to shoot for."

"Kim, do we really need that rainforest tape going during the day now?" Rory asked as his oldest sister (by three minutes) walked out of the bedroom where she had put Kayla down for a mid-morning nap. "As if listening to it each and every night weren't bad enough, now we must endure it in the daytime hours too!"

"And what's most ironic about that concept is the fact that the tape hasn't yet done one bit of good," Reed added. "The neonate still insists on proclaiming her profuse vocalizations every night."

"Well, it always did the trick at home," Kim contradicted him. "If it bothers you that much, you can always get out your guitar or something, Ror."

"Not a bad idea," Rory responded. "I could go for some great jazz right about now, while the wonderful aromas from the kitchen come wafting through. Sounds like the perfect combination."

Too soon, our time in Oklahoma drew to a close. We said our good-byes and promised to keep in touch and then once again prepared to embark upon the rest of our journey.

"Um, Dad, you might not want to go very fast, at all," Reed advised after Mom had closed the doors and gotten everything situated. Uncle Rick and my brothers had slept in the motor home for the past several nights, so the blankets and pillows all needed to be stowed away and their beds turned back into couches.

"I don't think we ever need to worry about Dad going too fast," I said.

"No. I mean really, really slow," Reed clarified further.

"Hey, what's that smell anyway?" Kim asked. "I think it's almost worse than Nebraska."

"That's what I'm trying to explain," Reed said. "I was suffering from a bit of intestinal discomfort last night and had to rid myself of a fair amount of unnecessary byproducts of metabolic activity—"

"Okay. Go no further, Reed," I demanded. "I think we all have the picture."

"With everything else going on, I'm afraid that emptying the toilet tank on this here rig was the one thing that got neglected," Rick said.

"And now it must be dealt with without further delay," Rory said meaningfully. "It's just a good thing that neither Rick nor I had similar issues to contend with last night or things would've been in a sorry state indeed!"

After that little quandary was taken care of, the rest of the day passed without further incident. The next day was a different story, however. The motor home once again broke down and needed major repairs. After the final figures for this tour were all tallied, they indicated that we had lost over fourteen hundred dollars.

"But we're not in this for the money," Dad reminded us. "Even though I have to admit it would've been nice to at least break even."

"Looks like there's some road construction ahead," Rick noted.

"Oh, come on," Rory moaned. "We're less than an hour away from home, and now we have to—"

"Come to a screeching halt," Reed finished for him as our vehicle skittered to a stop.

But it wasn't the normal type of gradual slowing that construction of this nature usually required, and I knew that once again, something had gone quite awry.

"Right near the town of Faith we are, no less" Rick said with a dry laugh. "And stuck as we can be."

"Hopefully some people of Faith will get us out of this mess," Reed said. "But how did we manage to get in said mess? I'd like to know."

"The motor home and trailer are both so heavy and loaded down that we just got totally stuck in the mud," Mom replied in a voice too tired by this time to have much emotion left in it.

Once more, a tow truck had to be called, and then we all sat and waited for it to arrive.

"Well, Kayla, would you like to drive?" Dad asked. "We won't be going anywhere for a while, so you might as well come up here and enjoy the view from the driver's seat."

The fussing baby was retrieved from the bathtub and passed to the front, where she thoroughly enjoyed her time up with Grandpa, pounding on the steering wheel and looking at all the knobs and levers.

"I just wonder if the Lord is trying to tell us something," Mom mused. "Maybe we just aren't supposed to do music anymore."

"I can tell you right now that that isn't going to happen," Rory said in no uncertain terms. "One way or another, I know already that music is going to be a huge part of my life. This is only the beginning as far as I'm concerned, which means I'll likely have a lot more adventures just like this one, but that's okay."

"What about the family ministry, though?" Mom wanted to know. "I think it might just be too hard now with the girls having kids of their own and everything. We can't just keep taking big risks like this if God isn't going to make it plain that we're doing the right thing."

"I don't know if that's a decision we need to make," I answered thoughtfully. "And definitely not right here and now. The way I look at it, God will just keep showing us the next step as we keep seeking His will. But I doubt He'll ever show us the whole game plan all at once. If He did that, there would be no free will and no stepping out on faith involved."

"I think one of the things we might have done wrong this time was not finding out enough of the specifics in advance," Kim said reasonably. "But that's why we live and learn and will hopefully know better next time around. God isn't obligated to honor everything we try if we aren't doing whatever we can to prepare for what's ahead."

"Yeah. I mean, when you think about it, the fact that our audiences were so small really shouldn't have been very surprising," I said, "if you consider that we're basically completely unknown in that part of the country."

"And even though things didn't exactly turn out the way we hoped, I think it was still a good trip, by and large," Reed added. "Like you said, we don't know what changes the future might hold, but at least we'll always have this time together to look back on."

"Anytime I get to play music is a good time in my book," Rory said. "Not to mention all the good food we got to indulge in. And just think, the generator actually worked the whole time. That alone is worth counting our blessings over. We could've been without the use of the computer or stereo or air-conditioning the whole time, and that sure wouldn't have been very fun."

"That's right. It could always be worse," Reed said. "Never underestimate the power of Murphy's law."

"It's just a good thing we didn't know when we first started our trip that the best part was destined to be the concert we did in Rapid City right at the beginning, before we ever even left our home state," Kim said, "or else we never would've gone. And then think of all the adventures we'd have missed out on."

"I believe I'd rather not think about those adventures right at the moment," Rory responded. "Maybe in a year or two, it will be fun to look back."

"Here comes the tow truck," Mom said.

"Well, all I know for sure is what I said a few minutes ago," Rory reiterated as we slowly began to emerge from the mud that surrounded us. "Music is in my blood, and there's no getting around that fact. So I'm willing to do whatever it takes to pursue it because not to do that would be letting what God has obviously given me just go to waste. And that doesn't make any sense."

"That's a good attitude to have," I told him. "I think you've just barely begun to scratch the surface of what God has in store. You and Reed have your whole lives ahead of you, and I can hardly wait to see how He's going to use you in the years to come."

Contact the Author

Rory and I love to hear from our fans. Just go to: **www.facebook.com/rorystory**, where you'll be able to receive updates on my future writing endeavors and Rory's life as a Nashville musician.

listen|imagine|view|experience

AUDIO BOOK DOWNLOAD INCLUDED WITH THIS BOOK!

In your hands you hold a complete digital entertainment package. In addition to the paper version, you receive a free download of the audio version of this book. Simply use the code listed below when visiting our website. Once downloaded to your computer, you can listen to the book through your computer's speakers, burn it to an audio CD or save the file to your portable music device (such as Apple's popular iPod) and listen on the go!

How to get your free audio book digital download:

1. Visit www.tatepublishing.com and click on the elLIVE logo on the home page.
2. Enter the following coupon code:
   84f9-9c65-c0ec-2d4a-d929-2957-ce81-ff2f
3. Download the audio book from your elLIVE digital locker and begin enjoying your new digital entertainment package today!